BROKEN SOULS

BOOK THREE

LISA HELEN GRAY

To my readers,
Keep a hold of those friends who become family.
They are keepers.

PROLOGUE

EMILY

My pulse races to the beat of music bouncing off the walls. I sit at a dressing table, and the woman who stares back at me in the mirror is someone I don't recognise.

My foundation is a darker shade than I would normally use, and my eye makeup—something I got help with—is smoky with a hint of sparkle. My lips, a dark shade of red, match the lingerie set I have on.

This woman is a fraud.

None of this is me. Not the real me.

The real me wants to be a hairdresser. She wants to be at home in bed. Instead, the only job I could find in the town my grandma and I moved to was at a strip club. We couldn't go back home. There was nothing to go back to.

Years ago—before I turned sixteen—my parents nearly killed me. I was asleep in my bed when the cigarette my drunk dad forgot to put out set fire to the sofa. They got my sister and themselves out, failing to remember I was upstairs asleep. By the time they realised, it was too late. The fire had spread, and I was trapped upstairs, screaming for someone to help me.

I'm the accident of the family. I was never supposed to be born, and the only reason I was, was because my mum didn't go to the abortion clinic until it was too late. She's let me know my entire life how much of an inconvenience I am.

My parents might not have beat me every night, but what they did do was so much worse. They didn't love me. I was used as a verbal punching bag. If my dad lost a job, it was because I caused him stress. If we got a visit from a social worker, I was to blame. If my mum couldn't afford something, it was my fault. All the damn time it was my fault.

My sister, Reign, didn't receive the same treatment I did. She got birthdays and Christmases, and parents who wanted to know how her day was. I never even got to join them on a walk to the shop. Reign was the child they planned for and wanted; until they realised parenting wasn't for them. I was the daughter they didn't want, and they treated me like a modern-day Cinderella. Only, there wasn't a Prince Charming to save me, or a Fairy Godmother.

Or maybe there was. Joyce, my grandmother, saved me the day she took me from their care. She fought tooth and nail with the courts, and finally, with a statement from me, she got custody of the child her daughter neglected. She wanted better for me, and at one point, she wanted better for her daughter. Only, there was no saving Shelby from the life she was leading. She enjoyed living it up too much.

And honestly, I'm glad it worked out that way. I loved living with my grandmother. She's one of those women who when she speaks, you listen. Her wisdom got me through some rough years of my life. We were happy, but then, on my nineteenth birthday, she got sick. A year later, she was diagnosed with early onset Alzheimer's. It started off with small things like forgetting where she put something, or asking me to repeat the same things. And then it wasn't. It was big things like leaving the stove on, or forgetting she couldn't drive anymore.

My parents saw an opportunity to get money when she became sick. My mum started to come over and help with her care. She didn't take it seriously, and the only time she showed an ounce of sympathy for her mum was when other people were around. Behind closed doors, she was snapping at her and complaining.

When my grandma got rushed into hospital because of an overdose, I knew it was my mum. Her expression said it all. When it came back in her toxicology report that it had been happening frequently, I couldn't risk us staying there.

So, we sold her home, moved an hour away, and I got us set up in a two-bed house. Things were great for a few months, until my grandma's health deteriorated to the point I couldn't be the one to care for her full-time anymore. My Carer's Allowance wasn't enough to get by, and since we only received so many hours of free home care, I had to find the difference whilst also still being able to live. I couldn't touch my grandma's money because it never felt right. I wanted to be the one to care for her since she did so much for me.

We tried a care home while she was lucid enough to make the choice herself, but they lost my trust after a string of incidents happened that—in my eyes—they didn't take seriously enough. I didn't want to judge all care homes by their standards, but it was the tipping edge for me. She had been unsettled and seemed more lost, so we went back to full-time home care. Until I couldn't.

Now, I'm working at Tease, which gives me more pay for less hours and the time to care for my grandma during the day, when she needs it the most. A night nurse takes care of her during my work hours. A larger chunk is funded during the night, so it made sense to look for a job that had night hours.

My eyes water as I picture what I'll need to do out there. I've been given training, enough to show me the ropes, but none of it prepared me for the real thing. The past few months, I've been given lessons on how to dance, worked the floor wearing the shot girl outfit, and been given shifts behind the bar. Tonight, however, our boss, Dave, wants me to work the private booths because one of the girls called in sick. If I don't get out there soon, I'm going to get fired.

Olivia, a girl who has been showing me the ropes for the past few months, steps into the room, adjusting her underwear. She is stunning, with long legs, a slim frame, and gorgeous thick black hair. I'm jealous of how well she carries her confidence. Her shoulders don't slump when she's walking around the club, and I've never seen her shy away from approaching a male.

"Hey, babe. You ready for your first night in the booths?" she asks, before throwing her gum into the bin.

Was anyone ever ready? I will have to take my clothes off, something I've been lucky to avoid since starting here.

"Not really."

Seeing my expression, she drops down in the chair next to me and swings my chair around until I'm facing her.

"You don't have to do it. Dave will never force you to, and he'll understand if this job isn't for you."

Dave is the manager of Tease, and he's been nothing but kind and patient with me as I learn the ropes. I always imagined a strip club owner to be old, fat and sleazy, but he's far from it. He's athletically fit, nearing thirty, and is good to his employees. Even if he yells a lot at some of them. It's never out of anger, but out of frustration.

My hands shake as I drop the dressing gown from my shoulders. "I don't have a choice. My nan is sick, and I don't get enough allowance to afford what we need. If I lose this job, I'll lose the funding I get towards her care, and I can't afford to pay for it privately. It took me a long time to get this one," I tell her, before taking a breath. "It's just… The thought of taking my clothes off makes me sick."

"I get it. When I applied, it was the only job available. I care for my siblings, and at first, I didn't need the job because I received benefits. But my life revolved around cleaning, packed lunches, ironing, and doing school drop-offs and pick-ups. I needed my own identity, which is why I work four days a week. Don't get me wrong, working nine-to-five would be easier and less stressful, but I wouldn't make the same tips as I do working here."

"I'm so sorry. I sounded really judgemental. I didn't mean to offend you," I promise, hoping like hell I haven't lost the first friend I've made since moving here.

She surprises me by laughing. "It will take more than that to offend me. You forget, I live with three terrorists. Nothing can get to me. Well, except Trixie, but she knows what buttons to press."

I smile at her words. "She is full on."

"That's one way to describe her," she muses. "But seriously, don't stress about it. If you don't want to do it, don't. And if you do, just close your eyes whilst you dance, or don't look at them. It makes it easier."

"Is that what you do?" I ask, and fluff out my hair, knowing I'll have to cut this conversation short in a minute.

"I did at first. Now, I stare the fuckers down. It makes them think twice about saying anything crude."

I get to my feet. "Well, wish me luck."

"You don't need it. You'll be fine."

I stop at the door and let her see how badly I'm scared. "No, seriously, wish me luck."

She laughs. "Good luck, babe."

THE LIGHTS in the booth are like hot beams, causing sweat to trickle down my cleavage and spine. They're like a kaleidoscope of colours, blurring my vision as I dance for a groom here on his stag party.

The doorman—whose name I can never remember—is outside, which doesn't make me feel any better. He doesn't make me feel safe, not like the others do. He's a big guy, with muscular arms, and could probably take out a bunch of people before getting hurt. His mind, however, isn't on the job. It's either on us or the other female patrons who come into the club. If a guy touches a dancer, he takes his time to pull them away or break it up. His job is to prevent them from getting too close.

And this guy I'm dancing for wants his money's worth. I'm worried the doorman won't come in if this guy becomes too much.

"Take it off, you slut," he slurs, spreading his arms wide and resting them on the back of the booth.

He looks like an ordinary, run-of-the-mill businessman, but his behaviour doesn't fit the mould. He has no control, for starters. The more he drinks, the more aggressive he becomes. And I'm willing to bet he treats his fiancée like this too. This isn't a man blowing off steam. This is the real him, and it's the suit he hides behind to fool those around him.

He reminds me so much of my dad.

I can feel tears burning the back of my eyes, and my fingers shake as I reach behind me to unclasp my bra.

I'm not moving quick enough, because he stands and rips the flimsy red lingerie from my body. The foul odour of cigarettes makes me gag.

"I want to see some tits. I'm not wasting my money here."

I cry out, clutching my bare breasts so he doesn't see. His fingers dig into my wrist, trying to tug my hands away. "Get off me!" I scream.

A breeze cools the sweat on my back, and the guy in front of me glances up at whoever pulled the curtains open.

Please be security.

The groom snarls at the newcomer. "Wait your fucking turn."

"Let the woman go," my saviour growls, and his voice, although smooth like milk chocolate, has a hint of darkness.

And I can't believe I'm comparing a voice to chocolate.

"You want some?" the groom declares, and shoves me hard enough to knock me off the podium. My head smacks against the wooden shelf that holds the music player, disorientating me.

"Please don't make me ruin this suit; it's a rental," my saviour states.

I glance up at my avenging angel, and my breath catches in my throat. He is gorgeous. Tall, built, dark hair, strong jaw, and incredible bluish/grey eyes. He is a sight to behold in his black suit.

His warning goes unheard as the man who attacked me charges at him. Suit guy barely moves. He simply leans to the side and waits for the perfect moment to bring his elbow down hard between the groom's shoulder blades. He goes down fast, but before he hits the floor, the doorman who is meant to be protecting me is there, dragging the guy out.

"Sorry, man."

I'm so focused on watching the groom get dragged away that I don't see my saviour until he's kneeling down in front of me. I flinch away, and his expression softens. No words are exchanged as he removes his jacket and wraps it around my shoulders, covering me.

"Are you okay?"

The tears that were threatening to slip free earlier finally drip down my cheeks. In my shock, I admit, "I don't know if I'm cut out to be a stripper. This is my first night, and I feel sick. I thought I could do this but I can't."

"Let's go and get you cleaned up. Your head is bleeding," he states softly.

I lift my hand to where the throbbing is and it comes away with dark, red blood. "Oh no."

He helps me to my feet, his touch gentle, comforting, and for the first time tonight, I feel safe.

He turns around, ordering softly, "Put the jacket on."

I do, and use the privacy to lift the soft material up to my face, smelling the intoxicating aroma. It's woodsy with a hint of spice, and it's soothing.

"Done," I declare awkwardly, not knowing what else to say.

"Come on, let's get you cleaned up."

"I'm sorry, but you aren't allowed out back; our boss doesn't allow it," I tell him, bravely making a stand.

He smiles, and it holds a secret. "That's okay. Me and the owner go way back. He'll be fine."

"Still, I'd rather not. I need this job, and I don't want to lose it."

"Come on," he demands, and takes my hand.

I follow him out, and lo and behold, Dave is heading towards us. "Is everything okay, Cole?"

"One of the punters got too handsy. You need to fire that fucking doorman. If I hadn't been walking past, she would have been seriously hurt, and all because he was busy talking to another dancer."

"You okay, doll?" Dave asks, and his jaw clenches at the sight of my head.

"I'm okay," I lie. Because I'm not okay. And the only reason I'm not a mess is because of the man who is holding my hand.

"I'm going to get her cleaned up," he tells Dave.

Dave doesn't even blink, which means Cole was telling the truth about them being friends. "Alright," he replies, then turns to me. "After, head home. You can take the night off." I go to argue, but he lifts his hand and continues. "With full pay, girl."

7

My shoulders drop with relief. "Thank you."

We head through to the back halls, and instead of continuing down to the changing rooms, he pulls me into Dave's office. He doesn't stop, pushing a door masked as a shelving unit to take me into another room. My eyes widen at the black sleek office and living space. There's a black plush sofa, a large television mounted on the wall, and a small kitchen space in the corner. I have to wonder how close to Dave he is to know this is here.

"Take a seat," he orders.

I do, my entire body shaking. I watch his broad back tense as he reaches up to grab a first aid box. I stay silent, the shock of what happened finally hitting me.

That man could have seriously hurt me. If it wasn't for this guy, no one would have helped me until it was too late.

More tears slip free as he takes a seat on the pouffe and begins to clean my head. "I'm Cole, by the way."

"I'm Emily," I reply, keeping my voice low and soft.

His gaze holds me in place. "You okay?"

"I will be," I admit, unable to look away. "I just hope I still have a job. Dave already took a chance on me since I have no dancing skills at all."

"I thought you didn't want to be a stripper?" he reminds me, before warning, "This will sting."

I flinch when he dabs a cotton ball into the cut. "I have no choice."

"What do you mean?"

I let him see everything I'm feeling, but the intensity of his gaze has me backing down. "It doesn't matter," I reply, and avert my focus to the desk as he finishes cleaning up the wound.

"It does if you are being forced to work here," he tells me, throwing the used supplies into the bin.

"I'm not. Forget I said anything," I plead, not understanding what's come over me. I'm not usually this open with my personal life. Years of living with my parents did that to me. They made me believe my voice didn't matter, so I stopped speaking and instead, listened.

He walks over to the mini bar and pours two drinks. When he comes back over, he hands me a glass. "It will take the edge off."

I take a sip, trying not to gag at the foul taste. I've never been a big drinker, and I can't say I'm a fan of vodka.

But after taking another sip, warmth fills my veins, so I take another. "Thank you."

"Now, explain to me why you are working a job you don't want to do," he demands.

His authoritative tone has me answering. "My grandma is sick. It's a long story, something I don't want to talk about, but she's getting worse. I can't care for her alone, and to qualify for more help, I must be employed. I also need to pay our bills, and I don't want to use my grandma's money to do it. She spent so many years looking after me. I want to give back and care for her."

"Do you not have family who can help?"

I let out a dry laugh. "My family are awful people. They don't care about me, and they don't care about her. She's all I have."

Understanding flashes in his eyes. "I know how you feel when it comes to family."

"My life is a mess. I'm supposed to be the one who has everything figured out, but I guess my parents were right. I'll never make anything of myself. I'm a nobody. And my sister, she's waiting for me to fail. And she's right to think it. I can't even get this right," I choke out, and he moves, leaning forward to grab my hands.

"You don't seem like a nobody to me. You seem like someone who has the world on their shoulders and has no one to help her carry it."

I meet his gaze, and it's not the alcohol warming me. It's him, and the way he's watching me. "Why are you being so nice? You don't know me."

"No, but I know what it's like to be the person who works shitty jobs just so you can have better. I get it. But you need to know, you haven't failed," he declares. I lean into his touch when he tucks my hair behind my ear. "You're a fighter. You have to be to do a job like this when you don't want to. And truth be told, my day hasn't been going so well either. Until now."

I'm not sure if it's the shock, the alcohol, or hearing his kind words

—something I've never had from anyone but my grandma—but I lean in and kiss him.

I forget that it's my hand keeping his jacket closed around me, and I forget that I've only just met this man.

When he doesn't respond, embarrassment consumes me. I lean back, unable to meet his gaze. "I'm sorry. I don't know what came over me."

I barely get the words out before he's on me, kissing me until he steals my breath. I fall back on the sofa, letting him tower over me, and I know in this moment, I'm not just giving him my body.

I'm giving him me.

This might have happened unexpectedly, and it might be a huge leap for me, but something about this feels right.

All those years of verbal and physical abuse, of not feeling loved or wanted, have led me to this. Led me to him. And I can't deny how good it feels.

For once, I'm taking something for myself.

And I'm going to enjoy every second.

1

EMILY

Rain pelts down on the black umbrella I hold in my hand. People pass by, offering their condolences, but I know if I speak, I will break. And I can't do that today. It's not what my grandmother would have wanted. Not with my parents lurking close by, sucking up the attention her death has given them.

Losing my grandmother has left a heartache no time or person can heal. But it's also a love no one can ever steal from me, not even my parents.

My grandma showered me with love daily, even on the days she forgot who I was.

I'm glad we got to share what she wanted for her funeral before she became lost in her own mind. I got to give her one last gift before she died, and it was beautiful.

With most of her friends and close relatives already gone, it's time to leave. I kept the service small, like I promised I would. Everyone here today loved her, and she touched their lives in a small way. She wasn't a lady who appreciated grand gestures or extravagant things. She lived a simple and blessed life, and that is how she wanted her goodbye to be.

Our goodbye has been one of the hardest things I've ever had to do. With that said, I know she'll never be fully gone. She will always live on in my heart, and in the garden we created together. I'll see her in the birds and hear her voice every time I sing my daughter her favourite lullaby.

Today has been a tough day, but I've been preparing for it since she was first diagnosed. And I know I'll move on tomorrow thinking of her back with my granddad. I'll picture her up there, drinking tea and telling her love everything he missed.

"How are you holding up?" Harriett whispers, standing strong and supportive next to me. She looks beautiful in her pencil dress. And to honour my grandma, she pinned a white rose to the bottom of the strap. All my girls have one, including me.

"I'm doing okay. I will need to leave soon to sort through her things."

"You don't need to do that today," Gabby tells me softly. "You can sort that out when you're ready."

I paste on a smile. "It's what she wanted. I promised I wouldn't hold on to her things when she was gone. She said I didn't need them, that she'd always be watching over me."

"Do you want us to help?" Olivia offers, brushing her black hair over her shoulder.

I lean in to her, grateful for her offer. "No. It's something I want to do alone."

"I know this isn't the time to bring it up, but are you sure you aren't adopted?" Gabby asks.

I look over to where my mother is dramatically sobbing, soaking in the attention people are giving her. Her dirty blonde hair has grown darker, with shades of grey showing her age.

"I don't know how I'm going to go on without her," Shelby cries, always the drama queen.

"Sadly, I'm sure," I reply, answering Gabby.

"Has she said anything to you?" Harriett asks quietly as people pass us by.

I snort. "Aside from glaring at me, no, she hasn't."

"Well, she's about to because they're walking over here," Gabby rushes out, and I feel everyone become alert.

Shelby, in a white blouse and tight mini skirt shorter than my sister's, walks next to my father as they make their way over. My dad, who hasn't bothered to make an effort, is wearing jeans and a dark blue shirt. The shirt is clearly new, and something I'm surprised they splurged on since they spend every penny on cigarettes or booze.

"Hey, Mum. Hey, Dad," I greet when they reach me, before turning to my sister, who, unlike me and Mum, doesn't have natural blonde hair. Hers is sadly a box dye, and poorly applied if the dark orange patches are anything to go by. Her cheeks are sunken and at odds with the weight she carries around her lower half. "Hi, Reign."

Reign lifts her bag higher up her shoulder. "We've come to get the address for the wake. Since you didn't bother getting her own daughter a car, we have no idea where we are going."

I sigh, because I've been waiting for this. "Grandma didn't want cars, and she didn't want a wake. She said they are too depressing."

"How would she know what she wanted? She probably forgot she was dying," my sister announces, sounding just like our mum. "This is you being a stuck-up bitch and pocketing the money."

"No, Reign, it's really not. We made these plans before her health declined. I have it in writing."

"I'm her daughter, Emily. You shouldn't have been allowed to make these decisions without me. I should have been a part of this," Mum scolds, trying to save face in front of my friends.

"Mum, if you want to contribute, I'm happy to take some money towards today's costs."

The colour in her cheeks fades to white. "Oh, so now you want my help. No. You should have thought about that before you decided to keep me out of it."

I want to pinch the bridge of my nose and snap back, but I don't have the energy. "Mum, I invited you to come with me to the funeral home, but you were busy. I just wanted to get it done, like she wanted me to do. I didn't mean to upset anyone."

"Well, you did," my dad admits, rubbing his hand over his large stomach.

Mum takes a breath, steeling her spine. "We want your address to collect a few things. We want Joyce's wedding rings and a few other pieces from her collection. I'm also going to need access to her accounts so I can begin to get them transferred over to me."

And this is why they're really here. "Mum, Grandma has given me those rings. It's all in her will. And everything that wasn't sentimental, she donated or sold years ago."

"You mean you stole it," Reign snaps. "Grandma would have wanted us to have something of hers."

"It's in her will," I repeat, hoping she can detect the truth. "I have no control over it, and it was done before she even got sick. I have some of her favourite scarves, pictures, and children's books she kept if you'd like to go through them."

Her lip curls. "No, thank you."

Mum, coming out of her shock, steps forward. "I don't believe this for a second. You're lying."

"Mrs Hart," Harriett interrupts. "It's been a long day for everyone, so maybe we can revisit this conversation another day."

Shelby ignores her, glaring at me. "It's bad enough you turned her against me, but now you are keeping her things from me. You won't be getting her money. I'm her next of kin, and I have rights."

"Mum, I don't know who will inherit it. It's still going through the firm that was hired in the wake of her death. I don't want to do this with you."

"We put money in the car to get here," Dad tells me. "We bought clothes for this thing and now you're making us leave empty-handed." He turns to Shelby. "What kind of daughter did we raise?"

"You didn't raise her," Gabby snaps. "Her grandmother did. And when she got sick, Emily was there, caring for her."

"Because she never gave us a chance. She's always acted like she's too good for us," Reign barks.

"Because she is," Harriett replies.

"Now leave. She's just said goodbye to her grandmother, who she loved dearly. She doesn't need to hear this," Olivia states. "She wants to get home to her daughter."

Shelby's lip curls. "You still have that thing?"

"She's not a thing. She's my daughter."

"And how will she feel knowing her mother took everything that belongs to us?" Reign asks.

"I'm leaving," I announce. "I'm grateful you came today. It would have meant a lot to Grandma."

"How are we meant to get back? We have no petrol money," Shelby hisses.

I sigh, and as I reach into my bag, Gabby warns, "Don't you dare."

"It's fine," I reply in resignation. "Here, take this."

Dad is quick to take the money out of my hand. "It's not much, but I guess it will do."

I turn to my girls. "Thank you for coming today. It means a lot to me. I'll see you tomorrow."

Harriett pulls me away from where my parents are arguing. "Are you sure you don't want us to come?"

"I'm positive. It's something I need to do alone."

"What about Poppy? Do you want us to take her for the night?"

I force a smile. "Thank you, but we will be okay. I'll speak to you all tomorrow."

I give them all a hug and a kiss on the cheek, before making my way to my beat-up car. Since the crash last year, I haven't been able to afford anything else, but it gets me from A to B and that's all that matters.

When my family begin to screech my name, I close the door to my car on them. It mutes them, but what really drowns them out is my nan's favourite music artist. Frank Sinatra was her go-to musician, so I listen to one of his songs as I pull out, leaving behind the chaos my family will bring down on me for leaving.

Because even after years of being separated from them, they still hold some sort of power over me. I still want to give in just so I can have peace. They're like kids who are naughty, so to stop the yelling and tantrums, you give in and let them have the toy they don't deserve.

And I can't do that to my grandma. Years ago, she made me

promise to not let them take those rings or any of her other jewellery, so I'm not going to break it, even if it would be easier.

I just need to get through today.

———

SITTING on the floor in the living room, I watch my daughter play with her Trolls and doll house. They are her favourite toys. She can spend hours playing house with her Trolls.

The joy I normally feel while watching her is gone. I'm trying, really trying, but my heart is still with my grandma. I should have been here with her in her last moments, but instead, all I have is a picture in my mind of her sleeping in bed.

All her things are bagged and ready to be donated, equipment we had for her care is being picked up in the morning, and lastly, all her cabinets and drawers were picked up not long ago by another charity shop. Grandma wanted me to use the room as a room for Poppy, but I'm not there yet. I don't think I can go back in there again, or at least, not for a few days.

The doorbell rings, and Poppy looks over at me. "Nanna?"

"No, sweetie, it's probably Auntie Harriett, Gabby and Olivia," I tell her, and lift her up in my arms.

I had a feeling they wouldn't stay away, but as much as I would love their company, I want to be alone with my daughter.

I pull open the door and jerk when I see Dave, my boss from Tease. I know why he's here. A few weeks ago, we were at a barbeque at his home. My world came crashing down around me that day. First, I got the phone call that my grandma had passed, and then, Poppy's dad —a man who knew nothing about her prior to that day—saw Poppy for the first time. We went over two years without seeing each other. Two long years. From the moment he came back, I tortured myself over how to tell him he had a daughter.

But he knew.

He knew, with one look at the girl I held, she was his.

"Dave," I greet, then lower Poppy to the floor. "Go play with your Trolls, baby."

She rushes off without a fuss, and Dave's gaze snaps up from watching her. "Can we talk for a minute, please?"

I don't want to have this conversation outside, so I pull open the door a little wider, giving him room to come inside. "Let's go into the kitchen," I tell him.

Since this is the first time he's been here, he takes a look around, and for the first time, I'm ashamed of where I live. The paintwork was done by me, and since I could only afford magnolia at the time, it's plain. But at least it hides the fact I can't paint. My sofa has seen better days. Not even the grey throws can hide the stains my child and grandma have made.

Everything is either second-hand or was bought for me, and although it doesn't look all that great, it still does what it needs to. My money went to the two people who needed it the most. So when grandma needed a new chair because of her back, I got it. When Poppy needed new clothes or a play set, she got it. I made sure my daughter had everything new, and got the best of the best, because it's something I never got.

As we reach the kitchen, I close the gate to keep Poppy secure in the living room and head to the kettle. I flip it on, bringing two cups down. Just when I think he's not going to break the silence, he does, clearing his throat.

"I'm sorry for your loss. Me and Lin wanted to be there but after everything that has happened, we thought we would give you space," he announces. "I see you got your flowers?"

"I did, thank you."

I finish making the tea before placing his mug in front of where he sits at our small table. I sit down, closing my fingers around the mug.

"I knew, you know." My nose begins to burn and the back of my throat swells as I force the tears back. "Well, I always assumed. I thought if she was his, you would have told me."

"I couldn't tell anyone," I tell him, my voice cracking. "My friends found out a few months ago when he first came back to the club."

"Why, Emily? Why would you keep this from him?"

"I never planned to keep it from him. The day after our night together, you called me into your office. Do you remember?"

"Yes. Cole wanted me to put you on as a bartender and not a dancer."

"He did?" I ask, surprised.

Dave's eyebrows pinch together. "I thought you knew."

"No, I thought I was a terrible dancer, so you didn't want me up on the stage."

"No. He came to me that night and told me he didn't want to see you on the stage or in the booths, and to put you behind the bar so you could keep your job. That same night, he gave the bartenders a raise."

I clutch my stomach, feeling sick. "I didn't know."

"Then why were you bringing it up?" he asks.

"Because that same night, I walked out of your office and ran into Trixie. She asked me what I was doing with the manager the night before and if he'd said anything about her. I wasn't sure who she was talking about, but then you walked out—"

"And I said he was there, and pointed out that you talked to him," he finishes.

"Yes, and that's when I realised I had slept with my boss," I reveal. "I thought he was a friend."

"He's more than that. He's my family, Emily."

"I'm sorry," I tell him, and feel the tears fall. "I didn't find out I was pregnant until a few weeks later. By that point, I was ashamed. The girls were already mad that I got put behind the bar and given a raise. I didn't want to go to you in case it got out who the baby's father was. I didn't want people thinking I slept my way to my position. So, I waited, and kept waiting, but then so much time passed, and I was too scared to do anything."

"You could have come to me," he declares.

"And what would you have done? Told him? What if he wanted me to abort the baby? I couldn't let that happen. As hard as this has been, she's my world, Dave. I loved her before I met her."

He pinches the bridge of his nose. "He's not speaking to me. He's mad because I didn't tell him, and the only reason he hasn't showed up here is because he got called to the sister club. Someone burnt it down."

Well, that answers why he hasn't been here. I've lived with constant dread for the past two weeks. Every time someone has knocked on the door, my stomach has turned, and I've wondered if it's him.

"I appreciate you coming to see me, but I need to get Poppy into her bath and get her ready for bed."

He takes the hint and gets to his feet. "I'll let you get on with your evening. But if you need anything—anything at all—call me."

"Thank you, but we'll be fine."

We head back into the living room, and Poppy immediately struts over to me. I lift her up into my arms. "Bath?"

"Yes, sweetie, you're going in the bath."

She waves to Dave. "Bye."

He smiles and taps her cheek. "Bye, Poppy," he replies, then turns to me. "Speak to you soon."

We say our goodbyes, and instead of dwelling on our conversation, I head upstairs. I still have a few more hours to go before I'm finally alone. Then, and only then, will I let out everything I've been desperately holding in all day.

2

EMILY

For two days, I've walked around like the ground beneath me will crack at any given moment.

My world turned upside down, and I'm struggling to find a balance. I've always been able to pull up my big girl knickers and forget about yesterday so I could live for tomorrow, but I'm still living the day I lost my grandma, and I can't fast forward or rewind. I'm trying to move forward. I really am. But all I can manage is to put one foot in front of the other.

I couldn't even get shopping right. First, the trolley wheel broke, so I had to go out and get a new one, and then the strap on Poppy's nappy snapped because I had used a smaller size by mistake, so when she wet herself, it managed to leak through the sides. I then went to go and pay for what I did have, and my card got declined.

After getting back in the car, I checked my account and realised the funeral directives had taken out the funds for the rest of the funeral costs, even though they promised me I could pay monthly. They took everything, including the savings I had in there.

All I have are the tips I have in a box under my bed, and that needs to get me through till the end of the month.

"We're home, baby girl," I promise, and she settles a little. "Let's get you changed out of those wet clothes."

"Yes, Mummy." I slide out of the car and head straight to her, unclipping her out of her seat. She immediately clings to me, wrapping her little legs around my waist. "Love you, Mama."

"Love you to the moon and back, sweet girl."

As hard as these past few weeks have been, she's been my shining star. She always has been. I love my grandma with everything in me, I love my friends, and my friends' siblings. I love hard. But my daughter… It's another type of love. It's not that I love her more or less, but differently. It's an unconditional love, one I know I'd die for, go to war for, and kill for. She's my entire world. There's nothing I wouldn't do for her.

She lays her head on my shoulder, and I brush her blonde locks away from her eyes. I fight back the tears that threaten to fall. I feel like I've failed her so much lately, and I know I need to do better. *Be* better.

Letting myself in, I jerk back at the mess in my living room. It's like someone has come in and turned it upside down. Furniture is tipped over or broken, pictures have been ripped down and shoved off the mantelpiece. A few toys have survived, but the contents in my cabinets haven't. There are papers ripped, photos torn, and knick-knacks smashed.

Who would do this?

"Poppy," Poppy cries, pointing to her favourite Troll toy who, frustratingly, is also called Poppy.

"We'll get Poppy in a minute, sweetie. Right now, Mummy needs you to be quiet. Can you do that?"

She nods, and I continue through the house to the kitchen, stepping on broken parts of my life. I've never been one to buy things for the sake of buying them. I don't need the latest tech or the newest décor design. Nearly everything I own is sentimental. But it's mine; it's home, and someone has come in and destroyed it. None of it is valuable—except my grandma's rings, and I'm wearing those on a chain around my neck.

Everything in the kitchen is the same. All my kitchenware is smashed, and the cupboards and drawers have been emptied. The backdoor is open, but the window is smashed, which explains how they got in. My keys are above the door on a hook still. I put them there so Poppy didn't get them to unlock the door, and at one point, so my grandma couldn't get out.

Backing out of the room, I go to the stairs that are between the kitchen and living room. Slowly, I begin to creep up them. I haven't heard anything to indicate someone is still in the house, but that doesn't mean anything. The bathroom up ahead is in the same state as downstairs, and from a quick glance in the mirror, I can see there's no one hiding in the shower. But there is water on the floor, something I'll sort out later.

Our room is next, and the mess of it brings tears to my eyes. They clearly spent the most time in here because everything from my walk-in wardrobe has been ripped out, and the boxes all emptied.

I check my grandma's old room, but since it was empty, no damage has been done. I go back into our room and quickly lower Poppy to the floor.

"Let's get you out of these clothes," I tell her, and rummage through the mess for a nappy and a spare set of clothes.

"What happened, Mama?" she asks, cuddling one of her Trolls to her chest.

My hands shake as I take hers. "It's going to be okay. Mummy will clean it up soon."

I quickly change her, and once I'm done, a thought occurs to me. "My tips."

I race over to the bed and find the box immediately. Just as I feared, it's empty. "No," I cry.

"It's okay, Mama. It's okay. Don't cry," Poppy tells me, patting her warm hand over mine.

Tears fall as I pick her up. "Yeah, baby, it will be." I grab my phone, dialling nine-nine-nine. I quickly run through the events, forcing my voice to remain calm so I don't scare Poppy any more than I already have.

Once they promise they are on their way, I head downstairs, my legs threatening to give out. I need to be strong for Poppy, which I've had to do for weeks now. But with every broken piece of my life I pass, my legs grow heavier and I want to buckle under the unfairness of it all.

I freeze when I reach the bottom, hearing glass crunch in the living room. "The police are coming," I call out, hoping it scares them away. "Leave!"

"I'm not here to harm anyone," the intruder explains, and I quickly take the last step and turn into the living room, not believing my ears.

The last person I expected to turn up at my house, and the last person I needed to turn up at my house, is here.

Cole Connor.

The man who changed my life, who has been the centre of my dreams and the cause of my daydreams. He's here. He might look as good as I remember, in his white crisp shirt and black trousers, but it doesn't erase the fact he's frowning at me.

"Mr Connor," I breathe, and like my heart, the kitchen explodes.

I rush me and Poppy further into the living room and turn back to watch the remaining parts of the ceiling fall to the floor, water following.

How is this my life?

When did it become so chaotic?

And it's only bloody Monday.

I left to get a few bits of food for the week, something normal, since lately, I've felt so discombobulated.

Now, it's like my world turning upside wasn't enough; fate had to give it a good spin too.

Realising no one has spoken, and my daughter isn't crying, I pull back to check on her. She isn't watching the disaster unfold in front of us. She's watching the man beside us, her greyish-blue eyes—like her father's—round with wonder.

"She really is mine," he whispers. I glance up, and the hurt shining back at me makes me want to hold him. I gulp, not knowing what to say. "Why didn't you tell me?"

I look down at the floor, focusing on a broken toy. "I never saw you again."

"But you could have got my contact information from Dave."

I close my eyes, hiding the shame, before finally confronting my worst fear. "I was young and scared. My grandma was deteriorating, I was working at a strip club, and I knew it was going to be hard."

"And telling me could have made it easier," he replies, unable to check his stern voice.

"I wanted her, Mr Connor."

"It's Cole," he snaps.

I duck my head and take a moment to think of what my friends would do. Harriett would snap back, Olivia would probably punch him, and Gabby would have some witty comment. Me; all I have is the truth, and that's what I'll give him.

"I loved her before I even met her. I didn't even think of any other option but to keep her. That was the only thing I was certain of. Going to you made everything uncertain. I didn't know where you were, who you really were, or if you would want me to keep her. But I was also scared of trapping you. I was always planning on telling you, but then months passed with no word or visit from you, and the longer it went on, the more nervous I became. I didn't mean to hurt you."

"Well, you did. You kept a daughter from me. For over two years."

Tears well up in my eyes. "I'm sorry."

"I plan to be in her life," he declares.

"You can see her. We can make a plan for visitation, if you want."

"Of course I want to see her. She's my daughter, who you kept from me for two years," he growls, and I know he's keeping his anger in check for her sake. But I can see it in his eyes, in the way his whole body is tight, that he's struggling.

I sniffle. "You can come here whenever you like. We can—"

He snorts and curls his lip in disgust as he takes in the room. "I'm not leaving her in this shit hole. It's unsafe. There are stains on that sofa that don't look recent."

My heart bottoms out. "Please, don't do this."

"What did you think I was going to do? You work at a f—" He stops himself, his gaze moving to Poppy briefly. He lets out a sigh before finishing his sentence. "A strip club. And if you haven't forgotten, there's a killer on the loose."

"I haven't forgotten," I tell him, steeling my spine. "My friend is lucky to be alive, so please, you don't need to remind me. The sofa isn't what's important. And yes, I work at a strip club that *you* own, so you know I don't strip. I work behind the bar."

"I'm not leaving her here. I will go to the courts if I have to."

My worst fear is coming to life. "We can work this out. It doesn't have to be like this. And once she gets used to you, we can arrange overnight visitation."

He lets out a breath and smacks his fist against the wall. Poppy cuddles up to me, and I quickly look down to find her falling asleep.

"You're the reason she doesn't know me. I've stayed away out of respect for your nan dying, and the fact I wasn't completely sure she was mine. But I'm more than certain she is mine. I want to be in her life, like I should have been all along."

"Please," I beg, feeling more tears fall. "Don't do this."

"You can't live here with her. The place is falling apart, and it clearly hasn't been cleaned in a while," he barks. "I'm not leaving my daughter in this place. Your ceiling has just fallen through, and I'm pretty sure as I parked up, there was a drug deal going on across the road. I am not leaving her here with you."

"Please, you can see her whenever you want. I won't stop you. But it doesn't need to be like this. I can fix all of this."

"This can't be fixed. And you've already been asking for extra shifts at work. Are you going to need more? Because no, I'm not comfortable with this."

"You can't take her from me," I choke out. "Please, you can't do this. I'm all she knows. She needs me. I need her."

His eyebrows pinch together. "Emily, I'm not taking her from you. You can come too."

"What?"

"You can't stay here. This place is a mess. I have a home close by. I can get furniture ordered in for…"

"Poppy. Her name is Poppy," I tell him. "She has my grandma's middle name."

"Poppy," he whispers, and the heartache nearly cripples me.

"We don't need you to help us. I have friends I can stay with, and we can arrange times to see each other."

He loses his soft expression. "It's not up for discussion. I am willing to take this to court if I have to, but I hope you won't let it go that far. And from the looks of it, I can't see them siding with you when you don't even have a safe home to sleep in."

"You can't do this," I argue.

"Pack whatever you need. I can buy anything you are missing, and I'll have someone come and collect the rest of your belongings."

"No, stop. This is insane. I'm not going anywhere with you. I hardly know you."

"You knew me well enough to sleep with me," he retorts harshly, but then stops to take a breath. "Sorry."

"No. It's good to know how you really feel about me," I snap.

"Please. I want to get to know my daughter. Please, let me have this."

Dejected, I reply, "I'm going to put her down in the car. Can you watch her and let the police know I'm inside?"

"You called the police?"

My eyebrows rise. "Take a look around. I've been burgled," I snap. "Believe it or not, it doesn't look like this normally. I do clean. And it might not look like much, but we don't need much. I have everything I need right here, and Poppy has everything she needs."

"Emily, I—"

"Didn't think? Clearly, I wasn't either when I thought you were a nice guy," I snap. "So will you watch her whilst I get some stuff together?"

"Yeah," he replies, and follows me outside.

As I get her settled in her seat, I avoid Cole at all costs. I know I did wrong in keeping her from him. If roles were reversed, I would be mad as hell, too. But I wouldn't say or do the things he has.

But he is right. He has missed nearly two years of her life. He missed out on all the beautiful things I got to witness. But I'm not the only one who made a mistake. He did when he left me to get dressed and never came back.

I do owe Poppy. She deserves to know her dad, but what she doesn't deserve is to be in a home that is falling apart. She deserves to be warm tonight, and to have food in her stomach. And as much as it pains me to know I won't be able to give her that, I'm not stubborn enough to cut off my nose to spite my face.

Which means, we are moving in with Cole Connor.

As I leave to grab our things, I have to wonder: who exactly is Cole Connor?

3

COLE

I have a daughter.

A beautiful daughter who looks just like... I shake away those thoughts, the memory too painful, and glance in the rear-view mirror. Emily's still following, which is surprising since I didn't think that death trap of a car would get her to the end of her street. I also expected her to drive away and hide behind those friends of hers. Dave already warned me not to cross her, that it will come back to bite me in the arse with her friends. I believed him. I've seen the security footage of their escapades.

Still, I wish I had pushed more to get her to carpool with me. Her car isn't safe. I'm not sure how she managed to get it through an MOT test.

I've spent the past two years living the high life. I've been invited to red carpets, to events where I've won awards for the outstanding work I've done, all while she's lived in a home that's closer to a box, with only essentials inside. Emily brought one suitcase, but our daughter has more, which is why we loaded up my car too.

I also know she's worked extra shifts, and at times, had to take an advance on her wages, something I agreed Dave could do for those who truly needed it.

All this time she could have come to me. She didn't need to do any of that. I would have helped her, and not just financially. I could have given them both more and helped with childcare.

Which sounds ridiculous coming from me. Children were never on the cards for me. I've always been dead set against it. The night we slept together, so much had happened with my family, and I wasn't in a good place. Then, the woman I had been sharing a life with, who I finally gave a chance to, gave me an ultimatum. It was marriage and kids or nothing. Being with me wasn't enough. And back then, kids were a big no. I didn't need to think about it, but she couldn't accept that. I had so many reasons, but none I could explain to her, so she left.

The same night, someone stole a cash box from a sister club that held over fifty grand inside. As I was leaving to sort it, I heard *her* cry. I own over a dozen strip clubs around the UK, so I'm used to beautiful women. However, Emily Hart wasn't just beautiful. That night, I saw something in her that surpassed all the beauty in the world. She held a vulnerability that called to my soul. She was a kindred spirit, and I knew without any words that we would understand each other.

What made her more attractive was her brutal honesty and lack of knowledge over how stunning she truly was.

But it was all a façade; a lie to keep me from seeing the real her.

She kept this secret from me for over two years. I missed out on my daughter's life. I missed it all. From the moment I saw the little girl across the garden, I knew she was mine, and I've never wanted anything more.

Emily kept that from me. She stole my choice, our time, and I can't get that back. Which is what made me go there today. I didn't want to lose any more time. I got fed up of waiting, and Emily has had years to come to me. But even after I found out the truth, she still didn't come, which left me with no other choice. I didn't plan to threaten her with lawyers, but after seeing their home, I knew I couldn't wait for her to get used to me before moving them in. I had to act immediately.

That day in the garden, I discovered that not wanting children didn't matter. It didn't matter how careful I was, or how sure I was that I didn't want to be a dad, I could still love my child. And I do love her. I love her with everything I have inside me, which means I would do anything for her.

Getting closer to home, I say, "Call Gia." Immediately, ringing echoes through the sound system, and I wait for her to answer.

Gia has been my personal assistant for a good seven years. Before that, the woman volunteered her time at a few charity centres I run. However, it was her ambition and determination that got her the job as my personal assistant. Now, she runs my day to day and keeps things running smoothly with my other companies.

"Good afternoon, sir," she answers.

"Gia, I need you to find me a suitable place to purchase items for a twenty-two-month-old girl."

"Like a gift store?" she asks, and I hear the clicking of a pen.

"No. I mean for everything they'll need. Clothes, toys, bedding, safety items, and anything else they'll need."

"Excuse me for being blunt, but what is this for?"

"It's a long story, but it turns out I have a daughter."

"With Cassandra?" she asks, speaking of the woman who left me over two years ago.

"No. Like I said, it's a long story. Can you do that for me?"

"Um, yeah, sure. I can do that. I'll send you the link."

"Please make sure they offer next day delivery," I tell her, before ending the conversation. "I have to go, but thank you, and I'll speak to you later about the GHR report."

Pulling up to the gates, I press the fob to open them, and drive up to the double door garage. The three-story home is placed on the nicer side of Coldenshire. It's not a gated community, but all the homes have incredible security, with gated drives and fenced in gardens.

For the past two weeks, I've had decorators and interior designers come and go. I wanted to make sure it was liveable since I haven't stayed here in a while. I've been worried about Emily not approving of the decor, but after seeing her home, I can't see that being an issue. She will have everything she needs and more.

And since I know nothing about our daughter, I've been waiting to fill her room with furniture and toys until I got Emily's opinion and approval.

I wait for Emily to park and take a moment to calm myself and take a breath. This is happening. We're moving in together. Am I happy about it? No. But she shouldn't have kept my daughter from me.

Some of the anger I've been holding inside seeped out earlier, but there's still so much there. This time, I can't fuck someone until it's out of my system, and I can't hit the bottle to drown it out. I can't hide from this, and I don't want to. She's my daughter.

Sliding out of the car, I meet Emily at her car door. Red-rimmed eyes stare back at me, and I want to feel for her, but I don't.

"I'll get some of the bags now, but I'll grab the rest after showing you around," I tell her.

"Cole, what are you doing?"

My brows pinch together. "Helping you."

She exhales. "Okay, then what is your plan? How long do you plan to keep us here? Have you even thought this through?"

"What did you think was going to happen? You kept her from me. If I had known from the beginning, we could have worked out a plan. I would have been in her life, watched her grow, but you took that from me. I'm not missing another day."

She sniffles, and tears slip down her cheeks. "We can still do that. It doesn't have to be like this."

"Stop with the waterworks. This is happening, Emily. I want to be a part of her life, and this is the only way."

She wipes her nose on her sleeve and narrows her eyes at me. "You weren't there. You left, and you never came back. Don't put this all on me. You didn't exactly leave me your number."

No, but she's the reason I watched security footage, and the reason I stayed away. I was scared of what happened between us that night, and what it meant. It was one night. One night, and I felt like she made my world better. And it scared me.

Instead of telling her that, I snap, "Is that why you kept her from me? Because I didn't leave you a number?"

She snorts. "Please. Do I look that shallow or petty? No. But when you have sex with a woman without a condom, you should at least check in," she snaps. "There were two of us that night, but only one of us had to face the consequences. Me. I had to go through morning sickness alone. I had to go to appointments alone. And I raised our daughter alone with a sick grandma. Don't you dare put all this blame on me."

She goes to the back door and pulls it open, before gently lifting out our sleeping girl. Her words echo in my mind, and for the first time since finding out, I see it from her point of view. I was so blinded by my rage, I never gave a thought to what she went through.

"Emily," I call.

"Where can I take her to lie down?" she asks, and there's a cold mask in place, and I know I've fucked up.

Don't let her fool you.

I head to the boot and lift it open to grab two suitcases. "Follow me." We head up to the house and I use the key lock to let myself in. "I'll give you the code and a fob for the front gate once you are settled in."

She doesn't speak, so I drop the cases just inside the door and direct her to the living room. I clear my throat. "This is the small living room."

"Can you just show me where we'll be sleeping? I also need to call my landlord and inform him about the house, and then I need to go through my emails."

"Okay," I reply, and head back out of the room. The staircase leads up to the first floor, where there are four bedrooms and two bathrooms.

We pass the first door, which is the second biggest room on this floor and shares a bathroom with the next bedroom. "That room will be Poppy's once I have everything delivered." I hand her a card, and she takes it. "Email me, and I'll send you the login details and you can pick some things she will need. Send me a list of foods you like and don't like, and any allergies. My assistant will have food delivered this evening, and I'll order in food when you are ready." I stop at the second door. "This will be your room. The bed is high, so if you aren't comfortable sharing with Poppy, I can bring up one of the camping beds for her from the garage."

"No, she's fine with me," she tells me, still not meeting my gaze. "We share a room, so she doesn't need one of her own."

"I want to be able to put her to bed, or wake up with her," I admit. "I'll have cameras and monitors in her room that we can both watch from our rooms in case she needs us."

"Okay," she whispers, and her broken words nearly make me give in.

I push open the door and wait for her to enter before following.

"That door leads to a bathroom that joins on to Poppy's room," I explain. "And that one is a wardrobe and dressing room."

The king-size bed is pushed against the outer wall, coming out into the room, a bedside table either side of it. In the corner, against the entrance wall, is a seating area with a sofa and television. Near the window is a reading nook with a light. By the entrance sits a table with some decorative items. The colour scheme of the room is neutral and warm, so the interior designer filled the space with beige, soft browns, and cream. Then the stylist who came in filled it with ornaments and faux pampas.

She moves over to the bed and gently lays Poppy down, then begins to place pillows near the edge of the mattress so she doesn't roll off.

"I know this isn't what you wanted, and I get this is a big change for you, but please, let me get to know my daughter."

"I would never stop you from getting to know her, but you have to know this isn't going to work. It's not practical, and it's confusing to Poppy. She is going to want to know why we can't go home."

"This is her home," I croak out.

"But for how long? Because I don't think you've thought this through. What happens when your girlfriend starts asking why we are here?"

"I don't have a girlfriend."

She flicks her blonde hair over her shoulder. "Okay, so what if you start dating, and she wants to know why we are here?"

"Look, I don't have all the answers, but please, give me this."

"I can't live on a whim," she admits. "I can't live here not knowing what it means for us, or what our future holds. She needs stability. What we want doesn't matter. Only she matters."

"Which is why she should be here. Emily, your house just fell apart, and you were burgled. You don't have to worry about that anymore. Security here is great, and I can replace anything you lost."

"And what happens after? What happens in the future, when it turns out we can't live together? Where does that leave me and Poppy? Because I'll never leave her. You can threaten me with lawyers all you want, but I'll never stop fighting for her."

"If it doesn't work, you can keep the house."

"You can't give me your house," she scoffs.

"It's just a house. I can buy another one. And I will get it in writing if it will get you to give this a chance. I know I went about this the wrong way, but you said it yourself: you'll never stop fighting for her. Well, neither will I. She's my daughter, and I want to be her father. So please, give me that. Please. All I want is to get to know her."

She seems to be truly thinking about it, and hope fills my chest. I knew getting her to leave with me didn't mean I had won. It just meant I left her with no other choice. Getting her to stay will be a fight for tomorrow.

"I don't need it in writing, but I need you to promise me: if this doesn't work out, you'll let us leave and we can arrange visitation."

I step further into the room and stop when I reach the bed. "I won't leave you without a home, so I'll promise to leave if it comes to it. I have a flat in the city centre I can go to."

She nods, and fiddles with the strap on her bag. When no more words are exchanged, I take a step back. "I'll bring up the rest of the bags and leave them outside the door so I don't disturb her. I'll put all of Poppy's things in her room."

"Thank you," she whispers, and I close the door behind me.

I lean back against it, closing my eyes when I hear her begin to sob. I want to go back in there and tell her I'm sorry. But it doesn't matter how much she makes me care, she still lied to me, and I'm allowed to be mad about it.

She can hate me all she wants, but she'll soon see I'm doing her a favour. I can give her everything, and she doesn't need to be alone anymore.

We don't need to be alone.

4

EMILY

Waking up in a strange home, with a man somewhere inside who is angry at me, brings tears to my eyes. I've made so many mistakes, all of which I've paid for in some way, but never like this.

The beautiful memory I've cherished for close to three years has been ripped away from me. And I'm not sure what hurts more. That I no longer have it, or that it was a lie.

No longer do I see the caring man who took his time to clean my wound. I don't feel his gentle touch or hear his soft words. I don't see the same emotion from that night when he looks at me now. It's gone, and in its place is something ugly that I can't even run from.

He threatened me with lawyers, and his expression said what he didn't say out loud. Who would let a stripper keep their daughter instead of someone financially well off? Cole may not have said those words, but he didn't need to. I felt them. I might not strip for a living, but considering what I wear to work, I may as well. And he's right. Who would side with someone like me over him?

It won't matter to them that I love my daughter with all that I am, or that I care for her and make sure she has everything she needs.

They'll just see the girl behind the bar in short shorts. They'll see a woman working nights away from her daughter, instead of seeing a woman providing for her daughter.

I come from a broken home. My parents might not be separated, but they were broken. They were cruel and selfish, and I knew, even before I got pregnant, that I never wanted to be like them. I wouldn't care how tired I got, or how low life could get; I would always make sure my child knew they were loved, wanted and cared for. And that is what I've strived to achieve and have done.

Being here doesn't magically fix what he missed. I understand why he doesn't want to miss another minute—I'd be the same—but he must know it won't work like this.

"Cry?" Poppy asks after slipping her thumb out of her mouth.

"No, baby. Did you have a good sleep?"

She nods. "Where man?"

My heart skips a beat, because I know this is the moment where her life is about to change. She might not understand my words or remember them in years to come, but I will. And I'll know I did the right thing. "That man, he's your dada. Like I'm your mama. Can you say, dada?"

"Baba."

"Da-da," I repeat slower, smiling at the crease in her forehead.

"Dada."

"Good girl," I cheer, and lift her up into my arms. "You are such a clever girl."

"Pop," she demands.

"Come on, let's go find your sippy cup and make you a drink."

I want to hide away in this room, but Poppy's needs come first, and my girl needs a drink. Poppy waits for me to get off the bed before raising her arms to be picked up. I muster up a smile for her as we make our way out of the room.

As promised, he has left our bags outside the door. Taking her backpack, I swing it over my shoulder and warily make my way downstairs.

I'm beginning to regret not taking that tour, because I have no idea where I'm going. At the bottom of the stairs, I take in my options. To the right is another room, and I can see from peeking in this must be the *large* living room. It runs down the side of the house that leads out onto a patio area. It's beautiful and reminds me so much of River's in that it doesn't look lived in. There are no personal touches, or anything to give me an insight into who Cole Connor is.

To my left is the *small* living room, which I comment on with sarcasm. It's bigger than my entire house. I decide to follow the hallway between the stairs and the small living room and make my way down until I reach the kitchen, which has an adjoining dining room.

Sat at the breakfast island with a hot cup of something is Cole. His beauty makes me want to cry, because I know it's not real. He's proved that today by showing me a lot of ugly.

"You're awake," he declares, closing his laptop.

I should ask how he knew I fell asleep, but I don't. I don't care, not in the grand scheme of things. But him bringing it up reminds me I still need to call my landlord.

"Dada," Poppy calls, stopping Cole from getting up.

He looks right at me and lets me see what I've refused to see. He really does only want to get to know her. "You told her?"

"Yes. She, um, she doesn't understand the significance, but with time, she will."

He clears his throat. "Thank you."

"Can I make her a drink, please?"

His brows pinch together. "You don't have to ask. This is your home too. Only the attic is locked, but other than that, please move around freely."

"I'm not quite there yet," I admit.

"Right," he replies. "Um, I don't have any squash."

"She doesn't drink squash. Too much sugar. If you don't have milk, water is fine."

"I have milk," he declares.

"Down, Mama," Poppy demands.

I gently lower her to the floor, and she immediately takes her bag. I smile as she gets out her sippy cup and runs it over to Cole.

"Looks like you're making the drink," I state, feeling uncomfortable. Now I'm no longer holding Poppy, I don't know what to do with my hands. It's a stupid thing to be focusing on, but if I drop them to my sides, I feel like a robot; if I cross my hands in front of me, I feel like a nanny waiting for instruction. And now, I feel like a freak act, so I decide to fold my arms across my stomach. "Do you have anything to make her a sandwich? I didn't pick anything up from home because it was ruined during the break in."

I miss out the part where I didn't have any food, or any of my tips to buy anything. He'll only use it against me.

"I think I have a jar of jam and some bread. I'm sorry it's not much. My assistant has ordered food, but it won't be delivered until later tonight."

"No, that's fine. Just show me where it is," I ask.

"Actually, can you lift up the laptop screen and start going through stuff she'll need for her room? I've picked out a few things, but I'd really appreciate your help," he declares, and I cave at the overwhelmed tone in his voice. "I can make her a sandwich while you do it."

"Um, okay," I reply. "She needs it cut up into small squares."

"Pop," Poppy demands, smacking the cup against his leg.

I watch a smile light up his face as he takes the cup from her. "Want to help me?"

"Yes," she replies. "Up."

His expression brings tears to my eyes, and I watch as he hesitantly picks her up. His gentleness and care nearly breaks me, and I have to look away before he sees how much this is affecting me.

He might not believe me when I tell him, but this is all I ever wanted. For her and for him. She deserves to have two parents who love her unconditionally. She deserves everything the world has to offer.

And every day, I've wished for this for her.

Keeping my secret had been easier than telling the truth, but I realise now how very wrong I was.

All my life I've had to lie. To teachers, to social workers, to my grandma and friends. It was engraved in me for as long as I can remember. The lies had been easier to deal with than the consequences. And when I left home to move in with my grandma, and I finally revealed the whole truth about my upbringing, I made a promise to myself that I would never do it again.

But some things don't change. I'm forever finding myself back in that place with my parents, and something drives me to keep the truth from people.

A voice inside my head tells me it's to protect me from being hurt, or maybe it's from years of emotional abuse; I don't know. There's no excuse for my behaviour, and I see that now as I watch them from the corner of my eye. I caused more hurt by keeping this from him.

I wish Poppy was the end of my deceit, but it's not. There's still something he doesn't know. Something no one other than my grandma knew.

I even have a secret from my friends, because I don't want them to look at me differently. I want to fit in. But I think now is the time to finally trust those around me, even if I get hurt in the process.

The laptop boots up, and immediately, I'm greeted by a list of items in a basket. My stomach drops at the amount. "Holy sugar," I hiss.

"What? Did I get the wrong things?"

"It's all toys," I point out.

He rubs the back of his neck. "I went on to a few sites, and this is what's popular. Is it wrong?"

"Cole, it's at two grand already. She doesn't need all of this."

"I want her to have everything," he rebuffs. "I noticed she had some Troll stuff, so I ordered them too."

"Poppy," Poppy cries, and Cole looks at me for answers.

"It's her Troll. I've left it in the room."

"We'll go and get it," he promises.

I scroll down. "You've got her a massive beanbag," I point out, as if he didn't already know. "And a massive chair."

"If you go on the next tab, there's a page with nursery sets. The cots change into toddler beds, but I didn't know which one you'd like."

I hold my breath as he walks over and clicks on the tab in question. In front of me is a grid of pictures of nursery set ups, and although I'm here under duress, I can't deny how gorgeous they are. I've always wanted to do this for her.

"Which one do you like?" he asks Poppy, and points to the screen.

"That one," she squeals, and points to the one with the canopy princess top.

"Is that one okay?"

"This is too much. Way too much. I can't let you do this."

"I want to. So please, help me, because I don't want to mess up and get the wrong thing," he orders. "I've added a car seat for my car, but please, add the rest to it."

I apply the set to the basket on a sigh and continue searching. "I'll add a booster chair for your dining room chairs, and stair gates. You'll also need to get some safety clips for the drawers in here and probably move a few things in your living room. It's not really child friendly."

"I have someone coming tomorrow to baby proof everything, so don't worry about those things. He'll fit stair gates to the stairs and kitchen too."

"Doll," Poppy demands.

"Let's go and get your doll," he tells her, and together, they head off into the house.

I continue to add a few things to the basket, feeling uncomfortable with doing so. All of this is extravagant and not needed.

It's also a slap in the face because it's everything I'll never be able to give her.

Sliding off the stool, I move to the large bay doors and look outside. It's a fairly large garden, and beautifully done. He must have a gardener come in, because it looks professionally done. I tried to maintain our garden at home, but aside from my grandma's flowerbed, everything was overgrown and filled with weeds. With my grandma sick, raising a toddler, and working nights, it got neglected a lot.

Thinking of the flowers my grandma planted saddens me. I wanted to keep them growing, so her memory could live on.

"Why do you look sad?" Cole asks, startling me.

"I was just thinking of my grandma's flowerbed back home. It will die now I'm not there."

"I can have it transported here," he tells me.

"It's fine," I whisper, still staring off outside. A building running alongside the left part of the fence catches my attention. "What is that building?"

"It's the pool house. It's heated, so you can use it whenever."

I nod without saying more, and I hear him move away. I take a quick look to find him steering Poppy over to the plate of food he made.

I go back to my gazing and admire how beautiful his home is. I guess there are worse places I could be kept.

Hopefully, over time, he'll see this won't work out, and he'll let us go.

I know I only have to make one phone call and my friends will be here, helping me break free. The only thing stopping me is that he's right. I do owe him this. Leaving won't fix anything; it will only make things worse, and I can't risk losing my daughter. I don't want weekend visitation or to go without spending holidays with her.

So, I'll play this his way.

For a while.

5

COLE

My first night putting my daughter to bed, and it's an overwhelming feeling. Everything she does scares me. We bathed her, and I was worried the water was too hot and deep. We put her to bed, and I worried she'd fall out in the middle of the night, even though Emily fixed a bed guard next to her to stop that from happening. She ate her dinner, and I was worried she'd choke. I saw everything around her as a danger, and all I wanted to do was protect her. Emily even slipped from her mood and laughed, which I hoped was a good thing.

I've never cared or worried for anyone like this. I always thought something inside of me was broken. It's why relationships never lasted. I never loved them enough to fight for them. But with Poppy, and in turn, Emily, a strong emotional connection has surfaced. It's almost domineering, like I see them as mine.

Emily has been upstairs awhile. I'm beginning to think she'll hide away up there for good. But as soon as the thought enters my mind, light, hesitant footsteps sound on the stairs.

By now, I'm normally deep in work in my office, but I wanted to be here in case either of them needed something.

My gaze is still on the doorway when she enters. "Did she settle okay?" I ask.

She nods and walks further into the room to take a seat on the sofa opposite. "There's actually something we need to talk about," she announces, running her hands down her thighs.

"If this is about our arrangement, I thought we cleared that up?"

Her nerves are showing. There's a tremble in her hands, and her leg begins to bounce. She does nothing to hide it, which means she isn't aware she's doing it. "No, it's about my pregnancy. I've waited until we were alone to discuss it."

I put my laptop down on the sofa next to me and sit up, giving her my full attention. "Okay. I'm listening."

Her eyes are swimming with tears when she looks at me, and there's a heartache shining back at me that I've only ever witnessed through loss.

"I was pregnant with twins. During my first trimester, I had two scans. One to confirm the pregnancy because I had been bleeding, and another for a dating scan. The first scan I had showed twins, which may have been the cause for how sick I was. During the second scan, they could only find one baby. They called it vanishing twin syndrome. It's not uncommon to have, and most of the time, they don't pick up on it since it happens so early in the pregnancy," she reveals, and I drop back against the sofa at the news. We lost a baby. "I wasn't keeping this from you, I promise. I was just trying to find the right time. It's not easy for me to talk about. In fact, until now, I've not spoken about it. No one else knows."

So not only have I learned that I'm a dad, but now I'm finding out it would have been twins. She went through this loss alone, and even though a voice is telling me she made it that way, it kills me that she had to. I should have been there.

"I'm so sorry, Emily. I can't imagine what that was like for you to go through. Alone as well."

She wipes away a tear and replies, "It was tough. I didn't want to face it. I never miscarried. I didn't even know whether they were a boy or a girl; I just knew I lost a baby and my pregnancy absorbed it. But you needed to know."

"And Poppy, she had no problems?" I ask, regretting that I missed it all.

"She was a little early, but only by a week. It's horrible to say, but before I lost the twin, I was weak and sick, but I started to regain strength again a few weeks later."

"I wish I had been there."

She hesitates for a split second, before deciding to go for it. "For what it's worth, I'm sorry you weren't. I know it means nothing now, but please, understand I didn't do this to hurt you."

I run a hand over my face and nod. "I'm not there yet, and I can't promise it will go away, but I'll try."

"I understand," she whispers.

"She's a clever girl. Poppy, I mean."

My comment brings a smile to her face. "Yeah, she's forward for her age and is above average on all her growth checks."

"She is?"

"Yeah."

"Does she go to nursery?"

"She does get fifteen hours per week, but that will change once she turns three. I mostly used those days to take my grandma to her appointments."

"I heard what happened. I'm sorry for your loss. I know you were close."

"Thank you."

When she doesn't say more, I ask, "Who has her when you're at work? Dave said your grandma had dementia, so I don't want to assume you left Poppy in her care."

"Never," she reveals, shaking her head vehemently. "I'm good friends with my neighbour. She works part-time, so she had Poppy at mine on Thursday and Friday nights. On some weekends, her daughter, who is sixteen, had her. But the night nurses didn't mind either and often took a little extra money to watch over her."

"And you did that while working until three-four in the morning?"

She shrugs. "It gave me more time with Poppy. It was hard at first because I was tired, but I guess I got used to it. I napped when she did, which worked out well 'cause it was usually the time my grandma went to lie down."

"And what if she was ill? I only ask because I had someone look into Poppy, and they found she's had a lot of doctor visits."

Her eyes narrow a little. "I never once went into work if she was sick. She has always come first, Cole."

"I wasn't stating otherwise."

"Yes, you were."

"Look, I'm sorry. I just want to know everything. I'm not judging you."

"Would life have been easier if I worked nine till five? Probably, but then I would have missed so much time with my daughter, and I didn't want to do that. I didn't have the luxury of not working. I did what I needed to do."

She flips her blonde hair over her shoulder, gazing down at the floor. I cross my hands between my legs and lean forward. "I didn't mean to upset you. I'm just trying to understand how you did it all."

She nods but still doesn't meet my gaze. Not even a day, and I'm already fucking this up.

"Speaking of work, I need to know how it will work now. The only reason I had good childcare was because we lived next door to each other. I can't see Mel letting her daughter stay over here."

"You don't need to work."

She stiffens and cuts me with a sharp look. "Yes, I do."

"I can give you money. You can spend all your time with Poppy, like you wanted."

"It's not about that anymore. I love being a mum. I don't want to imagine a life without her, but that's not saying I don't need my own identity. I need my friends. I love working at Tease, and I just got a promotion."

"But you don't need to now. Harriett has left, and I'm pretty sure I recently read that Olivia has gone on maternity leave whilst Gabby is still recuperating at home."

"Harriett still pops in and sees over the dance routines. Olivia should be back in a few weeks, and Gabby is already back at work. If you've forgotten, she was kidnapped by a serial killer. At *your* club."

"Exactly. Which means it's not safe for you."

"It's not safe for anyone."

"They aren't my child's mother."

She blows out a breath. "I get that you want to be a part of Poppy's life, and I'm supporting that because it's not about me. It's about her. But you do not get to have a say in my life. I don't care who you are, what pull you have, or if you threaten me; I'm not leaving work. And I'm not going to quit working at the gym either."

"I'm not trying to tell you what to do. But you said it yourself: this isn't what you want to do. You wanted to be a hairdresser."

Her eyes widen at the comment, and I know she's going back to the first night we met each other. I didn't want to give myself away, but I've never forgotten that night or the things we discussed. No amount of sex ever erased that night from my mind. She was all I saw in other women's faces. It was her I was touching. It was her I was fucking. And it was her who took me with their mouth.

"I'm not quitting. Not now. Dave needs all the help he can get since he has pulled others from the bar to work the stage."

"You still have another two weeks off, right?"

"Yes."

"Then we have time to come up with an arrangement. I can hire a childminder."

She's surprised I've given in. "You would do that?"

"Yes," I agree.

"Thank you," she replies warily.

"But I do want you to think about going to college to study hair. And before you begin to argue, this isn't me telling you what to do. This is me telling you, you have options now. You don't have to work stupid hours to make a living. You aren't alone anymore. I'm here."

"Funny, because it sounds a lot like you telling me what to do."

"Put it this way, is this what you want to do for the rest of your life?" When she doesn't answer, I continue. "You can still work at the club. You just don't need to do those long hours anymore to make money."

"I like working there," she admits, but I can hear what she isn't saying. She wants to go to college.

"I'm not saying you don't," I reply.

"Speaking of money, if we are staying here, I want to help towards bills and food."

"God no," I retort without thinking.

Her gaze narrows. "You wanted us here so you could co-parent. The least you could do is let me help."

"I really don't want to sound like a dick when I say this, but I have enough money to pay for it all."

"Good for you, but I work hard for my money, and I expect to pay my own way."

"And I've missed two years of my daughter's life, so think of this as me giving you everything I missed out on giving from the start."

"You need to stop throwing it in my face because there's only so much I'll take."

I pinch the bridge of my nose. "The house is paid for outright. If you want to help with shopping, then fine. It's not like I'll know what to get anyway."

"You eat, don't you?"

"Yeah, *out*. I've rarely eaten at home, hence the empty cupboards."

Her eyes widen at the declaration. "Then I'll cook to help out too."

"You aren't here to be my maid or cook. This isn't a give and take scenario where we keep score. All I want to do is help. I didn't bring you here to take your money or your time. I'm not trying to rub what I have in your face, and I'm sorry if it's coming across that way. I would have done this for you from the moment I found out you were pregnant, and I'm not sure if you've noticed, but I'm a very persuasive man."

"Then we'll agree for me to do the shopping from now on. If there's anything you need, we'll have a list on the fridge you can add to. I enjoy cooking so it won't be any hardship, and if it's okay with you, I'll do the cleaning. I can tell from how clean it is that you have a maid come in and do it."

"Actually, no, I do it. I like to keep my life private, so the only hired help who comes here is the gardener."

"You clean?"

"Yes," I reply, and I know I've shocked her. "We aren't going to get all the answers today. It's going to be a work in progress, and it's not even been a day."

"I know. I just don't like not knowing."

"Back to the work issue. There's actually something I've been keeping from everyone."

"Please don't tell me it's true, and you're closing."

"No, although it has crossed my mind during recent events."

"Then what?"

"It came to my attention that some of the girls have outgrown the stage and want to stop stripping."

"What? Who? What does that even mean?"

"Let me finish?" I demand, arching a brow.

She settles back into the sofa, letting out a breath. "Sorry."

"As I was saying, some girls want to stop stripping, so I've been looking for a space near the town centre to open up some sort of coyote bar." Her jaw drops, and her eyebrows rise. "The hours will be different. It will be open from seven till two in the morning, which is more reasonable. And to keep business flowing, we have room to have open mic nights and put on shows during the week. And no one has to strip, which will give us room to open up auditions for new Tease dancers."

"I… Who… Did…" She stops rambling to take a breath, gaining her composure. She wants to ask if it's because of her and her friends. And she'd be right in assuming that. I heard them talking about it, and not to mention, I've had reports about it from Dave. "Did someone tell you about me and my friends asking for a coyote night?"

I lie when I reply. "It was just brought to my attention. I'm not aware of who brought it up."

She can't mask the excitement in her gaze. "You have no idea what this will mean for some of them. Olivia's eldest sibling found out about her stripping, and ever since, she's felt dirty about dancing. The same goes for Gabby, since she's now technically a new mum. I just want to be where they are. None of us are ashamed of working there. We love it, and it's not what society says it is. But this would change their lives."

I smile. "When the contract comes in, I'll have to show you the plans."

Suddenly, there's a buzzing in the room, alerting me to the front gate.

"What is that?" she asks, startled.

I grab my phone and log into the app to show me who's there. "It's the food," I reply, and buzz them in.

She stands, announcing, "I'll come help."

"No, I've got it. Didn't you want to talk to your landlord?"

She bites on her bottom lip, and I have to shove my hand in my pocket to stop myself from reaching out and stopping her.

If anyone is going to bite that lip, it's me.

Shaking those thoughts away, I miss what she says. "I'm sorry, what did you say?"

Her brows pinch together. "I said I'll go back upstairs. I can call him from the dressing room."

"Alright."

"If it's alright with you, I think I'm going to head to bed right after. It's been a long day."

I stop at the front door. "Emily, this is your house now. You can do whatever you'd like."

"Not there yet," she mutters, and I swear, it's her favourite sentence today.

She heads off upstairs, and I go to the door. With time, she'll understand why I'm doing this and agree it was the best decision. I may still be angry with her, but it doesn't mean I don't want what's best for her too. Especially now she's revealed the loss she endured whilst pregnant. I can't imagine what that must have been like for her. To be pregnant, working, and caring for a sick grandma. She had the world on her shoulders. I'm willing to bet she pushed her grief to the side and didn't reveal it to those around her.

I've spent years watching her. I've seen her grow into her confidence and into her role at the club. She reminds me of a flower growing through a crack in the pavement.

I don't know what our future holds, but I'm not going anywhere. Not now. Not ever.

6

EMILY

Continuous tapping stirs me awake from my restless sleep. It has been unsettling trying to sleep in a strange home. Every noise, creak or buzz was new, and it kept me awake half the night. Crying myself to sleep during the day probably didn't help, and it wasn't until Cole walked past the bedroom at gone two in the morning that I finally drifted off.

The tapping continues, and I fully wake when I hear the front door open. Voices drift up the stairs, and I slide out of bed, careful not to jostle Poppy. I open the door a crack and hear a woman's voice float up the stairs.

"We are here because your assistant accidently emailed your father a link to a baby shop. We called this morning, and she congratulated us on becoming grandparents. What on earth is going on? There must be some sort of mix up. We didn't even know you were dating, Cole."

"Mum, please, keep it down. They are still sleeping," Cole warns.

A deep voice joins the conversation. "Son, what is going on?"

"I found out a few weeks ago that I'm a father to a little girl. She'll be two soon. The email you received was meant to be for me so I could get her the things she needed."

"What?" his mother cries. "When? How?"

"Honey, if you need to know how…" the deep voice teases.

"Now is not the time, Joe," she scolds.

"Can we do this another day?" Cole asks. "They're sleeping upstairs."

"No. I want to know how you've only just found out about this daughter, how you know it's yours, and why she is here."

I hear a weary exhale. "Because I've been running the sister club, trying to get it back on its feet after the fire, for the past two years," he replies. "I only came back recently, which is how I found out."

"Why on earth didn't she tell you before?" Joe asks.

"Oh my gosh, she's a stripper, isn't she? I warned you not to get involved with those girls."

"Mum, stop," he warns.

"Is your mother right?"

I hear Cole let out a breath, whilst I hold mine, waiting for the answer. "She works there, but she doesn't strip. We spent one night together, but I swear, she isn't who you probably think she is."

"I bet she probably is," his mother scolds.

"She's right, son. You don't know this woman."

"And how do you know the kid is yours? This woman could be saying it to get money out of you."

"If that was the case, why didn't she tell me I had a daughter? She could have gotten money from me from the very beginning, but she didn't. I only found out because I saw her, and she looks just like Lana."

Lana? Who's Lana?

Does he have another kid?

"Have you done a paternity test to confirm it?"

"I don't need to," he argues. "I know, Mum. I know!"

"Alright, everyone needs to calm down."

"No, I won't calm down. He has a stripper living with him. She could be involved with the wrong people, or here for the wrong reasons."

"I invited her here," Cole tells her. "Can we move this into the kitchen?"

"I could do with a coffee," Joe replies.

"Mama," Poppy calls, and I startle, like I got caught. "Up."

I rush over to the bed, and Poppy immediately moves the sheets off her. "Did you have a good sleep, baby?"

"Wet," she cries, her nose scrunching up.

"Let's get you changed," I offer, and move over to the bag where the nappies and wipes are. I've been trying to potty train her for a few months now, but it's a work in progress.

As I begin to work on changing her, I take my time, hoping I give Cole enough time to get his parents to leave. I don't want to be this person, but after listening to them talk about me, I can't see my presence here being a good thing. I also don't want to subject Poppy to that kind of energy. It messes with a kid, and she already had to listen to us argue at the house yesterday.

"Tea," Poppy demands, asking for the one thing I treat her to in the mornings.

"Why don't we sit up here and read a book?"

"No. Poppy want food," she whines, rubbing sleep from her eyes.

Letting out a breath, I quickly tie my hair up and lift her into my arms. "Come on then, baby."

"Dada?"

"He's downstairs, waiting for you."

"Yes," she cheers.

As I make my way down the stairs, I can still hear the heated argument happening in the kitchen.

"What if she's after your money? Why does she need to be here? Don't give up your life for a woman you had a one-night stand with."

"Are you asking me to give up my daughter?" he asks, aghast.

"Of course not," she replies, equally upset over the accusation.

"Then stop. I'm not giving up my life, I'm adding to it."

"Alright, son, we get it," Joe replies.

"I don't," his mum replies.

"Dada," Poppy calls, revealing our arrival.

I lower her to the floor, and she immediately runs over to Cole, who easily lifts her into his arms with a smile on his face.

His parents are enamoured with her, watching as she gives him a kiss on the cheek. The woman, who I'm guessing is his mum, has dark brown hair perfectly styled to frame her round face. She's wearing a cotton pencil skirt with a cream blouse that shapes her curvy frame.

His dad, who bears no resemblance to his son, has silver hair, naturally slicked back. Unlike his son, he doesn't wear suits. Instead, he has on dark navy jeans and a plaid blue shirt. He's a large, handsome man.

"Food?" Poppy asks.

"You want breakfast?"

"Yes!" she sings.

"Cereal?" he asks.

"No," I call out. "It has too much sugar, which upsets her stomach."

"What does she normally have?" he asks, acting like his parents aren't here and we've been doing this for a while.

Aware of the audience and not wanting to cause a scene to prove their argument right, I reply, "She likes scrambled eggs and toast."

"Scrambled eggs it is," he reveals, and lowers her to the floor.

Noticing the two newcomers watching me, I lamely wave. "Hi. I'm Emily. This is Poppy, our daughter."

"I'm Poppy," Poppy giggles.

"It's lovely to meet you," the lady greets, and there's a warmth in her eyes as she kneels down to Poppy's height, running her hand over the troll's head. "And who is this lovely lady?"

"Poppy, my troll," Poppy explains, and hands her the Troll doll.

She takes it with care, running her hand over the spiked hair sticking up. "She's lovely."

Poppy takes it back, and I move to pick her back up. "Why don't you take a seat at the table while I help with food?"

"Okay," she answers, and I lower her onto a chair. "And tea."

"And tea," I agree, tapping her nose. "Remember, call me if you want to get down."

She goes back to playing and I make my way over to the kitchen counter, bravely speaking up, even if I can't meet their gaze. "I know you have questions, and I know you have your reservations about me, but please, if you don't mind, keep them to yourselves whilst Poppy is here?" I whisper, beating some eggs into a bowl to keep busy.

Cole places his hand on the small of my back, and I try hard not to react to it. His touch is like fire, and I can feel it all over.

His mother inhales sharply, distracting me from his touch. "You heard?"

"I did," I admit.

I won't cry.

"I'm so sorry you had to hear that," she tells me, and her words sound sincere. "It's a shock, and we don't know you."

Joe stands next to his wife, offering his support when I finally find the courage to look at them. "Georgia didn't mean anything bad by what she said."

I meet Georgia's gaze. "It's okay if you did. He's your son, and you love him. I get that. I'd be the same if it was Poppy. But I'm not here to take anything from your son. I don't actually want to be here," I ramble. "He's asked to get to know Poppy, and I won't stop him. Please, be assured, I'm not after his money, nor am I trying to trap him. If he asks us to leave, I will. Happily."

"You aren't going anywhere," he growls under his breath.

Georgia steps forward. I'm not sure what she's going to do, until she opens her arms and hugs me. "I'm really sorry for judging you. It was unfair of me."

I awkwardly hug her back, my posture rigid. "It's okay."

Joe clears his throat. "I bet this news has been a surprise to your family as well."

I hand Cole the eggs to put in the pan and reluctantly reply. "Actually, I don't have much to do with my family. My grandma raised me from a teenager, and she passed away recently. So aside from the funeral, we've not seen them."

I mentally slap my forehead for being so honest. Georgia shares a look with Cole, and there's a silent conversation going on there that the rest of us aren't aware of. "I'm sorry to hear that."

"Mum and Dad have a big family," Cole reveals. "They expect everyone else to as well."

"I do not," his mother scolds softly.

Joe laughs. "Yeah, honey, you do."

"Oh stop," she replies, laughing. "Although, I can't wait to tell everyone we have a grandchild."

Cole groans. "Let me get to know her before you start telling everyone. I'll never get rid of Aria if she finds out."

"Aria is his sister," his mum explains.

"She's a little wild," Joe admits.

"Kit is just the same," Cole states, his posture and words such a contradiction to the man I've come to know. He's relaxed around them. More himself. "Where is he now?"

"He's actually on his way home from Australia," Georgia announces.

"His brother can never settle. He needs to be on the move, seeing new places," Joe explains.

"What about Dave? Is he your brother too?" I ask, remembering Dave saying they were family.

"Oh, Dave is—" his mum begins, but Cole interrupts her.

"Dave isn't that kind of family. We were brought up together, and he became a part of the family."

There's a tension in the air, and I know they are keeping something from me. Although his words ring true, I feel like there's more to the story.

"Me and my friends are like that. We became our own family since most of us didn't have a good one growing up."

"They don't see their families either?" Georgia asks, and although it wasn't said nastily, I can detect judgement.

"Harriett's mum died when she was younger, but she has a close friendship with her dad. Olivia's dad forgets she exists until she reminds him, and her mother—before she died—wasn't really a mother. Olivia is raising her siblings. Gabby doesn't have a good relationship with her parents because she's gay, but recently, she reconnected with her mum. We're all like sisters—except for Olivia and Gabby, who are now dating," I declare. "Sorry. I ramble when I'm nervous."

"Don't be nervous. I can't wait to meet these friends of yours. Do they work at Tease too?"

Heat floods my cheeks. "Harriett is practically a doctor and has degrees in so many fields. She doesn't work at Tease anymore. I think she only did it because at one point, she was going to be a professional dancer. Not a stripper dancer," I remark quickly, wishing I was the one sitting at the table with Poppy so I could distract myself.

"And the others?" Joe asks. "Do they still work there?"

"Sort of. Olivia is on maternity leave at the moment because she got custody of her mum's newborn. She died giving birth," I explain. "She might actually be going to university to do nursing, but it's just an option right now. Gabby loves dancing, but she's taking time off to recover from her kidnapping."

"She was kidnapped?" Georgia asks, aghast.

I inwardly groan. I'm really not making a good first impression. "I'm sure you read about it in the news. She was taken by the serial killer."

"Oh my lord. Is she okay?"

"She's doing a lot better. She bounced back pretty quickly."

"They still haven't managed to find him, have they," Joe states.

I shake my head. "No, but they've got new information now so it's only a matter of time."

"What new information?" Cole asks, sharp and alert.

"He mentioned a brother to Gabby," I admit. "He said a bunch of stuff, but her memory of that night hasn't fully come back to her yet."

He pushes up from his chair. "Can you finish helping Poppy? I just remembered I need to go and make some calls."

I move over to the table. "Um, sure. Is everything okay?"

"Yeah, I just forgot to move an appointment back," he explains, but it's a lie. "Mum, Dad, why don't we have dinner here at the weekend?"

"I think that's our cue to leave," Joe remarks.

"It's okay. We're actually going out for breakfast," she promises. "We'll come for dinner on Saturday."

"Good," he replies, and I can see he's eager to leave.

Georgia turns back to us and makes her way over. "It was lovely meeting you, Emily."

"You too, Georgia."

"Goodbye, sweetheart," she tells Poppy, and presses her lips to her head before looking back at me. "Would it be okay if I took Poppy out shopping before dinner on Saturday? I would love to treat her to some new things."

I bite my lip because I'm not sure if I'm comfortable with that. "I'm not sure you can get her anything new. Cole went overboard and bought an entire shop."

"I'm sure we'll find something she wants."

When I don't reply, Joe butts in. "It's okay, darling. We're new, and she doesn't know us."

"It's not that I don't trust you. You seem like great people. And with how Cole has been since we got here, if she wasn't safe with you, he would have already refused. It's just… she doesn't really know you. I don't really know you."

Georgia grasps my shoulder. "Then let's change that. We'll make it a girl's day and use the time to get to know each other. Unless you have other plans?"

I give her a warm smile, glad that she's not taken it to heart. "I'd love that."

"I'll get your number off Cole later, and I'll message you with a time."

"Great," I reply. "See you Saturday."

As they leave, I can't help but watch Cole. He seems distracted. I'm surprised he didn't push them out.

What did I say that made him react like that?

Poppy dropping her fork brings me back to the present and I reach down to pick it up. I'm not going to get answers from him. It came to me when I was lying in bed last night: he asked a lot of questions about us yesterday but always managed to evade the ones about himself. He did it skilfully so I wouldn't question it. But a woman's midnight thoughts pick at every waking moment.

I'll have to be just as skilled to get answers.

Because neither of us really know who Cole Connor is, and that needs to change.

7

COLE

After handing over a tip to the team who assembled Poppy's bedroom and made it look more like a little girl's room, I bid them a good day.

I wanted to be the one who put it all together since I never got to do it for her as a baby, but I saw all the boxes, with screws and bolts, and lost confidence that I could make it safe. So I called in reinforcements, who not only helped assemble everything but switched out screws for bolts and made it as safe as it will ever get for our daughter. With their service came an interior designer, who made it look like a little girl's dream room. She has a colouring section, a reading corner, and even a play area where a massive doll house was added.

Tomorrow, they'll be back to sort through the new deliveries arriving. I've ordered her another colouring table and a few more toys to keep downstairs, and whilst browsing their website, I ordered a play set for the garden, which will take a few more weeks to arrive. Everything is coming together, so hopefully, they'll both feel at home.

Closing the door, I head into the kitchen, where Poppy and Emily are preparing dinner. Emily has been quiet for most of the day and detached herself from any of the arrangements. I didn't think it would be smooth sailing, but I didn't expect this. I thought after this morning, we had reached some sort of middle ground to do what's best for Poppy.

She even won over my parents, though I knew, deep down, they were treading carefully so they didn't make things worse.

"Do you want to see your new bedroom, Poppy?" I ask, my tone still foreign to me. I'm used to being sharp, unforgiving, and stern. I'm unapologetic with whoever I speak to. But Poppy, she brings out a softer side, something I didn't think I'd ever have.

"Mine and Mummy's?" she asks, her button nose scrunching up.

"No, you'll have your own bedroom," I explain.

"Sleep with Mummy," she tells me.

Taking pity on me, Emily intervenes and lowers the spoon so she can kneel in front of Poppy. "No. You'll have a big girl's room now."

"But I'm a baby," she argues.

Emily chuckles. "Yes, you're my baby. But now you'll get your own room. It will be fun."

"You sleep with me?"

"Hey, why don't we go check it out and you can decide for yourself?" I offer.

She blinks up at me, and I realise I sounded like small print on a contract.

"You go on upstairs with Daddy, and he'll show you your new room."

Reluctantly, Poppy agrees and strolls over to me to take my hand. "Are you coming?"

Emily shakes her head and forces a smile. "I'll finish dinner. It's nearly done, so I'll call you when it's ready."

Not wanting to push her any more than I already have, I lift Poppy up and begin to make my way up to her room.

Reaching the top of the stairs, I close the gate behind me and lower Poppy to the floor.

"Are you ready?"

"Yes!" she cheers, and I push open the door, letting her see what we've all been working on.

After deciding to skip a cot and go straight for a bed, I was a little bit worried about the dangers. But now, seeing the grey-framed bed sat on the floor with only the mattress for height, I'm not as worried. The guards on the sides make it look like a massive floor mat. A soft, salmon-coloured canopy on the roof-shaped top has lights that fall on either side, giving it a princess feel.

The stylist did good at making it look inviting. Along with the massive Troll bean bag, they chose a large grey chair, which again is floor level so there isn't a risk of Poppy trying to climb it. And since she has her chest of drawers in the walk-in wardrobe, I don't have to worry about those either. The bookshelf and unit that houses her pens and crayons are also bolted to the wall. And to be even safer, I had them bolt the two tables to the floor. It will take some work to be repaired when she outgrows the table, but it will be worth it.

Warily, Poppy steps inside, her Troll dropping to her side as she gazes at everything. "Wow!"

"It's all yours, Poppy," I tell her.

Her hair swings as she turns to me. "Mine?"

"Yes, this is all yours now. This is your room."

She picks up a doll with round blue eyes and long blonde hair. "Poppy's?"

"Yes, baby, it's yours."

She squeals, and the sound brings me joy. She runs over to the paper set strategically out on the table. "Poppy's?"

Her happiness is infectious, and I find myself smiling wide. "Yes."

"Poppy," she squeals, pointing to her favourite Troll on the bean bag.

"This Poppy's?" she asks, and I know she's not asking if it's hers. She's asking if it's her troll's.

"It's for both of you," I promise, then step over to the bed. "And this is your bed. Do you like it?"

"Love," she squeals. I almost have a heart attack when she goes to dive on it. Luckily, I'm quick, and I manage to lift her up by her waist and gently lower her onto it. She laughs and rolls around on the bed until all the sheets and pillows are a mess.

"Me sleep here?"

"Only if you want to," I tell her, knowing now that the room divide isn't just hard on Emily, but Poppy too.

"I'm a big girl," she tells me, and lies down on the pillow before jumping back up. She wobbles out of the bed and heads back over to the beanie, where she lays Poppy down before covering her with a blanket. "Poppy sleep too."

Movement at the door catches my attention, and I turn to find Emily leaning against the doorframe, a mist of tears in her eyes as she watches her daughter.

"What do you think?"

"It's incredibly beautiful."

"Mummy," Poppy cries and races over to the door, taking her mum's hand to pull her into the room. "Mine."

"I know, it's beautiful."

Poppy takes a doll, giving it to her mum. "Mine too."

"What else can you show me?"

"My bed. Look," she demands. "You can sleep too."

Emily lets out a laugh, but I think it's more to cover up a sob. "Thank you."

"Look, I didn't understand before, but I see it now. If this is too much, we can change this into a playroom," I tell her.

Her gaze breaks me. "No. This was always going to happen. It should be now."

"I've put the screen by the side of your bed. You can log in on your phone too, so you don't need to keep bringing it up and down when she takes a nap."

"Where are the cameras?" she asks, gazing around the room.

"One is on the shelf in the corner so you can see the entire room, and then," I begin, walking closer to the bed. I point at the end of the bed. "That one will show the entire cot."

"Cool," she muses. "Dinner's ready, by the way."

"Eat here?" Poppy asks, pointing to her colouring table.

Emily beams at her daughter. "We don't want to get spaghetti bolognaise all over your nice new table, do we?"

Poppy shakes her head. "No," she replies, then races over to the beanbag to give her troll a kiss. "Be back!"

I immediately lift her in my arms. I'll never get tired of this feeling. It's as if I have the whole world in my arms. I've never in my life, ever, felt anywhere close to what I feel for our daughter. It's like I had nothing before her, and now I feel like I have everything.

"I tell you what, if you eat all your dinner, we can come up here and draw some pictures. What do you say?"

"Yes!" she cheers, squeezing her arms around my neck.

Emily clears her throat. "We both know it won't matter what she eats. You'll still come up and draw."

I grin because she isn't wrong. "And that's a bad thing?"

"No, I just never would have pictured you to be like this."

"Honestly? Neither did I."

That's the last she speaks as we make our way downstairs. Which is fine, because Poppy speaks enough for the both of us.

WALKING upstairs from my office later that night, I expect the house to be quiet since it's two in the morning.

However, the kitchen counter light is on, so instead of heading up to bed, I go to investigate why Emily is up, just in case it's because of Poppy.

In a pair of silk pyjamas and an oversized cardigan, Emily sits at the breakfast bar with a cup of tea in her hand. I take a minute to look her over. She's still got the same slim frame as when I first met her, but she's wider now in the hips, which looks good on her. But there's something else, something I haven't been able to put my finger on. She's grown in confidence, and there's a fight in her tone. But even with that, I still can't pinpoint exactly what is bothering me. Or why it does.

She looks up at the sound of me taking a step inside the kitchen. "Sorry, did I disturb you?"

"I was downstairs in my office," I answer, my feet light on the floor as I make my way round the counter.

Her nose scrunches up. "There's a downstairs?"

I grin as I flip on the kettle. "Yeah. It's a man cave. Where did you think all those danger hazards went?" I tease, bringing up the ornaments and glass vases I had removed from Poppy's reach. "Did you not take a look around today?"

"The garage?" she replies, completely ignoring my other question.

I chuckle as I pour the hot water over the tea bag. "What has you up this late?"

"A bunch of things."

"Want to share?"

"The police still don't know who broke into my home."

I take a seat opposite her, fighting back the urge to sit next to her. She looks so sad right now. "It could have been anyone in that neighbourhood."

"I've lived there for a while, and I've never been broken into. And despite what you think of the area, everyone looks out for one another. Nothing bad really happens there."

"Did they pick up anything from the fingerprints?"

"No. Whoever it was, they wore gloves."

"I get that it's stressful. However, for some reason, I don't think that is the reason you are looking so gloomy."

When she meets my gaze, her eyes are filled with unshed tears. "It's nothing."

"You can talk to me," I tell her, hoping my words carry the truth. I don't want her to think it was a demand.

She lets out a dry laugh. "You already think the worst of me."

"You don't know what I think of you."

She wipes under her eyes with frustration. "You've said plenty."

"In the heat of the moment, yes," I agree. "Now, what is it?"

She lets out an adorable puff of air. "My grandma's funeral was costly. Her estate is still being looked through, so the funds won't be released until then. The funeral directives knew this and agreed to a payment plan until the rest of the funds were released. The day you came to mine, I had just come back from shopping. My card had been declined, and after investigating why, I found the funeral directives had taken the entire amount and left my account in debt. I went to get my tips from the club, since we had bills coming out and needed food…" She chokes on a sob.

"And it's been stolen."

She nods. "I'm in a strange home, I'm no longer sharing a room with my daughter, and I have no money. I feel trapped and just needed to take a breather."

"Then let me help you. I'll have my assistant transfer funds into your account."

She stands with her cup in her hand, moving over to the sink. "No. I didn't tell you because I want your money."

"I know. And I know this isn't a story to hint at getting some either."

She swills her cup out and leaves it on the drainer to dry. "So, you'll be okay with me declining the offer."

"No. I won't. I don't want you to feel trapped here. If having a little bit of money in your account makes you feel a little less trapped here, then it will be money well spent. I want you to feel at home here, not like a prisoner."

"Then you shouldn't have forced me here," she snaps, but the fight immediately leaves her. "I'm sorry."

"No, you're right. I should have gone about this another way, but I don't regret it. Because you're both here. Where you should have been all along."

"Have you ever been forced to be somewhere you don't want to be? It's not a great feeling. I get why, but it doesn't make it hurt any less. I feel like I've lost a part of my daughter and myself along the way. It's going to take time to come to terms with that, not money."

I take her elbow to stop her from leaving the room. "I've felt trapped before. I've been locked in Hell and fought to get myself out. But I didn't do it alone. I had people who loved me unconditionally, who helped me out of the darkest depths of Hell. And because of them, I learned that I didn't need to do it all alone. You don't either. You might not like how you get to where you are going, but I can promise you, when you get to where you want to be, wanting for nothing more, it will be worth it. Because you fought to get there." I take a breath, knowing I revealed more than I wanted to. "You want Poppy to have everything you didn't. I see it in the way you speak to her, the way you brush her hair, and the way you listen intently to her, even though she's speaking incoherently. You don't care because you'd give her everything. Your time, your love, and your life if it came down to it. If you are willing to do all of that for her, then why not this? Why not give her the life we can provide for her, together?"

"You're right. I can't keep thinking of what should've, would've or could've been. I need to think about right now. And right now, she needs to know her father. She needs to grow up seeing that love can come in all forms. My parents didn't love me, and I grew up knowing it. Poppy has two parents who love her, and she doesn't deserve to have me getting in between that."

"For what it's worth, I wish things didn't have to happen like this."

She forces a smile. "Me too," she replies, before whispering, "Goodnight, Cole."

"Goodnight, Emily."

8

EMILY

It's late Friday evening and my phone hasn't stopped blowing up with messages and calls. None of us are working tonight, and my friends want to know where I am. I've been able to keep them in the dark all week, but now, all bets are off. If I don't go to the pub, they'll phone the police and start a search party. And if I do go, I'm not sure whether I can pretend everything is okay.

Keys clang in the bowl at the door, and I hold my breath, waiting for Cole to reach the kitchen. He's been gone for an hour, seeming smug about something before he left. In black trousers and a white crisp shirt with the sleeves rolled up, he oozes sex—somewhere my mind should definitely not be going when I look at him. But it does. Every single time. I can't help it. I shouldn't find him attractive after everything he's said and done, but I do. Sadly, my hormones don't factor in all that he's done.

My phone lights up again, vibrating across the counter. "That's been going off a lot today. Everything okay?"

"It's my friends. We are meant to be meeting for a drink tonight, but I still haven't told them what happened or that I'm here."

"From what Dave has said, you four don't keep secrets from each other."

I glance away, unable to meet his gaze. He already thinks I'm a liar. This is just more evidence I'm not honest with those in my life. "We don't keep secrets from each other. Sometimes, I think they know me better than I know myself."

"Then why not tell them you are here?"

This time, I do meet his gaze, giving him a piece of me in the hope he understands. "Our friendship is something I've never had in my life before. I've never had people care for me or love me like they do," I explain, holding back the emotion those words cause. "My grandma loved me, but it was a maternal love. My friends… it's different. They don't just need me, they want me in their lives, and it goes both ways. They made me stronger. We make each other stronger."

"And you don't want them to see you as weak for giving in to me and moving in," he finishes, seeing where I am going with this.

"I guess in a way, I am," I whisper. "All three of them are so strong. They are a force to be reckoned with. I don't want them to see me as weak or treat me differently. They are the only people I've had in my life who have seen me as their equal."

He leans over the counter, his broad shoulders tensing. I gulp at the sight of his muscles and remember to keep breathing. "And what do you think will happen if they see you as weak?"

I open my mouth to reply, but then stop, not knowing what to say. Our friendship is like a strong family bond. There is no jealousy. There's no time-keeping on how long it takes to reply to a message, or how much time you spend with another person. It's not about what is given. And we never had to worry about us all falling for the same person. Things that other friends fall out over don't even factor into our friendship. We don't expect to be anyone's main focus because we know, come good or bad, we are there for each other. We aren't a one-way friendship. It's how we roll. But having him question it out loud has given me pause. I don't know what I'm scared of. I'm not even sure if it's a conditioned reaction from my childhood.

"I don't know," I reply.

"Then tell them. You've been here nearly a week, so they'll find out sooner or later."

"Yeah, I guess you are right. But I don't have a sitter since—"

"I'm here."

"I can't ask you to babysit."

The flesh between his eyes scrunches together. "I'm her dad, Emily. You aren't asking me to watch our daughter. Just like I wouldn't ask you to watch her. You aren't doing this alone anymore. If we both have plans, we can ask my parents to watch her until we hire a childminder. But until then, we can do this together."

"I'm sorry. I didn't mean it like that. I promise," I assure him before letting out a sigh. "I guess it's going to take some getting used to."

He slides over a set of car keys. "You can take your new car to meet your friends."

"I don't have a new car," I tell him, eyeing the keys suspiciously.

"Yes, you do. It's what my call was about earlier. It was ready to be picked up."

"I have a car," I tell him, letting my voice drop. He needs to hear how serious I am.

"I'm surprised that scrap of metal made it here. I'm having it towed tomorrow. It's not safe for you or Poppy."

"You're being serious, aren't you?"

His dark eyebrows pinch down. "Deadly."

"I'm not taking that car. And you aren't taking mine. I'm not your girlfriend, and I'm not your responsibility. You can't just do things like this, Cole. It's not normal," I snap. "Get whatever you want for Poppy, I won't stop you, but leave me out of it. I don't need you throwing this in my face."

"Emily, wait," he calls, but I grab my bag hanging over the chair.

"Stop. I'll be back by half eleven," I tell him.

He calls my name, but I continue, angry that he can make me feel so cheap. I might not own expensive things, but I don't see the point in living above my means. I have everything I need or want. Although the gesture is sweet, it's also patronising. I can get my own damn new car when the time is right.

Getting into the beat-up vehicle, I throw my bag on the passenger seat. I need to get out of here. I can wait until I'm far enough away to pull over and message my friends to tell them I'm on my way.

I shove the key into the ignition, and I'm greeted by a jittering sound. I twist the key again, pressing my foot down on the clutch, and I'm greeted with the sound once more before it quickly dies.

I slap my hands on the steering wheel as knuckles tap on the glass window. I don't move my gaze from the steering wheel as I wind the window down.

"I didn't buy it," he tells me. I slowly meet his gaze as he holds the keys through the window. "One of our client's sons owed the club in London a lot of money. His son set fire to one of the booths after he found his dad in there with a dancer. To thank me for not pressing charges, he offered us a new car through his dealership on top of the money he covered for damages. I was going to decline it, or give it away, but then I saw your junk of a car and thought of you. This wasn't about anything more than that. I promise."

"I didn't know."

He smirks. "You never asked."

"Neither do you," I wearily let out. "You should have spoken to me first."

"I knew you would say no. I thought if you saw it, you wouldn't turn it down."

He steps away from the window, and I get a good look at the blue Toyota. It's beautiful, and in my favourite colour. Cole jangles the keys. "Can we agree to scrap this car now?"

I reluctantly take the keys. "You should have told me it was blue to start with. I'm a sucker for blue."

He laughs as he pulls open my door. I grab my bag and slide out. "I'll remember that for the next time."

"There is no next time. I'm serious about this needing to stop. I'm not your responsibility. I can take care of myself."

"Okay, I promise to speak to you first. This will be the last time I do something without you knowing."

"Why does it sound like there's a but?"

"But… you can't keep bringing up stuff I've already done."

"Okay," I agree.

"Promise?"

"Okay," I repeat, rolling my eyes.

I can make the promise because I know he has promised to stop too. I unlock the car, hoping I can keep the excitement off my expression. It's so posh and clean, and I'm pretty sure I can see a screen for a built-in sat nav.

"Have fun. I'll call you if I need anything," he tells me, and begins to retreat into the house.

I pull open the door and rest my palm over the top as I reply. "Cole?"

"Yes?"

"Thank you for the car."

He doesn't react for a second, probably surprised I said thank you. I've not exactly set a good example of myself since all this began. "You're welcome."

I give a nod before sliding into the brand-new car that is mine. I've never owned anything like this in my life. I don't think I've been in anything this fancy. It smells new with that polished woodsy scent.

Starting the car, I let my thoughts drift back to my friends. I have to tell them. I owe them that much. It wasn't that long ago we all cornered Gabby into sharing.

Gabby has always kept herself closed off. Unlike me, she does it because of friends she lost growing up. They all made her think she wasn't enough, and that she was too needy. I do it because of previous emotional abuse and being forced to lie about my life. I had to fake being happy, and I never grew out of it. I had to show the world a different face, one they wouldn't question. No one ever cared enough to look past the façade to find out the truth. My friends, they'll see past it because they know me. They love me and won't stop until they have answers. It's why I managed to avoid telling them who's Poppy's father was. And why they never saw how much my grandma's illness affected me. I isolated myself from them so they wouldn't see.

Now, they need to know everything. They need to know the whole truth.

AFTER TAKING a seat in the vacant chair, I regret not giving them the real reason it took me so long to find a babysitter. Luckily, they were calling earlier to say they were running late, so my excuse wasn't questioned. And why would they when they know there are times I can't get a babysitter.

I only read the messages after parking in the car park down the road. I didn't want to risk them seeing the new car. And the walk gave me enough time to prepare for what I was going to say.

But then the girls arrived in a taxi outside the pub, and I knew something was wrong. Gabby was crying, and with Gabby, that's never a good thing. She mostly cries when she's angry. I knew my issues had to wait, which is why I told the white lie that I was waiting for a babysitter. It's only a half-truth. I knew Cole would watch Poppy for me if I asked, but they didn't know about Cole and where we were living.

"What happened?" Harriett asks, coming to take a seat in her chair. She hands out a round of drinks she ordered from the bar and places her purse in the bag hanging over her chair.

Gabby crosses her arms over her chest in a puff. "The fucking media is what happened."

"Are they still hounding you?" I ask after taking a sip of my cocktail.

I already know most of it. The media somehow got her private number and started calling her, to the point she had no choice but to change her number. I don't think it would be hard for them to get her new number though.

The media have been ruthless, even camping outside of Tease, waiting for dancers to start or leave work, hoping one of them will finally break and tell their story.

"Hounding me? They are sleeping outside our door," she remarks.

"They aren't," Olivia corrects, rubbing her hand up and down Gabby's back.

I want to say it feels weird to see them as a couple, but it doesn't. Nothing has changed other than they like to show PDA and have sex.

They are still the same bickering, fun, loving Gabby and Olivia. The two are perfect for each other.

Who knew two sides of crazy made the perfect match.

Gabby rubs at her arm. "Okay, so they don't have tents pitched up outside, but they are there all the time. I'm scared to piss."

Olivia coughs into her hand. "The bathroom is at the back of the house."

Gabby snaps her head in Olivia's direction. "Whose side are you on?"

"Yours. I agree, they need to go, but giving them a batch of Charlotte's cookies when you know she's not recovered from your ordeal wasn't going to fix anything."

Oh God. I place my hand over my mouth, trying to cover my laughter. Charlotte's baking has caused hospital visits in the past. Even those with a strong stomach haven't made it. Then she met Drew, and it changed. But it's still a hit or miss. If she's getting some, she bakes good. But when she's stressed or worrying, we're back to having toxic cupcakes and stone-like scones.

Gabby snorts. "It got rid of half of them, didn't it?"

"Not the point," Olivia reminds her, struggling not to laugh. "Tish attacked one of them with her bag," she adds, speaking of their neighbour.

"He shouldn't have had explosive diarrhoea on her front garden," Gabby snaps. "She was protecting her garden."

"If you're handling it, what is the issue?" Harriett asks after taking a sip. "We could do a drive-by and hit them with paintballs."

"Did you pack them when you moved into River's?" I ask.

"Yeah. River saw them and now wants to set up a course near the house."

"Most of them are harmless. There's only one we're really bothered about, and Gabby is projecting that on the rest," Olivia admits. "He's following Lee to school. He's tried talking to us at the kids' school. He's hounded us during shopping trips, so we switched to ordering online. But then he snuck a recording device into our oranges. He hasn't stopped trying since then to find new ways to get information."

"What? Have you reported him?" I ask. "They aren't allowed to do that."

"He thinks because I won't share my story, I'm making it up. First, he thought it was to get more money, but now, he's accusing me of being silent so I don't risk getting caught out in a lie," Gabby explains. "I'm not above lying, which is what he's published online."

"You're fucking kidding," Harriett snaps.

"What the hell did he publish?" I ask, mad on her behalf.

Olivia glances at Gabby, chewing her lower lip. "He wants to convince or prove to everyone, beyond reasonable doubt, that she is lying."

"There are witnesses," I point out. "Trixie had her finger chopped off. I know she's had it reattached, but it's still smaller than the rest."

"He hasn't gone there yet," Olivia explains. "He's concentrating on showing proof she has lied."

"About what?" Harriett asks, and Olivia glances at Gabby, silently gesturing for her to answer.

"I lied on my application form for Tease," Gabby bursts out. "I didn't think it would matter since you don't really need an A in English to slide up and down on a pole. I put higher marks so Dave didn't think I was stupid. This guy is using a bunch of examples so people don't believe me."

Olivia clears her throat. "He even brought up her lying about her dad's death."

"He *is* dead to me," Gabby argues.

"And that she told someone she was an assassin working for the CIA."

Gabby arches her eyebrow. "*Did it* or *did it not* stop Mathew—or whatever his name was—from doing his next girl dirty?"

"No one is going to believe him," I assure her, hiding my amusement about Olivia's ex-boyfriend.

"The thing is, people do. I had to read threads of people posting that I deserved it. I'm not a criminal. I'm not a paedophile. I fucking dance," she tells us, raising her voice. Her tone gains the attention of other punters. "That's it, you heard it here. I strip and shake my titties and got kidnapped."

"Calm down," Olivia gently orders, placing her hand over Gabby's. "We can sort this. We can go to the police."

"They aren't going to do shit," Gabby replies, her shoulders dropping. "He still kidnapped me."

"Babe, what is really going on in your head?" Olivia asks. "You're not you, and I'm worried."

Gabby's eyes water with unshed tears. "The more they write about me, the more the killer knows," she heaves out, her voice shaking. "I'm scared he's going to come back for me."

"Oh, Gabby," I choke out, tears springing to my own eyes.

Real fear is on her expression. She's tried to play this off and argue that she doesn't care, but we can see it. She's truly scared for her safety.

"This isn't some twat discriminating against me for being gay. It's not my dad being a prick. He's a killer, and I don't want to die."

Harriett, choked up with emotions like me, leans over the table to take her hand. "I know you didn't want us to, but me and River are going to pay for you to have some security put in. No one should feel scared in their own home."

"It won't matter. Her mum has bought us a house. We just have to wait for the sale to go through," Olivia admits.

"Oh my god, congratulations," I tell them both.

"It still won't hurt," Harriett mentions. "And I'm happy for you both."

"It won't stop him," Gabby tells us. "I don't want to talk about this. It's not why we arranged to come here."

"Was there meant to be a reason?" I ask, unaware there was one, since we normally do something together.

"Yes, we want to know if you're okay," Olivia replies.

"You've been distant. And you haven't been answering your door," Gabby adds. "We even tried your neighbours, but they weren't in either."

"Or answering your phone," Harriett points out.

"I've just been dealing with things. I'm okay. Really," I promise, forcing a smile.

"Are you sure? I know what it's like to lose someone you love. We are here if you need to talk," Harriett tells me.

I bump my shoulder with hers. "Honestly, I'm doing better. I'll never truly get over it, but who does? There will always be that ache. I just need to sort through that in my mind. It's a big change for me."

Olivia gives me a warm smile. "We love you and just want to make sure you're okay."

"I'm good. But we should contact Hayden and see if she can get her cousin's fiancé to stop this reporter," I evade. "I'll go order us some drinks, but you should call her."

Gabby's nose scrunches up. "I didn't think of that."

I slide out of the chair and make my way over to the bar. I give my order to the bar lady, and it isn't until I'm finished that I realise I have no way of paying for these drinks.

My heart races with each drink she pours. I can't find the words to stop her, or to turn to my friends for help.

"That will be twenty-six, sixty-nine," she tells me, and I reluctantly tap the card on the card reader. My cheeks flame, ready for the embarrassment of having to ask my friends to pay, but when the beep of it going through dings, my eyebrows shoot up in surprise.

I take out my phone, quickly logging into my online banking app, and see three thousand pounds in my account.

"What?" I gasp, searching down to see a Cole Connor debited the money into my account a few days ago. Our conversation from earlier comes flooding back.

I promise to speak to you first.

This will be the last time I do something without you knowing.

You can't keep bringing up stuff I've already done.

He worded it like that for a reason. Cole knew I wouldn't like this. And he made me promise.

"Everything okay?" Harriett asks, startling me.

I quickly drop my phone in my pocket. "Yes. I just need to leave a little earlier tonight."

"Is Poppy okay?"

"She's great. I just need to get back a little earlier tonight to relieve the babysitter."

Her brows pinch together. "Are you sure everything is okay?"

"Yes, just tired. I keep having weird dreams." It's not a lie because I have been having weird dreams. But I know that isn't what she was asking.

"I've been having them too since Gabby was taken. My worst fear came to life that night."

"They'll find who is doing this," I assure her.

"They have to," she murmurs, her voice drifting off.

Her thoughts have gone where mine have. I know they have. How could they not when we're all scared this will end up with one or all of us dead.

She heads off to the table first, and I follow, hoping they don't ask if I'm okay again. Gabby steered the conversation earlier because she doesn't like the attention being on her. But this reporter is really bothering her, so I'm not going to make tonight about me. I'm not the one who was kidnapped. She was.

I don't matter right now. She does. And I want to make sure she enjoys herself tonight and relaxes.

Everything else will still be happening tomorrow. It's not going to stop.

And when the time is right, I'll tell them.

I'll tell them everything.

9

COLE

Last night, I got to sit with my daughter alone. It was the first time where it was just us two together, and although I was on edge the entire time, I wanted to take advantage of it. I knew I wouldn't get many chances like I did last night. Emily wouldn't have left me with her in the first place if she wasn't so worried about her friends.

As much as I would have loved for Poppy to be awake, I was content with watching her sleep. She adapted to her new room rather easily, and I couldn't help but be proud of her for it.

It also gave me time to run over how much my life has changed. I've always had properties to go to, but I never stayed in one place for long periods of time. They were never a home to me until now. My life revolved around work and sex. And I did both a lot. I needed them to function. But since Emily and Poppy moved in, none of that appeals to me anymore. I want to be where they are, and right now, that's at home. And I've not really felt at home since I left my parents' house at eighteen.

My time with Poppy got cut short. I wanted to stay with her until Emily got home, but instead, I went to bed early to avoid bumping into her. Emily found out about the money I sent her. I had been waiting for her to mention it, and was prepared, but I still didn't want to ruin her night by arguing about money, so I never replied to the message she sent.

I won't pretend to be someone I'm not. Emily needed money and I have plenty. If I can't spend it on my daughter and the mother of my child, then what's the point? My clubs have been my only responsibility. My family can financially take care of themselves, and my clubs make enough money that they practically run themselves. Emily and Poppy are now my responsibility, and I want to provide for them.

This morning, she was too busy taking care of Poppy to question me over the money, and the minute I got the opening, I snuck off downstairs to my office.

Now, I can't hide away, so I head upstairs in search of them. My mum will be here any minute to take them out for the day. I want to make sure Emily is comfortable with spending the day with my mum before she arrives, because I've come to learn that Emily is a people pleaser. I don't think she notices it half the time, but it's something I've picked up on throughout the week when we've spoken. I don't want her to leave with my mum just to make everyone happy. I want her to go because she wants to.

I find them in the living room, Emily putting on Poppy's shoes. "Hey. Did you have a good night?"

She gives me a side eye. "I'm surprised you weren't there to pay for my drinks."

I chuckle at her sarcasm. "So, you finally realised I transferred you some money."

"Yes, and the first chance I get, I'll be giving it back."

I cross my arms over my chest as I rest against the doorframe. "No. We spoke about this last night. You said you weren't going to bring up what I've already done. I promise it won't happen again without us talking about it."

She finally meets my gaze. "Why do I have a feeling you'll still do it even if I say no?"

"Look, it's just money. I have more," I tell her. "Plus, didn't you want to be able to buy your own food and drinks today?"

She finishes zipping up Poppy's coat before letting her go back to playing with her dolls. "Do you take after your mum or your dad?"

I arch an eyebrow at the question. "What does that have to do with this?"

"I want to know if your mum will actually let me pay."

I laugh, which is uncommon for me. "You already have her sussed out."

"Great," she mutters.

"Did you speak to your friends?"

She tucks her blonde hair behind her ears. "I never got a chance to. Gabby is having issues with some reporters. One in particular is trying to make her out to be a liar."

My eyebrows pinch together. "What does he think she's lying about?"

"All of it. He thinks they set the whole thing up to try and cash in on it."

"From my understanding, the police have pictures of the crime scene. They matched DNA to some of the previous victims in that cave."

"It doesn't matter to him," she admits. "He doesn't care. And it's not helping those who already look down on dancers. She's been getting a lot of hate, and she's already scared enough."

"Is there anything I can do? I have connections with people who work in that field."

"I'm surprised they aren't hounding you for information," she mutters. "I'm not sure there's anything you can do."

"Oh, trust me, they are. Gia, my assistant, deals with them," I tell her, letting out a breath. "I can't promise anything, but I'll look into it."

"Thanks."

"How is your friend? I got updates through Dave, but he's been taking it hard. He's blaming himself for it all."

"Are you two speaking again?"

"About business," I evade, not wanting to go there.

"You can't punish him for my mistakes. He didn't know. And he seemed cut up about your falling out when he came to see me the day of my grandma's funeral."

I step away from the door. "He saw you?"

"Yes. He wanted to see how I was, and to get me to talk to you. But I was grieving, and my grandma was all I could talk about."

I nod, needing to change the subject. Dave is the one person I thought I could rely on. He might not know about mine and Emily's night together, but he must have known something. I never took an interest in any of my dancers, let alone decide to put one as beautiful as Emily behind a bar. With a raise. "Have the police given you any more information about the kidnapping?"

"No. Everyone seems to be pretty closed off about it."

"How did you find out where she was?" I ask. I've wanted to know this from the minute I was told two of our employees were taken and it was her friends who found them and not the police.

"We have connections too," she muses, throwing my words back at me. "It wasn't easy to find her. What we had was based off insubstantial evidence. Or at first it was."

"What was it?"

"Moss," she replies. "There were traces of it on each victim, so although it was filed into evidence, no one really looked into the importance of it."

I sit down on the sofa next to her. She twists on the floor to face me and rests an arm on the sofa cushion. "But what made you look into it? Into any of it? I don't understand why you'd risk being put in his crosshairs."

Her thick, dark lashes flicker. "Aisling was our friend. We only saw her at work, but we all liked her. She didn't deserve to die. None of them did."

"No. She didn't."

"You knew her?"

"Yes. She came to me asking for advice about opening a studio for a youth dance club."

Her eyes crinkle in the corners as she smiles. "She was amazing with kids. She met Poppy at one of the barbeques Dave hosts, and she was so good with her," she muses, before letting her eyes drift closed for a second. "She was a professional dancer before an accident ended her career. I guess it's like an Olympian after an injury. You can no longer do it as a career. Aisling just wanted to dance, even if it meant stripping or teaching."

"So, you did all that for Aisling?"

"Yeah. We had help from our friend, Hayden Carter, and her family. She has a blog where she posts real life crime stories, so she was already doing her own research. We got together to go over everything we knew, in case we could tell the police something new. The moss was a start, so we had her cousin look into it for us."

"It was risky putting yourself in danger like that. You have Poppy to think about."

"It wasn't like that. We didn't purposely go looking for him. That was never our plan, I swear," she promises. "We did it to find our friend. We've been living with this threat for months, and all of us are at risk. Hell, it should have been me who was taken that night. I was the one who was looking for Trixie. Gabby told me Trixie went for a smoke, so I went to get her. Gabby stopped me and said she'd do it." She glances down at her lap. "She only went outside for me. I had so much to do, and she wanted me to win the new position we were all competing for. It should have been me."

My breath gets trapped in my lungs. "I didn't know that. I'm sorry."

If she had been killed that night, I would never have known about my daughter. Poppy would have been without a mum or any family.

"I still wish it had been me. I feel guilty she got hurt."

"I don't care if this makes me sound like a dick, but I'm glad it wasn't you." Her lips part at my admission. I clear my throat. "You have a daughter who needs you."

She shakes herself out of it and replies, "It doesn't matter now anyway. My friend is safe, and I don't regret looking for her. It wasn't just the right thing to do, but what we needed to do."

"If we could close Tease until this was over, we would. But too many people need this job to survive, and we can't afford to keep paying for staff with no income to the business. And although we have a waiting list for potential stage dancers, they'll still need training, which is something we won't have time for. And we don't know when this will be over, or if it ever will."

"We all get it. Businesses all over town are closing down right now because of the economy. We understand that if Tease closes again, it won't recover, and there will be cutbacks and staff layoffs for the first year. Dave gave us all the chance to leave, and he made it clear it wasn't time sensitive. We can leave when we want, and he'll understand. He'll even keep our jobs open until it is over. But Dave has supported every single one of us. It's no secret dancers don't have a good reputation. It's not classed as a respectful profession, and we live with that every day. Even shot girls and bartenders are labelled the same just by association. Dave makes sure that doesn't touch us inside those walls. He doesn't let our information get leaked, and he bans any form of photography or press unless given written approval by the dancers themselves. Any trouble we get inside, he shuts it down quickly, and any complaints about sexual harassment are dealt with quickly," she explains. "But Dave isn't just our boss. He's our friend. He's there for all of us, and is the first to offer support or help if one of us has something going on. I don't know any other boss who would do that for their employees. Which is why we've all stayed. We aren't blind to the fact this is killing him. He's not sleeping, he's stressed, and he doesn't have the same banter with the girls as he did before. It's been weeks since he last threatened to fire one of my friends."

If Dave could hear them, he would play off Emily's words by making out it wasn't a big deal. He's always been like that. He never takes credit for anything he does. He's always believed an act of kindness shouldn't come with strings.

"It would mean a lot to him to hear you say those things. He went through a lot of loss growing up, though he probably won't like me revealing that to you," I begin. "It didn't make him grow resentful or become closed off. If anything, it made him care more. He knows how short life can be, so he made it his mission to make sure those around him know he cares." I look past her, not wanting her to see what I'm feeling inside. "He's a better man than I'll ever be."

She lets the words linger between us before finally replying, "We both know he wouldn't like to hear me say those things. He doesn't take compliments well at all."

I laugh at her words. Her attempt to lighten the mood has worked. "Yeah, you're right, but it would still mean a lot to him. He loves managing Tease. He threatens to leave at least once a week, but if I ever gave him the choice, he would stay. It's all a front. He cares for you all. You're all like a family to him."

"And family should stick together," she points out. "Which is why we would never let him down by walking out when he needs us the most. None of us blame him or wish he would shut the club down. We know how much the place means to him."

"I'm going to keep applying pressure to the police. We want them to do a regular drive-by or get more police presence near the club."

My phone beeps with an alert for the front gate. After checking who it is, I buzz my mum in.

"Is that your mum?"

"Yes," I answer. "Before she comes in, I wanted to double check you are okay with going out with her today. I don't want you to feel pressured into going."

"No. Your mum is right. We don't know each other, and she doesn't know her granddaughter. We can't fix that until we've spent time together."

"She didn't mean the things she said. She said them out of concern," I admit, talking about their first meeting.

She gives me a smile that lights up her face before getting to her feet. "It's okay. I understand where it came from and why she would think those things. Was it nice to hear? No. But she also didn't treat me unfairly. She was nice and kind, and more than apologetic afterwards. Her words came from concern for her son. I will not hold it against her or any of you," she promises. "I have a mother who doesn't care. She would never have questioned your motives, or even tried to protect me. You're lucky to have a mother who is always on your side."

This isn't the first time she's mentioned her parents in a negative way. I'm not blind to the horrors this world can produce. I've lived through some of my own. I also know she's not the problem in their scenario. It's her parents. What I'll never understand—even more now that I have a child of my own—is how a parent can cause this much pain for their child. From what I can see, Emily is a daughter they should be proud of. She took care of her sick grandma for years, she's worked her arse off so she isn't another statistic living off government funding, and has raised our daughter alone. She's accomplished a lot for someone so young.

I want to ask her more about it, but now isn't the time. She has no reason to open up to me, and I have no right to ask. Maybe once this phase of our life is over, she'll give it to me freely.

A knock on the door pulls me away from my thoughts. Before I leave to answer it, I say, "Thank you for being so understanding. She really does mean well."

"No problem," she quietly replies.

I head over to the front door and pull it open. I greet my mum with a smile. Long gone is her fancy dresses and outfits. Instead, she is wearing dark jeans and a white woollen jumper, which she has on under her beige, long coat. She wants to fit in with Emily, probably to make her feel comfortable. It's one of the things I love most about her. She has a huge heart, ready to give those around her all her love. Her hair she didn't dress down. It's the same as always: immaculately styled, her curls framing her face.

"Mum," I greet.

She steps inside, leaning up on her toes to press a kiss to my cheek. "Where are my girls?"

See, she's already pulling them into her fold. "They're waiting in the living room."

Brushing past me, she walks to the living area, stopping when she spots the girls. "Hey, Poppy. Are you ready to go shopping with your grandma?"

"Grandma?" she cries excitedly and begins to rush to the door. Emily tags her around the waist, pulling her close.

"Grandma is in Heaven, remember," Emily whispers. "She's with Grandpa."

Mum places her hand over her mouth. "I'm so sorry. I didn't…"

"It's okay," Emily promises. "If it's okay with you, she can call you nan, or nanna."

"I would love that," Mum whispers.

Emily turns Poppy and lifts up her chin. "I know you miss Grandma. I do too. But she's resting now up in Heaven."

"No more boo boos."

"No more boo boos," Emily tells her.

We have spoken about this briefly. Although her grandma never personally took care of Poppy, they still spent a lot of time together. Poppy was the only one her grandma never got upset or confused with, so they had a special bond. Emily told me that sometimes, Poppy would sing one of her favourite nursery rhymes to her grandma, which helped her fall asleep.

"So, are you ready to have a fun day with Nanna?"

"Nanna," Poppy repeats, testing those words out. It brings a smile to my face, because my girl is good.

"Good girl," Emily cheers. "You ready to go?"

"Yes!"

Mum laughs at her enthusiasm and is quick to reach down and lift her up when she charges at her.

"You ready to buy some new clothes?" Mum asks.

"Princess dress?"

"We can do princess dresses," Mum replies, before turning to Emily. "Are you ready? I thought we could go for lunch too."

Emily grabs her bag from the sofa. "I am."

"Is Dad coming later for dinner?" I ask.

"Yes. Your brother and sister will be coming too."

"Kit is back?"

"Yes. He arrived late last night and was still sleeping when I left."

"He didn't go home?" I muse. He lives three hours away, where he owns an art gallery. It's why he travels so much. He takes pictures and then sells them in his studio.

"He didn't see the point when we invited him to your dinner."

"Alright, well, I'll leave him a message and see what he's doing," I tell her, then lean down to press a kiss to her cheek, before doing the same to Poppy, making her laugh. "Bye, Poppy."

"Bye, Dada," she replies.

I step back and immediately turn to Emily, my body jerking.

There's an awkward moment where neither of us know what to do about it. I had moved to make the same gesture to her as I did with my mum and Poppy. I don't know why I went to, but I can't take it back.

She smiles and pats me on the shoulder. "It's okay. I don't need a farewell kiss," she teases.

I rub the back of my neck. "Sorry. Didn't mean to."

We do nothing but stare for a second, until she clears her throat, breaking the spell. "Georgia, I have a car seat I can transfer into your car."

Glancing at Mum, I see she has a smug smile on her face. "It's okay, dear. Joe has had one fitted in mine."

"Perfect." Emily beams.

I rub the back of my neck again. "Alright, well, um, I guess I'll see you all later."

"See you," Emily calls, and is the first to step outside.

Mum full-on smiles. "Bye, son."

I narrow my gaze on her. "Be careful."

After another goodbye to Poppy, I close the door and lean back against it. What was I thinking? And why am I so cut up about it? I'm not this man. A woman has never made me act like a schoolboy.

Never.

So what makes Emily Hart so special?

10

EMILY

I've always compared people's parents to my own. It's a habit I've never grown out of. At school, I wondered what my peers had that I didn't. What did they do for their parents to attend school events or for them to be taken out for the day? It was the same when I saw Harriett's dad pull her in for a warm hug. He hung on every word she said, and asked her questions that my parents would never have asked me.

Georgia is no different. She's got such a huge heart and loves her son fiercely. She's not how I imagined her to be. She comes from money—a lot of it, from what I can gather. But she doesn't act like she does. Money hasn't made her act like everyone is beneath her.

I'm actually enjoying our time together. She's told me stories about her daughter's escapades growing up, and even mentioned how beautiful Kit's artwork is. I feel like I already know them. She's spoken about Cole's other businesses too. I'm surprised she hasn't given me any embarrassing baby stories yet.

We're making our way through town to a restaurant she wants us to try. Poppy is asleep in her pushchair, unbothered by the noise going on around us. Part of the path is being dug up beside us, there's a busker singing an Ed Sheeran song not far in front of us, and there are hundreds of people milling around, going about their day.

"Cole said your home was broken into," she states. "Did they find out who did it?"

"No. And none of the neighbours saw anything either."

"What was taken?"

"Meaningless jewellery and money. Some of the jewellery pieces were real, but it was all replaceable. I had the two things that matter most to me: my daughter and grandma's rings that I have attached to a necklace my granddad bought his wife."

"It must have been scary," she soothingly replies.

"It was. It was the same day Cole turned up."

She lets out a soft sigh. "Why don't we stop here and sit down on this bench before we go in."

I pause to steer the pram over to the concrete bench. "Did I say something wrong?"

"Of course not. But I feel as Cole's mother, I need to apologise."

"For what?" I ask as we take a seat.

"Cole has asked me not to reveal personal information about himself. He wants to be the one to share those things," she reveals.

My eyebrows rise. I don't know what she means by the comment. I don't know if what he has to say is good or bad. "Okay."

"He told me what happened that day. He said some things that I know he regrets."

"Respectfully, you weren't there. He said those things because somewhere inside him, he felt them."

"My son is fierce when it comes to business. He can mingle and socialise and know exactly what to say because he can read people very easily. He's always been like that. You and Poppy are an anomaly to him. He never planned for you, and he doesn't know how to speak to you. But I can tell you, he means no harm or ill-will to you or Poppy. He just wants to do what's best for you both. He said those things because he was hurt."

"I know. I understand it was said out of hurt," I admit. "But he still said some awful things to me that I can't magically erase from my mind. I could sense he was holding back, but he still implied stuff, and that hurt the most."

"He really is a good man. I'm not just saying it because he's my son. He truly is. So please, give him a chance to make this right between you both. He knows he did wrong by approaching you the way he did. But he wants to be a father to Poppy."

"I'd never stop him. That is not what I was doing. I wasn't keeping her for myself like how he sees it. It was never a custody issue with me. If he wanted to see her, I wouldn't have stopped him. If he wanted nothing to do with her, I would have understood because he never asked for her."

"I can't speak for my son and tell you what he would have wanted. I don't know the answer to it. But I know he would have supported you in every way he could," she tells me, keeping her voice soft. "It saddens me to know I missed so much. I love my family, and I've been waiting for grandchildren for a while now."

Her words aren't meant to cut me, but they have that effect. It wasn't just Cole who missed out on so much. It was his family. She has grandparents, and an uncle and aunt.

"I know this doesn't mean anything to you now, but I am sorry you missed her life. I was so scared when I found out I was pregnant. I had a sick grandmother to think of, and I hadn't been at my job long. But one thing I knew for sure was that I wanted her. I never knew I could love someone that soon or so much."

"A mother's love is the purest love this world has to offer. There is no stronger bond."

My shoulders drop with relief that she understands what I'm saying. I clear my throat and continue, hoping I don't mess this up and say the wrong thing.

"As beautiful as our night together was, I didn't really know Cole. I didn't know what he would want me to do or how he would react. So I waited to tell him because then, he couldn't force me to get an abortion. And then *too much* time passed. When I finally saw him again, I didn't know *how* to tell him. I never meant to hurt him. I never meant to hurt anyone."

Her cold hand touches mine in comfort. "I see that. So does he deep down."

"I don't think he does. I don't blame him for not trusting me. I've not given him reasons to."

"He'll come around," she promises.

I force a smile. "I hope he does. I've lost my deposit on our home because we left on such short notice. I don't know when he'll come around and let us leave."

She lets out a laugh. "He's not holding you hostage."

I arch an eyebrow. "He threatened me with lawyers so I'm sure it's breaking some sort of law. I'm there under duress."

"You said your home was broken into. I'm assuming that means things got broken. Am I right?"

"Yes," I warily answer.

"And Cole mentioned a ceiling fell through downstairs, which I'm assuming wasn't a result of being broken into?"

"Kind of. I was waiting for the landlord to fix the plumbing, so there was already an issue. Whoever let themselves in must have knocked a pipe for there to be that much water in there."

"And plumbing issues like that aren't easy fixes. It would take weeks, if not months, depending on your landlord, to be fixed. Being where you are is the best place to be. Your friends would have taken you in because they sound like great friends, but I think I know you enough to guess you would have felt guilty and a burden to them by being in their space. With Cole, you have your own space. He wants people to believe he bought that house as an investment, but I think deep down, he was waiting for the right person to fill it. He would have sold it by now if he wasn't. And if he liked it that much, he would stay there instead of the flat he has on the other side of town, but he never did. Until you."

"My friends don't actually know where I'm staying right now. They don't know anything," I admit, ducking my head in shame. "And I'm guessing you've heard that Cole offered to give me the house."

"Your friends will understand," she replies, and again, her words are soothing, like she knows it bothers me that my friends don't know.

"And his lawyer is a family friend. I believe Cole is waiting to give you the deeds to sign."

My eyes widen at her statement. "I can't take his home."

"It's not a home without you or Poppy."

"He doesn't even like me."

"Then you don't know my son," she tells me, and there's a hint of taunting, or maybe even disappointment. I'm not sure, because like her son, she has a way of making you feel like you are missing something.

"Sometimes I feel like I don't know myself," I admit. "I've worked for everything I have. It might not be much, but I did it. I got us to where we are. Receiving gifts of that magnitude doesn't happen to me. I feel like there's a string attached."

"Not everything comes with strings, my darling girl. Sometimes people do something because it's the right thing. And it is. Because Poppy isn't just your responsibility now. She is his. And he wants to do right by her."

"Then why does the offer make me feel so dirty?"

"Because women are sadly conditioned to be care providers. We've spent years being the ones responsible for children. Mothers are the ones who are left to carry the weight of being two parents whilst most men can go about their day like they don't have children," she explains, and sits back, crossing her legs. "A mother I met through a charity I support has three kids and works part-time. She was struggling to provide everything her children needed and often went without so they didn't. Their dad, who worked full-time with no commitments, didn't have to pay for child support. They expected the mother to live off the bare minimum whilst supporting three other people, but it wasn't the same for the dad. It's not fair that he got paid three times as much as she did, and their calculations said he only earned enough to support himself. My son isn't him. He isn't offering it because he wants to prove a point or show you up. He's doing it so you don't have to. He's doing it because he values what you have done for Poppy and is stepping up."

"I never looked at it that way," I whisper, glancing at the thread on my jeans.

"I grew up with a single mother who, like yours, didn't care much for me. She slept with a rich, married man and got pregnant with me. She expected him to leave his wife and give her the life she wanted. When he didn't, she took her disappointment out on me. I know conniving women. You, my darling girl, are not one of them. And I'd be disappointed if my son ever made you feel like that."

"Is that why you said those things that morning?"

She closes her eyes for a split second, but I see the guilt before she masks it. "I guess in a way it was. My son is a wealthy man. I didn't want him to get hurt when he's already been through so much."

"What about your dad? Did you see him growing up?"

"Yes. My father made a mistake with my mum. He got drunk one night and my mum seduced him. He regretted it immediately the next day when he realised what he had done. My step mum—who I call mum—is nothing like my mother. She's sweet and kind. She forgave my father because she believed she was the reason he got drunk. They had not long gone through another miscarriage when the doctors told her they had to remove her last fallopian tube. She wouldn't be able to conceive, so she broke up with my father. She knew how much he wanted to be a dad, and because she couldn't give him that, she let him go. He didn't go out that night planning to cheat. He didn't know what he was doing."

"Oh God, that must have hurt your step-mum when she found out about you."

"It did, but not in the way you think. She was hurt that he cheated, but she wanted him to be in my life. When my mother kept threatening to abort me if he didn't do the things she wanted, my step-mum was beside herself. They knew each other since they worked in the same office, so she knew my mum wasn't lying. My dad gave into her demands during the first few months of her pregnancy. He gave her a promotion. He gave her money. He took her to appointments and acted the part to appease her. When I was born, he told her he wouldn't leave his wife, so she used me as a tool to get back at him. She would make him jump through hoops to see me or punish him by not letting us see each other. It went through courts, and she set him up each time. He never stopped trying though."

"What happened in the end?" I ask, invested in her story.

"It was the weekend after my ninth birthday, and it was my dad's weekend to have me. By this point, I only saw him once a month. We went back to his and they arranged a pool party for me. My step-mum had bought me a new swimming costume, and she asked me to go change. I did, and layered a T-shirt over it. Halfway through the party, the material began to grow heavy and irritate my skin, so I took it off," she reveals, and her eyes gloss over with unshed tears. "I remember everyone stopping to stare at me. It wasn't until I saw my step-mum's face crumble with tears that I realised what they were seeing."

"What did they see?" I whisper, feeling my throat close up with emotion.

She meets my gaze dead on. "All the bruises my mum's boyfriend had left on me. I never told anyone. I was too scared to because my mum had already gone mad at me for telling her. My dad refused to take me back home after that, and my mum, not wanting to lose her new cashpoint, didn't put up a fight. My dad got full custody, and I never looked back. But I saw what she did to him. I remember it vividly, and I guess I jumped to conclusions when I found out the news about Poppy. I was taken back to that time in my life, and I didn't want my son to go through that. I can see I was wrong, and I apologise sincerely."

It's my turn to comfort her. I take her hand in mine and meet her gaze. "I will never do that to your son. But more, I would never do that to Poppy. I can promise you that."

She sniffs and pulls out a hanky to dab the corner of her eyes. "I know you'll never do that. I knew it the moment I saw you walk into that kitchen with Poppy clinging to you. Only a loved child would hold their mother like that. I also knew it when you told us not to talk about it in front of Poppy. You were protecting her. Only a mother who loves their child does that."

Her words bring tears to my eyes. "Thank you."

She clears her throat. "Enough sadness now. I brought you out to have a girl's day. Now what do you say about going for this lunch?"

"I say I'm starving and can't wait," I tease, getting to my feet.

"There you are!"

For a split second, I freeze with dread. I never expected to run into my friends today. They'll know I'm a fraud and a liar the minute I turn around. I deceived them; the very people who I love most in the world aside from my daughter.

And I don't know how to make it right.

11

EMILY

Taking a breath, I turn to face all three of my friends. Gabby has both hands on the pushchair with a sleeping Carter inside. Olivia stands on her right, and Harriett is on her left. And not one of them looks pleased with me. I gulp as a coldness seeps into my bones.

I knew that one day, my secrets and lies would eventually catch up to me. I just never pictured it to be like this; out in the open, and with them coming to me about it. I always pictured being the one to go to them with it.

"Hey," I greet lamely. I cross my hands behind my back to stop myself from waving. "I thought you were going to the police station today to make a report?"

Gabby snorts. "Do you take us for amateurs?"

"We knew something was up with you," Harriett adds.

Olivia nods in agreement. "We know you lied to us."

"I…I don't…" I close up, my worst fear coming to life. I'm going to lose my friends.

"Why don't I take Poppy inside the restaurant," Georgia offers.

"Poppy isn't going anywhere with you, lady. We don't know you," Gabby warns, pointing at Georgia. "Step away from the girl."

Oh God.

"Who are you?" Harriett asks.

Step up and tell them.

I gulp and drop my hands to my sides. "Guys, this is Georgia Connor. She's Poppy's nan."

Each of them drops their unapproachable façade, and Gabby is the first to move. She takes Georgia's hand, giving it a shake. "Hey, I'm Gabby. It's nice to meet you. I swear, we were just worried for our friend." She turns to me, arching an eyebrow. "Do we like her?"

I smile despite the situation. "Yes. We like Georgia."

"Can I take Poppy inside so you can talk?" Georgia teases, as she shakes Harriett's hand.

All of them nod, not saying a word. "Thank you," I tell her, and she takes the pushchair, making her way inside the restaurant. Once she's gone, I turn to my friends. "I'm so sorry. I didn't mean to keep this from you. I swear, I've been meaning to tell you."

"Emily, we know you. You are our friend, and we love you," Harriett begins. "Which is why we never call you out on stuff. We understand it's your way of processing, and you'll tell us when you are ready."

"You had a shit childhood. It's only right it's going to mess you up a bit," Gabby declares. "Look at me, I have daddy issues. I'm one of *those* girls."

"What do you know?" I ask, ashamed it had to come out this way.

"Well, we know you haven't dated at all," Gabby offers.

"Yeah, Gabby snooped through your phone after Harriett tried to set you up with that doctor. You said you couldn't go on a date because you were speaking to someone else, but you weren't. We never understood why you wouldn't just say you didn't want to date," Olivia admits.

Gabby lightly backhands her arm. "You weren't supposed to tell her I went through her phone."

"Dude, ouch!" Olivia snaps. "I thought today was all about honesty."

"Stop!" Harriett warns. "This isn't what we had planned."

"It's fine," I promise. "I was ashamed. I wanted to fit in with you all, and I was embarrassed to admit Cole was the only man I slept with."

"Woah, wait up. The only one? I just assumed it was after Poppy, but woah, this is big news," Gabby reveals, her jaw dropping.

"Shush," I stress. "People can hear you."

"Please tell me you at least took care of yourself," Olivia pleads.

I roll my eyes. "Of course I did."

"Why would you hide that from us?" Harriett asks, masking her emotions. I can't tell where her head is at, and that hurts the most.

Tears spring to my eyes. "No answer I give will sound right."

"Tell us," Harriett pleads. "We're your friends."

"Because I didn't want you to think something was wrong with me," I admit on a cry. "I spent my whole childhood being told I was weird and a loner. I finally had friends and I didn't want to lose you because I wasn't one of you. I know you would never judge me. It's not about that. But I…"

"Spent years being judged so you didn't trust anything different," Gabby finishes. "We get it."

I drop back down on the bench and Harriett follows whilst the other two stay standing in front of us. I lower my head. "I'm so sorry. It seems pathetic now I've said it out loud. I swear, I'm not a pathological liar."

"Babe," Harriett soothes. "Just because you wait to tell us what's really going on, that doesn't make you a pathological liar. It's how you're programmed to deal with it. All of us process things differently."

"We don't care how many people you've slept with, or if your life is perfect. You forget, we bonded because our lives weren't perfect," Gabby reveals. "We're imperfectly perfect."

I lift my head and find Olivia staring at Gabby with wonder in her gaze. "Why do you hide this side of you? You go from not making a lick of sense to this deep person with kind things to say."

Gabby winks. "Got to keep you thinking."

Harriett's hand runs down my back. "We know your life isn't perfect, Emily. We want to make it better, not worse, which is why we never pushed. We aren't blind though. We know you haven't had it easy. Which is why we know it's hard for you to open up about how hard you are finding things."

"You should know us by now. We love each other despite our flaws," Olivia tells me.

"And now isn't the time to isolate yourself from us. You need to put an end to this way of thinking for all our sakes. We need to be a united front more than ever right now. And that means you need to be transparent with us about everything. No more hiding, Emily. Stop giving your parents this power," Harriett softly demands.

I burst into tears at the truth in her words. My parents do still have power over me. And I let them have it. But more, it's the disappointment in her tone that I can't take. "I'm sorry. I'm so sorry."

"Don't apologise," Olivia scolds gently. "We aren't here for apologies. We're here for our friend who we are seriously worried about."

I wipe the tears away, even as more flood my cheeks. "How did you know to find me here?"

"We tracked your phone," Harriett admits.

"Which is why we know you've not been at home all week," Gabby replies.

"We also looked through your window and saw your house had been cleared of most of your things," Olivia states. "But we want to hear it from you."

I nod. "First, I need you to know, I never meant to keep anything from you. I always tell you in the end. But there's a voice in my mind that tells me not to share things with you until I've fixed them."

"Because your parents are assholes," Gabby retorts. "We aren't blaming you."

"I know. I just needed you to know that," I reply.

"What happened at home, Emily?" Harriett orders. "Why aren't you there? Why didn't you come to us?"

"Because everything just seemed to happen at once. In the first fifteen minutes of being awake on Monday, I kicked a doorframe, stepped on a toy, ran out of milk, and found the bread was three days out of date. I went shopping to mostly get out of the house, but then my day just got worse. My card got declined at the till, so I went back to the car to check my online banking, only to discover the funeral directives accidently took out a lump sum for the funeral, which emptied my account. I went back home to get my tips and found I had been broken into. The place was torn apart. Not a lot survived the break-in, not even my tips. My life was in pieces around me. Literally."

"Wait, your house was broken into?" Olivia asks, kneeling on the ground in front of me. "I thought you were just having a clear out."

"You can't keep these things from us," Gabby stresses.

"We should be out there hunting whoever broke into your home," Olivia continues. "God, you both must have been so scared."

I pick at the lint on my jeans, and through thick tears, I watch as Harriett's hand reaches out to cover mine. "It was. For a split moment, I wanted to give up. I wanted the world to stop turning because I didn't know how much more I could take."

"We would have taken it for you. Let us carry it," Gabby pleads.

"I don't like that you were alone and feeling like that," Olivia adds, her eyes watering with unshed tears.

Harriett's hand squeezes mine. "We aren't going to keep telling you what you should have done. I think you know what you should have done. So instead, I'll tell you we care, and we want to know about everything. We want the good and bad, and the in between. Because we love you, and no one on this earth could make us stop. Not even you if you asked."

I wipe under my eyes with the sleeve of my coat. "It was for a split second. Just that second. But then I put one foot in front of the other and did what I needed to do. I got Poppy changed out of her wet clothes and was about to call one of you when I heard I had a visitor. Cole was there."

"What?" Harriett gasps.

"Cole turned up?" Gabby asks, her eyes widening. "Oh God."

Olivia clears her throat. "What did he say? What did *you* say?"

"Nothing worth repeating," I reply.

"What does that mean?" Harriett demands.

"Nothing," I sigh. "Long story short, he moved us in with him. I don't know who broke in, and I went with Cole because I owed him that much. I didn't tell you because I didn't know how to explain it, which sounds ridiculous now that I'm saying it out loud."

"You owe him nothing," Olivia argues. "What the fuck did he say to you?"

"I'd rather not say."

"Emily," Harriett warns. "You need to be honest with us."

I slap the palms of my hands down on my lap. "He threatened to take me to court."

"He fucking didn't," Olivia snaps. "I'll kill him."

"Calm down," Harriett tells her. "Emily, what else has he said?"

"That's the thing. He didn't need to say anything. He implied it. And that was enough. He thinks because of where I work, the courts will side with him. He's right. They will."

"This is what we are going to do," Harriett begins. "We're going to get Poppy, go grab your things, and then you are going to move in with me and River."

I give her a warm smile and take her hand. "This is why I never told you. I knew you'd do this for me."

"Because you'd do it for us," Gabby replies heatedly. "I don't see where you are going with this or why we are still sitting here."

"He's her dad. He's missed out on her life," I start.

"That doesn't give him the right to order you around," Olivia declares.

"It sounds much worse than it really is. He's really good with her."

"He could visit sick children in his spare time and help old people cross the road; that doesn't give him the fucking right to treat you like this," Gabby snaps.

"River can totally take him if that's what you're worried about," Harriett declares.

"Please, don't," I plead. "It started off bad, yeah, but he really is trying to make up for it. Poppy loves him. She loves her room. She loves her new home."

"I don't like this," Harriett admits. "I don't like the hold he has over you."

I meet her gaze. "I kept his daughter from him. If the roles were reversed, what would you expect me to do?"

"Okay, she has a point, because if Olivia kept the kids from me, I'd probably bury her," Gabby tells us.

"Hey," Olivia barks.

Gabby's eyebrows rise. "I said probably."

"He deserves to get to know her. He's done nothing wrong. He reacted badly, but he's only human."

Olivia scoffs. "Stop defending him. He's taken you from your home."

"I was broken into. There was nothing left before the ceiling in the kitchen fell through."

"The kitchen ceiling fell through?" Harriett asks.

"Yes. Just as I got downstairs and saw him," I admit on a sigh.

"We're worried," she replies. "What he's done isn't right."

"I know, but he's trying. It would be bad if he didn't want her, but he does."

"What are you going to do when you have to leave?" Gabby asks. "He has to know that can't be a permanent situation."

"Get this, he wants to sign the house over to me."

"Shut the front door," Olivia cries.

"Seriously?" Harriett murmurs.

"I'd take it," Gabby offers. "You need it more."

"Gabby," I snort. "I can't take a home from him."

"Yeah, you can. He made you leave yours," Harriett points out.

"Are you sure you want to stay there, though?" Olivia asks. "This isn't another way for you to hide your feelings from us?"

"It's fine. He went about it the wrong way, but he's been good to us since we've been there. I won't lie, it's been jarring, but I'll get there. Poppy deserves to have everything," I explain. "And I promise, I won't hide how I'm really feeling from you anymore. I'll let you know what's going on."

Harriett nudges me with her arm. "You'd better."

"It's such a relief now that you know. I'm meeting the rest of his family later, and I'm nervous about it."

"Did his mum react badly?" Olivia asks.

"She was concerned for her son. It's actually what we were

discussing before you arrived. She was apologising about her reaction to the news."

"Was she mean to you?" Gabby demands. "She seemed so nice."

"She is nice. She wasn't mean to me. She didn't even know I was there, and she was quick to apologise."

"I want you to know that if you change your mind at any point about staying there, you can come stay with us. We have the room, and we'd make sure Poppy is comfortable," Harriett promises.

"Thank you. We're okay where we are at the moment. She's enjoying her time with him. And he really does love her."

Gabby pats my leg. "We'll be the judge of that."

"No. You can't start hassling him. If things go sideways, I don't need him telling the courts my friends are crazy," I warn.

Gabby rolls her eyes. "We don't need to say anything for people to come to that conclusion."

"We might not need to do anything. He might not fuck up again," Olivia cheerfully adds.

Harriett grabs her bag from the floor. "We really do need to go to the police station now. Are you sure you'll be okay?"

"Um, yeah," I answer, surprised they're leaving. I thought for sure they'd come join us for lunch.

She presses her lips to my cheek. "Stay safe. And no more ignoring our calls or messages."

"I won't," I promise.

"Catch you later," Gabby declares, giving me a hug.

Olivia does the same. "We'll call you later."

"Let me know how it goes," I lamely reply.

With one last goodbye, I watch them head off into the crowd. I'm left feeling stumped by their quick departure.

Shaking myself out of it, I head to the restaurant. The conversation went better than I had hoped. I know it won't be the last time it's brought up, but at least now, that crippling anxiety inside me won't take over. I don't need to pretend everything is okay. Whether or not those old fears resurface is another story.

It's a battle for another day.

12

COLE

I've been sat watching my phone, waiting for it to light up with a message from Emily, for hours now. It's driving me crazy. I don't want to check in and come across as a creeper.

The house feels strange without Poppy and Emily here. It's quiet and still, something I normally find comfort in but now dislike. I should have gone with them, or at the very least, stayed with them until I knew for sure they'd be okay.

I slide my phone across the counter, feeling ridiculous about it. They're fine. They've gone years being fine without me.

My phone vibrates, and I lean over the counter to grab it. My heart races, ready to go get her, but it's not a message.

It's the front gate.

Buzzing my dad and brother in, I let out a breath and mentally slap myself. I need to get a grip.

As I make my way to the front door, I fire off a text to Emily asking if everything is okay. Dad and Kit are getting out of the car when I pull open the front door.

"Are the girls home?" Dad asks.

My phone beeps with a message from Emily. "This is her," I tell Dad.

Emily: We'll be back soon. We've taken Poppy to a soft play park.

Cole: Is that safe?

She sends a picture of Poppy in a pit of balls. It's only a small, caged area with a short slide.

Emily: Perfectly safe.

Cole: All right. See you soon.

"So, the prodigal son returns," I greet Kit.

He greets me warmly, pulling me in for a hug and smacking my back twice before stepping back. He's the same as he's always been. Black, unruly, curly hair. Tanned skin under the artwork of tattoos covering his body. His wardrobe hasn't changed either. I don't think I've ever seen him wear anything that isn't black.

"And I hear the disciplined workaholic is now a dad," he greets back.

I move aside to let them in. "You heard right."

"So, it's true she's a stripper?" he asks, and there's judgment in his tone.

"No. She works there, but she doesn't take her clothes off," I answer, heading into the kitchen.

"Kit, just be happy for your brother," Dad warns.

"Fuck that. Some chick comes into his life, tells him he has a kid, and he just what? Believes it?"

I jab him in the arm as I pass him to reach the kettle. "You've got no idea what you're talking about. It's not like that. And FYI, she didn't tell me. I found out. I've been through this with Mum and Dad."

"And I've already told him all of this too," Dad admits.

"Do you have anything stronger than tea?" Kit asks.

I sigh and reach for the key in the draw. I throw it to him. "Make sure you lock it back up."

"And he keeps the alcohol locked away," Kit mutters.

"Because I have a daughter who can reach it," I mutter back.

"How are the girls settling in?" Dad asks.

"Should be kosher for her, living in digs like this," Kit remarks.

I ignore him and answer my dad. "Poppy loves her new room."

"What kind of name is Poppy? You didn't even get a say on her name," Kit butts in as he comes back in with a bottle of whiskey.

"It's my daughter's name, Kit. You've been here five minutes. Don't ruin it by being a prick," I warn. "I will put you out."

"Bro, I'm just saying. You have no reason to trust this woman. She could be playing you."

"Because you don't know her. If you did, you wouldn't be standing there with your sly fucking remarks."

"Alright, boys. That's enough now."

Kit pours himself a hefty drink. "Sorry. I'm jet-lagged."

"Your mother messaged me earlier to say she's having fun getting to know Emily. I'm pretty sure she's already adopted her into her fold. You know what your mother is like."

"Yeah, she's too nice for her own good."

I slam my mug down on the counter. "Kit, what is your problem? Did some girl break your heart? Did Mum not cuddle you enough as a kid? Seriously, snap out of it."

"Sorry," he mutters. "It just came out."

I glare at him for a moment longer before turning to Dad. "Is Aria stopping by?"

"After work."

Kit's phone beeps and he pulls it out of his pocket, glancing at the screen. "Dad, that friend I told you about—Llam—who does security, said he can pop by yours sometime during the week. He has something he's working on right now, but he will make time in the week as a favour to me. I'll pass on your details to him."

"Something wrong with your security system?" I ask.

Dad rubs the scruff on his jaw. "Not sure. There are time lapses in the feed."

"I looked it over and I think someone is switching it off," Kit admits. "Which is why I called in the favour."

"How long has it been going on?" I ask.

Dad ducks his head. "A few months. But you know me, I'm not tech-savvy. I know the basics."

"Nothing has gone missing in the house though, right?"

LISA HELEN GRAY

"We have checked, but everything of value is there. Your mother has locked a few bits in the safe to be sure, but like I said, nothing has gone missing."

"Better to be safe though."

"Yeah, your mother is starting to think I'm the one who is messing it up. But we've had it long enough that I know the basics."

Kit slaps him on the back. "It's alright, Dad. Liam is good at what he does. He'll sort it for you."

"When do you go back home?" I ask.

Kit shrugs. "I don't know. I've been thinking of staying here in Coldenshire and opening a gallery."

"Seriously?"

"Yeah. It seems like you lot need me," he mutters. "Look what happens when I'm gone."

I roll my eyes at the snide remark. "Pretty sure we can take care of ourselves."

"Are you saying you don't want me to move here?"

"I didn't say that. It will be good to see you more. When you aren't being a dickhead, that is."

"It would be nice to have you around more," Dad announces. "We miss you."

"Well, I plan to stick around for a bit. I'll have to go back at some point to check in on the gallery and pack up if I decide to move."

"Jesus," I comment. "What happened to you in Australia?"

He snorts. "Can't a guy just want to be closer to his family? I've been travelling for months. I'm not saying I won't go do it again, because I will, but it would be nice to have people to come home to."

"I'm not judging. Just surprised. You've always liked being on the move and not tied down," I tell him.

"Must be because I'm getting old then."

"Why don't we get a start on dinner? We can put the spag bol in the slow cooker, then go sit in the garden and catch up more," Dad suggests.

"I'm good with that," I reply, and leave to go get the slow cooker out of the pantry. Really, it's an excuse to get a breather for a few minutes.

I want Kit to like Emily. I need him to accept her because she's always going to be a part of my life. I messed up once by speaking to her like shit; I don't want to make a second mistake by allowing my brother to as well.

I GRAB Poppy out of her car seat, careful not to disturb her.

"Should we wake her?" I ask as I secure her tightly against my chest.

"She'll wake up on her own soon. I think she's tired from all the running around," Emily admits.

"I forgot how energetic children can be," Mum teases.

"Will she sleep tonight?" I ask.

"Yes. I'll give her a bath and let her play a little longer," Emily answers.

A blue car pulls onto the drive, and my sister waves as she sees us.

"Mum, I'm gonna go in and lay Poppy down on the sofa."

Emily follows me into the house. "Her pushchair is in the kitchen. I'd feel more comfortable with her being close."

"All right," I reply, and walk down the hallway to the kitchen.

My brother's gaze immediately goes to Emily, his eyes narrowing slightly until they land on our daughter. He watches as I sit her in her pushchair and clip up her straps.

"Kit, this is Emily," I announce. "Emily, this is my brother, Kit."

"It's nice to meet you," Emily offers.

He grunts, not speaking a word. I'm about to call him out on it when I hear heels clicking on the floor, coming towards us.

Emily lowers her head and steps aside as my sister walks in with my mum. Her peach-coloured hair is curled to frame her angular face. She's dressed up a bit today. She's swapped out her leggings for dark blue jeans, but her top is similar to her other clothes. It shows off her midriff, but to keep warm, she has on a fleece jacket.

"You have a baby? Why didn't I know you had a baby?" she cries.

"Shush, you'll wake her," I warn, and step to the left so she can see Poppy asleep in her pushchair.

She throws both hands up to cover her mouth, and her eyes glisten at the sight of my daughter. "She's beautiful, Cole."

"That she is," I boast.

"Will she wake up soon? I want to meet her."

"Let her sleep," I tell her.

She gives Poppy one more glance before giving me a big, dopey grin. She closes the space between us and pulls me in for a hug. "Hey, brother. It's been a while."

I hug her back. "I'm back for good now."

She pulls back, still grinning. "When can I meet the woman who tamed my big brother?"

"She's standing right there. And we aren't together," I point out.

She spins to face Emily, who has straightened away from the wall. "Hey," Emily waves.

Rushing over to her, Aria pulls her in for a hug. "Hey, it's so nice to meet you. I'm Aria."

"It's good to meet you," Emily tells her, smiling back.

"Shall we wait for the little one to wake up before eating?" Dad asks. "Smelling that for the past two hours has made me hungry."

"Honey," Mum lightly scolds. "Have a snack."

"No, we can eat dinner. I can put some aside for Poppy," Emily announces.

"You'll be joining us?" Kit asks, a bite to his tone.

"Ignore my brother," Aria bites out, though there's no heat behind her words. "He's always grumpy."

"I can take Poppy upstairs whilst you all eat," Emily whispers.

"We came to meet our niece," Kit points out.

"Enough. This is Emily's home. You're the guest here," I warn him.

"It's okay," Emily promises. "I'm not that hungry."

"No, you'll sit and eat dinner with us," I tell her, my words coming out harsher than they need to.

Aria snorts. "Of course she will. She's family now."

"She's not my family," Kit retorts.

"Enough, son," Dad snaps. "You will respect Emily in this house, and you'll be polite to her."

"I'll get the plates," Mum offers.

"I'll get the pasta on the stove," Dad adds.

Aria links her arm through Emily's. "I want to get to know the mother to my niece."

As they make their way over to the table, I head towards Kit, and keep my voice low when I reach him. "One more step out of line, and you'll be out that door before you get the chance to apologise."

"Alright," he growls, and heads into the pantry, most likely to loot the alcohol fridge or cabinet.

Mum steps over to me, placing her hand over mine. "I'll talk to him."

I watch her follow him, and I take a minute to gather myself. I meant what I said to him. I will kick him out. She's the mother of my child, and they come first. I won't have anyone disrespecting them in their own home. Not even my brother.

13

EMILY

His brother hates me. I don't know what I did for him to resent me this much. It's suffocating. I can feel his glare on the side of my face, and it's making me uncomfortable. If I was a person who could handle confrontation, I would have called him out on it already. I nearly have a few times, but then I remembered, they're family. I'm the outsider here, not him.

His sister is bubbly and talkative. She doesn't seem to hold any ill-will towards me, which has made the evening more bearable. But only just.

Dropping the pot of pasta onto the heat mat, Cole then takes a seat next to me. I let out a breath when he blocks his brother's view of me.

"So, my mum says you bartend at Tease," Aria states.

"I do. I'll be back at work in a few weeks."

"Do you not worry about what your daughter will think of you working at a strip club?"

"Kit," Joe warns.

"It's a question. I want to get to know her."

"It's fine," I quietly reply.

"No, it's not," Cole growls.

Kit scoffs. "It's a valid question."

"To answer your question, I'm proud of my profession. I go to work every day, I pay my taxes, and my bills. I would hope working to provide for my daughter would make her proud. I'm not ashamed of what I do. I'm not ashamed of where I work. I enjoy it."

"You must get a lot of attention from men. How will that work now you're living here?" he asks.

"I do. But it stays at work. And I don't return those advances. I don't lead them on. And I'm not sure how living here relates to that."

"He means, how will you bring a man back here," Cole bites out.

"Well, since Cole is the only man I've ever been with, I don't see how that is relevant or why I would start now," I blurt out.

I close my eyes as everyone's gaze falls on me. I didn't mean for that to come out, and I know I can't take it back now. There is no way for me to lie my way out of this one. An alarm saves me from everyone's questions.

"Someone's breaching the side fence," Cole warns, getting to his feet.

I look out the window, and my eyes widen when I see Gabby hanging from the fence. Her leg is stuck in the vines going up the wood.

"Oh shit," I hiss, and slide my chair back. "I'll sort it."

"I'm calling the police," Cole warns. "Don't go to the door."

"Don't. It's my friends."

Hearing the truth, he replies, "I'll call the company and make sure they don't send the police out."

"Why on earth are they climbing over the back fence?" Georgia asks.

I head outside and begin to jog over the grass to where she is.

"I'm still stuck," Gabby hisses.

"What are you doing?" I ask.

She blows out a breath and looks up at me, beaming. "Hey, Em. Surprise! We've come to see you."

"And you couldn't use the front door?" I ask as I help untangle her leg. She drops into the bush, and the other two follow, climbing down.

I step back to give Gabby room, and she brushes off the dirt and leaves from her clothes. "It was locked."

"There's a buzzer," I muse.

"We wanted to come and see if you were really okay," Harriett explains.

Gabby waves, and I turn to see Georgia and Aria waving back. "Who's the girl?"

"Cole's sister," I answer.

"Is she being nice?" Olivia asks.

"Yeah, but I think his brother hates me," I admit.

"The tall, dark-haired, brooding one?" Harriett asks, her expression turning stern.

"Yeah."

"Who's the silver fox?" Olivia gushes. "He's hot."

"And you're in a committed, loving relationship," Gabby reminds her.

"I didn't say I was going to date him," Olivia snaps, poking her in the shoulder.

Gabby shoves her back. "Well, how would you feel if I said the girl was hot?"

"You didn't need to. Your expression said it all."

"Alright you two. Pack it in," Harriett demands, pulling them apart.

Gabby pushes her hand down her leggings. "A fucking fanny wedgie hurts like hell," she groans.

"Girls, why don't you come in and have some dinner?" Georgia offers, her voice carrying over the garden.

"We would love to," Gabby calls back, and tags Olivia's hand, pulling her towards the house.

"Why don't you think the brother likes you?" Harriett whispers as we follow at a slower pace behind them.

"He keeps making little digs," I explain. "It's fine, though. Nothing I can't handle."

"Where's Cole?" she asks.

"Informing the security company that it's a false alarm."

Her eyes widen. "Well shit. It's tighter than Fort Knox in here. It was the only way in we could find or attempt."

"Or you could have pressed the buzzer," I tease.

She laughs. "Where's the fun in that?"

We step inside, and I hear Georgia introduce my friends to everyone.

"Sorry for the drop in. We just wanted to surprise our friend," Gabby announces.

"Was there something wrong with the buzzer on the front gate?" Joe asks.

Gabby's nose scrunches up. "How would it be a surprise if we announced our arrival?"

Aria laughs. "You're the chicks Dave wants to fire every week, aren't you?"

"He said that?" Gabby asks, her jaw dropping. She turns to Olivia, her eyes glistening with happiness. "He talks about us."

"He's lying," Olivia assures Aria. "He'd be lost without us."

Gabby nods. "He really would."

"Didn't you start a brawl not long ago?" Aria asks.

"Technically, the reporters did. They wanted the dirt on Aisling, a friend of ours who was murdered, and it didn't go down well. We did Dave a service," Gabby explains.

"Gabby is right. I was there that night, and we did him a favour," Harriett admits.

"If you ever need a plus one on a night out, call me," Aria demands softly.

"Really?" Kit asks, his lip curling.

"Ah, so you're the guy with a stick up his arse," Gabby cheerfully greets. "You should smile more. It will make you more approachable."

"You should go to the club. Wind down. Live a little," Olivia remarks, unable to hide the sarcasm.

"Or the next time you make a snide remark, you'll find laxative in your drink," Harriett tells him sweetly.

"Right, can we have dinner now?" Cole asks, and I watch the blood drain from Gabby's face as she tenses.

"What's wrong?" I ask her, and the others move, noticing it too.

"You," she accuses shakily as she turns to confront Cole.

His eyebrows pinch together. "Me?"

She growls low in her throat, and I know that sound all too well. It's her fighting growl.

"Get him!" she cries, and before I can reach for her, she's diving on him, knocking them both to the floor.

Chaos erupts around us. Cole's mum screams while his dad holds her back so she doesn't get hurt, and his brother moves to his rescue.

"What is your damage?" Cole roars, trying to shove her off without using force.

"Babe," Olivia cries, trying to pull her off.

"It's him," Gabby yells.

Harriett and I move, helping Olivia pull her off. Gabby continues to fight, slapping and kicking with all her might.

"Stop!" Harriett pleads.

"No. No. What are you doing? Get him," Gabby demands, her voice breaking. "It's him."

"We have no idea what you're talking about," Olivia tells her, wrapping her arms around her to stop her from hurting herself.

"Stop. Don't let him get away," Gabby sobs.

"Gabby, it's Cole," I remind her, wondering if this is the break we've all been waiting to happen.

She meets my gaze dead on. "I recognise his voice. It's him. He's the one who kidnapped me. Who killed all those girls."

"What?" I breathe out.

"I haven't killed anyone," Cole argues as his brother helps him to his feet.

"I think you have the wrong person," Georgia tells us, tears pooling in her eyes.

"Are you sure?" I ask Gabby.

"You can't seriously believe her?" Cole growls. "I've never killed anyone. I'm not the man who kidnapped you."

"Then why do you sound just like him?" she spits out.

"I don't know, but it's not me. I promise you," he argues, before turning to me. "You said you fought him and he had blood pouring from his head. Do I look like I've been in a fight recently?"

"It's been weeks. Those injuries would have cleared up just like Gabby's," I answer warily.

I don't know what to believe. He's the father to my daughter. We've been sleeping in the same house for weeks. Wouldn't I have known if he was a serial killer? Aren't serial killers supposed to have some quirk that is proof they're a killer? Or am I one of those people who star in documentaries, who tell the world they didn't know and that he was a nice guy?

Oh God, I think I'm going to be sick.

"Maybe he's right," Olivia warily announces. "Hayden hit him pretty good, so he would have some marks."

"And I was in London the night you were kidnapped," Cole adds, and I relax a little.

"Why are you explaining yourself? The bitch is crazy," Kit declares.

"No, I'm not wrong," Gabby snaps. "And I'll show you fucking crazy."

Harriett helps drag her back. "Can you prove you were in London?"

"This second?" Cole spits out. "No. But I have plenty of witnesses who can vouch for my whereabouts."

"Wait, the killer said he had a brother," Harriett begins. "What if you're his brother?"

"I've been out of the country until early this morning, when I arrived back," Kit remarks. "Jesus. This is fucking nuts. You need to phone the police and get them out of here."

"Wait," I order. "She wouldn't react like this for nothing."

"Sweetie, my son isn't a killer," Georgia promises, and the heartbreak in her voice breaks my heart.

Harriett scrunches her nose up and steps closer to Cole. Her gaze goes from his to his brother's, and back again. Both brothers stare back at her. "You aren't blood related. His eyes are set apart more, and you, Cole, have a stronger jawline. You look nothing like your sister or parents."

"I'm adopted. I don't know what that has to do with this," he replies, flexing his jaw.

My breath catches. I didn't know this. I didn't see it. I had told myself he and his dad shared the same appearance qualities.

I saw what I wanted to see.

I step forward, my voice shaky. "The first morning here, I mentioned the killer talking about a brother and you freaked. Why would you react like that if it wasn't your brother?"

"My brother is standing right next to me," he growls.

"No, your biological brother," I point out.

Pain flashes across his face, and he lowers his head. "My biological brother is dead. He died years ago in a prison riot."

"Is this what you wanted?" Kit spits out. "This has nothing to do with you."

"Then why did you run off that morning?" I ask, ignoring his brother.

He glances up. "Because the police already questioned me. They questioned everyone. A team of behaviour investigator advisors were in on the questioning. They asked me a bunch of questions about crimes and reports made against Tease. Then they went through my own personal life, asking if anyone held a grudge. My brother was the only person who came to mind."

"Why don't we give Emily and Cole a minute to discuss this privately," Georgia offers.

"No offence, but I'm not leaving her with someone who might be the killer or related to the killer," Gabby argues.

"He's not the killer," Kit bites out.

"You're mistaking me for someone who cares about what you think," Gabby snaps.

"Are we really not going to call the police?" Kit growls. "First you break in, then you attack my brother, and now you stand in his house calling him a murderer."

My gaze meets Cole's, and I'm frozen under his spell. His silent plea is almost deafening. He's telling me, without words, that he isn't the killer and to believe him.

And I want to. So badly.

"Can you all leave us?" Cole demands, still not looking away.

"We aren't leaving her with you," Harriett remarks.

He looks away, meeting her gaze. "I would never hurt her. I would rather die than ever see her in pain. I know you have no reason to believe me, but it's true."

Harriett slowly turns to me. "We can wait outside in the garden for you."

"He said leave," Kit demands.

"And if you speak to her like shit one more time, it won't be her boyfriend you need to worry about. It will be all of us," Olivia snaps. "Same goes for Emily."

"Can they wait in the garden?" I ask, letting him see with just a look that I need this. I need them here. It's not that I don't feel safe with him. I just feel safer knowing they are here.

"Yeah," he answers.

"Do you want us to stay?" Georgia asks.

"I'm good, Mum. We can arrange dinner for another day," he replies.

"I'm not going anywhere," Kit announces. "Why should her friends be allowed to stay?"

Olivia snorts. "She's five-foot-two, can't even kill a spider, and you're worried about *her*."

"Kit, I'll call you later," Cole promises.

"Son, call us if you need us," Joe pleads. He closes the space between us and reaches down to kiss my cheek. "My son is a good man."

"Call me if you need me to come back," Georgia offers, kissing my cheek before moving to her son.

Harriett pulls me away as they say their goodbyes to Cole. "Are you sure you're going to be okay alone with him?"

"I don't think he will hurt me," I admit. "This has to be some sort of mix up."

"Trust me, it's not," Gabby replies. "I can agree, he's not the killer, but he's definitely related to him. It's faint, but a memory is being brought to the surface. The killer has his lips to my ear, and before he shoves me into the water, he tells me to ask Cole. I'm not imagining it or making it up."

"I don't think you are," I assure her. "But something doesn't add up. I don't want to be one of those girls who are blind to the truth, but I do truly believe he wouldn't hurt anyone."

"You've been here a week," Olivia retorts. "You don't know him."

I meet her gaze. "But I do. It's hard to explain, but I do."

"We need to trust Emily on this," Harriett points out. "She knows him better than we do."

"I'm grabbing some food," Gabby sighs, and heads over to the table, where she picks up a plate and starts filling it with food. When she's done, she walks back over. "I'm not happy about this, but I'll follow your lead."

"Thank you."

Olivia slides open the back door, and they trickle out. When it closes behind them, I turn back to the room, finding we're alone.

I meet his gaze, unable to look away. "Explain."

14

COLE

I never thought I'd have to talk about my past to anyone. I'm not obligated to tell Emily either. I don't owe her anything. But there's a voice in the back of my mind demanding I do. For some reason, I need her to believe me when I say I'm not capable of this.

The hurt that shined back at me when her friend accused me of murder nearly brought me to my knees. It's almost like I've betrayed her, when in reality, I've done nothing to her.

"Explain," she demands.

I gesture to the table, and we both slowly walk over and take a seat. "Where do you want me to start?"

"From the beginning, but first, I need you to promise me you have nothing to do with the murders."

"I know we are still getting to know each other, but do you really think I'm capable of that?"

"I don't know what you're capable of," she answers.

"It's not me. I have nothing to do with this."

"And your brother; how sure are you about his death?"

"I had a letter from the prison notifying me of his death, so pretty sure."

She tilts her head to the side. "Did you bury him?"

"No. I washed my hands of him a long time ago."

"I need more than that. This person is killing my friends. He kidnapped my best friend. And you are the link that ties it all together. If, by chance, he is alive, then you know why he's doing this."

"As far as I'm aware, my brother died during a prison riot. It was in the news because a lot of inmates got hurt, as well as some of the guards. I got the letter two days later. I never took responsibility for the remains, and I never went to a funeral. I didn't get involved in any way. I understand that the evidence is damning, but it's still not enough for me to believe it's him."

She clears her throat. "He mentioned to Gabby that a woman was taken from him, that his parents didn't want him, and said his foster parents only wanted his brother. I'm assuming that's you."

I feel the blood drain from my face. "I need you to be sure. Did he really say those words?"

"I can call Gabby in and get her to tell you the rest, but that is the gist of it. Do you know what those words mean?"

I scrub a hand down my face. My whole life I've gone over memories to find answers. It kept me awake so many nights. I never understood how I could turn out okay, but he didn't. There was a time when I thought I was broken, and that something was wrong with me, but it was adolescence making me feel those things. As an adult, I can look back and see that it was my brother who was broken, or at the very least, something in his mind was.

"He's dead. I got the letter telling me he was dead."

She reaches over the table, taking my hand. "I think the letter was a lie. I think he's alive, and he wants revenge. What did you do?"

Shaking out of my shock a little, I reply. "It's not that easy."

"Then explain it to me. What happened to your parents? Start there."

"Our dad died in a car accident before our fourth birthday party. Rumours were he purposely drove off the bridge. My mum, she was never the same after that, and she took her life a few years later. My brother, Cyrus, is the one who found her. She had got into a full bath and sliced her wrists. They tried to home us with relatives first, but our parents didn't have many. Those they did have didn't want to take on three kids."

"Three?"

"I had a sister called Lana."

She swallows audibly. "What happened to her?"

"The official report says she fell down the stairs and broke her neck," I answer, and the grief that always consumes me when I think of her, rises.

"And unofficially?"

"Cyrus pushed her down the stairs. No one would listen to me when I said she didn't fall. Why would they? I was six and got told to be quiet. I might not remember much from that time in my life, but I still see that day vividly. We were sitting at the dining room table eating breakfast. Lana was in the chair between us when suddenly, she started crying. Hot tea had spilled on her dress and burned her skin. Our foster parents scolded her and told her to be quiet when she said our brother spilt it. She went upstairs to change, and because she was taking so long, our foster dad told my brother to go help her. I offered to go, but they wouldn't let me. If I did, she would still be alive."

"So, your brother pushed her?"

"I know he did. When we heard a commotion, we ran to the bottom of the stairs. Her legs and neck were twisted at a weird angle, and Cyrus was at the top, looking down. He wasn't upset or in shock. I can't explain it, but it was like he enjoyed it."

"What happened then?"

"We went to go live with another foster family. I don't remember much of them because I was so lost after my sister's death. I do remember they were nice though."

"The couple who was murdered were foster parents. Did you live with them?"

"I don't know. Everything during that time is a blur. Things happened in that house that I still can't explain, and I think I blocked most of it out. I can't even tell you what they looked like."

"What do you mean by things you can't explain?" she asks.

127

"Like things being stolen. Kids being clumsy, which resulted in broken bones. The family cat was found buried in the garden. His head was smashed in. And the fire brigade was called out twice that I remember to put out fires in the cellar. Both times we were lucky the house didn't burn down."

"You think your brother did all those things?"

I shrug. "I couldn't prove it, and by that point, I was scared of him. Dave had been my only friend, and even then, we had to be friends in secret. We knew Cyrus wouldn't like it, that it would set him off."

"Ah, that's what you meant when you said you and Dave were a different kind of family."

"Yeah. We're brothers in every sense of the word. Just not legally or by blood. He got homed with an aunt not long after the last fire, and luckily, ended up in the same town as me."

"What happened with your brother?"

"We got split up. My brother was moved to another home for better monitoring. I had to stay where I was because a couple wanted to adopt me."

"Georgia and Joe?"

"Yes."

"He said you took her from him. What did he mean?"

"I was at university when I next saw him, miles away from the group home. I thought he had changed, and I promised to keep in touch with him. And I did. He came out with me and my friends, and I thought I had my brother back. I never stopped thinking about him. I tried to get to know him, to find out what happened to him after he left, but he never wanted to speak about it. And I didn't trust him enough to tell him about where I ended up or what my family was like. I was right not to."

"Why?" she asks.

"Because it wasn't me he wanted. I was just a tool to get to a friend. Jack was my first friend at university. He came from a rich family, and Cyrus knew that. I don't know how but he did. I got a cryptic message from Jack one day, so I went to his house to check on him. My brother opened the door, thinking I was there to help him. It was crazy. He was crazy. Jack and his family were tied up on the floor in the living room, whilst Cyrus's girlfriend, Louise, was upstairs waiting for Jack's mum to open the safe. Jack's dad was lying on the floor unconscious, bleeding from his head. We got into a fight when the screaming started upstairs. I overpowered him and ran up to help Jack's mum. Louise was on top of her, trying to pull off her wedding band. His mum, not wanting to part with it, put up a fight. I tried to help, but there was a struggle, and Louise went flying over the banister. She died on impact. The police arrived on the scene as my brother went for me. He would have killed me if it wasn't for a neighbour phoning the police. He blamed me for all of it. He thinks I'm the reason Louise died, and why the police were there. He went to prison, and I never tried to contact him. I never went to see him either. He took everything from me that day. My friend, my degree, my life there. I couldn't stay in school after everything he did, so I moved back home. Then a few years ago, I had a letter forwarded from my old address announcing his death."

"So he could have sent that letter himself. If it was government issue, it would have been sent directly to you."

"Not necessarily. I have multiple homes in the UK."

"Yeah, but it was sent to the one he knew. That has to mean something. And excuse me if I'm wrong, but wouldn't you only be notified if you were his next of kin? You weren't. And I'm sure Jack's family would have been notified if he was leaving prison. Did you check if they got a message?"

"No. I couldn't face Jack after that. I'm not even sure if they live in that area anymore."

"So, it could be him?"

"But why? Why kill all those people when he could have come straight to me?" I point out.

"Because he wants you to hurt. If there's one thing we learned during Gabby's kidnapping, it's that. He is obsessed and wants to hurt the person he's obsessed with. If that's you, none of us are safe."

I duck my head. "He has to be dead."

"Do you want to risk another person being hurt because you didn't want to believe he's alive?"

How can she ask me that? "No."

129

"You acted weird that day I mentioned a brother. Where did you go?"

"To find that letter. I needed to go over it again, because I've had a bad feeling in the pit of my stomach for months now."

"Then listen to your gut now."

"We need to go to the police. They'll be able to find out if that letter is authentic or not."

"I think it might be best for me to go stay at a friend's house. It's not safe for us here anymore. He's after the person you love the most. I don't want Poppy mixed up in this."

"He won't find you here," I promise. "The house has never been in my name. It's been in a shell company's name until recently, when I changed the deeds over to you. It might be best to sign them now."

"I don't think he's that intellectual. He has other ways of finding us, and I don't know about you, but I'm not willing to put our daughter's life at risk."

"Trust me when I tell you this is the safest place for you both. If it is him, then it won't take him long to find you. I think for now, you need to remain safe within these walls. I know a guy who can install panic buttons in your car, in separate locations throughout the house, and one to keep on your person."

"I don't know," she stresses.

"If I thought for a second that I'd be putting you in danger, I wouldn't make you stay."

"It's easy for you to say; it's not you he'll hurt. It's me."

"You think it won't hurt if he gets to you?" I ask, coming off harsher than I intended. There's a moment of silence, both of us staring at one another. "Why don't I talk to the police first? They've already predicted he's going to take a new path. Gabby and Trixie messed up his original plan, so he'll probably come for me next. Not you. And if it is him, I'll make sure I work with the police to get him back behind bars, where he belongs."

"How will you do that?"

"Well, if it is my brother, and it's me he wants to hurt, I'll make myself available for him. I'll announce where I am in the papers if I have to, to make sure he sees and goes there. But we don't know if it's him. Not for sure. This is all guesses."

"I'm not a fan of you putting yourself in danger either."

"Why, do you care?" I ask, and her lips part.

"Of course I do."

I sigh. "Then please, stay. I don't want to lose more time with my daughter, and that's what will happen if we are living separately. We don't know how long this will take," I remind her. "I know I'm asking for a lot right now, and I don't have the right to ask for it, but she's my daughter. I don't want her to forget me."

"Only if you're definitely going to the police."

"Think of it as already done. You aren't the only one who needs answers. So do I."

"Is this what your mum wanted you to tell me? She mentioned earlier that you have things you want to be the one to share. Was it about this?"

"Yes. I have one photo of Lana, and Poppy looks just like her. I asked her not to bring up the adoption or anything personal because I wanted to be the one to share these things with you. It's not pretty. And I didn't want you to think I was using it to emotionally blackmail you. I lost all my biological family growing up, which is why I don't want to lose Poppy."

"All right," she whispers. "I need to talk to my friends. They won't like that I'm staying here."

My gaze goes to the window, where the three girls are talking heatedly to each other.

"I think they might already have your bags mentally packed."

She snorts. "I'll point out how good your alarm system was. They don't blame you. Gabby was just freaked. She went through a horrific ordeal, so you can't blame her for that."

"I don't," I promise. "Rest assured, if it is my brother, I won't stop until every one of them gets justice. He might be blood, but he's not my family. He never has been."

"Okay," she whispers.

"I'm going to call the policeman in charge of the case and see if he can set up an appointment with the detective running the case."

"Before you do, I want you to know how sorry I am that this is happening to you. If it is your brother, I know it won't be easy knowing all the horrific things he's done. I can't imagine what this is like for you, or what must be going through your head. But I am sorry it is."

Her words cut through me like a knife. They were meant to comfort me, to let me know she's here, but they have the opposite effect. Because I don't deserve her kindness. "Thank you," I choke out.

"Call me if you need me. I'll be outside with the girls," she replies, before leaving.

The backdoor closes behind her, muting her friends' voices. I glance down at Poppy, asleep in her pushchair. She is innocent in all of this. As innocent as my sister was. But I'm not a scared little boy anymore. I'm a grown man who can take care of himself.

I will kill him before he ever lays a hand on her.

I never thought I was capable of killing someone until her. For Poppy, I would kill. I would kill to save her.

I'd do anything for her.

That includes stopping him.

15

EMILY

The house feels empty without my girls here. After Cole called the police and explained the situation, they asked him to go to the station and answer some questions. He left, and my girls didn't feel comfortable leaving me here alone. They didn't want to leave me here at all and were ready to pack me up so we could leave. But one word from my daughter—dada—and they understood my confliction.

I was grateful they stayed for as long as they did. It gave us time to talk about what happened. None of us truly believed we'd ever get answers or find out who the killer was. Now the police have one, or at the very least, their first solid lead.

I head into the kitchen to find the key to the alcohol cabinet, which Cole keeps hidden. I'm not sure I'll be able to sleep tonight, so I'm hoping a glass of wine will help.

Cole got back twenty minutes ago and immediately went upstairs to take a shower. He was at the police station for nine hours so I'm hoping that means something. I didn't press him for answers because I knew the events of the night had left him unsettled. He looked so vulnerable when he walked in; a sharp contrast to the disciplined businessman I've come to know.

I hear a noise on the stairs as I pour my glass of wine. I look up to find Cole walking into the kitchen. He has a plain white T-shirt and loose grey joggers on, freezing me in place. Every girl has something they are attracted to. Always. Whether it's because they are in great shape, have a nice arse, or have gorgeous eyes. There is always something a girl is attracted to, that thing that hooks you and reels you in. Mine is clearly grey joggers and white T-shirts. I thought he looked hot in suits, but damn, seeing him in loungewear has me heating up. It could also be the fact I can see the outline of his cock in them, but that's another story.

"You're wet," he announces.

Yes. Yes, I am.

"Huh?"

"Emily," he calls out, snapping me out of it.

I feel wetness on the hand that is placed on the counter. "Shit!" I hiss, and quickly place the bottle of wine on the side. Cole is beside me with a cloth. "I'm so sorry."

"Is it me?" he asks. I want to say yes, that he distracted me with his grey joggers, which show the outline of his groin.

"What?" I ask, fully getting my head together.

"I don't want you to be scared of me," he reveals, moving aside to grab a glass.

"I'm not scared of you. I was distracted," I admit.

"I was surprised to see you still here. I thought for sure when I left that you wouldn't be here when I got back."

"You made some good points. I meant what I said when you first found out about Poppy. My intentions were never to keep her from you." He nods and heads into the pantry. I wait for him to return before asking, "What did the police say? You were gone a long time."

"They won't know if the letter is legit until morning. They did manage to get hold of the records from the foster carers that were killed, and they confirmed my brother was in their care after we got separated. It was only for a few weeks, and he only got put there because the male carer worked with troubled kids."

My heart breaks for Cole. "What about the others?"

"They can't find a link with the policeman, but that's not saying there isn't one. And for the young woman found in the reserve, the only connection is to Tease. She worked at the Blue Lagoon, which used to be Tease. We relocated that club to London, where I resided."

"I know this isn't what you want to hear, but it is looking more like it is him."

He scrubs a hand down his face, before pouring a hefty amount of whiskey into a glass. "Yeah, it is. I also found out that before he ran away at fourteen, he was being evaluated by a medical professional."

"Are they allowed to reveal all of that?" I ask. I thought it was all confidential.

"He's a risk to himself and others, so yeah, they can."

"What did they say?" I ask as a shiver runs down my spine.

"That he showed signs of sociopathic and a narcopathy behaviour. He was never treated, which explains a lot."

"You spoke about what he was like after your parents passed, but not before. What was he like then?"

He takes a large swig of his drink. "It's like my mind has been blocking it out. I remember being in hospital a lot. I picture my mum sitting next to me reading a story. But it's never the same room or the same nurses. They change, and I know it's because I was admitted for different injuries," he reveals, before blowing out a breath. "You don't need to hear all of this."

"I want to. I can see you're struggling with this, and I want to help."

"Because it's all fucking crazy. You read about this, you see it in movies, but you never imagine it can happen to you."

"I can understand that," I whisper. "Do you think your parents know?"

"I think they did because why else would they have separated us? We shared a room, but then we didn't. I was sharing with my sister until they could get the loft space renovated."

"If they knew, they were doing everything they could to keep you safe whilst still making sure your brother didn't feel singled out. I guess they knew it would make it worse for you and your sister."

"I want you to know I'm not him. I know I said what I did when I went to yours, but I swear, that isn't me. I'm nothing like him. I'm not saying I've never gotten violent because I have. I fought like any other kid, and I've got into it with men in the club. But I've never let my rage get the better of me or—"

"Don't do that," I gently warn. "Don't explain yourself, because I know you aren't him. I've seen you dote on your daughter. I've seen the love in your heart when you are with her. I have witnessed your kindness and received care from you. If you were anything like him, I wouldn't be working behind the bar. I wouldn't have been able to be there for my grandma. I know you aren't him."

The heat in his gaze as he watches me has me burning up. He shakes his head as he lowers the glass to the table. "It should be me making you feel better. It was your friend who was killed, and your friends who were kidnapped."

"Calling Trixie a friend is like someone asking for pepper and salt. It just doesn't fit," I tease.

He chuckles. "You know what I mean."

"I do."

He lets out a breath. "I should have listened to my gut months ago and said something. People would still be alive if I had."

"I don't think that's true. They've not been able to find who this is. What makes you think they'd be able to locate him? You read the papers, he was living in that cave and van. No one would have been able to find him. It's not like there are cameras with facial recognition up there. This might be a scene from a movie, but it doesn't have the tech like one."

"Why would he do this, though? It doesn't make sense. He could have got his revenge by coming to me."

"Harriett is big on mysteries and puzzles. She's always been the person to find answers, so she went looking. When we met up with Hayden Carter, who is also running the story on her blog and radio station, all we got were more questions. I'm not saying we didn't learn more by teaming up, because we did. And we all came to the same conclusion: he was looking for you or digging for information. Murders one to three were done in rage. Harriett read the reports, and the victims were tortured for fun, not for answers. They were revenge. The murder victims after were tortured for answers, besides Aisling. She had been tortured but was then killed mercifully. Or that's what they concluded."

"They'll know more tomorrow," he replies, his lips turned down. "What happened in that cave, Emily?"

"I only know the bullet points of it," I answer, not sure he really wants to know the truth.

"Please, talk me through it."

"Are you sure? It's not pretty."

"I'm sure."

I go to take a large swig of wine but end up downing the entire glass. I don't care how unladylike it is. I need it to get through this conversation.

Sitting down on the stool, I gather my thoughts before answering. "Gabby woke up in the cave to hear the killer yelling at Trixie. He had her tied to a chair and thought she was the woman who means the most to who I assume is you." I take a breath. "Actually, to make this easier, I'm going to talk like the killer is your brother and it's you he's after. Otherwise, this will get confusing."

"That's fine," he remarks softly, then his eyebrows pinch together. "Trixie is the ball buster who doesn't take subtle hints or direct remarks?"

"That's the one," I reply with a small smile. "We think Aisling told Cyrus that Trixie was the woman he's really after."

"Why would she say that?"

"We didn't understand that at first either. Not until the barbeque. I had gone by this point, but the girls filled me in. We asked all the dancers when they last saw Aisling, or if they knew who she spoke with last. It was you."

He closes his eyes for a brief moment. "I remember. She wanted advice on how to open a dance studio and what it would entail. I offered to invest, and even had a space in mind for her that I purchased as an investment last year."

"Yeah, well, we think Cyrus was watching you. He jumped to conclusions, assuming she meant something to you. When he took her, she must have remembered Trixie bragging about being with you."

"I've never been with her," he retorts, his expression twisting in disgust. I shouldn't feel this much relief at the news, but I do.

"Yeah, well, that's what my friends found out during the barbeque. Olivia asked if you had slept with Trixie, and one of the girls replied that Trixie wishes. She told them Trixie tried it on with you, but you were never interested."

"And that's why Trixie and your friend were taken?"

"Gabby was in the wrong place at the wrong time, but she's Gabby. She freaks under pressure and pissed him off enough to get answers."

"What did he say?"

"Basically, everything I told you earlier. No one wanted him, not even his parents. He said you took *her* from him, and that you had to pay," I reveal, before gulping. "He also said you were meant to be there, that he wanted you to watch, but because you weren't, he was happy to watch you mourn her."

"It was an accident. I was trying to pull Louise off Jack's mum. I had just got her away when his mum kicked out. Louise fell back, and because she was drugged up, she went over the banister."

"I believe you," I assure him. "Gabby said Cyrus was crazy, and he didn't make sense."

"I never thought he cared about her. When they came out with us that one night, she seemed more like a possession to him. He didn't treat her the best, but she seemed smitten with him and happy to do what he said."

"Most narcissists have that power, but she still made those choices. He wasn't there when she attacked the mum."

"No, he wasn't," he confirms. "I don't even know why they were still together. She made a pass at me at the club, and he saw. They got into a fight, and he sent her home. The last thing he said to me was that he didn't care. I had a feeling he did, but not because he was broken up over it."

"All we can do now is hope the police can get answers. The quicker we know whether it's him, the better. None of us are safe right now, and until tonight, none of us knew who to look for," I explain.

"Speaking of, we should talk about what to do next."

"What do you mean?"

"Well, I've called that friend who is going to fit those panic alarms, and he's happy to do it. But I think once we get confirmation that it is Cyrus, we need a contingency plan."

"If you're talking about setting yourself up to be bait, then no. That should be our last resort. Poppy needs her dad."

"I can take care of myself."

"I don't doubt that you can, but until we know what we're dealing with, we should let the police handle it."

"I'm going back in the morning. I want answers and they probably have more if it is Cyrus."

"I'll come with you. Poppy has nursery tomorrow, so we can drop her off then head over."

"Are you sure?"

"Of course. Unless you want your mum or dad to go with you?"

"We can head to theirs after. They've probably been worried out of their minds all night."

"Um, we can drive separately to the police station. I don't want to intrude with your family."

"You won't be. You're a part of this family too."

"Pretty sure your brother has my headstone picked out," I mutter.

He chuckles. "I wouldn't go that far, but for what it's worth, I am sorry for his behaviour. He's always been a grumpy fuck, but he's never acted like that before. I don't know what came over him."

"It's fine. I get treated like that by my own family, so I'm used to it."

His jaw clenches. "It's not fine. And it's not okay for your family to do it either. I will have a word with my brother, and if I ever run into your family, I'll give them the same memo."

"Please don't. It will only make your brother resent me more. I can handle it," I explain. "As for my family, I hope to God you never meet them."

"Why?"

"Because they're not nice people. I know you didn't think much of me before, but if you meet them, you'll want to take full custody."

He gets up and walks around the counter, and I turn on the stool when he stops in front of me. The touch of his knuckles under my chin sends shivers down my spine. My hairs stand on end when he meets my gaze.

"I never wanted full custody to begin with. It was never either/or with regards to Poppy. I wanted us to do this together as a team. As parents. Your family and their misgivings will never change that. I see you, Emily. I saw who you were the first night I met you. That hasn't changed, even if I did let my emotions cloud my judgement for a minute. I still see a woman who fought against all her odds to get to where she is. You're remarkable, and I can only hope our daughter gets your strength."

A lump forms in the back of my throat. I get paid compliments every night I work. My friends give them to me. But nothing like the words he just said to me. Aside from my friends and grandma, no one has ever made me feel like I'm a worthy person.

And no one, other than my friends, has truly ever seen the real me. Until now. Until him.

Unable to keep it together under his scrutiny, I flick my gaze away. The last time he caught me under his spell, I ended up losing my virginity. And we can't afford to get mixed up in each other. Not right now.

My gaze lands on the time glowing on the cooker, and I use it as my excuse to escape. "It's late," I whisper. "I should go to bed if we are planning on being out for the day."

He steps back, giving me enough room to slide off the stool. He doesn't move back entirely, and when his fingers close around my wrist, a small puff of air slips through my lips. Tingles spread up my arm and the back of my neck.

I look up, my lips parted as he stares down at me with so much desire, I have to press my knees together to quench the feeling between my thighs. Conflict passes over his expression, before he exhales and steps back, letting go of my wrist. "Good night, Emily."

I take a breath. "Goodnight, Cole," I breathe, my voice catching with emotion.

I leave the glass on the counter and make my way out of the room.

As soon as I'm out of the kitchen, I move quicker, escaping upstairs. The second my bedroom door closes behind me, I lean back against it and take a few steady breaths. Every nerve ending is on fire right now, and all because of how much I want him.

A man who may well be related to the person killing people.

He isn't Cyrus.

He's not, but it still doesn't make this any easier. If this is how he's making me feel a week into living with him, what's it going to be like in a month or two? How will I control my emotions and raging sex drive? I've managed to up till now because he's not been around. No other man has turned my world upside down and made me forget my own name. He has a control over me that no man has ever had before. And I'm not sure how I can control it.

Or if I want to.

16

COLE

My thoughts should be on what the police may have found, but all I can think about whilst heading up the stairs to the bright blue doors is Poppy and how we left her. I can still hear her cries, see how she distraught she was before we walked away. Emily said she loved nursery, but I beg to differ, since her reaction at being left there said otherwise.

"Maybe we should go back and get her," I declare, stopping just outside the door.

Emily looks in the direction of the car. "I should ring them. She's never cried like that before."

I reach for my keys and head back down the stairs. "We're getting her."

"Wait," she calls, racing down the stairs after me. "Let me call them first. They said it's normal for children to cry when parents leave."

"Did she cry before?" I ask, arching an eyebrow.

"No, but she's also never been a daddy's girl before now," she retorts gently.

"Are you saying this is my fault? That I did that to our daughter?"

Her lips tug up into a smile. "No, I'm not saying that. But she's clearly been enjoying the attention she gets from you. Have you not noticed she accidently falls a lot?"

I sigh with a resigned nod, glad she's noticed it too. "I've already researched if there's some sort of soft cushions we can put down to stop her from hurting herself. I'm surprised my heart hasn't given out yet."

She throws her head back, her golden blonde hair falling down her back as she laughs. "That's because she knows you'll go and fuss over her."

My eyebrows pinch together as I mentally question her sanity. This is no laughing matter. "I'm not following."

"She loves the attention from you. She knows you'll fuss over her if she goes to fall. If she needs help cleaning up, she acts like it's too much because she knows you'll help. She's also started dropping food because she knows you'll put more on her plate."

My eyes widen at the realisation. "Oh my god, our daughter is a little con artist."

She laughs louder. "That she is. Which is why I'll call the nursery and see how she's doing."

I shove my hands in my pockets. "Put it on loudspeaker."

She snorts at my mistrust and calls them. It rings a few times before a soft voice greets us. "Good morning, this is Rainbow's Day Nursery. How can I help you today?"

"Hi, it's Emily Hart, Poppy's mum. I'm just calling to check in and see if she's okay now."

"Hey Emily, it's Katie. Poppy settled right away. She's playing with her friends right now in the soft play area."

"So she's not crying?" I ask, butting in.

"That's her dad," Emily declares, struggling not to laugh.

"No. Poppy is a ray of sunshine here at Rainbow's. She's an absolute joy to have and loves playing with her friends."

"Thank you, Katie." Emily beams. "I'll see you later at pick-up."

"Enjoy the rest of your day," Katie replies, before the line goes dead.

"She was quick to answer the phone seeing as she has a classroom full of kids."

Emily chuckles. "You saw there is more than one person working there. And wouldn't you want them to answer quickly in case it was an emergency?"

She has a point. "Yeah, I guess I would."

She turns to look at the building. "Are you ready to go in there?"

"Is anyone ever ready?" I muse.

"I guess if you're in trouble, no. Luckily, we aren't," she replies.

"Let's get this over with. We need to know one way or another."

We head back up the stairs, and I push open the door, letting Emily through first. She waits for me inside the waiting area, and together, we walk up to the reception, where a middle-aged woman greets us with a stern expression.

"How can I help you today?"

"We're here to see Detective Inspector Raymond Douglas and PC Wallace," I greet.

"Take a seat and I'll go and get them for you," she orders, her voice deadpan and hard.

We move over to the seating area, but it's only Emily who takes a seat. "Sit down. That woman scares me, and I don't want her yelling at us."

I grin at her honesty. "She was a little sombre, wasn't she?"

"A little?" she asks, her voice pitching. "Her fingers kept clenching over her belt. That woman had a cell picked out for us."

"Relax. It's not like we're the ones in trouble."

"She doesn't know that," she remarks, and I take a seat, placing my hand on her thigh to stop her from bouncing it. Her lips part as she tenses, and I quickly jerk my hand away.

"Sorry."

"Mr Connor?" a male voice calls, and I look over to the side door, where Inspector Douglas stands. His uniform, which is different to a standard uniformed police officer, screams 'in charge'.

"Sorry we're a little late. We took our daughter to nursery," I explain as we both make our way over.

"Ah, if your daughter is anything like mine was, I bet the departure was difficult."

"Yours cried too?" I ask, forgetting the reason I'm here for a minute.

"Every drop-off," he reveals, before running his gaze over Emily. "Have we met before?"

She steps closer to my side. "Outside Tease, the night Gabby Thompson was taken."

"You aren't the one who yelled at my colleague, are you?"

"Um, no, that was Gabby's girlfriend, Olivia. I was working the night Gabby was taken."

I grit my teeth at his change of expression. It wasn't subtle, and I know the man is thinking the worst of her.

"Alright. If you follow me, we can update you on what we found out."

We follow him into the room he exited from. A table that takes me back to my school days is set in the middle of the room, two chairs on either side. He bypasses the table and taps his card across the fob by the second door. He pushes it open without a word, and the suspense is killing me.

"Did you find anything out?"

He glances over his shoulder but doesn't stop. "Surprisingly, yes. Our team worked quickly this morning to get answers."

He opens another door and steps to the side for us to go in. We enter a large conference-type room with a big oval table with paper-work scattered all over it. "Take a seat. PC Wallace will be in shortly. He's just grabbing some paperwork."

Emily sits down in the chair next to me, folding her hands over her lap. Not even a second later, PC Wallace steps into the room with a grey folder in hand.

"Good morning," he greets.

"You've met Mr Connor," Inspector Douglas greets back, before gesturing to Emily. "This is Emily; she's a dancer at Tease, one of Mr Connor's establishments."

"I'm not a dancer. I work behind the bar," she tells him, confidence in her tone.

"She's also the mother to my daughter," I reveal, hoping he picks up on my tone. I won't listen to him judge any of our dancers working at Tease. But more, if he continues with the remarks regarding Emily, he'll find himself out of a job. I'll make sure of it.

"You are in a relationship?" PC Wallace asks, pulling a pen out of his top pocket.

"No, we're co-parenting and living in the same residence right now," Emily explains.

"Is that wise considering the new information?" Inspector Douglas asks.

"Is that your way of saying the killer is Cyrus?" I reply.

"Did you manage to locate the letter you received informing you of Cyrus's death?"

"Why is that important?" I ask.

Inspector Douglas leans forward. "Because we must investigate all avenues, Mr Connor. There have been seven murders, and probably more we don't know about. You've been questioned multiple times since the connection to Tease began and failed to mention any of this."

He can't be serious. "And like I told you last night, I don't remember much of my childhood. I never even met some of the girls who were killed as I was at a different club. I didn't make the connection; Gabby Thompson did. I came to you as soon as I thought it was a possibility. I'm not hiding anything from you."

"I can vouch for that. He seemed as shocked as the rest of us," Emily announces.

Inspector Douglas doesn't look pleased with our answers. "We need that letter. The quicker we can get that filed into evidence, the better."

"My assistant is looking through my London flat. She'll send it right over if it's there," I answer, before pushing him. "But that doesn't answer my question about Cyrus being the killer."

"Cyrus Baldwin was moved to Bedford Prison from a category A prison six years ago. A few years ago, a riot began that resulted in multiple casualties. Cyrus Baldwin received a letter of recommendation after this for helping a prison guard get to safety. Under that recommendation, Cyrus was released. During our enquiries this morning, we found out the prison guard who gave the recommendation returned a favour to Cyrus under false pretences."

"A favour? What favour?" I ask.

"We're still waiting for a full statement, which a colleague in the Bradford Police department will be taking. The guard who wrote you the letter using prison stationary did it believing Cyrus was trying to make amends with you."

"By saying he was dead?" I ask, snorting. "That's ridiculous."

"By giving you the option to let go. Or so the guard believed. He was under the assumption Cyrus wanted you to be free of him, and that he was going to start over and become a better man."

I grit my teeth. "Please tell me the guard isn't going to get away with this. It's fraud, for fuck's sake."

"There will be an enquiry going into this, and yes, you are correct, but he felt like he was doing the right thing for the man who saved his life."

"This is crazy. He should be held accountable for all the crimes Cyrus has committed since being released. Everyone involved with his release should be," Emily announces, her words heated.

"Trust me, Miss Hart, there will be an investigation into all of it."

"So, he is alive. He is the person who is doing this," I retort, sitting back with a heavy sigh.

All this time, I thought he was dead. I won't pretend I held any love or loss for my brother because I didn't. I wanted to try at one point, because I wanted to give him what my family gave me to me. Unconditional love and a home. I didn't listen to my head back then, which resulted in a family being terrorised. So when I found out he died, I didn't shed a tear. It's why I never arranged a funeral or searched for where it was being held. I just moved on like nothing happened. And now, seven people have been killed and two injured.

Emily reaches over, taking my hand and gently squeezing. I squeeze back, letting her know I appreciate her comfort.

"Whilst the letter might have been false, we are still putting evidence together. We have no proof that Cyrus is the man we are looking for, but it's a lead we are quickly following," Inspector Douglas explains. "We didn't find anyone's DNA at the crime scene other than the previous victims', Gabby's and Trixie's. Our forensics are still combing through it all."

"We've also been doing a background search on you and your biological family. Was Cyrus ever left anything in the will by your parents?" PC Wallace asks.

Snapping out of my thoughts, I answer. "We all had shares ready for when we turned twenty-one. Because of my sister's death, the will then got split into two. Although, after his arrest, he lost his claim to his share. My biological parents had a clause in their will that I, as the eldest, would receive full beneficiary over their estate in the event one or more were mentally impaired, incapable, or committed a crime."

"So he doesn't have the funds?"

"I didn't say that," I reply. "When we reconnected before his arrest, I transferred some over to him and promised to do it monthly. He must have spent it if he went to those measures to steal from Jack's family."

The inspector and officer share a look. "What aren't you saying?" Emily asks, getting the same read as me.

"In Cyrus's statement, he claimed he wanted to punish Jack and his family, and it was never about money for him. You spent a lot of time with them."

It's not a question, it's a statement. "Yes, I was invited to family holidays and dinners. My family didn't live close to the university, so more often than not, I stayed with Jack's family during Christmas or breaks."

"We've gone over the police reports and everyone's statements. Were you ever made aware that Cyrus attacked Jack's dad because your brother spotted you both playing golf one day?"

"What? How? My brother had been back in my life less than a month, and I might not know exactly what I did during that month, but I know I never went golfing with Jack or his dad during the time we reconnected."

"And you're sure?"

"Yes, because his dad was recovering from a wrist injury from golfing. It was a week or two before my brother came back into the picture."

"Mr Connor, your brother had been fired from the golf club five weeks before the home invasion."

"I'm not sure where you are going with this."

"Like we said last night, your brother suffered with mental issues. We aren't exactly sure what since he never agreed to be evaluated. It's a rarity for criminals since most will use it to get a lesser sentence."

"Again, still not following," I grit out, getting annoyed now.

"But the one thing we have managed to pick up is that your brother is very jealous of you. It took us longer to get the last reports since they aren't exactly recent," Inspector Douglas begins.

PC Wallace clears his throat. "We went back as far as we could find, and I managed to get through to a teacher who used to teach you. Mrs Collins."

"I remember her," I agree. "It's vague, but I remember the cookies she would bring in to treat us."

"She's retired now, but the school gave us her information since she was the longest working teacher at the school. We have police officers travelling up to her home today to get a full statement, but what she told us over the phone was that she always had concerns about Cyrus."

"She remembered us?"

PC Wallace nods. "She did. She said she felt afraid of Cyrus. More than once, your parents were called in over incidents regarding him. Children were being burnt even though there was no appliances or fire. She found a lighter in Cyrus's bag on the hanger, but he denied it was his. She told us she caught him forcing soiled water down a little girl's throat, and when she confronted him, he threatened to slice open her throat. She remembered him even after all this time, and even confronted your parents about injuries you and your sister both sustained at home."

I scrub my hand down my face. The little sleep I got is catching up to me. "I don't remember all of this."

Inspector Douglas sits forward. "Most abused children don't. If it's true, and he was hurting you, children tend to block it out."

"For you to go to this much trouble, you must think it's him," Emily announces, her voice soft. "Why would you go to this much trouble otherwise."

Inspector Douglas lets out a heavy sigh. "He fits our suspect. We had behaviour analysts come in to build a file on the person we are looking for. The common term is profile. And your brother ticks every one of his boxes. It would also explain the strong connection to Tease."

"He's not the only person at Tease who came from a group home. Dave, our manager, is," she points out.

"We did a strong background check on David Finley, and he came back clean. We have no reason to believe he is involved with the person we're looking for."

"So what happens next?" I ask.

"Well, we're building a timeline right now for Cyrus. We've hit a dead end after his release, but that doesn't mean anything this early into the investigation. We have his criminal record with pictures, so once we gather more information, we will get that out to the media, but right now, we don't want him to know we're on to him in case it scares him. I don't think I need to tell you that if he gets in contact, you should call us immediately."

"Trust me, I don't plan on inviting him around for dinner," I reply with sarcasm.

"We will be in touch if we have any more questions, and we will keep you informed with what we find," PC Wallace announces, getting to his feet.

Getting the hint that they want us to leave, I stand, forgetting for a minute that I'm still holding Emily's hand. Inspector Douglas notices and arches a brow, but neither of us let go.

"If you can think of anything else, you let us know immediately. You can't sit on it like before. We don't want any more murders," Inspector Douglas states. "And I would make that letter your priority so we can rule you out as an accessory. We're doing our job."

Leaving before I lay into him, I tug Emily towards the door. "I'll get on that."

"Actually, before we go, there is something I need to say," Emily declares, pausing at the door. "My friend Gabby Thompson is being harassed by the media. She came in the other day so one of you could put a stop to it, and you weren't very helpful. Unless you want this information being leaked, I would get on to helping her."

"Are you threatening police officers?" PC Wallace demands.

My girl meets his gaze, unflinching. "No. I would never do that. But she's a scared woman who went through a horrific ordeal. She will do anything to get them off her back, even if it means setting them on you. She's been passed off as a criminal, when she's a victim, and she deserves to recover in peace. She has children, and a girlfriend who is hardly sleeping. I don't need to remind you of this, but I will; she is the reason you have made a break in your investigation. *Twice*. You would do well to remember that because she is a civilian, not a police officer."

My lips twitch, and I have to hold back a cheer of support. I always knew she was brave, even if she doesn't always show it. And the way she just stuck up for her friend, I want to pick her up and swing her around.

"We'll get some colleagues on to that. We do have more pressing matters to deal with right now, as you know," Inspector Douglas retorts.

"And yet here you are, bringing Mr Connor in to do more accusing and questioning instead of being out there looking for the killer. I'm not telling you how to do your job, but when you have civilians doing it for you, something has to give."

"We'll get it sorted," PC Wallace promises, and steps aside to let us go through the door first.

"Thank you," she replies, ducking her head.

We leave the room, and I don't let go of her hand the entire time. I'm not sure why, or what compels me to keep a hold of it, but it feels right.

And I have a feeling she needs the support after taking them on.

My girl has spirit.

17

EMILY

My palm is still clammy, still buzzing from the contact of holding Cole's hand. He seems so unaffected by it, whereas I'm a hot mess. I've been running my thumb along the crease of my palm to stop myself from hyperventilating. It's such a minor thing to be focused on considering where we were and what was said, but it's all I can think about.

Which is probably why I don't realise the car has stopped. I stare out of the window at the Victorian house with wide eyes.

"This is your house?" I ask, my voice pitching.

"No, it's my parents'," Cole replies, amusement in his tone.

"But you grew up here?"

"Yes. Why do you seem so shocked?"

I turn to him, forgetting about the fact we held hands, and that I didn't want to let go. "Because this is the length of three—maybe four —of the houses on the street I grew up on. This is huge."

He snorts. "This is a regular five-bedroom house."

"Five bedrooms? I lived in a two-bedroom house, where I had a mattress on the floor. I didn't realise until now how completely different we are."

"What are you saying?"

"I'm saying if this arrangement goes sideways, I know who the courts will side with. I grew up on the bare minimum. You grew up in a big house, with loving parents, and probably ate three times a day. I'm saying, I get why your brother is such an asshole to me. You brought in the riff-raff and he's protecting you."

"One, I was angry. I've told you that. And if at any point you want to end this arrangement, I'll leave. I've told you the house is yours, and my lawyer is bringing over the deeds later for you to sign. With all that said, I'm enjoying being with you both. I like how easily we've settled in, and how well we all get along. Do you not feel the same?"

I lean back against the seat, letting out a puff of air. "I do, yes."

"I grew up in a big house, Emily, but I worked for every penny I have earnt. I worked my arse off to get to where I am, and to pay off my student loans. The inheritance I received from my biological parents is in a savings account, and when the time is right, I'll transfer it to Poppy. I got a second chance at having a family, and I wanted to make sure they never regretted adopting me. I learned after I dropped out of medical school that that would never happen. They supported me and helped me find passion in my new path. As for my brother, he was out of line. He had no right to speak to you like that. I'll do my best to make sure that doesn't happen again."

"You went to medical school?" I ask, shocked by the news.

"Yes. I wanted to follow in my father's footsteps. He was a surgeon but is now a paediatrician at the local hospital. He doesn't work as much as he used to, but I admired his dedication to his work. Although I wanted to be a doctor, I think I wanted to for the wrong reasons. I love what I do now, and I'm good at it. I have charities, side businesses, and my clubs, and whenever I need something else, I find a new project."

"I'm sorry. I judged you for a minute because I see we're two completely different people. I think back to the day you turned up and what you said, and I know you don't feel like that now. But what if you wake up one day, see that person again, and decide you don't want to co-parent anymore? It scares me. Poppy is my world, and I never realised how much I wanted to be a mum until I got pregnant."

"We all have baggage, Emily. Are you going to wake up one day and leave because my brother is a homicidal maniac?"

I snort-laugh. "Okay, you have a point," I declare. "You should know, if I ever do decide to leave, it doesn't change anything between you and Poppy. You'll still co-parent and be there for everything."

"I know that now," he muses. "A lot has happened this week, and getting to know you has been one of them. I should have done that before kidnapping you."

I smile at his teasing. "If it's any consolation, I like being there too. The circumstances might not have been great, but it's worked out. But I do think if we don't get out and go fill your mum in, she's going to put her head through the window."

He looks through the windshield, laughing when he sees his mum's face pressed against the window. "We'd best go in."

I grab my bag from between my feet and push open the door. He shuts the car off and does the same, and we both meet at the front of the car. I nearly reach for his hand, and I inwardly groan.

He gives me a piece of string and I'm ready to pull.

The front door is pulled open, and his mum and dad are standing there, waiting. "Morning," Georgia calls.

"I hope it's okay I tagged along today," I greet.

She leans into Joe, and he puts his arm around her shoulders. "You're always welcome in our home," she tells me. "Where's Poppy?"

"She's at nursery today."

"On a Sunday?" Joe asks, his eyebrows rising.

"Yes. They run from six till three on a Sunday, and it will be her last weekend there. It's privately run, so they open Sundays for parents with special circumstances. They knew about my grandma and that I work night shifts, so they offered Poppy a Sunday spot. I won't need that anymore since we're co-parenting. The Sunday staff wanted one last day with Poppy to say goodbye. I think they're doing a little party."

"That is so sweet," Georgia gushes. "She must have made quite the impression."

"Oh, she did," Cole mutters.

"Come in, come in," she ushers.

"What do you mean, son?"

"She got a little upset when we were leaving."

I snort. "What he means to say is that Poppy is a daddy's girl and didn't want us to leave, and this one nearly went back to pull her out."

Georgia laughs. "Aria was the same. She was a baby when we adopted her, so we went through it all. The boys were much older and couldn't wait for us to leave."

Joe chuckles. "Because she wouldn't stop smothering them with hugs and kisses. She's the one who cried."

"Told you it happens," I tease, nudging Cole.

We enter a lavish living room. There's a huge half-moon sofa that takes up half the room, whilst two chairs are placed opposite. There's no television, or anything to suggest this is a room they sit in often. It's lavish and beautiful, but it doesn't feel lived in. It reminds me a lot of the main living room at Cole's. Since we moved in, I've only ever gone in there to clean. I've never seen Cole sit in there either.

"We're just having tea in the conservatory if you'd like some," Georgia offers.

"You have a beautiful home," I tell her as we move through the house.

"Thank you," she replies as we hit the conservatory. Harriett would love it in here. It has plants along each windowsill, and they didn't stop there. Vines run up the glass and over the top of the glass roof from the outside. It's like an indoor fairy house. The room is warm, inviting, and somewhere I'd probably nap a lot in.

Georgia takes a seat in the wicker chair, and Joe places his hands on her shoulders. "Is tea okay for you both?"

"I'll have a coffee, Dad. I didn't get much sleep," Cole admits.

"I'll have one too," I sheepishly reply, since I didn't get much either.

"Two coffees coming up," he tells us, and leaves through the door we entered.

"What are you doing here?" Kit greets, stepping in from outside.

"I've not had much sleep, or had the best morning, so don't start," Cole warns. "She's the mother of my child and I want you to treat her with respect before I beat it into you."

"She called you a murderer yesterday. She shouldn't be here. You have rights. You can get custody of Poppy. I've looked into it for you."

I step back as Cole speedily moves past me, grabbing his brother by the shirt and punching him in the face. His mother doesn't even flinch. "Don't mind them, dear."

"Please, stop!" I cry, ignoring her. "Do not fight over me. I will leave. It's fine."

Kit wipes his bloody nose with the back of his hand, glaring at his brother. "I'm looking out for you."

"No, you are being a fucking prick. You got lucky yesterday because Poppy was there, but she isn't here right now. I warned you to stop. I won't do it again."

"She called you a murderer. Do you know anything about her? What if this is all a set up to get money out of you?"

"I know enough," Cole snaps.

"Stop," I cry, and get between them when it looks like Cole is about to hit him. I turn to Cole. "Stop. He's your brother, and as much of a prick as he's being, he's still your brother. That means something. My sister wouldn't care enough to stick up for me. I got bullied in school and she was one of them." I turn to Kit next. "I understand you have concerns regarding me, but there's only so much I'll take before I get revenge. I'm not asking you to change your opinions about me, but I will ask you to keep them to yourself."

"This is messed up. You kept his daughter from him."

"Have you ever found something out, or had a secret you've been dying to tell someone because you know it will make you feel a little better, but you couldn't because of the repercussions?"

"Yes," Kit warily replies.

"That's what it was like for me. I didn't know whether he would make me abort the baby. I just knew I wanted her. Then I planned to tell him when I next saw him, but he never returned to the club again. I could have asked Dave for his details, but then it was one more person I had to tell. Then months passed, and she was born. I still didn't see him. Then she turned one, and he still didn't return. Then he did, and so much time had passed, I didn't know *how* to tell him. Believe me when I tell you I practiced it over and over, but I could never do it. How could I? So much time had passed, and I didn't know how he'd react. But I never once planned to not tell him. I was always going to. I'm sorry it took so long, but that is the truth." I pause, taking a breath. "I come from a family who hated me. They never showed me any love, and I didn't even know what it was until the day my grandma took me in. My parents never wanted me, and they made it known. Then my grandma got sick, and I returned the kindness she gave to me by caring for her. It was tough and it was hard, but I did it. I raised a daughter whilst doing it. So I know you don't know me, but know this. I've never intentionally hurt someone. I'm not a thief. I can't say I've never been in trouble with the police because me and my friends can find ourselves in tricky situations, but I can say I don't have a criminal record. I don't want your brother's money; I can make that on my own. So please, don't fall out with your brother, who has only ever spoken fondly of you, over someone you don't know. I can tell you honestly now, I'm not worth it. This fighting is not worth it. Okay?"

Clapping sounds behind me, and I turn to find Aria standing in the doorway. "You've got my vote," she teases, before turning to Cole. "I like her."

"I am sorry about yesterday. Me and my friends have had a rough few months, and we wanted answers."

"Did you get them?" Georgia asks.

Cole clears his throat. "Yes. Cyrus is alive. Whether he's the killer is still in question, but I really believe it is him."

Joe walks in with two mugs in his hand. His gaze goes from Cole to me, then to Kit, who is still cleaning his bloody nose. "I told you it would happen."

"Yeah, you did," Kit grumbles. "Look, I'm sorry. Some stuff has happened recently, and I've been lashing out at you because of it. I'm sorry."

"It's fine," I tell him, and take a seat in an empty chair. "Although, I will warn you, I wasn't lying about the revenge. Me and my friends have it down like a routine and can do it easily. Just ask Gabby's old homophobic neighbour who is getting male strippers at his door every weekend."

His lips twitch at the corners. "Noted. Consider me warned."

I turn to Georgia. "Me and my friends are truly sorry about yesterday. Gabby is the girl I was telling you about who got kidnapped. She was forced to watch as her abductor beat another dancer and then chopped off her finger. She died, Mrs Connor. It was for a minute, but she died in that cave. If we had been even a second later in finding her, we would have been burying another friend."

"Don't be silly, child. There is no need to apologise," she promises. "I can't imagine what it was like for her or any of you. I only got a glimpse yesterday, but I knew my son was innocent. He's a good man."

"I know."

"So, he's alive?" Joe asks, taking a seat next to his wife.

Everyone takes a seat as Cole begins. "The letter wasn't entirely forged. It's on legitimate paper, but the declaration is forged. There's an investigation into it, but long story short, Cyrus saved a prison guard during the riot we read about. The guard, grateful, wrote the letter believing Cyrus wanted to do something good."

"And what was that?" Joe asks, arching his eyebrow. "Because I don't see what good would come of that."

"The guard thought Cyrus wanted to make amends. Cyrus must have told him they had to tell me he was dead, so I would finally be free of him. It's messed up. I should have gone to claim the remains to be sure."

I reach out, placing my hand over his arm. "You weren't to know. It's like you said, he did some messed up things and you were done with him. No one can put any of this on you. You did what you thought was right."

Kit's gaze goes to where my arm is, and when he catches me looking, he clears his throat, averting his gaze. "She's right, bro. You aren't to blame here."

"Look at what's happened. People have died. Their families and friends will never recover from this. If I had just gone the day I received the letter, none of this would have happened."

His parents share a look before letting out a weary sigh. It's Joe who speaks up. "Son, I'm not sure how much you remember when you first came to live with us, but you barely talked. You would jump at the slightest touch, you had night terrors, and for a while, you wet the bed. We kept getting told you needed to adjust to new living arrangements, but me and your mum, we knew it was more."

"We sent you to a psychiatrist the week Kit came to live with us. Aria was just a baby and we noticed you didn't like Kit near her. And everything you were going through got worse," Georgia adds, and her husband takes her hand.

"During your sessions, a lot of stuff was brought up that the therapist spoke to us about. She gave us steps to follow because of it, and slowly, you adjusted to your new home and began to trust Kit."

"What came up?" Cole asks, showing a rare case of vulnerability. "I don't remember any of this."

"She did mention that might happen. You told her how your brother would smother you with a pillow, how he hurt you when no one was looking. The scars on your thighs? They are from where he would burn or cut you before your mum must have switched your rooms," Joe admits, and a gasp of air leaves my mouth.

"I was only a few years older than what Poppy is now," he retorts, distraught by the news.

Not caring if anyone says anything, or if they read into it, I take his hand, needing him to know I'm here.

I can't imagine what he went through. I picture Poppy, and I can't even fathom someone hurting her.

"We wanted to tell you," Georgia swears. "But when you started to settle, we didn't want to bring back bad memories."

"At first, we thought it was because you were separated from him. It was never our intention to separate you, but the agency said due to events they couldn't disclose, it was the best option. We didn't question them until we noticed your behaviour. We asked if we could at least arrange visitation for you both, and stupidly fought for it until they got back to us and explained why you were separated."

"It was because I was being adopted," Cole answers.

"No, son, it wasn't," Georgia shakily responds.

"Do you remember a fire at the home you were in?" Joe asks.

"There were a few."

"Well, during the last one, a neighbour accused Cyrus, in front of police and the fire brigade, of starting it. He called him a few choice words, which resulted in them finding dead animals in the garden."

"I remember. It was the foster parent's cat, I think," Cole replies.

"Yes, well, a week after that, your neighbour's daughter was pushed down the stairs. Their camera at the front and back of the house had been disabled, but the one inside wasn't. It showed Cyrus entering the home and going up into her room. It started off as him ordering her to jump off the banister, but when she wouldn't, he got angry and pushed her."

"What?" Cole breathes out. "How did I not know this?"

"You were homed with us shortly after. He tried to blame you, and swore by it, and even knew where you were to say he was there instead. But it turned out, the doctor you had been going to see was behind on appointments and you saw another doctor that day. Your brother didn't know that, so his lie didn't uphold. It was then other kids started to speak up about the abuse they endured, and that's when the agency sped up the adoption and we were told we were only getting one little boy."

"You were meant to get both of us?"

As sad as the story is, I'm glad they never adopted him. I don't announce it out loud, but all I can imagine is the damage someone like Cyrus would have done to a family like this. You can see all three children were loved and adored by Joe and Georgia. You can see they gave them everything they needed and treated them with things they would want.

"I barely remember much of my time before coming here. To find all of this out, I have to wonder what everyone didn't find. I knew he wasn't right, but to find out just how messed up he was... I don't know. I'm just shocked."

"I know it's a lot to take in, but me and your father spoke about it last night and decided you needed to know in case Gabby was right. We want you to be able to protect yourself. We were worried for you when you reconnected, and we were going to tell you that weekend when we came up."

"But then he attacked Jack and his family," Cole finishes.

"We are sorry. We're as much to blame in this as all the others involved," Joe adds.

"No, you aren't. You did what you thought was best," I tell them. "If anyone tells you otherwise, send them our way and I'll put them right. As harsh as this is, you could have renounced the adoption the minute you found out about the danger his brother posed. You didn't. Instead, you worked on making sure he felt safe with you, and his siblings and gave him a life he deserved. You chose to give him better." I turn to Cole, squeezing his hand. "I don't doubt your biological parents loved you, but what they did was cruel. They separated you, yeah, but as far as we've learnt, they did nothing to stop the abuse. They were probably blinded by their love for Cyrus, which didn't protect you or your sister. I'm pretty sure if any medical profession was involved with your brother before they died, it would have continued after. But the only time that was mentioned was during his time in foster care."

"There's only one person to blame here, and that's Cyrus," Kit declares. "What are they doing to protect you?"

"I can take care of myself," Cole remarks.

"I know you can," Kit replies. "But you aren't a killer. He is. You won't be able to do what needs to be done to stop him, and I truly believe that will be the only way."

"Well let's hope they catch him before it gets to that," Cole remarks. "For now, we're going to be vigilant, which means you all need to be too."

"You think he'll come for us?" Aria asks with a shake to her voice.

"From what Gabby pieced together, it's Cole he really wants. He took girls because he wanted to take away the one person who mattered the most to Cole. I think if he wanted to hurt any of you, you would have been on the list with the first murders. I'm not saying he won't, but that's what I believe. I can't tell you what his end game is, so I would still be careful whilst being out and about," I claim. "Also, it would be good to mention they think my friend derailed his plan. I'm not sure how those behaviour analysts work, but they seem sure that another girl won't be taken. They believe he'll go after who he's really after, which we know now is Cole."

"Then you really aren't safe with me," he whispers. "I don't know how to say goodbye to Poppy, even if I know it will only be for a little while."

He's right, but I don't tell him that. I'm not worried about me; I'm worried for my daughter. She's the one who is in danger now. "We don't need to decide anything today. All this is going on assumptions that it is Cyrus. We don't know if he knows you have a daughter. It's funny how the day you decide to show up is the day I'm burgled."

"You were burgled?" Aria asks.

"My house was turned upside down, and the only thing that was gone was the money hidden under my bed."

"Don't killers take something that means something, like a picture or a memento?" Kit muses.

I shrug. "I don't know. But he could have planned it knowing Cole would bring us back to his. He could be waiting for us to leave. I don't know."

"Does Evan Smith still do protective services?" Cole asks Kit.

"I can call him and find out. I know he still lives here. Has ever since his sister was kidnapped years ago," Kit replies.

"Who are they?" I ask. "Can we trust them?"

"Mum and Dad used to be close friends with their father. We can trust him," Cole promises.

"Their story is complicated," Aria assures me. "It happened before I was even born, but I went to school with their eldest daughter, Imogen. Their story is legendary around here."

"What happened?"

"None of us really know the real story about their parents, but the other part was all over the news and in the papers," Georgia explains. "It was all anyone could talk about. How they recovered is beyond me."

"And you want him to protect us?" I ask.

"Trust me, if anyone is good at it, it's Evan. Back when his sister was at school, a kid in their year raped a bunch of girls. He got caught attempting to rape the new girl after he drugged her at a party," Cole begins, and the story sounds so familiar. "It went to court, but the brother of the rapist wanted him out, so he went after the key witness, which happened to be Denny Smith."

"She's Denny Carter now," Aria muses. "She owns the best clothes shop in town."

"Oh my god, I know her. She's my friend's aunt. If I'm correct, Charlotte's mum is one of the survivors. Charlotte recently went through an ordeal of her own, which brought back memories for them."

"Well, Denny was kidnapped, and Evan changed careers into surveillance and bodyguarding. He's good at it. He fits security systems on the side, but we all get ours done by a guy called Liam. He's the best and the person who fitted mine," Cole tells us.

"Okay, I've never met Liam, but I've heard of him. If this Evan person will do it, I say go for it. You need to stay protected."

His eyebrows pinch together. "Emily, he won't be for me. He'll be for you and Poppy."

My jaw drops at what that means. I could be reading too much into it, but if he thinks I need protection, I must mean *something* to him.

As they continue to talk, I stare down at my lap, wondering if my heart will ever slow.

I can't mean something to him.

Can I?

18

COLE

I close the stairgate to Poppy's room on my way out and take one last look at her sleeping. She came home from nursery a little grumpy. Emily assured me it's probably because she's worn out, but as the evening went on, she got worse. She barely touched her dinner, and then screamed bloody murder during her bath time. That's when we both noticed she seemed a little warm.

Luckily, we have a nanny who is starting at the end of next week for a trial run, so she'll no longer be at risk of catching stuff at nursery. At least for a little while. Robin is in her mid-forties and has been doing her job for twenty years. All her previous employers couldn't praise her enough, and she recently reached her end date with her previous employer. Although she has a waiting list, we managed to snap her up by offering a pay rise. We wanted the best for our daughter, but also someone who could be trusted.

Emily is cleaning Poppy's toys away when I get downstairs. I fall down on the sofa, letting out a breath. "She's settled again."

She drops the last toy in its box before she turns to me. "Switch your camera off tonight. I've got Poppy if she wakes up, but that last shot of Calpol should do the trick."

"No, I've got her. You get some rest tonight."

She drops down next to me on the sofa. "You're the one who just had his world rocked. You didn't sleep last night, and don't you have meetings tomorrow?"

"About that. I've called Gia, my assistant, and she's going to arrange all my meetings to be done through Zoom. Until we get answers, I'd rather stay close to home. Thankfully, I had already been in the process of setting up an office here in Coldenshire. I might still have to travel from time to time, but I am going to cut back as much as I can."

"Please don't do that for us. We aren't going anywhere."

"I meant what I said when I told you I wanted to get to know my daughter. I don't want to miss a minute. You heard about some of my past, so you'll understand why kids were never on the cards for me. Firstly, I didn't want my child to be left how I was left when my parents died. Secondly, I was worried about them being like my brother. But the minute I saw her at Dave's, it was like a band inside of me snapped, and I knew I would do anything for her. I knew I wanted to be a part of her life and raise her. She was mine. I want her to know I'm not going anywhere."

She gifts me with a smile. "I feel exactly the same, but I can promise you, as joyous as that little girl is, there will be moments where you need five minutes. It's why I kept working after I had her. Working was my five minutes. Don't get me wrong, I wouldn't give her up or go back for anything. At first, I blubbered in the bath, feeling like the worst mum in the world. But I realised wanting five minutes doesn't make me a bad parent. It makes me a reasonable one. I've seen parents who don't, and they've got grey hairs before they're forty, forget to dress for the school run, and I'm pretty sure one mum had wine in her water bottle."

I laugh because I've heard similar stories from my parents. "I promise to take the five minutes. I've got six years before I get grey hairs," I tease.

"Good. So rest tonight. I've got Poppy."

"Is she sick like this often?"

"Recently? Yes. She gets stomach cramps a lot too," she admits.

"Have you ever had her checked out?"

"Multiple times. I've been doing a food diary for a while, so I know what triggers her cramps. I'll email you a copy."

"Thank you," I reply, before letting out a yawn. "God, today has dragged, even for a Sunday."

"Tell me about it," she muses, and tucks her feet up on the sofa. "I'm actually dreading going back to work. I've had so much time off, I've gotten used to it."

"Dave said you've asked for Saturday night off."

"Yeah. Me and the girls always have that weekend off together. When I said I'd go back, I wasn't in the right head space and didn't realise the date. Luckily, Dave didn't rota me in for the Saturday. He's always one step ahead, which I'm forever grateful for."

"Why? Do you have plans with someone?" I ask, hoping that didn't sound as accusing as it did to me.

"We're going to a scare fest. It's been closed for years now until they sorted their legal issues out. One guy had a heart attack and took them to court. Idiot had medical heart history, so the company sued him for loss and damages to their business. It's meant to be bigger and scarier, so we booked tickets a while ago."

"Is that really the best place to go considering what your friend went through?" I ask. "And don't you hate scary things?"

She bounces in her seat, grinning. "With a passion, but I love going to them."

"God, just don't ask Aria to go. She'd piss herself."

She laughs. "Aria's actually coming. Charlotte can't come because she wants to babysit for her cousin, Aiden. He has a little girl who Charlotte absolutely adores. She loves kids, and I'm pretty sure she'll have dozens of her own one day. It worked out well, since the last time she came, she was determined to make friends with the actors paid to chase us."

"When did Aria agree to this?"

"She gave me her number when you were talking to your brother outside."

"Jesus. It didn't take her long."

She laughs. "She also made me promise to let her be my bridesmaid when we get married."

I pinch the bridge of my nose. "Now that sounds more like my sister."

She shrugs. "I like her."

"Who else is going with you?"

"Aside from me and Aria, Harriett, Olivia, Gabby and Hayden are going."

"So, there's a large group of you. That doesn't seem so bad."

She looks away. "Yeah."

"What is that look for?"

"Nothing," she replies evasively. "When does that guy come?"

"Evan is sending Ben Donavan, an employee of his. Ben has worked for him since he was nineteen. He's now twenty-eight."

"He's not coming himself?"

"He's booked up at the minute but promised me Ben is the guy we want. All his jobs have specialised in stalkers. I have to trust he knows what he's doing."

"Anything right now has to be better than nothing. If either of us feel like he's not doing his job, we can talk to Evan," she tells me. "What time is he coming?"

I glance at my watch on my wrist. "Any minute. He wants to go over our schedules and what have you. That was the other reason I decided to switch things up with work. I want to be home as much as I can to make sure you're both safe."

"Do you really think he'll come for us?"

"I don't know anything, which worries me. I go into meetings knowing what I want, and I don't stop until I get it. It's like that in pretty much all aspects of my life. With Cyrus, I don't know what will happen, but I do know I won't go down without a fight. And not because I don't like to lose."

"Then why?"

"Because I have a lot to lose," I reply, getting lost in the depths of her gaze.

And suddenly, it clicks.

Emily's appearance may have changed a little, and she might have built her confidence, but the one thing I couldn't put my finger on—something that has been plaguing my mind since she first stood up to me—all of a sudden clicks.

She's comfortable with who she is and makes no apology for it. No longer is there a sadness lurking behind those gorgeous eyes. There isn't a broken woman who needs fixing. There's a survivor, a fighter, a warrior.

She's no longer at war with herself.

She's her own woman and doesn't need anyone to help her get through life. She can do it on her own.

And I've never wanted anything more.

"Why are you looking at me like that?" she whispers.

Because I want you.

I want all of you.

The gate alarm blares through the speaker, having forgot to switch it to my phone. It breaks the spell between us, and I finally look away.

"That will be Ben," I announce, getting to my feet.

There is no war inside my mind telling me this is a bad idea. In fact, it's probably one of the best choices I could have made.

There has always been something about Emily that has reeled me in. From the very first moment I saw her, I knew I wanted her, and I don't mean for one night. If Cassandra had turned up with my baby, I don't think I would have reacted the same as I did with Emily. Because if I'm honest with myself, when I saw Poppy across the garden, there was a moment where a heavy weight had been lifted from my shoulders. And all because I had been lying to myself for years by pretending Emily didn't mean anything. When truthfully, our night together is all I've ever been able to think about.

I've just reached the door when she calls my name. "Is everything okay?"

I duck my head. "Yeah, everything is okay."

I pull open the door as headlights shut off. Seconds later, a guy slides out of the car, brushing back his sandy blonde hair. He has sunglasses tucked into his leather jacket, and his boots crunch on the gravel.

And I know from one look at him that I don't need to worry about him protecting Emily; I have to worry about her falling for him. I'm a straight guy through and through, but I'm not blind. He's a pretty boy with a rough exterior, and the very thing women fall for. I've seen it time and time again with the girls at the club. I've heard them drool over them. It never bothered me because they didn't belong to me.

Emily does.

"Cole Connor?" he greets.

"Yeah, you Ben?"

"Yes. Is now a good time? I won't take too much of your time."

I push away the dark thoughts and jealously and step aside to let him through. "Just go through to the left," I order.

I watch him closely as we enter the room where Emily is in her beige lounge wear, tucked up on the sofa. She drops her legs as he enters, her gaze immediately going to me. "Is everything okay?"

It's then I realise my jaw is clenched. "Yes. This is Ben."

"Good evening. You must be Emily."

"Hi," she greets briefly, before focusing on me. "Why do you look like that?"

Way to call me out. "I'm fine."

I watch his gaze as I sit down close to her, staking my claim as my arm goes around the back of the sofa. "Evan said you've dealt with something similar to our situation."

He pulls out a pen and pad. "I have. It's my understanding you want me to watch over Emily and your daughter, Poppy."

"Mostly Poppy," Emily rushes out.

"Both of them," I order. "Evan said you'd talk us through the process."

"In situations like this, it's best to be clear about everything from the start. I understand you have a great security system here, but I always recommend our clients to have us live in until the situation is sorted. Even if you are present, I can use the time to scour the area or go through security footage. I've been informed that you think the immediate danger is to Emily and Poppy, is that correct?"

"We don't really know anything," Emily replies.

"I'm sure you've heard of the Night Stalker killer. We believe the person is my brother. If what the surviving victims said is true, he is coming after what means the most to me. That is Emily and Poppy."

"I've been brought up to speed on the situation regarding the killer. He's probably made contact, and it's so small, you haven't noticed."

"What do you mean?" I ask, sitting forward.

"As in most cases like this, he is watching you. He must have to capture those you've been in contact with. In that respect, it's not just them who are his prey. You are. My last client was a singer who travelled around the UK to play in concerts, weddings, pubs, clubs and even parties. During one of them, someone took a liking to her. I was working security for a band during the time she came on tour with them. One day, she noticed her hairbrush had gone, which for a girl, isn't alarming. But when her first pair of underwear was taken, I asked questions about other things and began to guard her under the order of the band. It was a week later when the letters started. Stalkers can't help themselves. They always take souvenirs."

"He's not my fan though," I point out.

"No, but you're the centre of his attention. He will have inserted himself into your life in some way, which may not be directly."

"And you think you'll be able to spot things that prove that theory?" Emily asks.

"I do. But even if there aren't any, I can still be here to help."

"And what will you need from us?" I ask, using my business tone.

"Your cooperation. I will only ask something of you if it's seriously important. But for this to work, I need you to follow. I'm willing to work with your schedule, whether that be living here or not. I can work with either, but I strongly suggest I stay. In cases like this, the middle of the night is when they'll hit."

"I have a spare box room upstairs at the end of the hall you can stay in."

"Is it close to the stairs?"

"No, Poppy's room is the first door up the stairs," Emily answers.

"Have you got room down here?"

"I have a games room downstairs with a pull-out bed, or the other living room. Downstairs is connected to my office and has steps leading up to the side door."

"The room downstairs is fine. If someone does come in, they won't expect anyone coming from below. I can set up extra cameras and will monitor them from there to give you privacy. You'll hardly see or hear me as I try to make myself as invisible as I can."

"And when can you start?"

"I'm finishing up my workload tonight, so I can start as quickly as tomorrow. But I'll need to know your schedules. If I'm shadowing Emily and your daughter, does that mean I'll be restricted to the house?"

"I'll be working from home, but on the days that I can't, I'll inform you in advance."

"I work at a strip club. And I'm not sure how well you'll blend in there," Emily counters.

"You are open to an attack on a stage," he announces. "Can you take time off?"

"I actually work behind the bar, and I'd prefer to keep my job."

"I can work with the bar," he states, writing something down. "Any other times you'll leave the house?"

"I'm going out with friends at the weekend, and then there are times I go shopping or out with my friends, but we mostly hang out at each other's homes."

He finishes whatever he's writing and looks up. "You and Poppy will be separated a lot. Who will be my main focus during those times?"

"Emily," I quickly rush out.

"What? No! Poppy is his main priority."

"I've got Poppy. I will die before I let anything happen to her."

"That doesn't make me feel any better because who will be there when you're dead? Who will protect her then?"

"I can take care of her," I promise.

"We always have our stay close standbys. We'll give you a panic button for those occasions," Ben explains. "We have standbys for situations like this, where priorities are divided at times. Our standbys cover those shifts, or if one of us are injured."

"Does that ease your mind?" I ask Emily.

"A little," she concedes.

Ben gets to his feet. "Good. I have to get back, but I will report in tomorrow afternoon. You can show me around and I can set up my equipment. Any questions in the meantime, you can call me." He hands me a card with his name, number and email address when I stand. Literally. No branding or any type of design that brings it attention.

"Thank you for coming on short notice," Emily announces. "And for doing this for us."

He jerks his chin up in reply. "I'll see you out," I offer, and begin to make my way over to the door.

Emily follows, and after bidding him farewell, I close the door behind him, before leaning back against it. I let out a weary sigh, already done with the day.

"You okay?"

I lower my head to meet her gaze. "Yeah. I know this has been going on a while for everyone and has only just begun for me, but I'm already done with it. I want this to be over so my brother can pay for his crimes."

"Everything will work out eventually. He can't play this game forever."

"You don't know my brother," I claim. "He can play the long game easily. You heard my parents today, but there's one thing they don't know. He's a master manipulator. I've seen it. I've been victim to it. He's been planning this for a long time. He's so far ahead, we might never catch up."

"No, but everyone eventually has to stop to take a breather. He did that after my friend escaped. He couldn't have predicted that. He probably didn't even entertain the idea that someone could. So whilst he's smug about being miles ahead of us, he's not looking over his shoulder. We can get him, Cole. We have to trust everyone around us."

"Easier said than done."

"No, it's not. Do you know why a lone wolf never survives?"

"No. Why?"

"Because he doesn't have his pack. We might all be leading different lives, but with this, we're together. We're a pack."

She's cute.

My lips twitch. "You do realise you are comparing us to, essentially, dogs?"

She grins. "I can't help it. I've been reading a shifter romance about a pack of wolves, and the metaphor was there. They are calling all their wolves home because someone is out to end their species, and then…" She closes her eyes. "Please erase all of that from your memory."

"I get what you're saying," I promise, and drop my hands on her shoulders. "And so you know, I will do anything to make sure you're both protected, even if it's the last thing I do."

She blinks her eyelids open. "That scares me. I don't want you to die for us. I want you to live."

"Stop, I'm beginning to think you like me," I tease.

Neither of us move, and I run my hands slowly down her shoulders. Her lips part, a gentle puff of air escaping her lips.

I want those lips.

I want her.

Under me.

Above me.

I want inside of her.

She clears her throat, unable to meet my gaze. "I'd best go up and check in on Poppy," she whispers, stepping back.

She forces herself not to run up the stairs to escape. I can see the tension in her body because of it.

She can't run forever.

And I'll never stop chasing.

19

EMILY

I flop down on my bed, giving myself a breather. I jinxed myself last night when I told Cole the Calpol would keep Poppy asleep. She didn't sleep longer than thirty minutes before she was up again for an hour or two. She's no better today, and because she's hungry, it's making her grumpier. Her temperature has gone down, which is a good sign because it means she can finally get the sleep she needs. It's what she is doing right now and has been doing for the last hour.

She isn't why I need a breather though. Something between me and Cole changed last night, and I don't know what. He's been in my space all morning, and I don't think I'm imagining it. I want to talk to the girls and get their opinion, but I'm waiting for them to arrive. When they heard Ben would be acting as a bodyguard, they all dropped their plans and told me they'd be here. Gabby doesn't believe he can protect us and is determined to prove it. How, I don't know, but it's Gabby so she could do anything.

Waiting an hour for them to arrive hasn't helped the dilemma I'm in right now though. Even with Ben here as a buffer, it hasn't stopped Cole from driving me crazy. He found every excuse to touch me, which had been the same all morning too. At first, I thought they were accidental touches, but then it continued. Every accidental touch, every brush of his hand or every time our gazes met, it sent me to mush. I can handle the touches, but there's something about his gaze locking onto mine that has butterflies fluttering in my stomach. It's like he can see the good, the bad, and every sinful, erotic thought that crosses my mind.

I don't know how to feel because I'm not sure if I'm imagining it. It could be years of pent-up sexual frustration.

There is also the fact he's Poppy's dad. The same guy who only a week ago took us from our home after threatening to take Poppy from me. He said some really shitty things; things that must have had a little bit of truth behind them otherwise they would never had reached his mind.

And then there's the fact his brother is a homicidal maniac.

My phone alerts me to someone pressing the buzzer, and thinking it's my friends, I buzz them in and slide out of bed. I don't know where Cole or Ben are, so they might not get the door. I grab the baby monitor off the side and head downstairs.

The house is quiet, and I don't hear any signs of Cole or Ben, which means they're probably downstairs in the office. I also don't hear my girls, which is surprising since none of us do quiet. I'm lucky Poppy adjusted to us talking and laughing, and normally sleeps better because of it. Since she's ill, that won't be the same, but there's a bit of distance between us since I plan for us to go sit in the big living room.

I pull open the door and it's not my friends there. It's a beautiful brunette with gorgeous upturned hazel eyes that are oddly cat-like. She has on a tight-fitting pencil skirt that enhances her curves, with a burgundy blouse tucked in.

"Hi, can I help you?"

She snorts before letting out a dry chuckle. "No, I've seen all I need to see."

Oh God.

My stomach sinks, and I feel bile rising in my throat. Is this a girl-friend he's been keeping from us? Not that he would be keeping it from us. He doesn't have to tell me a thing. But I did ask him outright if he had one, and he said no.

Going from her expression though, it's a strong possibility that she is.

She's beautiful—everything I'm not. She doesn't seem like the sort of person to ration food, nor to know what it's like to go shopping on a budget. Her Jimmy Choo's look like they've been worn once, where the fake pair I've got in my wardrobe should have been thrown out years ago.

I glance down at my leggings with bleach stains and the cropped T-shirt I'm wearing, and then back at her immaculate clothing.

Yeah, he definitely has no interest in me.

My chest aches at the thought.

"Wait," I call out before she can reach her car. "If you are here to see Cole, I can go get him."

"No thanks," she tells me, and my friends pull in beside her.

"Cassandra?" Cole calls. "What are you doing here?"

My friends, reading the atmosphere, slowly make their way over.

"I came to see if the rumours were true. I can see that they are."

"What are you talking about?" he asks before addressing me. "I'll be in in a minute."

"Oh, we aren't going anywhere," Olivia muses, giving him a defiant look.

Just then, Poppy crying through the baby monitor blares, and the hurt in Cassandra's eyes knocks me a little. She looks so distraught.

And angry.

So angry.

"I'll go get her," Harriett offers.

"Try to settle her first. She hasn't slept much," I whisper.

"Cassandra, what are you doing here?" Cole asks, his tone much tighter.

"You lied to me," she spits out. "You said you cared for me, but that you couldn't do the family thing. And then I find out you have a daughter who is two years old. Which means she was conceived when we were together. I begged you to start a family, and all along, you had some low-class skank on the side. I gave you everything and you ended it for *that*."

"No," he barks out, and Gabby jumps at the volume. "You don't get to come here and shit talk the mother of my child. What happened between us was between us. It had nothing to do with them. And I never cheated."

"What about your daughter? You don't think I should have known? We ended things because you didn't want kids, and now you're playing house with another woman?"

"No, we ended things because it wasn't working between us. We both wanted different things, and for different reasons. You had this wild concept that everything had to be done right then and there. You knew going in who I was, but you thought you could change me," he tells her, trying to keep his tone even. "My daughter has nothing to do with you. I'm not sure why you believe you had the right to know. We are over. Have been for a long time."

"I thought you loved me. I thought we had a future together, and you played me, Cole."

"I wasn't capable of loving someone back then."

She scoffs. "Are you being serious right now?"

"Deadly. I thought it was me, not you, but I've come to learn recently, it was us. We weren't a match. I gave the relationship a chance, and the minute I gave you that piece of string, you kept pulling on it. You couldn't let go and wanted it all. I told you I didn't want those things, but you kept pushing."

"You had a baby with another woman," she screams. "I gave up everything for you."

"Don't bullshit yourself. You gave it up for your job. It had nothing to do with me, so don't try to manipulate me into thinking otherwise."

"I hate you," she snaps. "You made me think you cared."

"I did, but that was all I could do," he admits, almost looking ashamed.

She turns her glare on me. "Take it from me, he will never love you. He just said himself he doesn't know how to, so protect yourself and your daughter, and run. He had me, and it was never enough. You're nothing to him."

I have no words. The same can't be said for my friends.

"Emily isn't you," Gabby speaks up, then hesitantly continues. "Even if they were romantically involved, she's not you. He was fucking lucky he got the first shot with her. And woman to woman, talking shit like that is only making you look like a disgruntled ex. Emily has a lot about her to love. You can't help but love her. I first fell in love with the way she spoke. Then her laugh, and for a time, I mimicked it. She's gentle, she's kind, and she has a huge heart, but don't mistake her for someone to walk all over. Take your anger out on him but leave her out of it."

"Please," Olivia finishes, earning a nudge from Gabby.

"We broke up years ago," Cole grouches. "I don't see why it matters now."

Cassandra's shoulders drop. "You broke my heart when you decided I wasn't enough. You only had to tell me *one day* and I would have waited."

"No, you wouldn't have, which is why you jumped into bed with the guy working at your firm. The same guy I had been telling you had a thing for you, and you said it was nothing."

Her eyes go round. "How do you know about Matt?"

"I know everything. I also know you are going through your second round of IVF, which is why you're really here. You can't hate me for your own misgivings and something I have no control over."

For a split second, my heart breaks for her. I can't imagine how much stress that is for her. But then she glowers at him, and I want to stand in front of him to spare him from that kind of hate. "I'll make sure my dad never works with you again."

"Whatever you need to do," he tells her, deadpan.

There is silence as she gets in her car, but as she backs out, Harriett's voice, over the baby monitor, echoes.

"His palms are sweaty…" she raps, and Cole's gaze drops down to the monitor.

His eyebrows pull together. "Is she rapping Eminem?"

"Our daughter loves rap," I reply sheepishly.

"And eighties music," Gabby adds.

"And Taylor Swift," Olivia grumbles.

Gabby grins. "You say you aren't a Swifty, but I've seen you belt out the lyrics."

"I can't help it. It's like the music begins and an unseen force takes over my body and mouth."

"You love her."

"Are you okay?" I ask Cole.

"I'm sorry you had to witness that. Cassandra is the woman I broke it off with before we met." He rubs the back of his neck whilst maintaining eye contact. "I'm confused as to why she came here today when her dad informed me she moved in with Matt and was happy. Honestly, I don't want to bad mouth her because our breakup was my fault, but I thought she seemed relieved that we broke up. She's never acted like she did today."

"There's a phrase for that. A spoilt brat throwing a tantrum," Olivia explains. "I'm pretty sure you were a jerk, but it's not like you hide it, and we barely know you. Women like that rile me because they know what they are getting themselves into but act surprised when it's pointed out to them after the fact."

"Maybe she was more affected than you thought she was about the breakup."

"I don't see why. She wanted things I couldn't give her. Or I thought I couldn't. I think it's more that I didn't want to," he admits, and his pupils dilate as he meets my gaze. "I don't feel like that anymore."

Gabby whistles. "Dang! I'd call him daddy and let him spank me."

Olivia snorts. "I once smacked your arse whilst walking past you and you swung a school bag at my face."

I turn to see Ben climbing up the ladder. At my silent question, Cole announces. "Ben's installing extra cameras."

"You took me off guard," Gabby whines. "And maybe I would like it if he did it."

"You're gay; I'm not."

"No, but you are in a loving, committed relationship," Gabby sings, earning a laugh and kiss from Olivia.

"That I am."

I let out a dreamy sigh. I love that they have each other. I love it for them, and I love it for us because we get to see our two best friends happy.

"She's settled back down," Harriett announces, and her shoulders slump. "Oh, the woman has gone."

"But we have a new arrival," Gabby tells her cheerfully. "Look at him."

Harriett barely spares him a glance. "Did you sort your friend out, because I'm not comfortable with the way she looked at Emily earlier. And I won't pretend I didn't hear raised voices."

"Harriett, this is his house," I rush out, eyes wide.

"Our house," he corrects. "I meant it when I told you I'd protect her. Not just from my brother but from everything."

"Are you really not going to look at the hottie coming down the ladder?" Gabby asks, missing the tension between us.

"I have my own man of deliciousness at home. He doesn't even compete," Harriett tells her, still not taking a second look at Ben.

"What about you, Emily? What do you think of Ben?" Olivia asks, wiggling her brows.

I feel Cole's gaze on me, and when I give him a brief look, I find him watching me intently. Clearing my throat, I admit, "I've not really thought about it."

"You've not thought about him once? You've not imagined climbing his body or—"

"I'm going inside," Cole announces rather loudly.

He storms off, and I give Olivia a glare. "You did that on purpose."

She shrugs. "The guy has a serious hard-on for you. His reaction just proved it."

"You think so?" I ask, watching the empty doorway.

"You can't want *that*," Gabby declares. "His brother is a maniac."

"You're crazier than his brother. The only difference is, he kills people, and you don't. I'm pretty sure I don't have room to judge," I point out.

She tilts her head, staring at me unnervingly. "You make a solid point."

"Do you like him?"

I meet Harriett's gaze, feeling a little unsettled when I answer. "I don't think I ever stopped. Does that make me a glutton for punishment?"

"It makes you human," Olivia answers.

"What are you going to do about it?" Gabby asks, popping some gum into her mouth.

"I don't know if he likes me. There have been signs all morning, but I don't know. I could just be seeing what I want to see."

"Oh, he definitely likes you," Gabby sings, grinning from ear to ear.

"And you aren't seeing things," Olivia adds. "He didn't ask you to leave for privacy earlier; he asked you to leave so you didn't have to witness his fuck up."

"It feels weird. It is weird, right?" I ask.

"If you like him, what's stopping you?" Harriett asks. "You already have a daughter together."

"Exactly. It could mess this up."

"If not telling him he had a daughter didn't do it, nothing will," Gabby offers. "Plus, it's not like you can't co-parent separated. You are doing it now."

She has a point.

"I don't think he likes me," I finally burst out. "Let's talk about something else."

Harriett grins, and it's slow, predatory, the same grin she gets when we're all about to get in trouble. "How do you feel about a shopping trip today to get something for the weekend?"

My eyebrows pinch together. "What would I need for the weekend? It's a scare fest."

Gabby, clearly reading Harriett's mind, grins too. "Ah. If you want to know if a guy likes you, all you have do is show a little leg, shake a little boob, and drive him nuts until he's on his knees."

I roll my eyes. "It might work at the club, but it's Cole. He works with strippers and has probably seen dozens of them naked."

"No, something tells me he doesn't mix business with pleasure. You were the exception. If he really wants you, he'll make a move. I have the perfect top for it. You can't wear a skirt, but there's a pair of jeans that will hug your hips. He'll be imagining what's underneath. You'll see," Harriett promises.

As I'm thinking it over, Gabby pushes, "What do you have to lose?"

"Aside from the clothes he'll tear off you," Olivia adds.

"Alright. Alright. I'll go and see if Cole is okay to watch over Poppy."

The girls high-five each other as I head inside. Is it a good idea to seduce the father of my daughter? Probably not. But I'm done not living. All my life, everyone else's needs have come before my own. Now, I want my needs to come first. Just this once. And I don't care if it makes me selfish.

I know he is worth it.

20

COLE

I check on Poppy, who is lying on the sofa watching a cartoon. She's still feeling under the weather, and since I didn't want to leave her, I decided to bring her downstairs so I can reply to some work calls.

Kit is bent over the pool table, taking his shot, but he glances up when I end the call. "Will you ever slow down? I thought that's what people do when they have kids."

"I like being busy."

"Yeah, to fill some void," he snorts, taking another shot.

"What about you? You going to tell me what's been going on with you? Mum and Dad are worried."

"They always worry," he mutters.

"Stop evading the question."

He parks his ass on the pool table, holding the cue stick between his legs. "I met a girl in Australia."

"Okay."

"We planned to come back together once my trip was done."

"It was that serious?" I ask.

"I loved her, bro. I had a ring picked out and was waiting to pop the question when we got here."

I throw my pen on a stack of papers. "What happened?"

"She didn't feel the same way. Could have been because she was already fucking married."

"Fuck, man. I don't know what to say," I tell him. Normally, I would comment that she's not the first married woman he's slept with, but something tells me this is different.

"Wasn't even the worst part. She aborted my baby and didn't even ask me what I wanted to do. She just wanted to make sure her husband didn't find out about her affair."

"Shit! That's low, man. No wonder you took Emily and our situation hard."

"It's fine. I got my own back. Emailed her husband a bunch of photos of us from our account, and some of her nude, and then shoved weed into the heel of her shoe. Pretty sure she's still in customs," he retorts, as the ringtone Ben designated for me blares.

"I need to get this," I tell him, and answer the phone. "Is everything okay?"

"You might want to come outside. We've just circled the block and there's a car parked outside yours. Emily informs me it's no one."

"Really?" Emily snaps. "He doesn't need to go out there. I can deal with them."

"I'll be outside," I tell Ben and end the call. "Watch Poppy?"

"Don't leave me. I don't know what to do," Kit stresses, but I'm already running up the stairs.

I leave the house in only a pair of socks. Ben doesn't park far from the gate, and I glance through the gap in the open gate to see a family of three standing against an old, beat-up car.

Emily's frowning as she slides out of the car and moves to address them. I stand back by the car as she does.

The woman reminds me of someone I used to know when I bought the first building to host Tease. She looked years older than she was, and those years weren't good to her. This woman looks like the world hasn't been good to her either—through no one's fault but her own—and she hasn't been fair to the world. I don't know how I know; I just do.

The old gentleman next to her looks bored, but the other woman is riddled with jealousy and resentment as she rolls her gaze over Emily.

"Mum, Dad, Reign; why are you here?" Emily greets. "How did you know I was here?"

My eyes widen a tad at the news they are her parents. I didn't see that coming since Emily bears no resemblance to these people. Emily is a blooming flower, and these guys are weeds that keep coming back. I step away from the car, on alert since Emily has shed some light on her childhood. These people are vultures.

"Well, after we found out where you lived through the funeral directives, we went by to see you and a young girl from next door gave us this address," the older woman declares, her lip curling as her gaze moves to the house behind us. "We want to make amends and fix the bridge between us."

I watch as Emily's shoulders drop. "You mean you want something," she guesses. "I'm sorry, but I don't have anything to give you."

"We came to discuss Grandma's belongings," Reign announces. "Don't pretend you don't have anything."

"I already offered for you to come and look through her things and you declined," Emily points out softly. "It's too late now as they've already been donated."

Her mum's eyes narrow, and the façade is dropped. "We aren't here for her clothes or stupid knick-knacks. I was promised those rings when I was a girl. I want them back."

"Mum, I have it in writing. The will is solid. And the one thing Grandma asked me not to do was to give in to your demands and give them to you. She knows you don't want them for sentimental reasons. You want to sell them because you know they are worth money."

"Our Reign has a lawyer friend. He said we have rights. And we will argue the will. You could stop this now if you just shared the inheritance between us," the dad announces.

Emily pinches the bridge of her nose. "Dad, she knew you'd probably try that too and she has things in place in case of that happening. Plus, her finances haven't been released to me yet."

"Yeah, but you have control over what to do with the money once it is. If you don't want to part with the rings, give us our share of the money," Reign spits out. "She was my nan too, and you took her from me. Don't even pretend you need the money. We know you have loads."

"I—"

"She was my mother, Emily," the mum argues. "She would want to me to have it. You turned her against us, and it stops now. You have this fancy house with your fancy clothes and rich man. You don't need it."

"You've always thought you were better than us, but look at you, sleeping with a man for his money," Reign spits out, and her gaze falls over my shoulder. "Or two of them. You disgust me."

I step forward, having heard enough. "Emily won't be giving you a penny. Her grandma's wishes are final, and if you try and make this difficult for Emily, I will have my lawyers sue you for emotional distress and whatever else we can pin on you. Whatever this is, it ends now."

"Are you going to let him talk to your mother like that?" her mum screeches at her.

I grab Emily's shoulders and tug her back against my chest. "I'm not going to tell you what to do, but I will tell you our daughter is watching. Don't let her see her mum get bullied by these people."

Her gaze goes to the side, where Kit has Poppy tucked close to his chest. Then she steels her spine to address her parents. "Grandma's wishes are final. I won't tarnish her memory by doing the one thing she asked me not to do. But even if she didn't make me promise, I still wouldn't. Because I'm the one who loved her. I was there every time she had a—"

"Blah, blah, blah," her mother growls, pinching her fingers to her thumb rapidly. "We don't care about what you or she wanted. We want what is owed."

"You just want to throw it in our faces," Reign growls. "You owe it to us. You live in that house, pretending to be poor, when in reality, you are rolling in money you don't even want to spend. It's fucking selfish. You gave not one thought to walking out on the people who fed you and raised you, who had to deal with your crying all the goddamn time."

"I slept on a blanket," Emily screeches. "I went days without eating, and spent years being abused by all three of you. You broke something inside me that I'm still trying to fix. I could handle you not loving me. I could handle you leaving me to die in a burning house. I was a child, and I had to. But I'm an adult now, and I make my own choices. I got what I have because I worked hard for it. I never had handouts or someone to fall back on. I had me. I don't owe you anything."

"You heard her. Now leave."

"You spiteful little bitch," her dad growls, and steps forward, going for Emily.

I push her behind me, not wanting her to get hurt. But Ben gets there first, moving fast as lightning. He pins the large man to the ground, and her dad's cheek presses against the tarmac as he cries out for help. "The residents have asked you to leave. And I would suggest you do as you're told," Ben warns them.

"We aren't going anywhere," her mum cries. "Get your hands off my husband."

"Don't even think about it," Kit warns when Reign goes to intervene.

"Leave, Mum," Emily demands, a flush working its way up her cheeks.

"And this is why I could never love you," her mum declares sharply. "You were a fucking cry-baby, always hard done by. It was never you; it was us. But it was you. You were the fucking problem. And I dealt with that. I put up with your constant fucking whining. Not your nan. Me."

Emily steps back like she's taken a blow, the colour draining from her cheeks. "Leave," she whispers, the strength leaving her.

"Then give us what we came for. You don't need it. I don't know how you make your money since you swear you don't strip, but you have a lot of it, which means you don't need my mother's things."

"Oh my god, it was you," Emily accuses.

I tug her against my chest, my eyebrows pinching together. "What do you mean?"

"You broke into my home. You stole my tip money."

Her mother's cheeks and neck turn red at the accusation. "I have no idea what you are talking about."

"I didn't hear it before because you distracted me, but you keep mentioning what money I have. You stole that money."

Reign scoffs. "You owe us. We lost money the day you moved out to live with Nan. I missed out on school trips, prom, and even college because of your selfishness."

"I needed that money," Emily whispers brokenly, before raising her voice. "I have a daughter to feed. I had bills to pay. I had a funeral to pay for."

I pull her back, placing a comforting hand on the side of her face. I tilt her chin up until she meets my gaze. "Concentrate on me, baby."

"I needed that money. We had no food. We had bills. And I had so much time off," she rushes out, her voice barely audible. "I wanted to die that day. For a split second, when it all became too much, I wanted to die. I gave up."

"No," I rasp.

And I made it worse by threatening to take her daughter.

"See, fucking cry-baby," her mother hisses.

"Get fucked," I snap harshly.

Kit, with Poppy still in his arms, steps forward. "You people make me sick. Get the fuck off his property before I call the police."

Ben pulls her dad up to his feet. "They will already be notified," Ben warns. "Expect to be served with a restraining order. The next time you come near Emily, I won't bother restraining you. I will beat your arse and then have you arrested."

As he orders them to their piece of scrap of a car, I focus on Emily. "Never, and I mean never, have those thoughts again. Poppy needs you." I press my forehead against hers. "I need you. We are a family, remember."

"I'm so sorry you had to witness that."

"I need to know you are okay. I need to hear you say it because, baby, I don't want you to ever feel like that again."

"It was only for a split second. I'm okay now. I would never have done it. I love Poppy too much. But my grandma died, I had no money, and I was so depressed."

I cup her cheeks, my gaze unwavering. Her pupils dilate, her lips parting. "You don't have to worry about any of that anymore."

"Um, I hate to break up whatever this is, but could, um, someone take the baby," Kit asks.

I step back, giving us both room, and turn to Kit. He's holding Poppy like she's infectious, and she seems to be enjoying it.

"Dada," she demands, giggling.

Kits eyes widen. "I'm Kit, kid."

I take her from him and cuddle her against my chest. "Mama cry?"

Emily pastes on a smile, running her finger down the bridge of Poppy's nose. "Mummy's okay, baby."

"You weren't lying about your parents," Kit mutters, rubbing the back of his neck.

She snorts. "Believe it or not, that's not even the worst of it."

Ben arrives back at the gate. "They're gone. I'm going to issue a restraining order. It might take a while and would probably go quicker if you had a solicitor."

"I can get that sorted," I announce.

"I should have known the break-in was them. I just didn't want to believe they'd stoop that low," she grumbles.

Kit's eyes widen. "Really? Because they remind me of extras from the T.V. series, *Shameless*."

She narrows her gaze on him. "Less of the commentary."

"I'm just saying," he defends.

"Careful, someone might think you like me."

He grins, flashing his teeth. "I can admit when I'm wrong."

"But you didn't," she points out.

His shoulders slump. "I am sorry for misreading the situation."

"And for judging me," she presses, twirling her hand for him to continue.

I grin when he narrows his eyes on her. "I'm sorry for judging you."

She laughs. "Thank you."

I turn to Ben. "Do you think we'll need to worry about them?"

"No. I heard the sister in the car. She was telling them to drop it. If I were to guess, she already has a criminal record and doesn't want to get into trouble again."

"I don't think they'll bother me now. They don't like putting in the effort. They've hassled me longer than they've kept a job, so I think they'll have given up today."

"I still wouldn't rule it out," Ben warns. "Greedy people get desperate."

"I know. And I won't. I learned what they are capable of firsthand."

"They really left you to burn?" Kit asks, as we turn to make our way back up to the house.

I grit my teeth as I wait for her to reply. "Yes, they did. But as soon as the fire brigade got me out, they acted like the doting parents."

As Emily and Kit continue to talk, unaware of the turmoil going on inside me, I think back on what was said.

She wanted to give up.

She was struggling.

And her parents left her to burn.

No child should have to live through what she has. I glance at Poppy, who is playing with the buttons on my shirt, and I can't imagine ever letting harm come to her. I would die before I let that happen.

I might not have had the best upbringing, but I got lucky when my parents adopted me. They showed me what it was like to be a part of a family, to be loved and less afraid. Now, I'm going to do the same for Emily. I'm going to show her how a family is meant to be. How love is meant to feel.

Because she deserves the best in life.

21

EMILY

My boots slide in the mud as we make our way to the back of the queue. Wind whistles through the air, and I glance up at the sky, hoping it doesn't rain. We've been waiting for this night for what feels like forever. The only other haunted house available around here is amateur at best. We were in and out within ten minutes of arriving when we went, and never screamed once. It had been like a house viewing, so we went back in and switched things up. The organisers weren't pleased and called the police.

Best night ever.

But this scare fest… it's epic.

Nothing beats being scared in a safe environment. It has your blood pumping and your heart racing in the best possible way. Me and the girls live for nights like this.

Noticing Harriett still glaring at Ben, I chuckle and nudge her with my shoulder. "Stop glaring at him."

"He wouldn't let us carpool together. Does he not realise we spent hours building that playlist," she remarks, not bothering to lower her voice.

"He's doing his job."

"And he would have been happier doing it to our playlist," she states.

"I'm with Harriett. You missed out on Michael Jackson's *Thriller*," Gabby announces.

Olivia snorts. "She nearly took my fucking eye out."

I arch an eyebrow. "Weren't you in the back?" I ask.

"Yes, but the crazy bitch moved like she was flagging down a plane."

I burst out laughing and reach for Harriett so I don't fall. "Where's Hayden?"

"She's coming. Maddison is coming with her," Harriett replies.

"Wait, is he coming in?" Gabby asks.

"*He* can hear you," I point out, and turn to Ben.

He's searching the area, alert. "I'll follow behind."

"Oh man," Gabby whines.

"What about Cole's sister; is she still coming?" Olivia asks.

"Yeah," I murmur, pulling out my phone. There's a message waiting for me from Aria. "She's here."

They help me scan the wooded area, where acres of land surround us. There's a designated car park close by, so she should be near us.

It's Gabby who spots her. "There she is," she muses. "I fucking love her hair."

"Me too," I agree, before yelling, "Aria, we're over here."

She spots us, and her shoulders drop. She beams, heading over to us. "I thought you guys had changed your mind and ditched me."

"Never," Harriett sings. "We're in this to win it."

The flesh between Aria's eyebrows creases. "There's a prize?"

"No, but making it out first is always our first goal," I explain, before making introductions again. "In case you've forgotten, that's Harriett, that's Gabby, and that's Olivia."

"Hey," she greets. "Are you the bodyguard?"

"Yes," Ben replies, not even glancing her way.

Is he gay?

Because my girls and Aria are gorgeous, and he hasn't checked them out once.

"Yo, bitches, who's ready to kill this?" Hayden announces from the top of her lungs. "Wow, I love your hair."

Aria brushes her hand over her short locks as she gazes at Hayden. "Thanks."

I laugh under my breath. I had the same reaction to Hayden too. She's a knockout, with a strong personality.

Hayden does a double take when she sees Ben, her eyes widening. "What are *you* doing here?"

I watch his jaw clench. "I'm working."

"For who?"

"Me," I reply when he doesn't answer. "Where's Madison?"

As if by magic, Madison appears, cheeks flushed. "You bitch," she hisses, stomping towards us.

Hayden doesn't even look affronted. She just arches an eyebrow. "I love these boots. I wasn't going to walk all the way from the car park to here."

"You jumped out when I was talking to the car park attendant," Madison argues. "You could have at least told me." She holds her finger up when Hayden goes to speak. "And don't give me crap about the boots. If you were worried about them, you wouldn't have worn them."

Hayden shrugs. "Okay, so I didn't want to walk. I was saving my energy for this."

We move forward in the queue and Ben leans down, his lips close to my ear. "You could have warned me the Carters would be coming."

I glance over at them and see Olivia introducing Aria as we move forward in the queue. "Why did you need to know?"

"Because I'm pretty sure they've got a screw loose, and I'm certain I saw her dad not far away."

I gulp, scanning the area, not seeing Max Carter. "Hayden, is your dad here?"

She tenses, narrowing her gaze at everything around us. "Why, did you see him?"

"Is he coming?" I squeak.

"Oh God," Harriett groans.

Hayden pulls out her phone, and her lips press together. "I swear, he won't bother us."

"It's your dad," Gabby points out. "Can't you get rid of him?"

"You don't get rid of my dad. I tried to ditch him in Tesco's as a kid, and he found me. Again at a fair ground. Then—"

"We get it," Olivia rushes out. "But what is he doing *here*?"

"Because he found out I was meeting you. He thinks you'll get me into trouble."

I melt at her words. However, Ben groans. "That's so sweet."

"Um, why would it be sweet?" Aria asks.

Gabby chuckles. "Because Hayden is known to cause trouble on her own. Their family are the definition of trouble."

"I went to school with Imogen, who is practically a Carter, so I know. But it still doesn't explain why you find it sweet," she muses.

I wave her off. "It just does."

"I need a pay rise," Ben grumbles.

"How is Imogen?" Hayden sweetly remarks, and although she's addressing Aria, she's looking at Ben.

What is that about?

Madison's brow furrows. "You saw her last night."

Ben glares at Hayden, before guiding me forward into the queue. "Don't get roped into her antics. I've heard they can be extreme."

I bite my lip to stop myself from telling him we're just as bad. "How do you know Emily?" Madison asks.

Aria smiles. "She has a daughter with my brother, Cole. We're family now."

Hayden arches a brow at me. "You told him?"

"He found out."

She nods slowly, like she's mulling something over. "How's that going?"

I quickly glance at Aria before lowering my gaze. "It's going good."

Aria snorts. "From what I know, he basically kidnapped her and moved her in."

Hayden meets my gaze. "I know a guy…"

Madison nudges her. "Stop. If she wanted someone's help, she would have asked for it," she argues, before turning to me. "You don't need anyone's help, right?"

I laugh. "We're good. I promise. He's been really good to us."

"And if it changes, we have a contingency plan in place," Gabby announces, earning a push from Olivia.

Hayden points to Aria. "His sister is right there."

Aria holds her hands up. "Hey, if he does something that warrants it, I'll help."

"He won't," I argue. "Honestly, things are… things are different."

Aria smirks. "I heard from Kit that you two had this gooey-eyed thing going on."

My cheeks heat. "We did not."

"You like him?" Hayden asks, watching me closely.

My cheeks flush, and I try to ignore the fact Aria is also staring, waiting for me to reply. "We are… We're just friends."

"Ladies, your tickets," a guy wearing a black grim reapers hoodie demands. We pass him our tickets and wait for him to scan each code. "We have to remind you that people with epilepsy and heart conditions are strictly prohibited from entering. Scare fest and Co. are not liable if you disobey these rules. You are forbidden to touch our actors. Any assault to our actors, and you'll be removed from the park, and the police will be called. Are those rules understood?"

"Yes," we call.

A woman dragging chains walks forward, her pupils glazed over from contact lenses.

"You may enter the maze at your own risk. You'll encounter all creatures from the dark underworld. Your only way to escape is to reach the tunnels to the haunted house," she taunts before cackling loudly. "Be aware, there are dangers lurking behind every corner."

We move forward to the archway made of hay, where another woman in chains approaches us. "Watch where you walk. There are traps everywhere," she cackles.

Hayden bounces on the balls of her feet as she jumps over the threshold. She holds her hands up. "What's the worst that could happen?"

I scream as hands push through the straw walls, grabbing her by her shoulder. She pushes off, and together, we rush into the maze.

I grab Aria's hand, laughing. "Come on."

"Oh my god," she cries when hands begin to shove through the gap near our feet.

"Fuck no," Madison screams as a zombie wobbles up to her. She refrains from attacking him or her—it's hard to tell with all the makeup.

The pathways are getting smaller the further we get into the maze. All the walls are decorated with lights or some sort of theme from a movie.

I'm shaking at the distant sound of screams. They sound like a woman is being tortured. A mist of fog falls all around us when Hayden stops. There's a painted red arrow on the wall in front of us, pointing to the left. We turn and find two girls running towards us, screaming. "Don't go that way. Don't go that way," they cry.

They pass us, and with wide eyes, I turn to the left, seeing a figure like the creature from *The Ring*. I scream, pushing Gabby in their path, and head right. Screams and laughter follow, and I push through the maze, not taking notice of where I'm going.

I come to a stop at another fork in the path, and I turn to Hayden and the others. "Where are Madison, Harriett and Olivia?"

Gabby bites her lower lip. "I have no idea."

Hayden laughs. "Oh my god, we need to beat them to the tunnels. Come on."

Just as we turn right again, we come to a stop, freezing at the huddle of zombies walking towards us.

We scream, racing the other way, and following the path down. A chainsaw roars to life, and I glance at Ben. "How far is the car park from here? Do you think we could make it back?"

"Don't you dare chicken out on us," Hayden warns.

"Did you not hear that chainsaw?" I breathe out.

She grins, taking my hand. "Let's go this way."

We slow down as the lights begin to dim. It's practically pitch black, and my heart is racing.

Screams pierce the air, startling me again.

"I hate this," Aria announces, a quiver in her tone.

We creep down the pathway as the sound effects turn daunting. It's like the music they play in movies when a killer is about to capture their prey.

And now we are the prey.

"Guys, are you sure we've not gone off track?" I ask.

"Keep going. Don't turn," Ben orders.

Hayden stops. "Why?"

"Because I think the building, or whatever it is, is up ahead."

She continues down the path, and we step out into the open, where the paths all meet. I shiver.

To the left, it's completely dark. I can't see how far it goes, or if it goes anywhere. To the right, there are whispers, like someone is reciting a poem. A creepy one.

The chainsaw roars to life again, and I scream, glancing behind me.

Up ahead, the shadows hug a large figure. He has a mask on, with the chainsaw close to his chest.

"Run," I shout.

I don't wait for them to follow. I push past Hayden and Aria and run as fast as my legs will take me.

I'm not going to be killed by a chainsaw.

22

EMILY

I stare down the gloomy stairs that are stained with blood, panting. The bricks have cracks running down them, and I'm pretty sure the spider webs are real.

A woman dressed up as a porcelain doll stands next to us. She's taking her job seriously, and each time she moves her neck, it's like a rusty hinge creaking. Her red wig goes well with the red lipstick she has on. Her eyes are black, and somehow, she got her skin to look shiny like a doll. It's creepy as hell.

"This is the small crawl space entrance. Are you willing to risk it?"

I stop biting my lower lip to answer. "How small are we talking?"

She breaks out of character, smiling widely. "Really small, ya know. But, like, I think you'll be okay with them. You're all so tiny."

"You've not seen my arse then," Madison mutters.

I rear back when the doll goes back into character, her entire expression flat. "Um…"

"It's okay if you move down to the next actor. He can invite you straight into the house."

"Anything else they need to know?" Ben demands.

"Are you not coming down there?" I ask, whirling on him.

"How can I protect you if I'm trapped inside a tunnel? I'll walk around and meet you at the exit."

Gabby snorts. "Chicken shit."

"Do you keep cameras inside?" he asks the doll.

She glances at me. "Are you, like, a celebrity or something?"

"Or something," Hayden mutters.

The doll woman looks to Ben. "Yes, there are. But it should be empty in there by now. I get alerts telling me when to let the next group into the tunnels. I think there's only one person left, and I hope he is still in there. He raced in there when he spotted me, so I never got the chance to explain the rules. I tried going after him, but he was gone, and I can't leave my post."

Ben nods and pulls me aside. "Do you still have the panic button I gave you?"

I tug my jacket aside, letting him see the silver chain he hooked it on. "Yes."

"Press it only in an emergency. Not because you're freaked out over a zombie."

I snort at the warning. "Okay. Go take the easy route."

He lets out an exasperated sigh and makes his way around the building. I sidle up to the others as the doll explains, "You have to be careful. Some tunnels have dead ends, but others have traps inside of them. The cage doesn't fall down for long."

"What? So we could be trapped down there?" Gabby asks.

"No. There are six exits from the tunnels. Then you'll need to make your way through the panic rooms," she explains. "If at any point you want to get out, yell red three times and we'll open up the emergency hatches from above."

"Come on, girls, let's go," Hayden orders, and takes the first step down.

Aria follows, her hands shaking as she uses the wall for balance. "I hate how realistic all of this is."

"There had better not be fucking bugs," Hayden hisses.

We walk into a tunnel that has dim lights on the ground to guide the way. The walls close in, and the ceiling drops down until we're on our knees, crawling through mud and water that has been stained red. The further we get in, the darker the tunnel gets. There is barely any lighting. The only good thing is it's no longer brick. It's metal we're crawling on.

Screams bounce off the walls, and my head bumps into Aria's arse. "Sorry," I grumble.

"What was that?" she cries.

Hayden takes the tunnel to the right as a voice whispers, "Come here, little girl."

"Fuck no!" Hayden bellows.

Aria races off to the left, and I follow her. I hear a scuffle behind me and stop to glance back. Gabby and Hayden are tangled up in a heap. "Oh my god, go, go."

"Don't fucking leave us," Hayden demands.

"There are eyes glowing," I point out.

She looks up at the glowing eyes at the end of the tunnel she was going down, and screams.

I turn back around and see Aria is up another hallway. I laugh, following her, or I do until I see more glowing eyes. She tries to back-track, but her jeans get caught on a twig. I untangle it and shuffle back a little when I notice a cage falling down to the right of us.

"Shit. Go, go, go," I cry.

I hear Gabby's screams in the distance and go the other way. What-ever has her screaming, I don't want to meet it. I head down another tunnel, this one a little wider, when I hear it.

"Help me!" a man bellows.

I freeze, and Aria knocks into me. "Why have you stopped? Go! I'm pretty sure IT, the fucking clown, is down here," she splutters through laughter.

I hear the man again. "Did you hear that?"

"Go. Do not be one of those girls who checks on a noise," she demands.

I keep going when the tunnel comes to a stop at a T junction. The sound of a cage slamming shut has me looking left.

And oh my god…

As I live and breathe, I will never forget this moment.

Max Carter looks up through the bars, his eyes wide as he screams out for help. "Get this fucking thing off me."

"Sir, you need to stop struggling," the clown demands. I'm pretty sure he's trying to free himself.

"Please, help me!" Max demands. "He's touching me."

"I'm trying to get you untangled," the clown barks.

Max's eyes squeeze together in a plea. "Inappropriately," he whispers.

Aria nudges me. "Don't fall for it. It could be a part of the act."

"That's Mr Carter, Hayden's dad," I murmur, as whispers race through the tunnel, followed by a mist of cool air.

"We're coming," they whisper.

I whimper. "I'm sorry, Mr Carter."

"Don't leave me here," he pleads as I go down the other tunnel. "Please! I have a wife and children who need me."

Laughing, I race to the end of the tunnel, my knees bruised from the ground. There's a red hatch door at the end, spurring me on. "There," I cry, moving faster.

"Come back!" Max bellows. "Come back!"

"Is he quoting the Titanic?" Aria wheezes through laughter as I push open the hatch door.

I scream as red water flows down in a stream at my knees. It feels like lumpy jelly. "Eww," I cry.

"Oh my god, I thought you pissed yourself," Aria splutters out.

I laugh. "Come on."

I squeeze through the small gap and fall into a treasure trove for psychopaths. In the centre of the room is a body missing half of its limbs. The fingers on the hand hanging over the table, twitch, and I shudder.

I quickly get to my feet, glancing around the small room. "I hope those tools are fake," I murmur.

Hanging above the table are all sorts of tools. There are body parts hanging from the beams above us.

Aria stops beside me, grabbing my hand. "What is that smell?"

It does smell a little funky in here. I wouldn't be surprised if something actually did die in here.

Movement from my peripheral vision makes me conscious of my surroundings. I glance in the corner, where the window is, and notice two glowing eyes. A man in a bloodied trench coat holds up a saw.

"Want to play a game?"

"Run," I scream, as the man steps forward.

Aria laughs and we make our way out of the door, going down a slim hallway. Bars and other effects and decorations are hanging off the walls and ceiling, and we slow our pace. I'm already scared out of my mind, and the effects are making it worse.

Smudges of blood stain the floor, like a dead body was dragged down there. And when I squint through the dim lighting, I notice a man sat against the far wall, his head flopped to the side.

We creep forward, wary of the gaps in the wall. A clown drops down in front of us at the same time a monster reaches through the bars. Aria tries to shove me, but I get there first, pushing her towards him. It's every woman for herself.

"Emily," she cries.

I charge through the door to my right, and a man hanging from a rope drops down, making a stomach-churning sound. I startle, spinning around to go back to Aria. We are safer in pairs.

The door slowly creaks shut, and my laughter dries up at the figure standing in front of it. Something inside of me senses that he doesn't belong here.

He doesn't look like one of the actors. In black trainers and a black jacket with the hood up, and a scarf hiding half of his face, he doesn't fit the part.

My blood runs cold. "Who are you?" I ask.

As he steps forward, the door is pushed open, knocking him back. Aria wipes the fake blood smeared on her face and glowers at me.

"You—" she begins, but her words are cut off by the dark, looming figure.

He smacks her head against the door, and she falls limply to the floor.

"Aria," I cry.

He straightens, and I glance at Aria's unmoving form, conflicted about what to do. When he takes another step, I run, hoping he follows me. I don't want her to get hurt again.

I push through the small door, screaming for help. He tackles me to the floor, and I cry out, stunned for a moment. When he grabs my hair, I twist, kicking and punching with all my might.

"Stop!" I plead.

"You will be mine," he demands, but his voice is muffled by the effects around the house.

"Hey," a voice demands, grabbing my attacker's attention. I use the moment of distraction to kick him in the stomach.

The actor steps between us as I crawl away, my heart racing. "You can't attack the visitors," he orders.

There's a flash of a knife, and before I can warn him, the attacker is slashing the blade through the air, laughing maniacally. The actor screams, and so do I, blood spurting all over my jeans.

This isn't a scene.

The blood is real, and so is the attacker.

I get to my feet and run, moving through the house with no idea which direction to take.

I hear piercing screams the further in I get, and when I push into another room, Hayden is there with Harriett, both of them in hysterics laughing.

"Run!" I cry.

Hayden untangles herself from the monster on the floor and whirls around to face me. "What the fuck!"

I'm tackled once more, and this time, we both go over a table. Everything tumbles off the table with us. My ribs protest as I land on something hard.

"Hey," a male voice snaps, as two hands grip my neck in a vice.

I slap his hands, unable to catch a breath. My temples pulse, and two tears roll down the side of my face.

Poppy.

I have to fight for Poppy.

I'm not sure who jumps on top of the attacker, but once he lets go of my neck, I inhale sharply. Hands tug at my wrists, distracting me from the burning pain in my throat. Hayden is there, helping me to my feet. She grabs a silver decoration bowl and smacks it across the attacker's head. The ping and vibrations of it hitting his skull echo over the sound system.

"Come on," Hayden screams, as she takes Harriett's hand. Harriett gets to her feet, and we all escape the room. We're moving down a narrowed hallway.

"Who is that?" Hayden asks, out of breath.

"I don't know, but he has a knife. Aria is hurt," I cry, my heart racing.

Harriett moves to a window, trying to break the boards off. Hayden and I squeeze in to help, but when the first board comes loose, there's nothing but brick behind it.

"Come on," Hayden demands, and we move up the stairs to the left of us. "I think we are still at basement level."

"We need to go back and find Aria. She's hurt. And so is one of the actors," I cry.

Harriett stops when we reach the top. "We need to get out of here first. We can't help her right now."

"Oh my god," I reply, and pull out the necklace hung inside my jumper, and press the emergency button. "Ben will come."

We head into the next room, and paid actors are still in character, unaware there's a real monster roaming the halls.

"Where is the exit?" Hayden demands. "We need to get out of here and call the police."

One of the actors steps out of his spot. "There's an emergency exit not far from here. Go up the next flight of stairs, then follow the hall down to the small flight of stairs. There's a room to the left. Go through that room and the exit is there."

A door behind us slams open, and we whirl around, screaming when we see the figure. Hayden tugs on Harriett's arm, and Harriett tugs on mine as we exit the room. We follow his instructions, my legs aching in protest as we make it up the stairs.

When we reach the next lot of stairs to go down, the attacker catches up to us. He grabs my arm, and my scream pierces through the air. Hayden tugs, which I don't think he expected as he falls into me. We tumble down the stairs, and every inch of my body aches as bruises form from the wood and decorations digging into me on the way down. Thankfully, there are only about eight steps.

We land in a heap at the bottom, and Harriett looks up at the same time as me. Separating us is the attacker, and her fear-filled eyes capture mine.

The attacker gets up at the same time as I do. I warily take a step back, panting.

"Run!" Harriett yells.

I do, and slam the door closed behind me. I hear a thud followed by a groan but keep going.

I have no idea where I am, or what other effects or jump scares I'll walk into. I quickly move through the building, closing all the doors as I do.

Down a long hall are three doors, and I quickly step into the first room, gently closing the door behind me.

Scanning the room, I shudder. There's a four-poster bed in the middle, chains welded onto the frame and blood stains on the sheets. A rocking chair with a doll sitting on it sways back and forth in the corner, and the curtains have seen better days.

The bed would be a good place to hide since there aren't many options in here, but I'm not stupid. I pay attention to horror movies, and those who hide under the bed always get caught.

Instead, I move to the cupboard and step inside, closing the door quietly behind me.

I can't outrun him.

I have to hide. And at least in here, I have room to move and run if I need to.

A hand clamps over my mouth, smothering my scream.

Oh God.

I'm going to die.

23

EMILY

My eyes widen with fear as a whisper of voices filter through the sound system. I feel a jaw brush along mine.

"There's a doll out there," Max whispers. "Don't let her find us."

My shoulders drop and I turn to him, gripping his biceps. "Max, we have to get out of here. There's someone trying to kill me. Aria is hurt, and so is one of the actors. Whoever it is has a knife. I'm not making this up. It's real," I ramble.

"I fucking knew it," he hisses, as the door outside the cupboard flings open.

Max covers my mouth and presses us against the back of the cupboard. I can hear my pulse beating because of how fast it's going. My knees tremble as the adrenaline begins to wear off.

I peek through the crack in the door, seeing my attacker move over to the bed opposite the cupboard. He kneels down, searching under it, and I close my eyes.

He knows I'm hiding.

I hold my breath, scared he'll hear me, and Max runs his hand over my arm. Boots crunch down on the floorboards close by, but I'm too scared to look.

"Emily?" Ben bellows. "Emily, where are you?"

The sound system cuts off, and I open my eyes. Lights switch on in the room outside, but it's the eye looking through the crack that has me screaming.

Max rears back, kicking the cupboard door open and knocking the attacker back. Max pushes us out of the cupboard, ready to fight, at the same time Ben stumbles to a halt in the doorway.

"Ben, he has a knife. He tried to hurt me," I cry, pointing to the attacker.

The attacker rushes at Ben, crashing into him outside of the room. Max pushes me behind him as Ben goes through the wall, the lath and plaster crumbling around him. The attacker goes to flee, but Ben kicks his foot out, knocking him to the ground.

More voices echo down the halls, and staff pile into it. Ben gets to his feet, but a larger man steps between him and the attacker. "Sir, you can't attack people," he thunders. "The police are on their way."

"No, stop him," I cry when the attacker gets to his feet.

Ben is blocked from following him, and he pushes the guy against the wall, his forearm pressed against the staff member's throat. "You fucking idiot. I was doing my job and you just let a potential serial killer go free."

"No," I rasp, wide-eyed.

Max wraps his arm around me. "You didn't think he was Mister Tickles, did you?"

"I thought it was just a random person. Do you think... oh God, I'm going to be sick," I breathe, and move to the side, emptying the contents of my stomach all over the dirty floor.

"I'm the one who brought it to your attention," Ben hisses, and I realise I've missed some of their conversation.

"We need to get to Aria," I pant, wiping my mouth with the back of my hand. "She was hurt."

The staff member lowers his head. "I didn't know. We had conflicting reports. We are just doing our job."

"And I was doing mine," Ben spits out, before walking over to me.

"Are you okay?"

"He had a knife," I whisper. "I knew he wasn't a part of the house as soon as I saw him."

"You did good hiding," he tells me, and wraps his arm around me. "Thank you for helping her."

"Just doing my bit," Max replies.

I give him a droll look. "You said you were hiding from a doll."

Max snorts. "Does it look like—" he screams, hiding behind me as a woman dressed as a doll stops outside the door. "Demon! Be gone!"

She rolls her eyes. "I thought you left."

Max scoffs. "Believe me, I tried."

"Well, it's a good job you didn't," I muse, rubbing my hands up and down my arms.

"We need to go outside and give a statement to the police," Ben orders, and guides me out of the room.

There's a line of other actors in the hallway. Their gazes and stares unnerve me as we pass them by. Ben keeps me close, his steps confident like he knows where he's going.

Harriett, Gabby and Madison are waiting for me when we step outside. There's a crowd forming behind them, all huddled into groups. Police are already searching the grounds, their torches lighting up the night.

I run to my friends, tears gathering in my eyes at seeing them unharmed. Harriett is the first to reach me and squeezes me in a tight hug. I grimace in pain when she presses down on some bruises. "Are you okay?"

"They think it was Cyrus," I whisper, letting her hold me. I need a comforting touch right now.

Gabby brushes a tear away from my cheek. "So he knows who you are. He could have attacked any one of us, but he chose you."

"Where are Olivia and Hayden?"

Gabby presses the palm of her hands to her eyes for a moment. "The crazy bitch went looking for him."

I freeze. "What?"

"I know. Hayden found some baseball bats and they've gone *hunting*," Madison reveals.

"I'll fucking kill her," Max retorts, his cheeks turning red.

"Where's Aria?"

"I'm here," she states, and I pull back from Harriett.

She's holding a bandage up to her head. Blood stains one side of her face, and I struggle to catch my breath. I reach for her, pulling her in for a hug. "Oh my god, you're okay."

She hugs me back. "Are *you* okay?"

"I wasn't the one who was hurt," I retort.

"No, but from what these guys have told me, you still got hurt."

The bruises will heal. "I'm good. I'm more worried about you," I admit, running my finger along the cut above her eyebrow.

"The actor is worse off than me. The knife cut deep, so the paramedics have taken him to the hospital," she reveals. "I wanted to see if you were okay before I went too."

"Will he be okay?" I ask.

"Yeah. But he'll need a few stiches," she replies.

I hug her again, glad she's okay. "I'm so sorry this happened."

"Hey, it's not your fault," she assures me. "But next time, can we do something without the theatrics? I know I asked for a good time, but I didn't think it would be this."

Harriett laughs. "We can liven a place up, but I promise, it's not always like this."

Gabby tucks her hair back behind her ears. "Well, we've caused a brawl a time or two, but it was a total accident."

Aria whimpers, but then her eyes widen at something in the distance. "Oh my god."

I spin around to find Olivia holding up Hayden, who is limping and covered in blood.

"Please no," Max rasps, rushing over to his daughter. "Medics! We need a medic!"

"Dad, stop. I'm fine," she snaps, brushing his hands away. "It's just a sprain."

"You don't look fucking fine. Where are you hurt?"

She slaps his hand away when he goes to lift up her jacket. "Dad, stop it. It's not real blood. I fell in the waste bucket from the tunnels. I twisted my ankle going down."

"You nearly gave me a heart attack," he roars. "That's it. You're moving home and I am handcuffing you to my wrist. You can have a few hours when me and your mum need time alone."

"Oh my god, Dad, stop. What are you even doing here?"

"To protect you. Why else would I come to this place of torture?"

She smiles, tilting her head. "I knew I was your favourite."

"You won't be if you're dead. Liam will be."

"Dad," she snaps. "Don't make me hurt Liam."

"Then don't do stupid shit," he remarks. "I'm being serious, Hayden. I got chased by a fucking doll. A doll. This isn't shits and giggles for me. I take this shit seriously, and I'm going to be scarred for life."

"Dad, they aren't real."

"You don't know that," he yells, and a few policemen take a step towards him. He snorts. "Don't even try it. If you had a daughter like mine, you would be doing the same thing."

"Dad!"

"Arrest her," he demands. "At least then I'll know she'll be safe."

"Dad, you are being dramatic. I'm safe."

"You went after a killer. You are not safe. I warned you coming here would be dangerous. But did you listen? *No.* I could have lost my only daughter. Again."

Her expression softens, and she loses her fight. "I'm sorry. I didn't mean to worry you."

He pulls her in for a hug. "Don't keep doing this to me. I take one thing seriously in this world and that's my family. No one prepared me for moments like this. They tell you to enjoy it whilst you can, but it never really sinks in. One minute, I'm changing shitty nappies, and the next you are finishing school, and I could handle that. But then you left home. You nearly died. Your brother nearly died. And now this. Nothing prepares you for this."

"Dad, this isn't your fault," Hayden assures him.

He pulls back, glowering down at her. "I know it's not. This is your fault. You should have listened to me when I told you not to come here," he remarks.

Hayden rolls her eyes. "You raised me. If you didn't want me to—"

He holds his hand up, covering her mouth. "This isn't about you. It's about me."

Ben joins our group. "Thank you again for helping Emily," he tells Max.

Hayden's eyes narrow. "Oh, so you can get involved, but I can't."

"If it makes you feel any better, it was an accident. He was hiding from a doll," I reveal.

Hayden bursts out laughing, clutching her stomach. "Oh, this is great. Wait until I tell the others."

"If you tell anyone, I will tell your mother about this."

Her laughter dies. "You wouldn't!"

"Oh, trust me, I would," he snaps. "Now come on. Let's get your foot looked at."

"Dad," she whines when he swings her up in his arms.

"Madison, you are coming too."

"What about my car?" she asks.

"Give me the keys and I'll drive it back," Gabby announces.

"You don't have a licence," Olivia points out.

"Um, yeah I do."

"Since when?" Harriett asks.

"Since I was eighteen," Gabby answers.

Olivia's eyebrows rise. "Then why don't you drive a car?"

Gabby shrugs. "Because I like my clothes. Tax, MOT, and insurance are expensive."

Olivia shakes her head, bewildered. "You honestly baffle me."

"Emily? Emily?"

I spin around to the deep voice and see Cole pushing through the visitors. His gaze is frantic as he searches the crowd for me. He spots me, and for a small moment, he freezes, relief evident on his face.

I turn to Ben, narrowing my eyes. "You called him?"

"Yes, it's my job. The police are waiting for the chief superintendent to arrive. He's now active within the Night Stalker case and wants to have a word with you."

I nod as Cole reaches me. He pulls me into his arms, surprising me. It's the last thing I thought he would do.

I bask in the comfort, holding him close.

"Are you okay?"

"Just a few bruises," I announce, pulling him close. Then a thought occurs to me, and my breath catches. "Who has Poppy? Please tell me she's not here."

"Kit is at mine with her. She's okay. She's asleep." He pulls back, cupping my cheeks. "What happened? I got the alert, and then Ben texted me saying you had been attacked."

"We were in the house, and he appeared out of nowhere. He attacked Aria first," I explain.

His gaze goes to Aria. "Are you okay?"

"Yes, but I need to go and get this sorted at the hospital."

"Mum and Dad are on their way. We'll follow you to the hospital so I can get Emily checked over."

"I'm fine. It's just bruises. I promise," I tell him. "Aria got knocked unconscious."

"It happened so quickly, I didn't know what was happening. One minute I was running into a room, the next I was being shaken awake by one of the actors."

"There's more," I tell Cole. "They think it was Cyrus."

"And where the fuck were you?" Cole accuses, glaring at Ben.

"Doing his job," I remark. "There are tunnels under the house that he didn't want to be stuck in, so he went to the exit to wait for us."

Ben straightens, like he had prepared for this to happen. "I had just got into the security room when she pressed the button. The location signal was spotty, so once I checked the location on the camera, I went in to look for her. It was barely minutes before I got to her."

Cole doesn't look convinced. I squeeze his hands and wait for him to look down at me before speaking. "It was the staff running this place who stopped him from doing his job. He was so close to getting him. So close. And if they hadn't intervened, he would have. This would all be over."

"Fuck!" he hisses, tugging me close. "Where is he now?"

"He is in the wind. They're still searching the grounds, but I think they are wasting their time. The police got here pretty quick. The first guy who got attacked called it in, so they were already on their way before I realised what had happened."

"Has he killed anyone?" Cole asks, his fingers tensing around my arm.

"No. They were minor injuries," Ben replies.

Cole glances down at me, and I realise I'm still in his arms. "Did he say anything to you?"

"He said: you will be mine," I admit on a whisper.

Gabby snorts. "Like his girlfriend? Because the dude doesn't have a chance."

"Or does he mean you'll be his next kill?" Olivia asks.

"I shouldn't have let you come," Cole declares, pinching his nose. "I should have made you stay home."

"Don't kick yourself over this. It's not your fault."

"But it is. I let you come."

Gabby snorts again. "You say that like you could have stopped her. Even if she did listen to you, we would have come and got her."

"She's right," Harriett begins. "It wouldn't have even mattered if you were in a relationship. No one but Emily decides what she wants to do."

"That's not what I meant," he reveals.

"Really? Because you just acted like the decision was yours to make," Olivia retorts.

"Emily?"

"They're right. I wouldn't have listened. I'm not letting anyone control my life, including him."

"The chief superintendent is here," Ben announces.

I glance at the girls. "You don't have to wait with me if you don't want to."

They glance at Ben. "We'll wait with you until River is here. But if you want, you can come stay at mine with us. We're going to get the kids and stay at mine."

"Thank you, but I want to get back to Poppy."

"We understand," Gabby promises.

I take in a breath and follow Ben over to where a group of policemen are standing. I just want the night to be over so I can get home.

Poppy isn't safe until we're back home with her.

24

COLE

Ben places the keys down on the counter when we step inside. I cradle Emily closer. She fell asleep at the hospital and hasn't woken up once. She didn't even stir when I picked her up, or when I put her in the car.

I was happy to get to hold her without any awkwardness. I could have lost her tonight, despite Ben's protests over Cyrus being there to kill her. He believes he was there to take her with him.

I'm not happy with either option. Emily is mine. I don't want her getting hurt because I couldn't deal with my crap all those years ago. If I had, I would have known Cyrus was alive, and I could have argued his appeal. I didn't. Instead, I closed myself off. I only let the relief I felt in the wake of his death sink in. Fuck everything else.

I blamed him for everything that went wrong in my life. He is the reason I took so long to grow attachments. My family worked hard to get me to love them. And he is another reason I didn't want kids. My fear was having a child just like him. But Emily was right, my parents are to blame for that in a way. If they had protected me like they did him, he would have gotten the help sooner.

"I'm going to check the security feeds then get a few hours' sleep," Ben announces.

"Ben, before you go, I want to apologise. I shouldn't have said what I did to you earlier. I'm sorry."

"I take what I do seriously, Mr Connor. You don't need to apologise. I will do better next time."

"Please, call me Cole," I order.

"Is there anything you want me to do before I head downstairs?"

"Actually, there is. I'm thinking of taking the girls away for the week—out of Coldenshire. I don't think Emily has a passport to go abroad, so I was thinking of one of my other holiday homes. I have one on a private beach, and another on private land in the Woodlands. It's a bit out of the way, and it's secluded, but the area is tight with security since there are many celebrities who hire cabins there. Would you consider joining us? I know the security is good there, but I don't want to take any chances."

I won't tell him the real reason I want to go. He doesn't need to know until we get there. I just want to enjoy the week with my girls, in case it's my last.

"Yes. When are you thinking of going?"

"After what happened, I would like to go tomorrow. We can leave around midday."

"I would prefer to get the lay of the land before moving to another location," he admits.

"I have the folders on my desk downstairs. It has everything you might need, but can we make this happen? Emily has been through a lot recently and I think this is what she needs right now." I lower my voice. "I also want to go over something with you, and I can't do that here when it's like he's constantly watching and waiting."

He glances down at Emily when she lets out a soft snore. "I'll go get those looked at."

I nod and make my way into the living room. I lower Emily down on the sofa, before going to search for Kit. He's not in the kitchen or in the other living room, and I begin to grow panicked. He wouldn't have gone downstairs because it's locked. Only me, Ben, and Emily have a key.

If he left Poppy here alone, I will kill him.

I head upstairs, praying he just went to put his head down for a bit, but when I see Poppy's bedroom door open, I peek inside. Kit takes up the entire bed and has Poppy asleep on his chest.

I pull out my phone as I step further into the room. I snap the photo, and the flash wakes him up. He glances around the room, probably wondering where the fuck he is.

When he spots me, he drops back down, pinching his eyes. "What time is it?"

"Half three," I reply.

He gently untangles Poppy, who has a tight grip on his T-shirt, and gets up, careful not to disturb her. I wait until the door is closed behind him before talking. "When I asked you to watch Poppy, I didn't mean literally."

He glowers at me. "You said she wouldn't wake up. She did. And kept crying about a monster. Bro, I had to exaggerate looking for something that wasn't even there just to get her to stop crying."

"And that's how you ended up in bed with her?"

His lip curls when he draws back. "You make it sound like I'm *that* uncle. Every time I moved, she would start crying again. I meant to wait until she fell asleep to move, but I closed my eyes for a minute."

I give him a droll look. "I'm teasing."

We head downstairs and he grabs his keys and phone from the side table by the front door. "How are Emily and Aria? I left my phone down here, so I've not had any updates since you messaged to say you were on your way to the hospital."

"They're okay. Aria needed stitches, and Emily has a few bruises," I reply, keeping my voice down. I don't want to wake up Emily.

"Was it Cyrus?"

"Yeah."

"Fuck, man. What are you going to do?"

"I have a plan, but I'm going to take the girls away for the week before I decide to do anything."

"Let me know what you decide. I want to help."

"No. I'm not putting you in danger."

"I've been thinking about that. If he's hurting the people closest to you, why not us? We're your family. You heard Emily's friends. They essentially said he hates that you got chosen and not him."

Shit! I never even thought about it in that regard. I meet his gaze. "What is his end game?"

"I don't know, but we will figure it out," he assures me. "Where are you taking them?"

"I don't know. I just know I want to get them as far away from here as possible."

"What about work? Didn't you say she starts back up soon?"

"I'm going to see Dave tomorrow and let him know."

"All right. Let me know if there's anything I can do."

"Thank you for watching Poppy," I tell him, opening the door.

He steps outside, letting out a yawn. "You didn't give me a choice. Again. You just left me."

"Are you complaining about watching your niece?"

He grins. "No. She's a cute kid. But you left me with her like you thought I knew what I was doing. I don't. So when you see duct tape around her nappy, don't yell at me. I broke the straps, and I couldn't find another one."

"You mean you didn't know how to put it on."

He chuckles. "Not a fucking clue."

"Thank you for staying and watching her."

He glances over at the stairs, a wistful look in his eye. "I'm happy for you, brother. I was wrong about Emily. I was wrong about a lot of things, and I'm truly sorry for the way I treated her, and in turn, you."

"It's water under the bridge."

"See you later," he announces, heading off to his car.

I close the door behind him and lock it. Moving back to the living room, I pick Emily up. "Alexa, turn landing light on," I call as I head up the stairs. "Alexa, turn living room lights off."

I lay her down on the bed when I reach her room, and she immediately tucks herself up in ball. I walk around to the other side and flick the lamp on before heading back out to turn the landing light off. The silence through the house is unsettling. I usually have to sleep with a fan on or some sort of white noise. I'm not used to complete silence.

After checking in on Poppy, I head back into Emily's room and drop down next to her, resting my back against the pillows. I don't want to leave her or Poppy. When I got that call alert today, I never felt fear like it. I didn't know what I would be walking into or if she was okay. All Ben told me was that Emily had been attacked, and to get there. When I saw her huddled up to her friends, I felt like I could breathe again. She meant something to me that first night we met, but now, she is everything to me. Her and Poppy are my life now. Nothing can happen to them.

I don't know if the need to stay close is due to the events of tonight, but I feel like this is where I need to be. Going upstairs, a floor away from them, feels like I'm abandoning them.

Emily stirs, and I glance down. Her eyelids flicker open, and for a minute, she looks confused. She glances around the room, her eyebrows pinching together.

She clears her throat. "Um, we're back."

"You sleep like the dead."

"Not always," she mutters, rubbing sleep from her eyes. "Why are you in my bed?"

"I can't leave you. Not after tonight."

"I told you I'm fine," she declares. "I should go and check on Poppy."

"I've done that. And you aren't fine. I saw those bruises."

Her lashes lower for a moment. "Cole," she breathes.

"I hate that you went through that."

"It's not your fault," she promises. "God, I hope I get some sleep before work tomorrow."

"About that," I begin.

"If you tell me not to go to work, I may actually punch you in the balls."

I grimace, placing my hand over my dick. "Look, I get you might want to hurt me—"

"I'm feeling stabby," she remarks.

I wince because I can see she's serious about it. "I'm not doing it to be controlling. You asked me to consult with you before I did things. This is me talking to you, so please, hear me out."

221

"But you aren't saying anything that is making this conversation better."

"You care about the girls you work with, right?"

"Of course I do. We're family."

"Then I think you should stay away from Tease. I'm not saying you'll be to blame, but I think to keep the other girls safe, we should both stay away from there. At least for a while. They've already been through too much."

"When you put it like that, I guess you are right."

"I know, and I'm sorry it has to be this way."

"What am I going to do? I need to work."

"I know, which is why I'm going to still pay you a wage as if you were working. This isn't you asking for time off. This is me ordering it. We might not recover if we have to close the club again. I'd prefer to pay an extra wage than have it completely shut."

"No, I get it. It makes sense," she murmurs. "I guess we don't need that nanny now."

"We need her. I was going to see if you'd organise a charity event for me for our local foodbanks. They need food more than ever right now, and their resources are becoming low."

"I can do that."

"But there's one more thing," I comment.

"What? Did the police find him?"

"No, they haven't. I want to take you and Poppy away tomorrow. I have some holiday homes. They are mostly where I go when I want to get away from people, and Ben has agreed to travel with us. I think it will be good for all of us, and as a family."

"What? We can't go away. What about Cyrus?"

"He'll never be able to find out what houses I own. I'm going to talk to Dave in the morning and explain the situation, then I thought we could pack up and head out. I was going to plan it for next year, when the weather warmed up, but I think now is the right time. You need to feel safe. You've been through a lot over the past couple of months—more than anyone should—and I want to give this to you."

"Are you sure?"

"Yes."

"Okay. Will there be stuff for Poppy to do?"

"It's in the middle of nowhere, but I imagine between the two of us, we can find some things to do. There's a heated pool, hot tub, and I can have the groundskeeper go grab some outdoor playthings and get it set up for our arrival."

Her eyes go round. "How long are you planning on us staying there?"

"Only a week. We can come back Sunday."

"Sounds good."

"How are you feeling? Do you need any more painkillers?"

"No, I'm good," she assures me. "Did the police give you any more information?"

"They only said they searched the house once more and didn't find anything. And with so many walking through there, there was no point in searching for fingerprints."

"He had gloves on, so it would have been a waste of time," she reveals. "Why don't you go get some sleep? It's been a long night, and if you want to travel tomorrow, you'll need it."

"If it's okay with you, I'd rather stay in here. I promise, there's no hidden agenda. I just want to be close to you both."

"Cole, I don't think it's a good idea," she tells me, her tone hesitant.

"Please. I know I've asked for a lot recently, but I'm asking for one more thing."

"Okay. This once," she declares. "Don't mistake me for a push over though. I just know how to pick my battles."

"Noted," I muse. "I might be gone before you wake up. I want to catch Dave before the club closes."

"Is it wrong that I don't want to get changed?"

I glance down at her outfit, grinning. The hospital gave her some soft bottoms to wear. Her jeans, shoes, and coat got ruined, but the rest of her outfit remained intact.

"You're warm. That's all that matters."

She slides the blanket up the bed, throwing it over her shoulders. "Good night, Cole."

"Goodnight, Emily." She rolls over, and I shuffle down, getting comfy. "Cole?"

"Yes?"

"Thank you for being there tonight. It means a lot," she replies softly.

"I'll always be there for you," I promise.

When she doesn't say anything else, I close my eyes, letting the strain of tonight pull me into a deep slumber.

I pray like hell my brother doesn't get to Emily in my dreams.

25

EMILY

Hearing Poppy crying pulls me from my deep slumber. I don't want to move. My body aches all over, and I don't think there is a part of me that isn't hurting. It also feels like I've only gotten a few hours' sleep.

I pat the bed beside me and find Cole is no longer there. He stayed with me last night. I don't want to know what it meant—if it meant anything at all. But he did, and the gesture was sweet and comforting. I felt safe.

Poppy cries again, and I jump out of bed, nearly toppling out when my ankle gets twisted in the bedsheet. It wasn't her hungry cry or her tired cry. It was the cry she makes when she's scared.

And from the sound of it, she's terrified.

The door smacks against the wall when I barge inside, only to stumble to a stop when I see Cole has her in his arms. But she is flopped back, trying to get away from him.

Weird. She normally loves cuddling up to him in the morning.

Cole stares at me, and I become self-conscious under his scrutiny. I glance down at my shirt, seeing nothing out of place.

When Poppy doesn't stop crying, I step forward, holding my hands out for her. "Hey, I'll take her."

She clings to my neck as I take her, shoving her face into my shoulder. "Dada," she cries.

"You want Daddy?" I ask, but when I go to hand her back to him, she clings to my neck.

"No. No."

I glance at Cole, who is watching me. "Sorry. I don't know what's gotten into her," I admit. "I thought you were going into work to catch Dave before it closes this morning?"

He clears his throat. "Just going there now," he explains.

"Are you okay? You sound funny."

"Just a dry throat."

"Okay," I reply, watching him closely. "Are we still leaving later today?"

"Leaving?"

"You said we were going away."

"Um, yeah. Yeah," he replies, stepping back to give me some room. "I should go see Dave."

"Okay. I'll see you later."

He leaves without saying goodbye, and I lift Poppy up my chest, feeling unsettled from the strange encounter. It's not normally like him to be so distant.

Did I say or do something in my sleep?

Shaking it off, I pull back to look at Poppy. "You okay, bug?"

"Want Dada."

"You said no to going to daddy, baby."

"Poppy scared."

"Of what?"

"Monsters," she whispers.

"Alright. Will some hot milk make you feel better?"

She shoves her thumb into her mouth, nodding. "Yes."

"Come on then. Let's go make you a drink."

"Wet, Mummy."

Instead of heading for the door, I move over to the changing station and grab a clean nappy. I lie Poppy down on the floor and tug down her pyjama shorts. I'm struck by the sight I'm greeted with.

"What on earth?" I breathe, picking at the duct tape, but it's welded to her nappy.

"Kat," Poppy declares, giggling. I love her nickname for Kit. "Fixed it."

"Uncle Kit taped you up like a cardboard box?" I ask. She nods, giggling louder. I lift her up in my arms. "Well, Mummy needs some scissors to get that off. And Mummy will be speaking to Kit."

I head downstairs and bump into Ben in the hallway leading to the kitchen. "Woah, everyone is up early today."

"I heard Poppy."

I grimace, heading for the kitchen. "I'm sorry."

"No need to apologise. I was set to wake up in a few minutes anyway."

"Can you pass me the scissors? It seems Kit needed to DIY the nappy to my daughter."

"Um, sure," he replies, heading for the kitchen drawers whilst I head to the table. I pull out the portable changing mat from under the pushchair and lay it down over the table.

"What the hell happened?" Ben asks as he passes the scissors over.

"Kit happened," I remark as I snip at the tape.

After removing the nappy and putting a new one on, I place Poppy down on the ground. "Do you want to stay in here with mummy whilst I make you a drink and some breakfast?"

"Yes," Poppy declares, and grabs her toys from the basket in the corner and begins to occupy herself.

"Do you want a drink?" I ask Ben.

"I'd love a coffee, but I can get it. You had a long night, and you must be sore."

I bring two mugs and a sippy cup down. "I've got it. It hurt when I woke up, but it feels better now I've moved around."

He takes a seat on the stool. "You are handling it better than I thought you would. I put your reaction down to shock last night, but you still seem okay."

I flip the hot chocolate machine and kettle on before turning to him. "You met my family, right?"

He tilts his head to the side, his eyebrows furrowed. "Yes."

"They prepared me for a lot. Not because they cared, but because they did shit so often, I had no other choice but to remain calm."

"Okay, but last night was a little different to being left in a car park," he remarks.

"How did you know I was left in a car park?" I demand.

Did he do a background check on me?

"You were left in a carpark? Jesus Christ, I meant metaphorically."

My shoulders slump. "Oh."

"Still, it's a lot different to that kind of trauma."

"What I'm saying is, I've dealt with a lot of stuff. Abusive and neglectful parents. I've been abandoned by them. I've been bullied. I had to care for my sick grandma. I lost Poppy's twin before she was even born, and I gave birth alone. I raised Poppy alone whilst caring for my grandma. I've been through a lot. This is just a blip."

He scoffs. "It's not a blip."

"Okay," I murmur, and try for a different tactic. "Have you ever been behind the wheel whilst being chased by a homicidal maniac?"

"Does chasing a homicidal maniac count?"

My eyes go round at the news, and I want to know more. Just not right now. "No. Trust me, it's completely different when it's them chasing you. I ended up crashing my car. It was not fun for any of us. Me and my friends have dealt with a lot, but we don't let it bring us down. If we did, we wouldn't be able to get up each morning. We've gone through bad break ups, shitty parenting, became single parents, and got through it. We've gotten into a pickle more times than I care to count. And don't get me started on the night we went looking for Gabby and ran into Cyrus. I've got this. I'm good."

"When you put it like that, how can I argue?"

I wave him off as I finish making our drinks. "The point is, I deal with things differently to most. Give it a few days and I'll probably be rocking in the corner."

"I'm sorry you were even in that position to begin with. It's my job to prevent you from being attacked."

I pass him his coffee and add some extra milk in Poppy's hot chocolate. "Poppy, baby, come get your drink."

She runs over and I hand it over to her. "Thank you."

"You're welcome," I reply, before turning to Ben. "It's not your fault. There are so many possible scenarios that could have played out last night and none of them were good in my mind. I kept thinking, if you had been with me, he might have attacked you before you saw it coming. I would have had no one to help me."

"You had Max Carter."

I arch an eyebrow. "The guy was running from an actress dressed as a doll."

"I wouldn't dismiss his capability. I've heard rumours about Max Carter, and he is not someone you mess with."

"Max? Really? No offence, but I don't think he knows how to tie his shoelaces."

"You have met his daughter, right?"

"Duh. Hayden is a rock star."

"Where do you think she gets it from? She's as looney as her dad."

"I wouldn't go that far."

"She single-handedly took down a ring of criminals for fun. I'm pretty sure she killed all of them."

"It was an accident."

"The Carters don't make mistakes," he points out.

"Whatever. The point is, I'm glad you weren't there when he first attacked. It was comforting to know you would come for me."

He clears his throat, glancing away. "Did Cole talk about the plans for today?"

"That we're going away?"

"Yes."

"He mentioned it last night. Are you sure this is a good idea right now? We don't want to be stuck in the middle of nowhere if Cyrus decides to strike."

Ben checks to see if Poppy is distracted before leaning in. "I don't like making assumptions in my line of work, but sometimes there are situations that call for it."

"And you think this is one of them?"

"I do."

"What is it?"

"I watched the footage last night. I watched the entire park's footage. He didn't follow you there, Emily. He knew where you were going and got there just before we arrived."

My blood runs cold. "What? How? Is he listening to us?" I search the kitchen like some hidden camera will pop out.

"I need you to think clearly. Where exactly did you talk about the event last night?"

"At Harriett's when we booked the tickets, but it would be hard for him to bug River's home. I'm pretty sure he checks for that sort of stuff regularly."

"Anywhere else?"

"Here."

"Already checked this place. It's clean."

I close my eyes for a moment, before meeting his gaze. "Wait, I mentioned it at Cole's parents' home. I invited Aria whilst I was there and sent over the details."

"Okay, but I swear I heard them saying the Connors have good security."

I nearly spill my tea when I lift up my arm. "Woah, woah, wait. When we were there, Kit mentioned about Liam installing a new security system because they kept having problems. Could it be their home that is bugged?"

He pulls out his phone. "I'll call Cole to get in touch with them."

"Hold up. Am I right?"

He stops, walking back to the counter. "I've had my suspicions about what is going on. They started the night I first got here and you made the comment about him not stalking you."

"Yeah, it's Cole he's stalking."

"What if it's not Cole?"

"I'm sorry, but I'm really lost. You need to explain."

"His anger is aimed at Cole. All of it. He's killing because of it."

"Yeah, he's killing the people who mean the most to him."

"Then why not start with the family who adopted Cole? If he wanted to hurt Cole, it would be to take those who are closest to him.

It would be his parents, his siblings, hell, even the bloke he grew up with and co runs Tease with."

Jesus. He's been here a week and already seems to know everything.

"He believes Cole took the woman he loved away from him. She died during an altercation that sent Cyrus to prison. He could be waiting until he has the woman first."

"I know. I've read the reports, which is why my mind went there first."

"So why don't you think it now?"

"Because he could have finished Aria off last night. He could have killed her. But he didn't."

"Maybe because he wanted me first."

"No. Which brings me back to the stalking thing. Everyone—including me—has jumped to conclusions by thinking it's Cole he's stalking."

"And you don't think it is?"

"No. I think it's his parents. I think its them who Cyrus is stalking. They're his end game. Not Cole."

"But why?"

"Because he has the one thing Cyrus doesn't have," he reveals.

I gulp. "What?"

"Love."

Poppy comes running over, smacking into my legs. I bend down, picking her up. "What are you going to do?"

"Call Cole and get someone at his parents' house to confirm if their home has been bugged."

"Then go. Go call him."

"I will be downstairs watching the cameras. Make sure you get those bags packed. The sooner we leave, the better."

"You think it's a good idea to leave in the middle of all this?"

"Now is the best time to leave. Once it's confirmed, I can get in touch with the police. We have been so busy watching Cole's back, and the places he visits, that no one has been watching his parents."

My heart stops. His parents have become family to me, and I don't want them in danger. "You think he'll hurt them."

"No, but to catch him, the police need to be watching them."

"I'll feed Poppy, then we'll go upstairs and start getting ready to leave."

"Call me if you need me."

I watch Ben's retreating form for a moment longer. If he's right about this, it changes everything.

We've been thinking this is all about revenge over a woman, but it's more deeply rooted than that. And with Cyrus' mental stability already being questioned, there is no telling what he will do next.

I've been fine up until now about the attack last night, because I came out unscathed. But now Ben has put those thoughts into my mind, I feel unsteady on my legs.

If Cyrus didn't plan to kill me last night, then what the hell did he have planned?

26

COLE

The decking is the only area lit up at the holiday home. Darkness swallows up the forest, and I can't wait to show Emily and Poppy how beautiful it looks during the day. They didn't get to see much when we arrived because Poppy wasn't feeling the best. By the time we got settled in, she had woken up from her nap and wanted dinner.

Emily is upstairs giving her a bath, whilst I nurse my glass of whiskey out on the deck, under the outdoor heater. Tomorrow evening, I will take the girls down to the fire pit. I'm hoping Emily will let Poppy have some s'mores as a treat.

Ben steps out through the French doors, taking a seat to my left. "I have spoken to Evan. He has sent a man to Mr and Mrs Connor's home."

I take a swig of my drink before replying. "So it's true?"

"Yes. He somehow managed to take over the feed instead of hacking it, which is why it wasn't flagged. Those glitches were to jump onto the feed without being caught."

"Liam is meant to be the best," I remark.

"He is the best. But he also told your dad to upgrade years ago."

"What?"

"Believe me, your dad is kicking himself over it."

I scrub a hand over my jaw. "Yeah, because he's a firm believer of 'if it's not broken, don't fix it.'"

"Liam will be there in the morning to update the system. He's already cut the feeds completely," he announces, sitting forward. "I might not have known you long, but I'm good at reading people. I know you have something planned, and whatever it is, I think it's a bad idea."

I meet his gaze. "He's coming after my family. He's killing people."

"Your parents are safe."

"I'm not talking about them. I know they'll be safe. I'm taking about Emily and Poppy. I only just got them in my life."

"Now the police know where to look, it's only going to be a matter of time before they find him, Cole. Don't do something you can't take back. He's dangerous."

"I know that. You think I don't know that? He's killing people. Because of me. And I'll be damned if I sit around and do nothing whilst he plans to hurt my family. No."

"What is your plan?" he demands.

"I have a friend who works at the radio station. He's going to let me go on air and talk about the killer."

"I thought the police said to not leak the information."

"I don't care. If I thought they were doing their job, I would leave it for them to deal with. But they aren't. They've got civilians doing their job."

He tilts his head, giving me a short nod. "And you think he has a radio?"

"How else is he being updated? He can't have a television because they think he was living in that cave."

He drops his elbows to his knees, leaning forward. "And what do you plan to do when you get on air?"

"Talk about it. Then piss him off enough that he comes to me."

"How will that keep Emily and Poppy safe?"

"I arranged with Dave to close Tease next Friday. I'm going to mention that multiple times through the interview and make it clear

I'll be alone in there. I'm hoping he comes for me. I want this done."

"He will kill you. If you antagonise him, he will kill you. I'm sure of it."

I lower my gaze. "Either way, this needs to end, and if that means me dying, I will do."

"Mr Cole, you have a family."

"Who were doing perfectly well without me before. I don't plan to go in there to die. I will fight until my last my breath. But it's a risk I'm willing to take. I cannot go on knowing I'm the reason so many families are grieving right now. Their lives have been changed indefinitely, and they will never move on from this. If detaining the man responsible for their loss eases their grief just a little, I will do it. It's not just for them. It's for the women who work at Tease too. I've only just begun to feel what they've been going through. Every day they go into work, they're scared they'll be next. I can make sure they aren't. I can make sure the mother of my child isn't next. I have to do this."

"Emily isn't going to like this."

"She doesn't need to know."

He sits up. "You aren't going to tell her that the main reason you've brought her away is so you can enjoy what might be your last week with them?"

"No. Because she'll try to talk me out of it, and I'm worried I'll let her. I'm doing this for her and our daughter."

"I think you should tell her. She deserves to know what is going on."

"No, and if you tell her, we'll have problems."

"This is risky, Cole. All of it. And I'm worried it's going to come back and bite you in the arse."

"It's my risk to take," I remark. "You won't talk me out of it, so stop trying to."

"Then let me help. I can see if there's a place close by where I can watch the feeds. I know a policeman who will be willing to be on standby too. If you are dead set on doing this, then we need to do it properly. And I'll have someone go through a script with you. You don't want him to cotton on to your plan."

I hear something clang against the counter inside. "Not another word about it," I whisper. "We can talk more on Friday."

"I'm going to take a walk around the area then go back to my room to watch the feeds."

"What feeds?" Emily asks, taking a seat next to me.

"The house feeds."

She tucks her legs up. "You think he will go there? He doesn't know we've gone away."

"I don't know, but it would be stupid of me not to keep an eye on them," Ben announces. "See you tomorrow."

He leaves and I turn to Emily. No matter how much I look at her, or what she wears, her beauty takes my breath away. "Did Poppy go to sleep okay?"

"Yes. She is loving the big bed," she admits. "You didn't need to put the mattress on the floor though. I brought the bed guard.

"She's been sleeping like it for a while now. I didn't want to risk her toppling out in the middle of the night."

"Do you have any news about your parents' home?"

I let out a weary breath. "Yeah. Evan has someone guarding them and Liam has shut down their feeds until he can replace it tomorrow."

"Oh God. I need to call your parents. See if they're okay."

I smile at her kindness. "You can do that tomorrow. It's late."

"Jesus, this is such a mess."

I kick my feet up on the table. "Tell me a memory that makes you smile."

"What?"

"Tell me. I want to get to know you better. I feel like I only have an outline of your life, and not much information."

She grabs a blanket from the end of the sofa chair she's sitting on, getting comfy. "A memory that makes me smile," she muses. "I think it would be the day I brought Poppy home from the hospital when she was born. The nurses had warned me her presence might unsettle my nan. It didn't. My nan cried when she saw her. She kept calling her Emily. She told me, Emily will be the prettiest girl in the world, and she couldn't wait to see her grow."

"I read that children or pets help patients with Alzheimer's. I'm glad you have that memory."

She lowers her gaze. "What about you? Do you have a memory that makes you smile?"

I grin because I have a few. "When I first met Dave, he was angry at everything. The first thing he told me was that he would never be my friend."

Emily beams. "Now you can't get rid of him."

"No. I can't. We would sneak downstairs in the night to get a snack. He would be the one to unlock the child lock whilst I gave him a leg up. We had to wait until everyone was asleep."

"They didn't give you treats in the day?"

"They did. But Cyrus would take them when they weren't looking."

"What about when you moved in with your parents? Is that your favourite memory of them?"

"All of it. I didn't show it to begin with because I was trying hard not to grow attached to them. I was scared they were going to be taken away from me like everyone else had. But every time they would read me a story, every time they asked me what I wanted for dinner, or asked if there was a game I wanted, is a good a memory to me. But I guess if I had to pick one, it would be the day they brought Aria home. She was only a baby. And they didn't favour her or pay her more attention. It was equal between the three of us. Kit was scared of her."

"Speaking of Kit, can you tell him not to wrap my daughter up like a broken parcel next time he changes her nappy."

I burst out laughing. "Fuck! I forgot about that. He mentioned it last night before he left."

"How did you not feel it on her?"

"In all fairness, I had other things on my mind," I reply.

She leans her head back against the cushion, letting out a breath. "You were right about coming away. I don't know what it is, but I feel less tense being here."

"Then my work here is done," I announce, unable to look away.

The intensity of her gaze has my breath catching. "I might kick myself later for admitting this, but thank you for everything you have done. I don't just mean last night. I didn't want to admit it to myself, but I was struggling. I work hard to give Poppy everything she needs, and I didn't realise how much pressure I was putting on myself to do it. Then you came in. You took that pressure and helped carry it. I'm so lucky she has you."

"Even if my brother tried to kill you?"

"You aren't your brother," she declares softly. "None of what is going on is your fault."

"I don't want to talk about him. Tell me what the birth was like?"

She laughs. "You might want to go back to talking about your brother."

I roll my eyes. "Tell me."

"Let's just say, I get why people say it's worth it in the end. I begged the midwife to just take her out. I pleaded with them to stop the contractions. Then I gave birth and any fear I had about raising her went away. I looked down at her beautiful scrunched up little face, and everything was right in the world. Nothing else mattered but her."

"I wish I could have been there."

"Me too," she replies softly.

"I'm here now. That's all that matters," I assure her. "I know things didn't start out the best, but I'm really happy about where we are now."

I know there's a story behind her smile. It's in her eyes, in the way she gazes at me. She liked hearing I'm happy.

And I want to make sure she is too.

"I'm happy too," she admits, unable to look away. When she eventually does, the spell is broken and she sits up. "I'd best go to bed. I bet you're tired too."

I am. But there's something I want to do first. "I'm going to finish my drink and then I'll go up."

She walks over, placing her hand on my shoulder, and I feel her touch all over. "Don't wait too long to go up. I know you want to fix what happened, and you're blaming yourself, but what is going on isn't your fault. None of it is."

"How long have you known me again?"

Her laughter is soft. "Feels like forever."

I place my hand over hers. "I promise to go up soon. I want to send a couple of emails so I can focus on you two for the rest of the week."

She lets out a soft puff of air. "Goodnight, Cole."

"Goodnight, Emily."

As soon as the French door closes, I pull out my phone, emailing Gia with a request. I might not be able to make up for the shit I said when I first went to Emily's, but I can try.

And I can start with the one thing I know will mean the most to her.

Then, I will get my brother out of our lives for good.

27

EMILY

After dishing up the last of the breakfast, I head to the French doors. Cole is out there with Poppy, showing her the beautiful landscape that surrounds us.

I hear her giggling when I push open the door. He's chasing her around the fire pit, two sticks in his hands. I bask in her joy and happiness. She loves her father, so much so she always wants to be around him.

And Cole... For a man who never wanted kids and didn't know what he was doing, he has perfected it quickly. The way he is with her warms my heart. This is all I ever wanted and was afraid would never happen. It was one thing telling your daughter that her dad doesn't know he has a daughter, but another telling her he wanted no part in her life. It had been my worst fear for so long, it became true in my mind.

Now, we're on a family holiday together, and he couldn't be more in love with his daughter.

Our daughter.

And I hate that I need to break it apart.

"Breakfast is ready."

Poppy stumbles to a stop, and her laughter grows louder. "Mama, bear."

"Is Daddy pretending to be a bear?"

"Yes," she replies, squealing when Cole lifts her up in his arms. "Dada."

"Come on, Mummy has made us breakfast."

"Yay!" she squeals.

I head back inside and move over to the kitchen side to grab the plates. The home is beautiful. It's a two-storey lodge that gives off such a homey vibe. I'm sure it is beautiful in the summer, but this place was born for colder nights and pit fires. The downstairs is mostly an open plan with beams separating each room. The living room has a deep-back sofa, with a humongous stone log fireplace. There's a fifty-two-inch television hanging in the corner of the room, and all the décor matches the fireplace.

The kitchen is more modernised with a dark marble countertop and dark oak cupboards.

The dark oak dining room table sits up to eight people and has three lights hanging down that are attached to a black metal frame. The corners of the metal frame have vines hanging down.

The entire house gives off that warm vibe. It's a home where you want to curl up with a book, with the fire crackling, and the rain splattering against the window.

I place the plates down on the table before going back for the rest.

Cole walks in with Poppy on his hip. "That smells amazing."

"Are you sure Ben doesn't want any?"

"He went for a run whilst scouring the area again."

"But maybe I can make him something to warm up when he's back," I offer as I place a jug of orange juice on the table.

He removes Poppy's coat. "He has a smoothie. He'll be fine."

"If you say so," I mutter.

"Mine?" Poppy asks.

I smile as I push the plate closer to her. "Yes, this is yours."

"I thought we could spend the day at a local farm. It's a twenty-minute drive. You get to pet the animals too."

"Animals?" Poppy asks.

"You want to go see the animals?" I ask Poppy.

"Yes!"

I laugh at her enthusiasm and meet Cole's gaze. "I guess that means we're going to the farm."

"I've heard they are good for toddlers."

"You've never been before?"

"I've been to a zoo. Does that count?"

I tilt my head. "Maybe?"

"You don't know?"

"Not really. I never went as a kid, and the one time we went to a safari park we didn't get past the camels before Gabby freaked out."

"What did she do?"

"One of them stuck its head in the car. Gabby freaked out and got out of the car, screaming it was trying to eat her. Then proceeded to be chased by four camels," I reveal, and he bursts out laughing. "We had to be guided out of the park and were told we were banned. Luckily, it was in the car I totalled after being chased by a homicidal maniac."

"Wait, what?"

"The car chase I told you about when Charlotte had her thing going on. We got into an accident, which means the park had that number plate and not the new one."

"Ah, well, she's not here this time, so you'll be fine."

"I'm just glad she didn't do it whilst we were in the lion part."

"Roar!" Poppy growls.

"You are such a clever girl," I cheer.

Cole smiles, running his hand over the back of her hair. "Do you know what sound a cow makes?"

"Moooo."

Cole chuckles. "Yep, your mum is right. You are such a clever girl."

"What time did you want to leave?" I ask.

"I thought we could leave after we're ready and make a day of it."

"I'll make up a packed lunch for us," I offer.

"No need. I went ahead and ordered a picnic basket from their café. It will be ready for us to pick it up around one."

I nod, trying not to show how giddy I am over spending the day together as a family. Our new routine has been hectic and tense at times. It will be nice not to worry over what awaits us at home. And finally enjoy a day together without a dark cloud hanging over our heads.

Clutching my side, I drop down on the picnic blanket, unable to contain my laughter. I wish Ben had been here to witness what I did, because it had been hilariously funny.

I grab the tea towel one of the members of staff gave me and hand it over to Cole.

He glowers at me as he drops down onto the blanket. "It's not funny."

Covered in muck and probably manure, he is a sight to see. We went to walk through the barn to take a look around whilst Poppy slept hugging a bunny. She didn't want to let the animal go, and the bunny seemed content with being with her. But the baby lambs wanted Poppy too. One pinched her favourite Troll toy, and Cole, being a knight in shining armour, wanted to get it back before it was destroyed. But mamma sheep didn't like that this tall, strong, man was messing with her lamb, and decided to chase him through the barn. He had just got outside when one of the alpacas came out of nowhere, knocking him to the ground. Mud and manure covered his entire front, and I'm pretty sure some got into his mouth.

Whilst he picked up his dignity off the ground, I collected the picnic basket and some towels from the staff and decided to eat in the field away from the other guests.

"It's pretty funny," I remark. "I thought Gabby was bad. But you screeched so loudly."

"Because it bit my bloody arse. I'm pretty sure I have bruises."

"You don't have bruises," I scold, unable to keep a straight face.

"Laugh it up. This coat cost me six-hundred quid."

"I'll get it out when we get home. Poppy loves getting dirty, so I've mastered the art of removing stains."

He rubs at his face hard. "I feel like I've ruined the day."

"Are you kidding? I've gotten over a dozen photos. This day will be memorable for the rest of our lives."

He stops trying to get the dirt off to grin at me. "You see us being like this forever?"

My heart races at his words. "We have a daughter. She will be ours for the rest of our lives, so yes."

He continues to scrub at the dirt. "I can't believe you took a photo whilst I was in distress."

"Believe it," I tease.

"Don't go showing any of the women at work," he warns.

"Why? It will be good for them to see you in a different light."

"I don't want them to see me in a different light."

I roll my eyes. "You intimidate them."

"Good."

I splutter out a laugh. "How is that good?"

"They won't think of asking for time off when they're hungover or want to go out."

"Dave deals with all of that though."

"Yes, but when they ask, and they don't take no for an answer, he will sigh and say: I'll have to bring Cole in and you can speak to him."

I drop the paper plates to the blanket, laughing. "Oh my god, is that why he drops your name?"

"Yes. We've been doing this a long time. They have to see one of us being reasonable, and one of us who doesn't take shit. Otherwise, they think they can get away with everything."

"Here, you missed a bit."

I crawl over the blanket, taking the towel from him. He tenses as I bring it up to his cheek, wiping away the remaining dirt he didn't clean off.

I meet his gaze, unable to look away. There is something pulling me to him, and I can feel my heart racing. He places his hand over mine, and my breath hitches.

"Did you get it?" he asks as he takes the towel.

I clear my throat and pull back. "Yes. All gone. Although you should get the anti-bacterial wipes from under the pushchair and clean your hands."

For a moment, he doesn't move, the towel still in his hand. When the spell is broken, he reaches under the pushchair, grabbing the pack of wipes. "Thank you."

"You're welcome."

"Should we wake Poppy up?" he asks, wiping the mud off his hands.

"Give her a few more minutes."

"I guess. She has tired herself out."

Although the weather is cold, and there have been a few showers of rain, it didn't take away the beauty from the scenery or the day. "I bet this place is beautiful in the summer. I can imagine this field being covered in brightly-coloured flowers."

"We can come back next year. Poppy will be old enough to go on a donkey ride then too."

"I can't wait to show her around the dinosaur trail."

"You mean you can't wait to see it," he teases.

I chuckle, grabbing his sandwich and passing it to him. "What can I say, I loved *Jurassic Park* as a kid."

He arches a brow. "As a kid?"

I laugh at his teasing. "Okay, I still love it," I admit. "What about you? What is your favourite movie?"

"I don't think I have one."

I rear back. "You don't have one?"

"Don't look so disgusted by it. I'm a busy man. I don't have time to really watch them."

"There's got to be something you enjoy watching." When he pauses, recognition flashes across his expression. "You just thought of something. I know you did."

"You promise not to judge or make fun of me?"

"Swear it."

"*The Great British Bake Off.*"

"No," I breathe. "Really?"

"You promised not to judge."

I hold my hands up, grinning widely. "No judgement. I thought for a minute you were going to say a teen drama like *The Vampire Diaries* or *Teen Wolf*."

His nose scrunches up. "I don't know what any of those things are."

I arch an eyebrow. "Really? Two of the most popular series in the entire world and you don't know what they are."

He peels off a grape, shrugging. "Like I said, I work a lot."

I tilt my head to the side, watching him. He seems embarrassed by his words. There is nothing wrong with working, but no one should make it their whole life.

"Maybe we should dedicate Sundays to family time. We could do day trips out or stay in," I offer, but he looks sad by my declaration. "Or even do it once a month. It's up to you."

He hands me a bottle of water from the basket. "I like the sound of it. You could introduce me to your favourite movies."

I rub my hands together with glee, hoping to lighten the mood. I don't know what has made him so sad. I just know I don't like seeing it.

"Be careful what you wish for. There will be no stopping me once I get going. And you'll find yourself watching romantic comedies. They are either cringy, which makes them funny, or they're actually good, and you'll die laughing."

"I'll bring the popcorn," he remarks.

I poke his arm. "Don't sound too excited. I might think you enjoy my company."

He meets my gaze, dropping his smirk. "I enjoy every moment I spend with you. You are a breath of fresh air, Emily."

Poppy breaks the spell. "Bunny!"

I go to reach for her, but Cole gets there first, and our hands collide. I inhale sharply, tingles shooting up my arm. "I've got her," he rasps.

I glance up to meet his gaze, and my stomach flutters. "I'll get her food ready."

As he gets her out of the pushchair, explaining softly that the bunny went back to be with his mama, I get her lunch together, ignoring the shake in my hands.

One look.

A touch.

And my mind is turned to mush.

28

COLE

Rain pelts down against the lodge's roof and windows, the sound so loud, it's almost soothing.

The weather cut our day short, but it didn't ruin our day. We picked up a few indoor games for Poppy to play, then had dinner and watched her favourite movie—*Trolls*.

I tuck the sheet up to Poppy's chin and reach down, kissing her forehead. The day has knackered her out. She was asleep before I got her out of the bath.

I stare down at my daughter, wondering when and how I got so lucky. She is the brightest star, a shining light, and everything that is good in this world. In the short amount of time I have had her, she has shown me what it truly means to live. She disrupted my life, just like her mother, and did it in the best possible way. I still believe you don't need a partner or children to feel complete, but they do complete me. From glitter pens to playdoh, and the chaos every morning, they complete me. They have filled a void I didn't know existed. And if Emily and I never slept together, I would not have known what it feels like to love someone this much. I would have missed out. They are the best thing that has ever happened to me.

Getting up, I head over to the door, closing the stairgate I picked up from home. The stairs to the lodge are made of wood and have gaps between each step. If Poppy gets out before Emily goes up to bed, I'm afraid she might fall through them. I'm glad we bought spares because it has come in handy this week.

Ben's door down the hall opens, and I glance down to see him stick his head around the frame. "Will you be okay for the night alone? Evan has asked me to go over your parents' footage. Liam managed to download nine months' worth of footage and encrypt it. Any time lapses have been restored. It's not the best, but he wants it gone through before I'm back."

"No. Go ahead. Anyone can walk onto this property, but they can't go unnoticed. We'll be informed, and the police will be called. And it would take a week to hack the feeds. By then, we'll be back at home. We're safe here. So do what you need to do."

"Just text me if something happens. I'll keep the headphones on so I don't accidently wake up Poppy."

"Thank you."

He heads back inside his room, so I take the stairs one at a time.

Emily is curled up on the sofa, watching the crackling fire.

"I'm sorry we couldn't make s'mores."

She sits up, taking the blanket with her. "Are you kidding? This is awesome. The rain pelting down, the fire crackling, this is a mood."

"A mood?" I tease as I walk over to the bar and pour myself a whiskey.

"Yes. A mood. We should come back here at Christmas," she announces. "Wait, we should all come down for Christmas. Your family, my friends, their kids and partners. It would be beautiful if it snows."

My hands shake as a lump forms in the back of my throat. "It sounds like fun."

"Well, your tone says something different," she comments. "It's okay if you don't think we'll be together at Christmas. I don't mean together, together. I mean as a family."

I meet her gaze. "When will you stop doubting me? I want this. I want us. If I didn't, I would tell you."

"You just seemed a little lost just then. Like you were wondering how to let me down."

"No, I was wondering what you wanted to drink."

She holds up a glass of rosé. "Oh, I've got a glass. The bottle is on ice in the bucket."

I glance over to the table, and sure enough, she has a bottle open, half of it already gone. "Plan on getting wasted, Miss Hart?"

"It was the mood."

"We're back to the mood?" I tease, walking back over to take a seat next to her. She lifts her legs up, dropping them into my lap. I place my hand over her ankle, enjoying her ease.

"Yes. The mood. This lodge is beautiful, Cole. You are really lucky to have all of this."

"You have it now too."

"No, I don't. This is yours. You act like we're married."

"We have a child together. So it's yours too. And Poppy's."

She tucks her legs up to her chest. "Did you ever take money from your parents before you started out?"

"You already know I didn't," I reply.

"And when you made your first profit, how did it feel?"

I exhale wistfully because nothing could beat the rush I got. "It felt exhilarating. The moment it happened, I didn't wait to start something new. I worked hard until I succeeded at that too. I had all this drive and passion to do more, which is when I built shops to offer affordable food sources."

"I'll get back to that after because I didn't know you had shops," she announces. "But that feeling, the accomplishment you felt, was because you knew you got there all by yourself. When I get this, I want to earn it. I want to know I worked my arse off."

She is such a stubborn woman. "Do you ever plan to get married?"

She freezes with the glass to her lips. "Weird question."

I pinch her toe lightly. "Answer me."

"Leave my toes alone," she warns.

"Yes, Miss."

"I guess one day. Why?"

"Do you plan to be an equal partner?"

"Isn't that what marriage is about?"

"Exactly. Equals. And for it to work, you have to share your lows and your highs. What's yours is his, and what's his is yours. Equals."

Her eyelids flutter, a small smile falling across her lips. "I never thought I'd hear you say something like that."

"Well, you've changed me. You've both changed me," I admit. "In the best way."

"I'm glad. I was worried we'd disrupt your life."

"Oh, you did, but I wouldn't change it for the world."

She nudges me with her toe. "Hey, you wanted us with you."

"Yeah, I did."

She drops her head down on the sofa. "God, the sound of the rain is beautiful."

So is she.

"Well, I have a surprise for you," I announce, and grab the remote off the coffee table and press the button. The white screen attached to the beam rolls down, and I click the projector on. "I've bought all of the Jurassic Parks for us to watch."

"You didn't?" she breathes.

"Oh, I did."

She throws the blanket off her legs. "I'm grabbing the popcorn." I laugh, watching her race to the kitchen. "Do you want sweets too?"

"I'm good," I call back. "Quick, I'm pressing play."

"Wait, wait, wait," she cries, and her panic causes me to laugh.

She enjoys the smallest things in life. It reminds me of our first encounter at her house. She told me she has what she needs, and she was right. I was a fool to put her down the way I did. Emily isn't the type of person who wants things, because she doesn't need more. She likes having what she has, and everything else in between is a bonus for her. Watching a dinosaur movie and listening to the rain in front of a log fire is enough for her.

And my god, I want her.

I want her so goddamn much, I think I'm in love with her.

Her outlook on life is inspiring. But her strength… my God, the strength she has inside of her is so strong. She used it to get through her childhood, she gained some along the way, and the way she stands —so tall and confident—will give her more strength going forward. It will get her through what needs to be done. What I need to do. Because I am doing this for her. She has fought her entire life to survive. She survived her childhood, her grandparent, and the loss of her baby. She got through raising a child alone, and the death of her grandmother. She got through so much, and this is something she doesn't need to go through. I can do it for the both of us.

She drops down beside me, placing the bowl of popcorn on my lap. I arch an eyebrow at the bowl overflowing with popcorn and M&M's. "You do realise I don't eat popcorn or chocolate?"

She snorts, her button nose scrunching up. "You say that now, but five minutes into the movie your hand will reach into the bowl, and ten minutes after that, it will all be gone."

"How do you know that?"

"Because it's exactly what you did when you walked into the living room and I was watching that murder documentary."

"I wasn't watching it," I defend.

"Dude, after five minutes of standing, you sat down next to me. Another five minutes later, your hand was in the popcorn bowl."

I laugh 'cause she isn't lying. I came up from my office to find her curled up on the sofa watching some true crime documentary. I was meant to get a drink and leave, but I found myself sitting down next to her and watching the rest of the season. I don't think we got to bed until at least three in the morning.

"Okay, you have me there."

She shuffles on the sofa until she can meet my gaze. "Thank you for arranging all of this. I thought coming here was going overboard, but now I see why you brought us here. I've not seen this side to you before now."

"What side?"

Her lips pull into a soft smile. "Relaxed."

I reach over, tucking a piece of wayward hair behind her ear. "How can I not be? I'm with you guys. And there is no one else I'd rather be with."

A puff of air slips through her parted lips, her eyelids closing. "Please don't say things like that to me."

"Why?" I ask, twirling a piece of her hair around my finger.

"Because I'll think you mean it."

"I do."

"But not in the way I'm interpreting it."

"And how is that?"

She meets my gaze, and for a split second, she looks like she wants to escape. From this. From what it means. "That you're the man I fell in love with after a one-night stand," she whispers.

Her words prompt me forward. I cup her jaw, tilting her head back, and kiss her. It's as good as it was the first time I kissed her. But unlike then, there is no hesitation. It's just me and her. And everything feels right.

She gets to her knees, and I use it to my advantage, lifting her up until she's straddling my thighs.

She kisses me with urgency, like I might pull away at any second. She doesn't realise I'm kissing her back just as hard, and I don't plan to stop this.

I reach for the silk top at her waist, lifting it up until it's off. I discard it, immediately groping her tits like a man who has never touched a woman before. They are bigger than the last time. A lot bigger. Yet still the perfect size to fit in the palm of my hand.

She moans against my mouth, rocking her hips back and forth, the friction causing my dick to harden in my joggers.

"What are we doing?" she whispers breathlessly.

"What we should have been doing all along," I answer.

She gets up, standing in front of me. The movie plays on in the background, and the fire roars to the right of us. Bare from the waist up, she is a sight to behold. Her beauty has always been there, but she holds it with confidence now, with assurance, and it's truly remarkable to see.

I reach for her silk pyjama trousers, never once looking away as I slide them down her thighs until they pool at her ankles.

I lean forward, cupping the back of her arse to bring her closer.

Her flesh smells like strawberries, and I take a minute to savour her scent before licking up her stomach to her navel.

She arches her back slightly, letting out a moan. I kiss her navel before lowering my head, peppering kisses across her flesh before I get to her pussy. I open her folds, licking her clit, enjoying the mewling sounds coming from her lips.

I suck, lick, and nip until her knees lock together. I lean back, pushing my joggers down my thighs to free my dick before reaching for her.

She doesn't need any coaxing. She straddles my lap like we've been doing this for years. "Once my dick is inside you, I don't think I'll stop," I warn.

She places her hands on my shoulders. "I don't want you to stop."

I line my dick up at her entrance, and before I can slowly coax my dick inside of her, she drops down, her walls clenching around my cock.

We both groan in unison as I grab her hips. Our lips collide as I let my desire for her take over. We have danced around this for a while now, and now it has all combusted, we can't take our hands off each other.

I throw away all the inhibitions I have about this. I wanted to wait until the Cyrus mess was over, but Emily has had me under a spell from the very first night I met her.

No man would wait to make her his.

No man would say no to her.

I flick my tongue along her jawline as she fucks me. I squeeze her hips, stopping her, before getting up with my dick still inside of her. I lay her down on the floor in front of the fire. She gazes up at me, her round, sky-blue eyes staring up at me. I tug her knee up to her chest and thrust inside of her.

My lips graze along her neck, before nipping at her collarbone. I lift to find her biting down on her lip.

"Mine," I growl, nudging her hand away.

The intensity of the desire shining back at me consumes me. My fingers dig into her thigh as I fuck her harder. She circles her other leg around my back, and I sink into her to the hilt.

Fuck, she feels good.

"Be mine," I demand.

Emily submits, nodding. "Yours," she breathes, her lips parting as I fuck her harder.

My balls ache, needing the release so desperately, but I don't want it to end.

Her hands slide across my chest, sparking a primal fire inside of me that I can't control.

Sweat beads my temple and runs down my spine. She's mine. She is finally mine.

I thrust harder; so hard, she jerks across the wooden flooring.

Her walls clench tighter the faster I thrust. It feels like soaring through the sky, and I don't want to come down.

"Yours," I pant, resting my forehead against hers. "God, you are so beautiful."

"Harder," she pants, her cheeks flushing.

She kisses me but breaks it off quickly when I push her thigh against her chest, applying pressure.

Our flesh slaps together, and her moans fill the air. "Fuck, you're tight."

"Oh God," she breathes, right before she inhales sharply, her eyelids closing as her orgasm tears through her.

Feeling her pulse around my cock has me coming inside of her. I pump the last bit of cum into her, before dropping down next to her, pulling the fallen blanket over our naked bodies.

She opens her eyes, and they glisten with hope and love. "What does this mean?" she whispers.

"It means you are mine."

"But I thought you didn't like me?"

I run my finger down her chest. "I'm sorry I ever made you feel like that, Emily. It's the biggest mistake I have ever made. I should never have stayed away. I should have come back for you."

She turns her head to meet my gaze. "Why didn't you?"

"Because I knew what kind of person you were. You were the type of woman who deserved a man who brought her flowers and showered her with affection. You deserved someone who wanted to put a ring on your finger. You deserved someone who wasn't as messed up as me."

"What has changed now?"

I hate the vulnerability in her tone. "Now I want it all. I want to give you these things. Being with you these past few weeks has made me become a better man. I want you, Emily. I want it all with you."

To prove my point, I kiss her softly, running my hand along her jaw and into her thick mass of hair.

"I want this too."

I kiss the tip of her nose, smiling. "Good, because I don't plan on letting you go."

She drops back, staring up at the ceiling. "This doesn't feel real."

I take her hand, placing it over my chest. "Feel how fast my heart is racing. This is real."

"And you just decided this tonight? You don't want to think about it for maybe longer than a minute?"

"I've spent years thinking about us. These past few weeks just cemented what I already knew. I want you, Emily. I want to be with you. I want us to be in a relationship and raise our daughter together. I'm in this for the long run, and I don't plan for this to end. I've been trying to think of ways I can win you over since the day you moved in. I fucked up big time, and I said things I wish I never said. But this… this is better because it came to us naturally."

She rolls to her side, running her hand along my chest up to my shoulder. "Then we really need to start having sex in a bed. Two times now we've had sex on a sofa and ended up on the floor."

Relief that she has accepted us being a couple causes a blinding smile to spread across my face. My lips kick up into a smirk. "Then let's rectify that."

I get up, and for a moment, she doesn't move, until I reach out for her to take my hands. "What are we doing?" she asks when I pull her up to her feet.

I swing her up in my arms, and they immediately circle my waist. "I'm going to fuck you. In our bed."

"What about the movie?"

"The movie can wait. We've got our entire lives to watch them."

She smiles, reaching down to kiss my lips. But as soon as she does, I feel like I've tainted her light in my darkness.

She has no idea what I have planned.

That I might not have a future after next week.

And I hope to God she can forgive me if my plan works.

29

EMILY

Poppy giggles as she throws the stick into the fire. It has become a game to her, and she's enjoying finding more to throw in there. She loves being here. Tonight is the first night it hasn't rained, but even when it did, she still wanted to go out and splash around in some puddles.

She even loved the hot tub and found joy in the bubbles. I'm sad that our time here is coming to an end. We have two more sleeps left, and I don't want to leave.

Since Cole and I took a leap, we've been unable to keep our hands off each other. I wanted to keep it from Poppy until I knew for sure this was real, and that I wasn't going to confuse our daughter.

But one touch, and I melted. I've never felt like this in my entire life. Not even with my friends. I feel liberated and free. I feel connected to this world in a way I have never felt before. And it's because of him. He has bewitched me, and I don't even care. These past few days, I've seen a side to him that I never thought I'd see.

He has shown me kindness, attentiveness, and most of all love. He listens when I speak. He knows what I want before I do. And he asks questions like he really wants to know the answers.

But when he touches me or kisses me… It's like the world stops spinning. Butterflies erupt in my stomach, and I get dizzy in his presence. It feels like home.

I go to sleep recanting our days, and I wake up smiling.

These past few days have been the best days of my life. We have laughed, we have teased, and we have shared. I've been so overcome with happiness, it's been hard not to cry. And I can't wait to share all of this with my friends. The only reason I haven't is because the signal out here isn't the best.

But damn do I want to talk to them. It's the first time I've been happy, where there isn't dread in the pit of my stomach. Any doubts I had left me the night he took me upstairs to bed. Because after he fucked me again, he didn't roll over and go to sleep. He held me. He asked questions, and answered mine. It wasn't just about intimacy that night. It was about us, and how well matched we are together.

He leans over, capturing my lips in a kiss. I pull back in a daze, smiling. "What was that for?"

"Because I know you are thinking of me. I can tell by that dreamy look in your eyes."

I chuckle at his honesty. "And that's a bad thing?"

He kisses me again. "It's never a bad thing. Because I'm thinking of you just as much."

"Kiss, kiss, kiss," Poppy yells.

Cole obliges, kissing me, and she laughs. "I can't wait to get you into bed later," he whispers.

"Maybe once she's gone to bed, we can get Ben to listen out for her whilst we enjoy the hot tub."

His pupils expand. "Oh, Miss Hart, I am more than happy to ask him."

I grin, nudging my shoulder against his. "You are shameless, Mr Connor."

"Here, try this," he offers, pinching some of the marshmallow off a cracker. He holds it up to my mouth, and I close my mouth around his fingers, taking the marshmallow.

I pull back, wiping the sticky sugar from my lips. "Woah, that is good."

"Poppy want some," Poppy demands, opening her mouth.

I tickle her belly. "You, miss, have had plenty."

"Pwease," she pleads.

Cole has already given in. I can see it in the way his shoulders drop, and he gets that droopy-eyed look. "Don't," I warn teasingly.

"Just a little bit?"

I sigh, giving in. "Just one more."

Poppy takes another cracker as Cole shoves the marshmallow onto the stick. He holds it over the fire, letting Poppy hold his wrist.

"We will make this the best one."

My jaw aches from smiling so much. It can't be helped though. I'm happy when I'm around them. This is everything I pictured us to be. It was a dream back then, one that has miraculously come true.

I watch as he puts the marshmallow in the cracker for her, before placing it in a tissue so she doesn't burn herself. "Wait for it to cool down," he warns gently.

"She's going to hate going home," I comment as she races off to sit down on the little deck chair he bought her from town.

He chuckles, grabbing his bottle of Corona. "She can come back whenever she wants to," he admits. "What is she like in the sun?"

"She's not a fan, if I'm honest. When we had the heat wave, she was miserable. I bought her a paddling pool with a canopy, but it burst within the day. The plastic just melted."

"I have a home abroad I want to take you both to. I'm thinking we should go when the weather is still warm, but not overbearingly hot."

"She loves the beach. She didn't used to. She hated the feel of the sand. But she is a winter baby."

"Does she like the snow?"

"She liked watching it from the window, but she was poorly last year so she never got to go out in it."

"I can't wait to share a first with her. I feel like I've missed out on so much already."

"Cole," I whisper. "You were there for more than you think."

"What do you mean?"

"You were there for her first night in a big bed, and in her own room. She called you dada. You were there the first time she said nanna. First time at a farm. You have so many more firsts to experience with her—so many more."

"I know. I just wish I could have been there for all of them."

"I really am sorry that you weren't," I whisper, letting him take my hand.

"I know you are," he assures me.

"All that matters now is that you are here. This is all I ever wanted for her. And you're an amazing dad."

"Did you doubt me?" he muses.

I chuckle under my breath. "Honestly, I thought you would be scared as hell."

"Oh, I am. It's a big responsibility, and Poppy hasn't reached the age where she understands danger. Did you see the way she jumped off the sofa the other day? I nearly had a heart attack."

I laugh this time. It had been the evening after we slept together. The rain wouldn't let up, so we decided to make a massive bed on the floor in front of the fire and watch some movies and play games. He went to go check on the dinner whilst I was putting away the game, and Poppy climbed onto the sofa. As he walked in, she dived off, wanting to land in the middle of the pillows. Our daughter would have been fine, but Cole overreacted and tried to reach her. He ended up stepping on a toy and falling flat on his face.

Poppy got up from her soft-cushioned landing and laughed at her father's fall. It was amusing as hell.

"I did, but you have no room to judge. You have bruises on your hip bone from where you fell."

"I thought she was going to hit the table."

"She was nowhere near the table," I tease.

"Poppy nigh, nighs?" Poppy asks over a yawn.

I smile as I get to my feet. "Come on, baby girl. Let's get you to bed. We can wash off all this yuck tomorrow."

"Yummy," Poppy amends, and when her sticky fingers go around my neck, I realise it won't wait until tomorrow.

I turn to Cole. "I'm going to wash some of this off her before bed. I'll meet you at the hot tub?"

He grins, picking up the empty packets of marshmallows and crackers. "I'll be there."

I lean over, pressing my lips to his. Poppy follows, smacking a wet kiss across his lips. His nose scrunches up, and I laugh. "You might want to clean up too."

"Oh, I do, do I?" he muses.

I laugh when he shoves his face into the crook of my neck. "Stop, you are getting me all sticky."

He pulls back, kissing the top of Poppy's head. "I'll be up to say goodnight once I've cleaned this away and put the fire out."

As I walk back up to the lodge, I can't keep the smile off my face. I have everything I ever wanted. I just wish my grandma was here to see it. She would love this for me. She would love Cole.

"Mummy happy?" Poppy asks.

I glance down at my daughter. "Mummy is super happy."

"Poppy happy too."

And this is how I want our life to be. Happy. Filled with love and joy. I want us to be a family.

I AM SPENT.

Not only did Cole fuck me in the hot tub, but the minute we sat down to watch a movie, he was on me again. It's been this way all week. I don't think we've gotten through an entire movie yet.

I grab Cole's grey T-shirt from the floor, pulling it over my head.

"Why are you getting dressed? I like you naked."

I arch an eyebrow. "And we've already taken too many chances today. I don't want Ben catching us."

"Ben knows how to do his job," he tells me, bringing me flush against his chest and kissing me until I forget my own name.

I kiss his shoulder. "Still, I'd prefer not to risk it again."

"God, I wish we didn't have to go back. I like it here with just us."

I pull the blanket over our legs as I respond. "Are you scared this will end when we get back home?"

"What has made you ask that?"

"I'm just worried this isn't real. That the minute we get home, you'll remember I'm the woman who kept your child from you and works in a strip club."

He cups my jaw. "There you go again. Doubting me."

I breathe out a sigh as I cuddle closer. "I know. I'm sorry."

He tucks my hair behind my ear. "Don't be. I put those doubts there."

"It just seems too good to be true. I'm not used to feeling like this."

"Like what?" he asks softly.

"When my parents treated me the way they did, and I moved out, it didn't matter. I didn't lose anything. I wasn't happy or unhappy about it. I didn't feel anything for the longest time because my parents didn't give me anything to mourn. I said I loved them because it was expected of me. I probably do love them deep down, but I don't feel it. My grandma was the only person I ever loved for the longest time. I grew so attached to what we had that I didn't want to lose it. Then I met my friends. It wasn't as quick as it was with my grandma, but I loved them. They mean everything to me, and I can't picture my life without them. They filled a void inside of me that I never knew existed."

He leans over, wiping a wayward tear that slips down my cheek. "Hey, no crying."

I smile, wiping it away. "My friends made me happy, and they were my world. Then I had Poppy, and now you. They may be my world, but you two are my life. I'm so deliriously happy that I'm afraid it's not real. I've never felt like this. I've never had this. I've watched my friends fall in love, but this, between us, feels different. And I'm scared it's not real."

"You know why I didn't want to get married or have a family. And I've told you I was wrong about it. But I haven't told you why."

"And why's that?" I whisper, tucking my legs up.

"Because of you."

My eyes go round. "Me?" I ask.

"Yes, you," he replies. "You showed me that it isn't about who can give who what. You showed me life can be beautiful in the now. I never saw it before because the women I dated were superficial. I had no one to show me what it was like to love."

"But your parents are in a very loving relationship."

"Yes, but as you know, a parent's love is very different from the love you feel in a relationship," he admits. "This is as real for me as it is for you."

"I've never done this before, and I think that's what is scaring me."

"Neither have I. Not like this. But together, we can figure it out."

"And you really want this?"

"I think I wanted this from the very first moment I saw you. I never understood what drew me to you. You started rambling about not wanting to take your clothes off, and I don't know... I felt a connection. I knew I liked being around you. I related to you in so many ways, and it scared me too."

"It did?"

He lets out a chuckle. "Fuck yes. Why do you think I stayed away for so long? I knew if I was around you, I wouldn't be able to keep my hands off you. It scared the hell out of me. I didn't want to unload my shit onto you."

"What made Cassandra so different? I know you wanted two different things, but you had a relationship with her."

"It might make me sound like a dickhead," he grumbles.

"I won't judge you, Cole."

"Cassandra seemed like the perfect choice. She didn't want hearts or flowers, and I guess it made her a safe choice for me. I could never hurt her the same way I could hurt you. She might have acted like a scorned ex, but I think it was more out of saving face than anything else. I was a prize to her. One she could show all her friends. It didn't bother me because our entire relationship was superficial. But when I knew it wouldn't end with just us being together, and she gave me that ultimatum, I knew it wouldn't end there. I didn't want to be trapped. Then I met you. And it was like karma had come to bite me in the arse because there you were, rambling about everything you had going on, and all I could think about was how cute you were. I was enthralled by you. Leaving that night had been hard. Then everything happened at the sister club, and I knew I couldn't bring you into my world. I thought sex was all I was capable of giving you."

"And it's not now?" I whisper.

"No. Because now I want to give you everything. I have never wanted anything as much as I want this. You and Poppy came into my life unexpectedly. It shook my entire world. You are like an organised chaos."

My lips tug up at the corners. I feel flattered by his words. "Organised chaos?"

"Organised chaos. It's the only way to explain it. It's a chaos I want in my life. It's organised in a way it fits perfectly."

"So what you're saying is: we're imperfectly perfect."

He laughs, the sound so beautiful and rare, it warms my heart. "Yes. That is exactly what I am saying."

I cuddle up closer, soaking in his warmth. "I thought I built you up to be this shining knight in armour because it's who I needed you to be at the time. For so long after you found out about Poppy, I believed what we shared was all in my imagination. It's why it hurt so much. I never thought we would ever be how we are now. Not once. But it didn't matter because of how much that night meant to me. I held it safe in my mind, where no one could tarnish it. I guess it's why I didn't tell my friends. I didn't want them to think I was crazy for feeling this much for a man I just met. Then there was the fact you were my first, and I read you can grow attached," I reveal. "Looking back now, though, I think we needed to lose each other when we did to truly appreciate how special our story is. We were both in bad places back then, and neither of us were ready for a relationship."

He presses his lips against mine. "I'm so lucky to have you."

I smile against his lips. "I'm glad we had this talk. I know you don't do the heart-to-hearts, but I think we both needed this. I've been wanting to bring it up for days, but I've been too scared you'll tell me my doubts were right."

"You are right, I don't do heart-to-hearts. But you make me want to be a better man, and that's what I'll strive to be for you. I'm not a stupid man, Emily Hart, so make no mistakes, I plan to keep you."

My stomach flutters at his declaration. "I plan to keep you too."

"Good," he murmurs, then peels the blanket off our legs. "Because I need to fuck you again."

I gasp when he lifts me up. Before I can protest about us being downstairs in the open, he steals my breath away with a kiss.

And my mind turns to mush.

30

COLE

Tonight will be our last night here, and I want to soak in as much of it as I can. We leave in the morning, and I'm not prepared for what I need to do. What I have to tell her. I know she will try to talk me out of it. She has a big heart and won't understand why I have to do this. I don't want to ruin everything we have built over the week by telling her either. I may not have known her long, but I see beneath the surface. This is the happiest she has ever been. I don't want to take that away from her.

I see the way she looks at me, and I feel it. I'm not blind to what it means. I may never have experienced this before, but I know it's love. Our conversation last night confirmed it. I thought I was going crazy feeling the way I do.

Everything with us happened so quickly. She went from being a memory, to being the mother of my child. I hated everything she took from me, and for a split second, I let it bleed into my feelings for her. For a split second. Then she proved me wrong the minute she begged me not to take our daughter from me. The second I saw that fear, I knew that no one who could love that much and that strongly could

269

be cruel. I wanted to retract everything I said, and give her everything she wanted, but there was a voice inside of me that was telling me to keep going.

I'm glad I listened because these past few weeks have been the best days of my life. Having her in my life has been like waking up from a dream.

"Hey, when you get a minute later, can we talk?" Ben asks.

"We can talk now if you want. Emily is upstairs packing our stuff. She doesn't want to leave it until the morning."

"Are you sure? It can wait until later after dinner."

"Yeah, it's fine. I've been meaning to pull you aside and ask if you found anything on the tapes."

"It's why I wanted to speak to you actually."

My eyebrows pinch together. "What did you find?"

"The data we found had timestamps for downloaded recordings. I've gone through every single one we could find, and they were all of your parents talking about you. About your childhood. The latest one was about how much Poppy looked like a Lana. I don't know who it is, but it seemed important because he cleared the cache data from it to make it clearer."

"Lana is our sister. I believe he's responsible for her death."

"It explains a lot."

"What do you mean?"

"Evan had someone look into her and noticed a grave in her name. He went there today, and someone has scrawled your name over the top of hers."

"What the fuck! And you think Cyrus did this?"

"We are monitoring the grave now. Evan has a live feed installed in a stone and placed it where it won't stand out."

"So Cyrus wants to bury me there?"

"I think so. We don't know how long it's been there either. But I think the behaviour analysts were right and Cyrus has changed his plans."

I scrub a hand across my jaw. "And you think that is my death."

"I'm looking at this as if it's a board game. Cyrus has all of you as his pieces and he's been moving you all around the board and making you and everyone else believe we are one move away from getting him. When in fact, I think he's one step from getting you."

"Which is why I'm changing the game. I'm going to end this once and for all."

"Then we need to do this properly. He's going to expect you to call him into a trap. He's probably waiting for it."

"Then what do you suggest I do?"

"I think we should use your sister's grave as a ruse and lead him to the club that way."

"How will that work?"

"Because we are going to make sure he knows it's a ruse and talk about you watching from the club."

I shake my head, because this is getting too chaotic. "So, you want me to call him to the grave, but then let him know we're going to be hiding out at the club? How the hell do you expect me to do that?"

"Because we found another feed."

My stomach bottoms out. "Where?"

"In your assistant's office. He has bugged her email."

"How? We have good software security."

"He jumped on an email she sent to your dad."

Fuck! I know exactly when it was. Gia accidently sent Mum and Dad the email about Poppy.

"And what is your plan?"

"We have a few men stationed in London who can go to the office on our behalf. If you can call your assistant and give her permission to give them access to your office, we can plant the email that way. You'll email her saying that you'll be out of office on the Friday, and she can reach you at Tease."

I scrub my fingers through my hair. "He has to pay for what he's done."

"He will. But we need to play this smart. Don't go in there if you aren't ready for what you might need to do."

"You mean kill him?"

"Would you rather he killed you?"

"I'll do anything to keep my family safe. I don't know if I'm capable of killing someone. I'm not him. I was planning to go in there and beg him to take me," I reveal, and his eyes widen. "If I have to die for him to stop hurting the people around me, then so be it."

"And what about us?" Emily whispers brokenly.

Ben lets out a breath, glancing at the ground. I face her, seeing the hurt in her eyes. "Emily, it's not what you think."

"So you aren't planning on dying? It's not noble, Cole. It's stupid."

"This is what needs to be done to stop him."

"And what's to say he will stop at you? What's to say he won't come for us after anyway? Did you think this through?"

"This will either end with him or me. I don't care which as long as it ends."

"You don't care?"

I scrub a hand along my jaw. "You are taking it out of context."

"Then explain it to me," she pleads.

"He's going to hurt you, Emily. He followed you to the haunted house and could have killed you that night."

"We handled it," she cries.

"You got lucky," I spit out. "He's not going to stop. You know that deep down."

"Is that what this week has been about? Your way of saying good-bye. Was all this a lie?"

I close my eyes at the truth in her words. "Emily."

"Oh my god. It is because of that. All this was a lie. I knew it."

"Stop! Don't put those thoughts in your head."

She curls her lip up in disgust as a tear rolls down her cheek. "They're already there, Cole. I poured my heart out to you. It was real, and it was special because aside from my friends, I have never been that honest with anyone. I never opened myself up because I was afraid of it being used against me."

"And I meant the things I said too, Emily. This doesn't change anything."

"This changes everything. You brought me here under false pretences, and then continued to hide it from me. It changes a damn lot."

"Don't do this. Please, don't do this. You have to understand why I'm doing this."

"No. I don't. Because if I meant anything to you, you wouldn't put your life at risk. You wouldn't put me through that knowing what my life has been like. And Poppy. She is your daughter. Have you even considered what this will do to her?"

"I'm doing this for her," I snap. "I understand why you're hurt, but you have to realise why I'm doing this. People have died. You and Poppy could die."

She swipes angrily at the tears slipping down her cheeks. "Is this why you acted so weird the morning we left?"

My eyebrows pinch together. "What are you talking about?"

"In Poppy's room. She was screaming, and when I asked why you weren't at Dave's, you acted weird with me. I excused it because I thought you were shocked over Poppy's reaction to you, but now I'm wondering if it was about this."

"Wait, what are you talking about? What morning?"

"The day we came here. In Poppy's bedroom. Stop acting like you don't know what I'm talking about."

"Emily, I wasn't there that morning. I left at four to go and see Dave. I didn't get back until after half eleven, and by that point, you were in the kitchen with Poppy."

"No, you were in her bedroom," she remarks.

"Um, Cole, she's right. You were," Ben announces, holding out his phone.

On the screen is the image of Poppy's bedroom. A man stands in the middle, holding a screaming Poppy. I take the phone, my breath trapped in my lungs. Because when the man turns, it's my face, but it's not me.

"It's Cyrus."

"What?" Emily asks.

"It's Cyrus."

"No, it's you," Emily remarks.

"Emily, we're identical. Me, Cyrus, and Lana are triplets."

Her face pales and she staggers backward. "What?" she whispers, sounding so hurt it cripples me.

"We're triplets, Emily."

"He held my daughter."

"Our daughter," I bite out, gritting my teeth as I look back down at the phone. Emily is taking Poppy off Cyrus, her lips moving a mile a minute.

"I need to leave," she announces.

"We're leaving tomorrow," I tell her as I follow her back inside.

He had been that close to my daughter. To Emily. And I didn't even know. I've done all of this so he never got the chance to get close to them. But he already had. Right under my fucking nose.

She brushes my hand away, her face bright red. "Don't touch me."

"Emily. If I had known about this, I would have told you."

"You should have told me you were identical. You could have told me so many times, but you didn't. You didn't even tell the police."

"Yes, I did."

"When?" she accuses.

I stop, trying to think of when it came up, but then the realisation hits me. "Fuck!"

"They've probably already found him all this time, but thought it was you," she screams.

"No, they have his records. They have our birth certificates. They know."

"But I didn't," she cries. "I didn't. You should have told me. We deserved to know."

"I thought I did tell you. I'm sorry."

"No, don't touch me," she snaps, then glances at Ben. "Can you take us back?"

"Emily, we can talk about this."

"You've had all week to talk to me about this, but you didn't. I'm going, and if you try to stop me, I will never forgive you."

I lower my gaze to the floor. "I'm sorry, Emily. I never meant for this to happen. Any of it."

"You made me believe you cared for me," she chokes out.

I meet her gaze, feeling helpless. "I do."

"Then why would you do something that is suicidal? Why did you lie to me? Why would you let Poppy grow up without a father?"

"I…" I stop myself, knowing if I tell her the truth, she'll forgive me. She'll try to talk me out of it, but I don't want her to.

She's right. This is suicidal, so maybe it is best if she hates me. It will be easier for her to get through if something does happen to me.

I know what I have to do, even if I don't like it.

"You're right. I did lie. You took my daughter from me and now you care if she grows up without a father. Don't kid yourself. I wanted you to feel what it's like to lose someone, and it worked."

"Cole," Ben warns.

"Fuck you," she rasps.

"You did that already," I snarl, swallowing back bile.

"I hate you," she whispers.

"C'mon, Cole," Ben demands.

I dismiss him and her, turning my back to look out at the forest. "Take her home. I'll have someone come collect my things in the week."

"Don't bother," she breathes, and I turn to find tears streaming down her cheeks.

She races off upstairs, and I glance at Ben. "Make sure she gets back safe."

"You didn't need to do that."

I glance at the stairs, where I can hear her crying. "Yes, I did. It was the only way for her to let me go. She was mad, yeah, but in a few days, she would have come around and come looking for me. She would have tried to stop me, and I need to do this without risking her getting caught in the middle. If I survive, I will fix this."

"And if you can't?" he asks.

"Then I've just lost the best thing that ever happened to me."

31

EMILY

Rain splatters against the windshield of the car. I turn away, resting my head against the window as I struggle to hold back tears.

I never said the words to him, but I know he felt my feelings for him all week. I never hid them. I gave him all of me. Something no one has ever had. Not even my friends. Not the same way as he did anyway

He took my heart, squeezed it in the palm of his hand, and shattered me.

If I have to die for this to end…

You took my daughter from me…

Those words will forever haunt me. He told me he forgave me, and it was a lie. All of it was a lie. The sweet words, the soft touches, the loving gazes. All of it had been a lie to reel me in, to get me so twisted up inside, only so he could tear it all apart.

This is what happens when you trust someone. This is what happens when you open your heart in a way you've never done before. It's crushed, along with all my hopes and dreams I had of our life together.

He slept with me because he knew his clock was ticking. He probably only did it because I was the only woman available right then.

My god, I am so stupid.

"You aren't stupid," Ben comments.

I lift my head, not realising I spoke out loud. "Yes, I am."

"You know why he's doing this, Emily. He's doing it for you and Poppy."

"No, he's doing it to right a wrong he didn't make. His brother is the one who took those lives. It was his brother who got himself arrested all those years ago. Cole is going to get himself killed, and for what? To let his brother get away with killing one more person. To let his daughter grow up without a father."

"He's protecting you."

"He's protecting no one," I argue, then lower my voice when I hear Poppy begin to stir. "You heard what he said to me."

"He said that out of anger."

"It must have come from somewhere."

"I've not known either of you long, so I don't know what to say. This entire situation is complicated."

"It's fine. This isn't your problem," I softly reply. "I can't believe he was holding my daughter. He was so close. He could have killed us then and there, but he didn't. I'm not complaining, but why? Why did he try to kill me at the haunted house, but then just leave us alive at the house? It doesn't make sense."

"I've been asking myself that same question since we found out he was in your daughter's room."

"Did you come up with an answer?"

"None that you want to hear."

I was afraid he would say that.

"Did you know he was a triplet?"

"Yes. But I didn't know they were identical. In the picture we had of Cyrus, his hair is longer, and he has facial hair. You could tell him apart from Cole easily."

"I thought they had to shave in prison."

"They do. But the photo we were given was from the day of his arrest. We haven't been given prison copies due to the investigation regarding the prison warden."

"Why would he not tell me? I've been looking for someone who shows resemblance to you, but all along, I just needed to be looking for Cole."

"I don't think he kept it from you on purpose."

"He didn't tell me, Ben," I stress, and quickly glance into the backseat to check Poppy is asleep. "When I was pregnant with Poppy, I was carrying twins. I lost one early into the pregnancy, and I told him. He could have told me then."

"I'm sorry you went through that," he tells me.

"When Gabby recognised his voice, he could have told us then. Or when we went to his parents after the police station. He had so many chances to fit it in, but he didn't. And I don't think it was accidental."

"Just give him time."

I glance back out the window. "I feel like such a fool."

"We are going to be back soon. You can call him from home and talk about this."

"I'm not going back there. It's not my home. Not now."

"Emily, Cole wants me to take you home."

"I don't care what he wants. I want to go to my friend's house. We have enough clothes and stuff to tide us over. And if I need more stuff, I'll get someone to go get them."

"This is putting me in a difficult position."

"Then fine. Take me back. But I'm telling you, I will get in my car and leave as soon as we arrive. Cyrus got inside without setting off alarms, and I don't know about you, but I don't want to wait for a second visit. And wouldn't you rather know I got to my friends in one piece?"

He lets out a sigh. "Okay. Tell me the address."

I rattle off her address before going back to staring outside. My heart is breaking, and I didn't think anything could hurt this much after my grandma passed. Albeit it's a different kind of pain, but it hurts just as much. I feel like I'm being crushed from the inside.

TEARS FALL down my cheeks as I curl up on the garden sofa, my legs tucked up against my chest. The rain still pours, splattering against the patio not far from where I'm sitting. I've barely said more than a few words since I got here, and Harriett hasn't hassled me with questions. She didn't need to. Me turning up, pleading for a place to stay, said enough. She brought us inside, fed my daughter, then waited for her to fall back asleep before telling me to go sit outside.

Harriett walks outside the French doors, keeping under the shelter. She places the glasses of wine on the table before moving over to the wooden chest placed against the wall.

I watch through blurred vision as she pulls out two blankets, bringing them over to us.

"Thank you for letting us stay with you. It will only be for a few days—just until we can find somewhere else."

"You can stay as long as you like. There's no rush," she promises, sitting down next to me. "Are you ready to talk?"

I open my mouth to answer, but the door sliding open again makes me pause.

"How badly do we need to hurt him?" Olivia asks, storming over.

I quickly dry my tears away. "What are you doing here? Where are the kids?"

"Hetty is watching them for a few hours," Gabby replies before turning to Harriett. "Do you know what happened?"

"I've only just asked her if she's ready to talk."

"Are you?" Gabby pushes.

I grab another tissue, dabbing under my eyes. "I don't even know where to start," I choke out.

"Oh my god, you slept with him," Gabby murmurs.

"If he's fucked you around, I'll make his brother look like a Tele-tubby," Olivia growls.

"The cute red one?" Gabby asks.

"Guys, now is not the time to be smart," Harriett remarks before throwing the blanket over my legs. "I can't sit here and ask you to tell us when you're ready. I can't because I know it must be bad for you to turn up at my house and ask for help. You need to talk to us."

"I did sleep with him," I confess, letting out a breath. "I know I shouldn't like someone who said all those things to me, but from the very first moment I laid eyes on him, I have been drawn to him."

"He's the father to your daughter," Gabby declares.

I shake my head because she's misreading what I'm saying. "No. It has nothing to do with Poppy. It's all him. When he looks at me, I lose my breath. He touches me and I get tingles all over. He kisses me and the entire world just stops. Have you ever had someone who makes you feel like you can do anything? Because he does. He had that kind of power over me from the very first time we met. It's only grown stronger being with him day in and day out." I swallow past the lump in my throat, glancing down at the blanket. "Has anyone ever made you feel like that?"

Gabby turns to Olivia with a dazed look in her eyes. "I've felt like that."

"I gave him all of me," I choke out. "I was so open with him, and it was all a lie. All of it. What is so wrong with me that no one wants to love me back?"

"Hey, we love you," Harriett replies fiercely. "We love you unconditionally. We love you because there is so much of you to love."

"Then why? My parents didn't love me. My sister can't stand the sight of me. And now him. What is wrong with me?" I choke out, my shoulders shaking with silent sobs.

Gabby kneels on the floor in front of me. "Fuck all, and you asking that question only proves there isn't. You don't ask it to be narcissistic. You ask because you care. You're kind, selfless, and have so much love to give to those you care about. You ask because you feel. What others have done to you says more about them than it does about you. Trust me."

Olivia joins her on the ground, bewildered. "I love you, Gabby."

"This isn't about me, but tell me again," Gabby replies.

"I love you."

"Why was it all a lie?" Harriett asks.

"Because it was for revenge," I begin, before telling them everything that happened. My heart breaks just a little bit more rehashing it to them. I feel like such a fool.

When they don't say anything, I glance up. It's Olivia who speaks first. "Girl, he said that to keep you away."

"What?"

"Trust me. If you had to do something to keep someone you loved safe, but you knew they wouldn't like it, you would push them away."

Hope fills my chest. "You think that's why he said it?"

"One hundred percent," Gabby answers.

"So I should try to speak to him again?"

"Fuck no!" Olivia declares sharply. "He still did you dirty."

Gabby picks up my wine, taking a sip. "I say sound the house alarm every hour, send a text saying, 'Got rid of the baby daddy. When can we meet?' then ignore his calls and messages," she reveals, holding her glass up. "Keep it toxic."

I splutter a laugh through my tears. "I can't do that."

"If you won't, I will."

I tuck the blanket up my legs. "Why would he lie to me about his brother? He could have told me so many times."

"It does seem suspicious," Harriett agrees.

"What am I going to do? I ache all over. One part of me wants to crawl into bed and never leave, but the other half wants to scream and yell."

Gabby places the glass down on the table. "I have an idea that might help. And you might not like it."

Olivia groans. "Oh God."

Honestly, anything is better than feeling like this. I hate myself for caring this much. I loathe that I gave him so much power over me.

If Gabby has a plan to make this all feel better, then I'm going to do it.

32

COLE

I step into the off-air zone, meeting the others who are waiting inside the booths. Ben is in the corner talking to Kit, their voices low.

My attention turns to Hayden Carter—who I didn't know worked here. She demanded to sit in and listen to the podcast where, Clayton Connor had one of his staff members interview me. She swings side to side on her chair, watching me with a blank expression. It unnerves me because I've only met the girl once.

"That is your master plan? Lure him to your club?"

How the fuck did she know that? "How?"

She rolls her eyes. "No one can fool a Carter."

"It's the only one I could come up with on such short notice."

"Is that why you broke Emily's heart?" My eyes widen at her announcement. "Yeah, you fucker, I know all about that."

I narrow my eyes. "It's none of your business."

A slow, predatory smirk falls across her lips, and I'm man enough to admit that it scares me. "Everything is my business when it comes to my friends."

I arch an eyebrow. "You have friends?"

She curls her lip. "What are you? Two? You hurt my friend again and I will destroy you. Slowly. That ticket you got yesterday will be just a blip of the things I can do to you."

"You got me that ticket?" I grit out.

She smirks. "You need sleep, Mr Connor; your tiredness is showing. Tell me, what is keeping you up at night?"

Fucking bitch. My house alarm has been going off every two hours non-stop since "Do you like this job? Because I have connections too."

"Ohh, don't threaten me with a good time. I might think you like me."

"I've not slept all fucking week, Hayden. Are you fucking crazy?"

"Don't speak to her like that," Clayton, Hayden's boyfriend, warns as he steps into the room.

Hayden slaps her hands down on her thighs as she gets up. "It's okay, Clay. Cole here is just a little tense."

"Are you single?" Kit asks.

Hayden grins and spins to face him. "Why do you want to know?"

Clay grabs her around the waist, pulling her flush against his chest. "No, she isn't."

Hayden pats Clay's cheek, like he's a fucking dog who needs petting or something. "My man hates it when someone hits on me."

Kit holds his hands up. "I get it. I get it."

She eyes him up and down. "I'm hot. No one can blame you for it," she tells him before turning to me. "And I didn't set the alarms. The girl you broke did."

Kit glances to the floor, but I see the smirk on his face before he can hide it. "Emily did it?"

"What did you think she was going to do? Say thank you for breaking her heart? Men, you're all fools." Clay coughs into his hand. "Accept you, handsome."

Ben steps away from the wall, pocketing his phone. "Sir, we have a problem."

"Is it Cyrus?"

He shifts, not meeting my gaze. "Um, no. It's Emily."

"What happened?"

Hayden drops back down in her chair, grinning. "This is going to be good."

"Talk," I demand, glowering at Ben.

"She's at the club, sir. That was Dave on the phone. He said to tell you to get down there."

"She's at the club? Are you fucking kidding me?"

"Why do you care?" Hayden asks.

I turn on her, my patience snapping. "Because I fucking love her and she's put herself in danger. Being her friend, you would think you would stop her. She has a fucking daughter."

She holds her arms out wide, glancing around the room. "Does it look like I'm with her?"

"No, but you were the day you went into the woods looking for Cyrus."

"No, we went looking for Gabby. There's a difference."

"Whatever," I snap, grabbing my coat. "We're done here."

I get to the door when she stops me. "Oh, and Cole."

"What, Hayden?"

"Ever speak to me like that again, and it won't just be me you have to worry about."

Clay folds his arms across his chest, narrowing his eyes on me. "Then who?"

"I will tell my dad you hit on my mum, and he will make your life a living hell. And I'll do that for fun."

Ben pales considerably, stepping forward. "Let's go."

He practically drags me out of the room. "I wasn't done," I grit out.

"Oh yes, you are. Not even I can protect you from Max Carter. He's a fucking lunatic. He makes Hayden look like a kitten."

"Is it wrong that I'm seriously turned on right now?" Kit asks.

"Yes," Ben and I snap simultaneously.

"Am I coming to the club?"

"No. You can go home to Mum and Dad's. I only let you come with me today to appease you. I meant what I said. I don't want you getting involved."

"Call me if you need me," he tells me as we step outside. He heads off in the direction of his car, and we head over to Ben's.

"See you later," I call out.

He lifts his hand to let me know he heard me. Once he's a safe distance away, I turn to Ben. "Do you think Cyrus will get the message?"

"Yes, the seed has been planted. We gave enough time for him to get wind of this. I will do my best to keep the police in line."

"Are you still worried they might intervene?"

He shrugs. "A little, but Evan has a lot of friends inside of the department. He assures me they are being cooperative. They want Cyrus as much as we do."

I unlock the car and pull open the door, watching him over the roof. "And what about Emily? You said you had someone on her."

He clears his throat, rubbing the back of his neck. "We did. But her friends are sneaky."

"Sneaky?"

"She was wearing a wig to match her friend's with the black hair. The three girls left, and he didn't realise it was Emily until the friend walked out twenty minutes later with a smug smirk. He was still canvasing the area for the vehicle when your friend called."

"Alright, let's go see what she's up to."

PERKS OF OWNING THE CLUB: I get to park right outside the front. Woods, one of our longest-serving employees, and the best in his line of work, steps away from the club doors.

"Sir, I didn't know about your situation. I would have turned them away."

"You think you could have turned them away?" I question.

He lets out a heavy breath. "No. I've been working with those girls for years, and I've never known them to listen to anyone."

I slap my hand down on his shoulder. "I know. I'm just learning that myself."

He clears his throat and steps back. "Yeah, good luck in there."

I straighten my suit jacket, taking a breath to compose myself. Ben flanks my left as we enter the darkly lit club.

I'm immediately greeted by one of the dancers who was taken not too long ago. Her name is lost in the back of my mind, but I know who she is because this is the same person Emily accused me of being with not too long ago.

"Cole, what a pleasant surprise. Did you come to see me?" she drawls, running her finger down my tie.

I grab her hand, gently pushing it away. "I'm sorry, but who are you?"

She glances to her friend, who is dressed in a short skirt and low-cut top. She pulls her gaze away from Ben to watch our interaction.

"I'm Trixie. Aren't you stopping by to say hi? The girls have thrown me a welcome back party."

"Whilst you are working?" I demand.

She fiddles with the strap on her bag. "No. I'm not officially back for another couple of weeks."

"Then enjoy your night."

"Wait. Maybe whilst you are here, we can grab a drink?" I go to walk around her, done with this, but she takes my hand, stopping me. "Or we can leave early, go somewhere quiet."

I take a step down, getting close, but not close enough it will trigger her. "Let me make this clear. I am not interested. Never will be."

She pales, stepping back. "Okay."

I go to leave again, but then stop a few steps up. "Have you seen Emily Hart in there?"

"Emily?" she spits out, before masking her disgust. "Why do you want to know?"

"Is she?"

"You're wasting your time. She doesn't date anyone. She's a lesbian."

"Funny. Because she's the mother of my child, and we belong to each other. She's mine."

"Emily?"

"Forget it."

"I knew there was a reason she got that pay rise," she remarks, but I ignore her, taking the steps two at a time.

I reach the top of the stairs, nodding in greeting at one of the members of staff, when I spot Harriett coming out of one of the private booths.

"Cole, I tried to get her to leave," Dave swears as he meets me in the V.I.P. area. "But when those girls have something in mind, nothing is stopping them."

"Where is she?"

"Emily?"

"Who else?"

He rubs the back of his neck, and I hear his groan over the music. "She's working in the private booths."

I see red. "She's giving someone a private fucking dance?" I grit out, not waiting for him to answer.

I rush over there, hearing Ben close by. "Sir, I'm going to secure the area, make sure Cyrus isn't here."

I nod, intercepting Harriett on my way over to the booth. "Where is she?"

I groan as she punches me in the gut. "If you hurt my sister again, I will remove your dick and shove it up your arse. Are we clear?" She smacks me on the back, leaning down until her lips are at my ear. "Yeah, we're clear."

I move over to the curtain, ripping it back, but only Gabby and Olivia are inside, making out.

"Where is Emily?" I snap, annoyed with these games.

Gabby arches an eyebrow at me. "Please, give me another reason to rip your dick off."

Olivia opens her mouth, but I put my hand up, stopping her. "I know. You all have this fascination with my dick." I stop myself, groaning inside at how stupid I sound. "Where is Emily?"

Olivia points behind me. "She's working."

Dumbfounded, I spin around, my eyes bugging out.

Because the woman I love is up on the stage, in a black fishnet dress that shows the thin thong she is wearing. She has no bra on, and

I can see the globes of her tits. There's something covering her nipples, something shiny and silver.

I gulp, running my gaze over her again. I've never seen her wear anything like this, or seen her hair styled and her face heavy with makeup.

And every man here is drooling over her.

Just like me.

33

EMILY

I stare into the mirror as memories flash to the surface of the very first night I stripped. I had been such a naïve young girl, scared of her own shadow and disappointing those around her. So much has changed since then. I looked into the same mirror, wondering how my life got so bad that I was stripping to make money. Then I was attacked by a client, lost my virginity, and got pregnant. I made friends for life, and I'm stronger because of them.

This place gave me life in every way imaginable. It gave me a purpose. Life. Friends. It gave me so much more than a paycheck.

It was only fitting I came back to the one place it all began. But I have to show Cole he cares for me. I have to show him I'm not going to let him order me around like my parents did.

I have to get him to see me.

See the woman who has fought her entire life, and who will fight for him.

I also have to get payback. Stripping is the one thing I was happy he took from me. Because he did it to protect me. He did it because he knew I wasn't cut out for it.

So I'll be going up on stage to show him I can handle anything. I can handle him. And hopefully drive him to the point of insanity where he drops the façade and lets me help him.

My phone beeps with a message, and I know it's time.

Woods: Girl, if I get fired, you owe me big time. He's on his way up.

I grimace at the message as I set my phone back down on the dressing table. I'm not worried about him being fired. I've heard people talk about Woods and how good he is at his job. They'd be a fool to let him go.

Heading out of the door, I walk to the curtained doorway, taking a deep breath. Through that curtain are the stairs leading up to the stage, a place that has been out of bounds for me when the club is open. Now I'm about to work it like I own it.

"You need to get up there now," Harriett orders as she rushes towards me.

"Can you see my nipples?" I ask, the only thing I'm wary about. I didn't want to stick plasters to my nipples, so Gabby sewed nude material into my dress, giving the illusion I was bare.

"No, but I still think you should lose the nude material. You have great tits. Use them."

I laugh as I fluff out my hair. "I'm not ready for that."

"Give him hell," she orders, smacking my arse.

I pull open the curtain, and pass Lou Lou on the stairs. Her flaming red hair is slicked straight, falling to her waist. Lou Lou is gorgeous but isn't so bright. She once gave a client her bank details, and instead of giving her account number and sort code, she gave them the long number and security code. Her bank was emptied within the hour. "They are hungry tonight," she announces.

I gulp. "Hungry?"

She laughs at my discomfort. "You're so funny."

I head up to the stage, and the light technician dims the lights, waiting for me to get into place.

There's a chair a foot in front of the pole, since I didn't want to risk falling flat on my face only working with a pole. My nerves will make me sweat, and there will be no gripping it if that happens.

I head to the pole, placing my back to it whilst facing the crowd. I lift my arms above my head, gripping the pole, and wait for the beat of the song we chose.

When Niall Horan's *Slow Hands* begins to play, the red lights fall from above, bathing me in a spotlight.

I sensually slide my back down the pole, closing my eyes. I know Cole is watching me. I can feel it. His intense gaze burning into me.

As I move back up the pole, I run my hands down my sides, my lips parting just a breath to make it more sexual. Harriett taught me well. She told me getting up here would make me feel powerful. Gabby said something similar, and so did Olivia. Men are at my mercy, and I've never felt this level of desire. Not for them personally but for how badly this will be getting to Cole.

I strut across the stage to the chair, turning my back to the crowd, where I know they'll be getting a great view of my arse.

The chair is facing the crowd, so I turn a little, lifting my foot up to the seat as I run a hand over my breastbone, down my stomach to my navel, before leaning my head back, letting my hair flow as I run the palm of my hand over my pelvic bone.

I straddle the chair, counting the beats to time my drop perfectly. Gabby said the crowd love it, and it will be enough to get Cole up on the stage. Or that is the plan.

I drop down, my arse cheeks slapping against the cool wood. I grip the back of the chair and lean back, making sure the chair doesn't tip with me.

The crowd cheers, some shouting lude comments. I close my eyes, focusing on the music and the dance I only had a few days to practice. I don't know how the girls do this all night, three times a week. Sweat is already trickling down my spine and between my breasts.

When I slowly sit back up, I run my hands down my thighs, lazily opening my eyes. And there he is, the man who wormed his way into my heart. Storming towards me, his expression is hard, taking me aback.

This isn't part of the plan.

He wasn't meant to be angry.

I get up at the same time as he reaches me. He doesn't wait for me to speak or stop before he lifts me up by the waist. The move is so quick, so efficient, I have to bite back a moan as I lock my legs around his waist.

"Cole," I whisper.

"Don't," he warns. "Not here."

I spot Harriett in the crowd holding her drink up in salute, believing the plan has worked. She can't hear the anger in his voice or feel the tension coming off him.

I screwed up.

Big time.

My body bounces as he takes the stairs, and I clench my eyes shut, humiliated when I spot another dancer going up them.

"Sir, is everything okay?" Ben asks.

"Stay at the entrance. Keep everyone away from the office," he orders, and slams the office door closed behind us. I hear the metal scraping across the floor, and I know we're going into *his* office.

He lowers me to the ground, and before I can utter a word, he's spinning on me. "What the fuck where you thinking?" he roars.

"No, what were you thinking?" I cry. "You—"

He towers over me, gently gripping my face as he slams me against the door. "You are putting yourself in danger by being here," he declares harshly, his gaze running over my face.

He's scared for me.

And turned on.

Feeling brazen, I lift my hands up, unclasping the straps holding the dress up with a flick of my fingers.

It falls to the ground, leaving me standing in front of him in only my thong and high heels.

His nostrils flare as he glances down, his pupils darkening. When he stares right into my eyes, I lick my dry lips, wondering what he'll do.

"Kiss me," I croon, caressing his shoulders.

He groans, slamming his lips against mine. I moan into his mouth. The texture of his suit is rubbing against my nipples, and the feel of his lips has me ready and wanting.

He grips my arse, lifting me until my legs go around him. He kisses me harder as he undoes his belt, his dick hard against my core.

Oh God.

He hooks a finger into my thong, moving it aside. I feel the tip of his dick, but he gives me no warning before plunging his dick inside of me.

With one hand now on my hip, the other grabs my chin, tilting my head up as he kisses me. Desire blazes in his eyes, dominating me to the point I can't look away.

He fucks me harder, with unrestrained force. I tear my mouth away, dropping my head back against the closed door, crying out.

My nails dig into his shoulders, and the heels of my shoes dig into his arse. My body shakes as he twines his fingers through my hair, pulling my head back to expose my neck. He licks, sucks and bites on the sensitive flesh, making me forget my own name.

He pounds me into the door, his thrusts unrelenting, like he's punishing me. But it's bittersweet. All of it.

My orgasm tears through me, and I cry out, gripping him tightly. He places his hand on my tit, squeezing me as he lets out his own release.

Panting and delirious from how good I feel, I'm barely able to catch my footing when he quickly lowers me to the floor. He doesn't meet my gaze, and I fold my hands over my chest, feeling vulnerable.

"Cole?" I whisper as he zips up his trousers.

"We can't do this."

Tears gather in my eyes, and I swallow past the shame and heartbreak. "Why? What did I do?"

He meets my gaze, hurt flashing in his eyes before he can mask it. "Because I have to do this, Emily. I have to stop him."

"Then why do you need to do it alone?"

"Because I can't risk you getting hurt in the process."

He brushes his fingers through his hair as he moves over to the desk. He pulls out a T-shirt from the top drawer, throwing it in my direction. I take it, quickly pulling it on over my head as a lone tear falls down my cheek.

"I'm already hurt. What you're doing is hurting me. You lied to me, yet I came back. You said cruel things, but I came back. I came back, Cole. I came back despite what my head is telling me to do, because I love you. I love you, Cole. And I don't want us to end like this."

He closes the gap between us, running the palm of his hand along my jaw. "I don't mean to hurt you, Emily. Just give me the weekend. Please," he pleads.

"I just told you I love you, and that is how you reply?" I choke out. "I love you, Cole. It's not an easy word for me to confess. My daughter, my grandmother and friends are the only other people I have ever said those words to."

He steps back, putting space between us, and looks away. "So because you said it, I have to? Just because you feel it, it doesn't guarantee I have to as well."

I swipe angrily at the tears that fall. "You're letting him win. He wanted to take away everything you ever loved, but he didn't need to do it. You did it all on your own. You're a coward."

"I'm doing this to protect you," he roars.

"I don't need you to protect me. I've been doing that my entire life. So don't lie to me. You're doing this to protect yourself," I scream.

"I'm doing this because I love you," he yells. "I love you so goddamn much it scares me. You came into my life and turned it all upside down. You are infuriating, testing, and I can't get enough. But I have to do this, Emily. I have to. You might have your views on all of this but hear mine. Hear that this is something I need to do. Hear how important this is. And after it is all done, I will fix this between us. And I will, because we belong together."

My voice breaks as I reply. "I don't want to lose you. We haven't had any time. We need more time."

He moves towards me, cupping the back of my head. He rests his forehead against mine, closing his eyes. "You aren't going to. I have something to fight for now. I wish I could hide us away forever, but I can't. I need to do this."

I nod as tears run down my cheeks. "Okay," I choke out.

He presses his lips to my forehead. "Ben will take you back to Harriett's."

He gently moves me away from the door, pushing it open. When he leaves, I drop to the floor, sobbing into my hands.

He's going to get killed, and I will have lost the only man I'll ever love.

34

COLE

The club feels eerie being closed. Only the spotlights on the floor are on, and a few overhead ones. It isn't the first time I've been in the club when it's closed, but it's the first time I've been in here alone with a potential life or death situation hanging over my head.

Dave insisted on staying, to make it look more authentic, but I didn't want to give my brother an excuse to go after him. Up until now, he has left him alone—and we have no idea why. Dave doesn't know why, because he didn't get along with Cyrus any better than I did. In fact, there was a time my brother resented him, which is why Dave and I kept our friendship quiet. The one time Dave stood up for me to Cyrus, he got violently sick the day after. When I questioned Cyrus about it—after finding an unknown substance under his bed—he told me that if I wanted to stay in the home, I had to stop being friends with Dave. He told me he would hurt him again if I didn't.

I'm not the same scared little boy as I was back then. I grew up. But Cyrus is still living the same life he was all those years ago.

And tonight, it's all going to end.

I have set up in the V.I.P. area, where he won't be able to sneak up on me. I can view the entire club from where I am sitting too, giving me another advantage.

I started out pretending to work, but then the hours passed, and I thought I might as well get something done. Patience has never been my strong suit, so I turned to the bottle and worked to try and pass the time.

Ben set up extra cameras in the blind spots, which I will be rectifying as soon as this mess is over. I didn't know we had some, but Ben took one look at the cameras and spotted ten straight off. He's monitoring the club and the cameras surrounding the building from a shop across the road. The owners let us use the space and will be compensated nicely for it. Ben and a team are ready to move in at a moment's notice.

They have plain clothes police officers monitoring the grave and a unit on standby to go in if he shows.

My money is on Cyrus going there, because it's three in the morning and he hasn't shown up here. The only people who have shown up are the punters who didn't get the message that the club was closed tonight.

I down another glass of whiskey, hoping to settle the nerves, when a message pops up on the screen.

Ben: Keep a clear head.

Cole: He's making me wait to unnerve me and it's working.

Ben: You don't know that.

Cole: I do. It's how he works. I used to stay awake as a kid so I wouldn't be struck blind by him. He knew. He stayed awake just to wait for me to fall asleep or let my guard down before striking.

Ben: The Lieutenant and Detective Douglas want to call it off. They don't believe he's coming and think this is wasting resources.

As much as I hate to admit this, I think it might be for the best. Cyrus must know it's a trap otherwise he would be here. I said enough bullshit to make him go after me that same night.

Cole: Twenty minutes, then we'll call it.

Ben: We tried. They are flying someone in to track him. He's meant to be good, so it's not over. We've just got to go about this another way.

I lean back into the booth, sighing. This was meant to be over tonight. I was meant to get my woman and daughter back home where they belong. It's not safe for them there until he's put behind bars or in a coffin.

I've always been able to keep a distance between me and anyone who comes into my life. Whether it be distant family, women, flings, or colleagues… I kept a barrier up and stayed aloof to everything. I've had people call me heartless, but I call it being ruthless, working to achieve everything I want in life. I make no apologies for it.

But then Emily came into my life and everything I was or thought I was didn't matter anymore. She got me to laugh—showing me I wasn't a robot. She got me to feel sadness—which showed me I wasn't callous to those around me. She got me to see there is more to life than work—filling my world with joy and chaos.

She showed me I could love, that I wasn't a cold and heartless man.

She took a chance on me when I gave her no reason to, and I let her down. I let her down when I lied and said she meant nothing to me. I let her down by fucking her against a door and then walking away like it meant nothing.

I let her down by not showing her she is my equal, my partner, my everything. As cheesy as it sounds, it's what she is to me. She has pointed out time and time again that we are two different people, but I never really heard her. When I took her out of her home, I made her believe it's because I had better. When I transferred money into her account, I made her think money could fix things. When I gave her a brand-new car, I made her think appearance matters.

But none of those things matter, and she has been trying to tell me that all along. I was too stupid and to set in my ways to listen.

What we have matters. What we feel matters. Material things and money only get you so far. It's who you have and what you share together that truly matters.

We could live in a broken-down home and ride a bus to work, and it will still be the richest I'll ever be because I would have her. I would have Poppy. We would be together and a family.

And now my brother has driven a wedge between us. She isn't safe with me, and she isn't safe with him still walking the streets.

Ben: Sir, you need to look at the order form for your table. It just pinged on my system.

My eyebrows pinch together as I grab the tablet from next to my laptop. Bringing up the order for the table, my lips part.

Have a drink on me. You are going to need it for what's to come. Did you really think I was stupid enough to fall for that?

See you soon.

C

The door to the dancer's entrance bangs open, and Ben and the policemen make their way over.

"Sir, there's more," Ben announces.

The detective clears his throat. "Your assistant's body was found mutilated about an hour ago. They've only just made the connection. A note was left at the scene."

"Gia?" I ask, swallowing past the lump in my throat. "Fuck!"

"He left a note," Ben announces, passing me a piece of paper.

No bitch tries to fool me.

I drop it on the table, glaring at the policemen. "He fucking knew. When did it happen?"

"They don't know. Her girlfriend was away working and the last time anyone saw her, was Wednesday."

"The day we did the radio podcast." Ben nods, glancing down at the ground. He's probably thinking the same as me. This is my fault. I turn to the detectives. "What are we going to do now?"

"Well, you need to keep out of the spotlight. Thanks to your podcast, the news has leaked a photo of Cyrus and it's being plastered everywhere. The last thing we need is our phoneline being filled with reports of seeing you."

I grit my teeth at his condescending tone. "Act pissed all you like, but I was doing something you wouldn't."

He jabs his finger towards me. "You jeopardised our entire case. You let him know we were onto him and now we'll probably never catch him. You got a young woman killed."

My hands clench into fists. I want to wrap my fingers around his neck and squeeze. Ben steps in, placing a hand on my chest. "Don't," he warns.

I narrow my eyes on the detective. "Shut the fuck up! You had nothing until recently and still did nothing. I wanted to do this to stop another person being killed."

"You did it to throw your weight around. You might be the big man in your line of work, but you aren't the police. You aren't above the law. If I had my way, you would be charged for your assistant's murder."

I rear back. "And you should be held accountable for every murder after the first one was committed. You are right. This isn't my job. It's yours. But in the time I have known about Cyrus, I have not sat behind a desk researching and looking into it. I've had people looking for him, and not just here in Coldenshire. I've hired extra security at the club and kept my family safe, something you didn't have the manpower to do. I am one person, Mr Douglas, and yet I have managed to keep three dozen people safe. You have yet to protect one."

"Look, it's late, and it's been a long night," Ben declares. "I think we should call it a night and get some rest. We know Cyrus found out about the trap and has probably already got something planned as revenge. We need to make sure we're ready for it."

"The murdered assistant was his revenge."

"Then you've not been reading Cyrus' file correctly," Ben argues. "He's narcissistic. Killing Gia is nothing to him. He probably did it to throw you off track. I'm not denying he did it to get revenge, but it wasn't revenge on Cole. It was on Gia for letting our team in to fix those emails."

"This is a fucking mess," Douglas hisses. "We have another body, and the public is getting angsty."

I grab my keys off the table. "Then do your fucking job and find him."

His colleague grabs Douglas' arm. "Come on, sir. We have to fill out all the paperwork from tonight."

He narrows his gaze on me, letting out a heavy sigh. "We will be at yours tomorrow afternoon."

"Looking forward to it," I reply, unable to keep the sarcasm from my tone. When they are gone, I turn to Ben. "How bad was it?"

"Bad. Her family is being notified as we speak."

"This is all my fault," I hiss.

"Thinking like that is what he wants. He wants you to feel guilty for the things he's done, but you shouldn't. None of this was on you. We had no idea he would go after Gia. If we did, we would have kept our team on her."

"Are Emily and Poppy safe?"

"Yes. River gave us permission to access his security system. We have night watch monitoring the feeds."

I shut my laptop and reach for my keys. "I'll tell Dave to keep clear of the club if he's alone. He was coming in at midday."

"Wise," Ben mutters. "Let's get back."

Tonight was a bust, and I can't help but ask myself: will this ever end?

I HATE COMING BACK HERE. It doesn't feel like a home, not without Emily and Poppy. I've not had this since the day I moved out of my parents—a place of belonging and feeling wanted. I had it all, and now because of my crazy-ass brother, I have to let them go. There is no way I can bring them back here. The first chance I get, I'm going to get her out of the country, somewhere she won't be touched, or worse—hurt. I have holiday homes they can go to.

"You okay?" Ben asks as we pull in.

"Been better," I reply, scrubbing a hand down my face. "I'll be fine when this is all over."

"I'm going to talk to Evan. I don't know if you know this, but he worked for a special unit in the police department. He used to infiltrate gangs and break the case down that way. He might know of something we can do that we haven't thought about."

"Haven't you already spoken about this to him? What could he possibly advise now, that he didn't before?"

"He gave me tips on what to look for, how to draw the killer out, but he's never once offered advice about how we can find him."

"Okay. If you think he'll help, then yes, do it. I just want this over with. I want to bring my family home before I lose them for good."

He pushes open the car door, and I follow, stepping outside as the first spots of rain begin to fall. "I'm going to get Emily out of Coldenshire until this is over. I don't want her getting mixed up in it. If he's going to retaliate over what I did tonight, then he might go for her next. She's the only person in the world he can hurt me with now."

"Wherever she needs to go, I'll transport her so she's safe."

"Thanks," I reply, pushing the key into the door. I take a step inside, exhaling. "We should get it done before he has chance to—"

Something hard smashes against my skull, causing my eyes to roll to the back of my head. Before I hit the ground and everything goes black, I watch as Ben hits the assailant.

35

COLE

I crack my eyelids open, squinting at my surroundings. Darkness fills the kitchen, the moon barely visible through the window due to the dark clouds swarming the sky.

A dull headache forms behind my eyebrows, my skull throbbing. I try to lift my head, but the heaviness weighs me down and my chin hits my chest once more. My eyes feel swollen, and spasms rack through my muscles to the point they feel like they might snap. Everywhere hurts, like I've been run over by a truck.

Everything comes flashing back. Pulling into the drive, heading inside, and being hit over the head by something hard. Clearly, he didn't stop when I passed out because I can feel the warmth of blood in my mouth and running down the side of my face.

The agony I feel isn't because of my own pain.

It's because I know what this means.

Who is here.

And I'm bound to a chair, vulnerable to his assault.

Boots squeak on the floor close by, and I push myself to lift my head.

The assailant kneels in front of me, pushing off his hood back to uncover his face. "Hello, brother."

"Cyrus," I bite out, coughing up blood.

He grins, splitting the cut on his lip. He hasn't changed a bit. His hair is still dark like mine, his eyes still that bluish grey, but his pupils are larger than mine, basically taking over the colour so they look black. There is nothing redeemable in those eyes. There's no hint of remorse, or life… He just looks dead inside.

"I've been waiting for you to wake up."

"You hit me whilst unconscious. Nothing changes," I grit out.

He grips my face with both hands, applying so much pressure my head feels like it might burst. "Keep answering back. I'm the one in charge here."

I spit out blood, narrowing my gaze on him. "Where's Ben?"

"Making a mess in your pantry. I would hate to be the one to clean that up."

Acid burns the back of my throat. "What is the point in all of this, Cyrus? You got free. You could have done anything, but you chose to kill innocent people."

"They weren't fucking innocent. That foster couple sent me away. You have no idea what happened to me because you were with your *new* family."

"You killed Lana. You hurt the neighbour's daughter. And you killed their pet," I retort, bewildered by his reasoning.

"She was a whiny little brat. She needed shutting up. As for the neighbour's daughter, she saw me kill the cat. She was going to tell."

"You disgust me. She was our sister!" I glare at the stranger before me, wondering how he got like this. "You didn't need to hurt anyone."

"The policeman had it coming. The day I got arrested, I heard him say it was no loss that Louise died and that I should have gone over the banister with her."

I rear back, because he almost sounds like he cares. "You actually cared for her?"

His deadpan expression drops and his face lights up with a smile. He forces out a laugh. "Fuck no. The bitch didn't shut up, and she was a slag. But she was still mine and no one gets to take what is mine from me."

"Is that what this is all about? You couldn't be the one to leave her, so you are seeking revenge? Grow up, Cyrus."

He jabs me in the kidney, knocking the breath out of me. I wheeze, coughing up phlegm.

"She was mine. You took her from me when you already had everything. You didn't need to take her. She might not have been much, but she was all I had. All you had to do was let us rob that family. We would have left as soon as we got what we needed."

"You were hurting them. You nearly killed their dad. What did you think I was going to do?"

"You were my brother. You were meant to be there for me," he spits out.

"If you needed money, I would have given it to you. If you told me what you were going to do, I would have given it to you."

He smiles, transforming his face into something more sinister. "And where would the fun be in that?"

"You had freedom, Cyrus, but you chose to kill instead. You took my sister away from me. Haven't you already done enough to me?"

He tilts his head to the side, his expression filled with pity yet smug. "I took more than that. Who do you think cut Dad's breaks?"

I glare at the monster in front of me. "You did?"

He grins, shrugging. "Mum's death was better. She thought she took paracetamol, but I swapped them out for her sleeping tablets. She fell asleep in the bath, and I sliced her wrists. Your face when I told you Mum was dead was worth it. If I knew Lana would cry that much, I would have drowned her in the bath."

"Why?" I croak out.

"Because they were going to send me away," he spits out. "I heard them talking about it. Mum was scared of me and what I would do next. They were more worried about you and Lana. Always fucking were. Dad planned to take me after our birthday, but I couldn't let that happen."

I struggle against the binds strapping me to the chair. "You're fucking sick. What is wrong with you, Cyrus? They were trying to help you."

"No, they were trying to help you and Lana," he roars, before leaning forward and biting my cheek.

I cry out, feeling the flesh break under his teeth before he pulls back. "You are fucking sick in the head. They should have taken you away sooner."

"You would have liked that, wouldn't you?"

"When I get free, I'm going to kill you," I scream. "I'm going to fucking kill you."

He stands, gripping my hair to bring my head down on his knee. There's a popping sound in my nose, and blood spurts out. My anger is the only thing I can feel. I've never felt like this in my life. Not when my parents died. Not when my sister died. Not even when I found out Emily hid my daughter from me for years. It's consuming me. I can feel the hatred and anger I have for my brother running through my veins, like it has its very own life force.

"How do you expect to do that? You are still a scared little boy," he spits out.

"No; the only boy I see in this room is you. You want to mess up your own life, fine, but you've destroyed other peoples, like a little boy throwing a tantrum."

He jumps up onto the kitchen counter, picking up a knife. He picks the dirt out of his nails, using the tip. "Are we really going there?" he asks, arching an eyebrow.

"I get that you're a psychopath. You've hurt people because it's fun to you, but what are you doing, Cyrus? What is your end game?"

"For someone who is a millionaire, you really are stupid."

"Hey, I made it in life because I worked for it. You got out of prison and used that time to kill people. If anyone is fucking stupid, it's you. There are only two ways this will end. You either dead or in prison."

He claps his hands together, grinning. "And ten points goes to Gryffindor."

"Why are you doing this, Cyrus?"

He places the knife down next to his thigh. "Most people in your position would be trying to talk me into letting them go. It's always: please, I have a mum or dad who love me. I have a child. Blah, blah, blah."

"Not always. Two got away."

"Oh, the infamous Gabby Thompson. I liked her."

"I'm sure she'll sleep better at night knowing that."

He laughs. "Did you know the crazy bitch with her asked for me to kill Gabby first? Practically begged if I'm honest. I like a cunning woman, but Gabby had more fight in her. I really thought I won a prize when I held her head under the water. If her friends hadn't have come when they did." He pauses, clocking his head to the side. "She would have been a goner."

"Why are you doing this? What did I do to you that was so bad, it resulted in all this chaos?"

"Because you had everything," he yells. "You and Lana were Mum and Dad's favourites."

"They loved us all equally. If they didn't, you would have been gone the first time you held my arm down on the hob."

"Then you were blind. Mum could never hold me the way she held you and Lana. When she did, her hands would shake. And the way she looked at me..."

"Can you blame her? You were hurting me and Lana."

"It gave her no right to treat me differently," he replies harshly. "Dad wouldn't kick a ball around the garden with me. He was constantly shouting at me. Don't do that, Cyrus. Get away, Cyrus. It was a relief when they died."

"When you killed them," I amend.

"They gave you everything. They even made that stupid clause in their will because they knew you and Lana would get it all."

"Is that what this is about? Money? Because I can give you money, Cyrus."

He jumps down off the side. "You know what happened to me after they split us up?"

I gulp. "No."

"I was in a home with crazy people. The worst of the worst were in there. Rapists, paedophiles, killers, and those who were just plain crazy."

"So you must have fit right in."

He swings his fist, hitting me across the jaw. "Do you know what they do to kids?"

I spit, aiming for the floor. "No."

"They hold them down and rape them. I was beaten, sodomized, and urinated on."

"Do you want me to feel sorry for you? Because I don't. You killed our parents. You killed my sister and countless others. You had no excuse for the first three murders. None whatsoever. You've been counting off what was done to you as a reason for your crimes, but what you did to our parents and sister was done before anything happened to you."

"I was a child."

"And you're a grown-arse man now. What's your excuse now?" I snap.

"It should have been you. It was meant to be you. I was meant to get the life you had. Maybe if I did, it wouldn't have ended like this," he roars.

"You had that. You had two parents who would have done every-thing for you. You took them away. You had a brother and sister who would have been there, but you ruined any chance of that happening."

"It wasn't meant to be like this. I was going to change. I was going to a good family, and would get the money Mum and Dad left me. But you took it from me. You took everything I was meant to have because you were always the favourite."

He's fucking delusional. Even now, he can't see what he's done, or that his actions led the path to this now.

"You really believe that, don't you?"

"I've had a lot of time to think about it. If I had the life you took from me, I would be free of it all. I deserve to have it."

"It's a little too late for that, Cyrus. If you truly wanted to change, I wouldn't be tied to this chair."

He jumps back on the counter, twirling the knife in his hands. "It was never meant to be like this."

My eyebrows pinch together at the change in subject. "What are you talking about?"

"Do you know why I robbed your friend's house?"

"Because you needed money?"

"No. Because I saw you at the golf course. You were with his dad, laughing and joking about something. He clapped you on the shoulder, and he looked proud. I didn't get that my entire life. No one ever treated me like that."

"Do you really need me to comment?" I ask, pulling at the ties binding my hands to the chair.

"I did it to take them away from you. I was never meant to be arrested."

"Good for you," I spit out. "I don't understand what that has to do with now."

"I went to prison, where the men weren't any better than the people in the looney bin. I stayed awake at night, picturing the perfect revenge. It wasn't meant to be like this."

"Then what was it meant to be like?"

"I was going to kill you then deliver you piece by piece to those who were in your life."

"And what changed?"

"I saw you with your adoptive parents. You were eating a meal at a restaurant with them and your siblings. And I realised killing you would be too easy. I had to do something more."

"So you started killing people who ever crossed my path."

"No, I was going to take everyone you loved before getting my revenge."

"Then why haven't you hurt my parents?"

"Why would I?"

"You just said—"

He laughs, jumping down from the side. "I'm going to take everything from you. When the police find your body, they are going to think you are me," he reveals. "Then I'll get the life I always should have had."

My eyes widen at the news. "And what? Take my place? It's a stupid plan. No one will fall for it."

"Oh, but they have," he announces, grinning. "Your sister did when I met her for coffee. Your brother did when I paid him a visit at his gallery and purchased an awful painting. And let's not forget your parents. They let me into their house under the impression I needed to get something from my old room." He laughs when he sees my expression. "I even fooled your pretty girlfriend. I can't wait to fuck her and show her how it's really done. She sleeps with one man, and it had to be you."

"Poppy didn't fall for it."

"No, she didn't, but I can make her death look like an accident."

The binds cut into my wrists as I struggle to get free. "Stay away from my daughter. I will kill you, Cyrus. I will kill you."

"You can try, but I have nine lives. Nothing can kill me."

"No one will believe you are me. None of them."

He pulls a phone out of his pocket, and I notice it's mine. "Let's see, shall we? If your girlfriend doesn't believe it's me, then it will help my way into your family's lives. They'll be so consumed with grief over losing her, they won't even notice the difference in my behaviour. They'll put it off as my own grief. I was going to make you watch me live your life so you could feel an ounce of how it felt to be me. But I'm just going to kill you."

"Don't. Emily has nothing to do with this. She is innocent in all of this."

"No one is fucking innocent," he spits out, slamming the knife onto the counter. "No one."

"Please, don't do this. Don't. Please. Take me. Take my life. You don't need to take theirs."

He holds the phone up to my face, unlocking the screen. "I'll kill anyone who tries to get in my way."

"Don't! Don't!" I roar.

My worst fear is coming true. The two people I wanted to protect are now in his crosshairs. I should have listened to Emily when she said it was a bad idea to move in.

I should have let her go.

Because being with me might just get her killed.

36

EMILY

I curl my legs up on the chair, watching the rain splatter against the patio through the sliding French doors. It is too early in the morning to be awake, but I couldn't sleep. I tossed and I turned but all I could think about was Cole and the danger he has put himself in. I don't care if he's protected by teams of people. If his brother gets to him, I know he won't be able to do what needs to be done. Cole isn't evil. He might be headstrong, competitive, and ruthless in his business, but he isn't cruel, cunning, or a fighter.

My life has been one thing after another, and I should be able to cope with this. I've faced much worse. But I can't shake this feeling that everything is about to blow up and go horribly wrong. I've just found the love of my life, so I don't know why I expect anything different. Any time I have something good in my life, something bad happens. I had my nan and she got sick. I got into college but then my nan got sicker and needed full-time care. I got pregnant and I lost my baby. There is always something that goes horribly wrong.

I swipe the tear that rolls down my cheek, silently praying he is okay. I'm not overly religious, but if there is a time to start praying, this is it.

Bare feet slap across the marble floor, and I glance over my shoulder to see Harriett entering the room. She closes her silk gown around her body.

"I had a feeling you would be awake."

"Did I wake you when I was making some tea?"

"No," she promises. She drags the other chair over to the French doors and sits down next to me. She curls her legs up, staring outside. "Are you okay? Has he messaged you?"

I glance down at my phone in my hand. "No. Nothing. I've wanted to message a few times, but Ben told me not to. I don't want to be the reason the plan fails."

She reaches out, rubbing my arm. "It's going to be okay."

"Then why is my stomach tied up in knots, and why does it hurt this much?"

"Because love makes you do and feel the craziest things. Trust me."

"I can't lose him, Harriett. I feel like we've not had enough time. What will I do if something happens? I've just lost Nan; I can't lose anyone else."

"You aren't going to lose anyone else. But if something does happen, you've got us. You will always have us. Boys… they come and go. Love can be found, lost and broken. But friendships like ours? They are built to survive the strongest storm. We've got you, Emily. We always will. And we will help you through it."

I force out a laugh, scrubbing a hand down my face. "I'm being stupid, aren't I?"

"No, you love him, and you care deeply. There's nothing stupid about that. I wish there was something I could do or say to make this better for you. I hate seeing you like this."

"You've said it," I whisper brokenly, my voice cracking. "You, Gabby and Olivia have been there for me through everything. The good, the bad, the ugly, and you stayed. You three have done more for me than you will ever know. You gave me hope. You showed me love. You brought me life. I'm so very thankful for that." I pause letting out a sigh. "This is different though. I thought Cole and I were meant to be forever. We were epic. And I don't know if you three will be able to get me through it this time."

She runs her index finger under her eye. "Now you are making me emotional. And there is nothing we can't do. You should know that. You've done the impossible for us too."

"God, why isn't he messaging me?"

"Maybe because it's four in the morning and he doesn't want to wake you up."

At her words, my phone beeps with a message. "It's Cole," I announce.

Cole: It's over, baby. Come home.

"What has he said?"

I glance up, a smile lighting up my entire face. "He said it's over and he wants me to come home."

Her shoulders drop, a huge sigh of relief passing through her lips. "It's really over?"

"Yes," I say, smiling so wide my cheeks hurt. I reach forward, hugging her tightly. "Or at least, that's what I think he meant."

"Text him back and see."

Emily: It's really over? They've caught him?

Cole: Yes. Come home. I need you.

Emily: Are you okay?

Cole: I am now he's gone.

Emily: On my way.

"Oh my god, it's really over."

"Are you okay?" she whispers when my shoulders start to shake.

"It's over," I cry.

She pulls me in for a hug. "I'm so happy for you all. Everyone will have justice now."

"We should wait to tell Aisling's mum tomorrow. She has been waiting for this moment ever since Aisling went missing."

"Agreed."

I glance to the hallway where Poppy is sleeping not too far away. "She is going to be so happy to see him."

"Yeah. I can bring her by in the morning. This should be just you and him tonight."

"Are you sure?"

She waves me off. "Of course I am."

I lean over, kissing her lips. "You're the best. Thank you."

"Go get him," she orders, smacking my arse when I get up. "And make him work for forgiveness."

"I will," I promise, grabbing my car keys and slippers. I don't bother going to get dressed since I don't plan to be wearing much of anything for long. "Love you!"

"Love you too," she calls out.

It's over. It's really over. I have missed Cole terribly this week. So much so, I don't know how I've gotten up every morning or how I've gone to sleep. Without him next to me, it's unsettling in a way I can't put into words.

Now we can properly explore what this is between us—without the fear we might lose one another.

THE HOUSE IS dark when I pull up, making me question if he meant to come home or to the club. I passed the club on the way over, and the place had been empty. There were no police cars or media crews outside—which surprised me since I thought there would be more activity. They have just caught a serial killer.

A chill touches the base of my spine, travelling all the way up to my scalp when I exit the car. The metal gate that leads through to the back swings back and forth, the creak echoing over the rain. The winds whistle through the trees, sweeping my hair around my face. I shudder, stepping away from the car, and close the door behind me.

Dread hits my stomach, coming out of nowhere. Maybe it's coming back here after everything that went down. Or maybe it's because I've lived in fear of Cole getting killed all week, and now the adrenaline has worn off.

I walk up to the house, realising I haven't brought my keys with me. I reach up, knocking on the door.

"Shit!" I hiss, stepping off the step to go back to the car, where I've left my phone. I don't want to miss Harriett's call, in case Poppy needs me. The door opens behind me, and I turn back to the house, needing to see for myself that he is okay. My breath leaves my mouth in a whoosh when I see he's unharmed aside from a cut on his lip. "Cole," I whisper.

But it's not Cole.

My body tenses for a split second, my heart racing to the point I can hear my pulse beating wildly. But I know if I freeze for a second longer, he will know I know he isn't Cole.

And that can't happen.

Not until I find out where Cole is and I can get out of here.

"Emily," he greets, and I want to sob at the sound of my name coming from his murderous mouth.

He doesn't get to say my name.

"You're okay," I breathe, hoping my words sound genuine. "Thank God you are okay."

"I wasn't going to let him take me from you."

I take a step up, steadying my hands as I take his. "What happened? Where is Cyrus?"

"Rotting in a prison cell, unless he died on his way to hospital. I got him good," he brags.

"Baby, you don't mean that. He's your brother. You care about what happens to him. Now you can get him the help he needs; maybe build a relationship like you wanted to," I lie.

He drops the smirk. "Maybe. But right now, I'm more bothered about getting you into bed."

He wraps his arms around my waist, caging me in. I place my hands on his chest, trying not to cry or vomit. "I actually can't stay. I have to get back to Poppy."

"She can go one night without you."

Not us. Me. Which is more evidence Cole is nothing like his brother. Cole would never say something like that.

"I can't," I whine.

His eyes narrow slightly before he masks it. "Come on. Don't make me ask again."

I force a smile. "Alright. Let me quickly go back to the car to get my phone. I'll message Harriett and see if she can get up with Poppy."

"Be quick. I've missed you," he orders.

I force a smile and make my way back to the car. I unlock it as my feet pick up speed. I have to get out of here and get help. For Cyrus to have Cole's phone, he must have him inside the house somewhere. Whether he's okay, hurt, or worse—dead, is still unknown. But I owe it to him to find out. He gave me everything I didn't know I needed. He showed me kindness and grace in the face of everything I had done. I have to help him.

And he has to be okay.

Not just for him, but for everyone who will miss him. His parents, his siblings, his friends. And me and his daughter. We can't lose anyone else. We can't lose him.

I open the door, leaning into the car.

"Hurry up," he calls out, startling me. I drop the keys and they fall in the gap between the seat and door. "What's taking so long?"

I lean out to face him, spreading my fake smile. "Just a second. I can't find it."

I reach back into the car, leaning over the chair to search for my phone. It isn't on the seat, and with the crap still in here from pole class, everything is all over the place. I panic, throwing bags into the backseat, when I feel a presence behind me.

"What's taking so long?"

I let out a dry laugh. "I'm so stupid. I've lost my phone."

"You don't need it for what I have planned."

"Maybe I should just go. I can come by in the morning and bring Poppy with me."

"Get out of the car, Emily."

"I can even bring you breakfast," I offer, sitting up to search for the car keys.

"Emily, don't make me ask you again," he warns.

My fingers wrap around a broken pole. "We can even get out of town—go away again."

"Stupid bitch!" he hisses before grabbing my hair. He pulls me back, only to slam my face against the steering wheel. Pain ricochets down my face. A sharp stabbing pain throbs against my cheekbone, the flesh under my eye throbbing from where I hit the steering wheel. I don't let the pain stop me. I grip the pole as he drags me out of the car. I scream as I swing the hard metal, hitting the side of his face. Pain like no other vibrates up my wrist and arm, forcing me to let go of the pole. The metal clangs as the pole hits the ground.

"You fucking whore," he snaps, holding the palm of his hand up to his bleeding wound.

I use his distraction to my advantage, and knee him in the balls. He drops the floor, and I run, heading for the back gate.

Small puffs of cold air escape my mouth as I whirl around to close it. I throw the black bin in its path and keep going, making my way along the side of the house until I reach the back.

The white net curtains blow in the wind through the open French doors. Every muscle in my body freezes at the sight of Cole tied to a chair. Flashes of Trixie being in a similar position not too long-ago surface, and tears burn my eyes.

Please be okay, Cole.

I draw in a long breath, crossing the threshold. "Cole," I whisper, running my hand across his swollen jaw. "Cole."

I shake him a little and a wheeze of pain leaves his mouth. He lifts his head slightly, his swollen eyes meeting mine. They widen slightly, a sliver of fear shining back at me. "Run," he chokes out. "Run."

The front door bangs open, and I quickly look around for a weapon, seeing nothing.

Run!

I get to my feet, quietly padding across the kitchen to the pantry. I stop to grab the house phone off the wall, and I silently thank Cole for having one installed. I had one because my nan didn't use mobiles. None of my friends have one, and I was surprised when I found out Cole did.

Hearing footsteps, I quickly duck down, crawling inside the pantry when my hand hits something warm and wet. There are dim, warm spotlights at the bottom of the counter, and I can make out an outline of a body.

It must be Ben.

I crawl forward, touching a leg, until I'm kneeling at his side. I

321

reach up, quietly tugging the drawer open that has all the spare dish towels and tablecloths. I pull some down as he whimpers.

I want to call for him to wake up, to find out where his injuries are. Instead, I place my hand over his stomach, since that's where the largest puddle of blood is, and feel for the wettest patch. I place the cloths down on his stomach, but it's that moment I'm ripped away from his body.

I scream, reaching up to grip the hands pulling my hair. I feel like my scalp is about to be torn off. I dig my heels into the ground, doing everything possible to stop him. It doesn't.

And when I go sliding over the tiled floor, I know this is it.

No one will be looking for me until tomorrow.

My hair flies over my head as I lift my head, staring into the monstrous eyes of my captor.

Fear prickles my scalp. It gnaws in my gut, and my entire body shivers.

Yet my words come easily.

"I will not go down without a fight."

He kneels in front of me, his hands dangling between his bent thighs. "And I love it when they fight."

37

HARRIETT

I can't shake this feeling that something isn't right. It has been eating away at me ever since Emily walked out the door and drove away.

I keep going back over the messages he sent. I might not know Cole Connor well, or for long, but I can't see a man of his calibre wanting the woman to go to him. He would have come here. He wouldn't have waited.

I pace the kitchen as the anxiety grows inside of me.

Fuck it.

I grab my phone and keys off the side, when my phone begins to vibrate in my hand. I let out a breath, but my relief is short-lived when I see Gabby's name on the screen.

"Hey, is everything okay?" I greet.

"I have a feeling," Gabby replies.

"Oh my god," I hear Olivia groan.

"A feeling?" I question.

"Yeah, a feeling. You know that's never a good sign."

"It's because you've got a black soul," Olivia jests.

"Funny, because not even an hour ago you were saying my soul is like a rainbow. All shiny and beautiful."

"Is there a point to this?" I ask, not having the patience to deal with this.

"Is Emily awake? Do you know if she's heard from Cole?" Gabby asks, a slight quiver to her tone.

"He messaged her not long ago saying it was over, but I've got a bad feeling."

"See, she's got a feeling too."

"Jesus Christ," Olivia groans. "There's nothing online about Cyrus but that's probably because it's too early in the fucking morning."

"Look, I'm telling you, something is wrong. He wanted her to go to him," I reply.

"Cole? I never thought of him as a man who would make the woman go to him," Gabby worriedly responds.

"That's what I said," I admit.

"Oh my god, let me try ringing her again," Olivia offers.

"You've already tried?" I ask.

"Yeah, when I started to get this feeling, I immediately called her. She hasn't picked up," Gabby replies.

"She could be having hot, sweaty, makeup sex," Olivia points out.

I rub my lower stomach. "No, I know I'm right about this."

"She's not picking up," Gabby whispers. "I don't like this."

"Me neither," I breathe out. "I'm going over there to check."

"Take River with you," Olivia calls out.

"Poppy is here. I can't leave her alone," I explain.

"Shit. We'll come meet you," Olivia offers.

"Should we ring Charlotte?" Gabby asks.

"Why would you ask Charlotte? She'll bring the entire family with her, and nothing could be wrong," Olivia argues.

"She has a boyfriend who even Max Carter doesn't argue with. She'll bring him," Gabby explains.

"Why don't I just go see if something is wrong first?" I offer.

"Fuck that. We need to stick together," Gabby argues. "I'll get Lee to watch my baby."

"Our baby."

"Look, I'm not getting into it with you, but he loves me more," Gabby points out.

"Now is not the time. I'm leaving. I just need to write River a note."

"Oh, tell him we said hi," Gabby calls out before I end the call.

I rush over to my gym bag, sliding on my gym leggings over my silk pyjama shorts. I replace the gown with a grey hoodie before quickly scribbling down a note, explaining where I went and to call the police if I'm not back in an hour. Then realise he won't know when I left, and add the time of leaving to the bottom.

It could be weeks of living with fear. It could be that none of us have been safe. But this gut feeling has never steered me wrong before. It's always been right.

I PUT my car into park behind Olivia's a few houses down from Cole's home. I get out, meeting them on the pavement.

"Are you sure you two aren't overreacting?" Olivia greets.

I rub my arms up and down, warding off the cold. "Do you want to take the chance? I don't know about you, but I'd rather interrupt makeup sex than hear in the news that she's been killed."

Olivia lets out a breath. "When you put it like that, I guess it makes sense."

"And I didn't?" Gabby whispers.

Olivia rolls her eyes. "You had a *feeling*."

"A feeling that has gotten us out of trouble a time or two. Didn't I say I had one on the boat before it blew up? And what about the time I said I had a bad feeling when we went abseiling? That rope snapped and the woman broke all her bones."

Olivia glances away. "It wasn't all of them."

"I'm telling you, I've got a sixth sense for this shit. It's why watching *Final Destination* fucked me up."

I nod in agreement. "I still can't drive past a lorry carrying logs."

"Alright, so best case scenario, she's having hot sex. Worst case scenario is what?" Olivia asks, waiting for an answer.

I shrug. "I don't know, but I don't think it was Cole who sent that message."

"Let's just get this done before the neighbours call the police on us," Gabby declares.

"Wouldn't be the first time," Olivia grumbles.

"Hey, that lady was a busybody," Gabby snaps.

I laugh at her reasoning. "You were pinching her ornament from her front garden."

"I thought it was public property," she defends.

"Babe, it had her house name on it."

Gabby stops before the gates, pouting. "But it was so me, and it didn't go with all her other ornaments."

It had been a glitter fairy gnome. It really was something Gabby would own.

The open gate pulls my attention away from what I was about to say. "It's open," I whisper, stepping in front of it.

It isn't the only door open either.

Up ahead is Emily's car, the driver's side door wide open. "You were saying about that feeling?" Gabby murmurs, her voice low.

"I take it back," Olivia replies. "This is bad."

"Really bad," Gabby agrees.

"So much for that makeup sex," I add as a scream pierces through the air. Gabby is the first to move, so I quickly pull her back by the scruff of her jacket. "Stop!"

"What are you doing?" she hisses. "That's Emily."

"And we can't go in guns blazing."

"So what do you expect us to do, because you know if we wait for the police, he will see those sirens and kill her."

"We go in quietly," I assure her.

"Quietly? Like fucking Santa Claus?" Olivia grumbles.

"Wait, we should split up," Gabby declares.

"Split up? Are you fucking crazy?" Olivia snaps.

Gabby snorts. "You knew that already."

"What are you thinking?" I ask.

Olivia steps closer. "You can't really think this is a good idea."

"Let's just hear what she has to say," I stress, knowing her concern is coming from her love for Gabby. She doesn't want to see her hurt again. I don't either.

"He has a side door that leads down into the basement," Gabby explains.

"It needs a key," I point out.

She pulls out a ring of keys. "Please, the minute she said it was locked, I got a key cut. People who keep a room locked have something to hide. I was waiting for the right moment to check it out."

"When did you… how did you…" Olivia shakes her head. "I don't want to know."

"I do," I reply, impressed.

"Remember the day everyone was distracted by the ex-girlfriend?"

"Yeah," I whisper.

"I swiped the key he gave to Emily, got it copied, and put it back before she could notice."

Olivia snaps her head towards Gabby. "The day Poppy's teddy went missing. You put it back then, didn't you? I thought it was weird when the doll mysteriously showed up on the sofa."

Gabby arches an eyebrow. "Maybe."

"Okay, so one of us goes up through the cellar. One of us should go around the back," I begin, glancing up at the house. "Isn't there a door in the laundry room that's attached to the kitchen?"

"Yeah. I did see that," Olivia replies.

"Wait, I have a better idea," Gabby announces.

"Oh God, what now?" Olivia groans. "Don't tell me you want to go in there."

"Actually…"

"You've got to be fucking kidding me," Olivia hisses. "No."

"Not a chance."

"Listen, okay," Gabby argues, holding up her hands. "You two have your phones on you, right?"

"Yeah, why?" I ask.

"Good. Harriett, you take the laundry room entrance, and Olivia, you take the cellar entrance. Message me when you know what room they are in, and if it's definitely Cyrus."

"What does it matter?" Olivia asks. "We heard her scream. We know he's in there."

Gabby cocks her hip to the side. "And what does he enjoy doing?"

Olivia's expression falls, her complexion going pale. "Torturing his victims."

"Well, they aren't going to be victims. They are going to be survivors," Gabby announces. "Once we know where they are, message me and I'll go up and knock on the door."

"And do what?" Olivia hisses. "Invite him for dinner?"

"No. Distract him so you can go in and free Emily and Cole. He will have them tied up and you know it. Probably Ben too."

"You can't be serious," Olivia argues, before turning to me. "Why aren't you talking her out of it?"

"Because it's a good idea. And the only one I think might actually work."

Olivia throws her hands up. "We could just phone the police and be done with it."

"He'll kill them before they could get in there."

"Fuck!" Olivia hisses. "Keep your phone on."

Gabby hands her the key. "Be safe."

I grab her arm before she can move behind the bush. "Wait, what are we doing when we get in there?"

"I'll call the police when you message me. If we have to, we fight like hell to save our friend," Gabby replies.

"And finally get him off the streets," Olivia adds.

I hug Gabby first, then Olivia. "If something happens, please know I love you and I don't want you to wear black at my funeral. Tell River I love him."

"What if he kills all of us?" Olivia asks.

"Then we'll find out if we really can haunt people from the other side," I reply, and begin to make my way up to the house.

This is going to end tonight.

38

EMILY

The side of my face feels swollen and bruised. He smacked my head against the side of the counter so hard, I felt the skin tear. Blood has pooled in my left eye, making it hard to see.

Cyrus has me tied to the chair, my back to the French doors, and he's turned Cole so he can watch as he beats me.

Cole's wrists are dripping with blood, a puddle at his feet where he's struggled to get free of his binds.

"I should have known a bitch wouldn't follow the rules."

"Fuck you," I spit out as he stabs a knife into my thigh. I scream, and if I could cry, the tears would be flooding my cheeks. "You will regret this."

"Do you know what it's like to grow up third best?"

I narrow my gaze on him. "Yes. My parents didn't love me. I slept on a dingy mattress on the floor that my sister used to piss on as a child. I didn't have new clothes. I was smacked a lot. And left to burn in a house fire whilst they saved themselves," I admit, and he arches his eyebrows, surprised by my outburst. "Don't you see? Your parents loved you. They could have drowned you in a bath and made it look like an accident. They could have had you committed. But a parent's love—something you know nothing about—is unconditional."

"And you've surprised me once again," he comments, running the knife along my cheek. "It's a shame we couldn't have played my game a little longer. We could have made a real go of it."

"You still don't see it. You are so far in your own head, you don't see it."

"See what?" he asks.

"That people go through shit every day. People have their own trauma, their own triggers, and their own horror stories to tell. They don't turn into murderous psychopaths. My daughter is better behaved than you. You remind me of the children in her nursery who throw tantrums when they can't get their way."

He backhands me across the face, and my head swings to the side, my hair covering the side of my face, sticking to the blood. "You don't fucking know me."

"I don't need to. Your actions tell me everything I need to know."

He grabs my hair at the nape of my neck, pulling hard. "Do you have any last words for her before I slit her throat?"

Cole struggles against the binds on his hands. "I will end you," he snaps out, once again fighting with the binds confining him to the chair.

"Nothing can end me. I will always be here. Whether I die tonight or in sixty years. I will be the monster in their dreams, I'll be the villain in the next Netflix movie. I'll never be gone," he roars. "Never."

I meet Cole's eyes, even though I don't think he can even see me at this point. My heart breaks for each blow he has taken. "I love you."

"Aw, ain't that sweet. She loves you," Cyrus teases, his laughter causing a shudder to sliver down my spine.

I keep my gaze on Cole. "When I met you all those years ago, I was broken. I thought I fixed it all by being a mum, having friends and a social life. Then you came back into my life, and I was still a little broken inside, and you made me realise that I don't need to be whole to be fixed. Because you are broken too. And it's okay. Because our two broken souls found love, and there's a beauty in that."

"Emily," he chokes out as Cyrus walks over to stand behind him.

Tears run down my cheeks. "Even if we die tonight, I don't regret a thing. I don't regret meeting you. I don't regret having a child or regret falling in love with you. Life isn't measured in time. Not really. It's measured in moments of happiness, love, and experiences—even the bad ones. You made me feel loved, Cole, in a way no other soul ever has. And I don't regret that."

"I failed you. I can't save you," he chokes out, pulling at the ties. Cyrus swings, smacking him across his face with his knuckles. Blood sprays from his lips.

"I love you," I cry, as movement from the corner of my eye gains my attention. Harriett ducks down in the laundry room doorway.

No! What is she doing here?

She isn't supposed to be here.

I need her to take care of Poppy when I die.

Tears slip down my cheeks as the situation finally sinks in. There is only one way out of this. I have to fight or die trying. At this point, I have nothing to lose. He's going to kill me anyway. I just have to make sure my friend doesn't go down with me.

"Go! You can't be here," I tell Cole, but my words are for Harriett.

Cyrus bunches his eyebrows together. "How hard did I hit your head?"

There's a knock on the front door, and I open my mouth to scream. Cyrus dives across the room, aiming right for me. His hand slaps over my mouth as we fall back, the wood digging into my spine as we hit the floor.

I whimper as I feel him lift his weight off me, reaching between us. I struggle against the binds, thinking the worst, and I notice the rope is loose. Instead of touching me, he brings up a rag instead, shoving it in my mouth until I'm heaving on the dirty, foul-smelling material.

"Make a noise and their death will be on your hands. Do you understand me?" he snaps.

Tears roll down my cheeks as I nod. He gets up, straightening the jacket I know he has stolen from Cole's wardrobe. Cole wore it the first time he came back to Tease. I remember it so vividly.

Cole hasn't moved or made a sound, but Cyrus grips his face, tilting his head back until he's looking at him. "If you try to make a noise, I will gut her in front of you and then make you eat her insides."

Cyrus drops his face and Cole's chin hits his chest. Cyrus leaves, and I frantically look to Cole. To my surprise, he lifts his head easily. "He's going to untie me at any moment because he thinks I'm too weak to fight back. Can you get free? If you can, run," he warns.

"Easy there, tiger," Harriett whispers, startling him.

"What…" Cole begins but freezes when we hear Gabby.

"Hey there, handsome. Is Emily in?" Gabby asks.

"She's in bed. Asleep."

"Can I just go speak to her real quick?" she asks sweetly.

"No," he tells her, and I glance to Harriett.

"Harriett, you need to leave," I warn. "None of you should have come."

"The police are coming," she explains, pulling a knife out of the drawer. "We've got this."

"But I'll only be a minute," Gabby pleads as Harriett moves over to Cole.

"What do you need her for?"

"I need to know if your psycho brother got caught or if the police need me to team up with them to catch him."

"And what makes you think you can catch him?"

"Puh-lease, I've watched every episode of Veronica Mars and every episode of CSI. I could get that dick in my sleep."

"Dick?" Cyrus grits out.

"She's playing with fire," Harriett hisses as she gets Cole free.

"Well yeah. Pussies are solid. They can take a good fucking and are capable of childbirth, and women don't act like we've been stabbed when it's knocked a little. Calling him a pussy would be a compliment. This dude is a dick. Doesn't always hit the mark, sensitive, and can't keep up."

Harriett gets my wrist free, and I hug her. "Thank you for coming."

"Get lost, woman," Cyrus demands. "Emily is asleep."

"Honestly, she won't mind," she replies, then continues to babble.

"We need to go," I hiss, and notice Harriett is texting on her phone. "Who are you texting?"

"Gabby. I'm telling her to get out of here."

"Where's Olivia?"

"Stuck in the cellar. Fucking Gabby only got one key cut. She's going back out now."

She helps me to my feet, and I notice Cole holding a stainless-steel frying pan. "What are you doing?"

"Ending this," he snaps, gripping the handle harder.

A plan forms in my mind. "Harriett, go and help Ben. He's bleeding in the pantry."

"What are you going to do?"

"Take him off guard," I tell her, then look to Cole. "When he comes in, pretend you've killed me."

"What?"

"He won't expect it. Then when he's checking if I am dead, hit him," I order. "Hit him hard and let him feel what it's like to be the prey."

Harriett nods in approval. "I'll go check on Ben. When the fight starts, I'll come back out. Remember your self-defence lessons."

I nod as I lay back down on the floor. "I've got this!"

"I guess I'll just see her tomorrow," Gabby whines. "But I'll never forgive you for this."

The door slams closed and Cole whispers. "Scream and stop suddenly."

"No," I scream, cutting off my cries, covering my face with my arm.

I hear footsteps pad into the room. "What the fuck?" Cyrus hisses.

"Now you can't use her against me," Cole murmurs, and I hear him stagger before the frying pan hits the counter.

"This wasn't a part of the plan," Cyrus snaps, his voice closer. His hands grip my side, turning me over. "This wasn't a part of the plan."

"Plans change," Cole replies, his voice filled with emotion. I hear a whistle in the air, and I open my eyes, meeting Cyrus' dead on. His pupils darken as he's taken aback by the lie. Before he can even take a breath, the pan strikes the side of his head, hitting him like a ping pong ball.

I kick Cyrus in the stomach, shoving him away from me. "I told you you'd regret this."

Cole takes a step, ready to attack once more, but Cyrus swings his arm out. To dodge the knife clutched in his hand, Cole slips, smacking his head against the breakfast bar. He falls to the floor—completely out cold.

Cyrus spits out blood, his hair falling into his eyes as he turns to me. "Your turn, bitch."

I scuffle backward as he lunges at me, pinning me against the floor. I scream, slipping my hands free to grip his face.

"You killed my friend," I scream, pushing my thumbs into the corner of his eyes. "You nearly killed my best friend."

"And I still might kill her. She's an annoying bitch," he snaps, gripping me around the throat.

A black strap with a ball appears in front of his face, and I notice Olivia standing behind him. She pulls at the strap, and the ball falls into his mouth, blocking him from talking.

Gabby rushes to our side. "And I'm not annoying. I'm eccentric," she snaps, slashing a whip through the air until it slices through the flesh on his cheek.

He growls behind the gag ball, throwing Olivia back and Gabby over to the side. She lands near the table, her eyes wide.

I reach up with my good leg, kicking him in the chest before trying to make my escape. I turn to my stomach as he grabs my ankle, pulling sharply. I scream out, turning onto my back to fight him.

Everything becomes a blur as he goes for me.

Olivia is getting to her feet behind him. Gabby is doing the same to my right.

Then Harriett is there, holding a bottle of wine above her head. She swings it down, smashing it across his head. He staggers, dropping to the floor on his side.

She throws the remaining bottle stem at his body. "That is for Aisling."

Olivia stomps down on his knee, and I hear a bone crunch as he wails in agony. "That is for nearly killing the love of my life."

Gabby brings down the whip, hitting him along his side and back. "And that is for making me trek through a forest."

Olivia glances Gabby's way, her lip curling. "Not for drowning you?"

"You call it drowning, I see it as baptising me," she retorts. "He doesn't get to keep any other trophy."

He spits out blood onto the tiles. "You're all fucking crazy."

I grab the knife that has fallen to the floor, and using all my strength, stab it through the hand he has palm down on the floor. "And you're finished."

"Find something to tie him up with," Harriett orders.

Olivia pulls out some handcuffs from her back pocket. My eyebrows rise. "Do I want to know?"

"We had a party last night," Gabby answers.

Cole coughs, sitting up. I crawl over to him, dragging my bloodied leg. "Are you okay?"

"Where is he?" he demands, holding his hand up to the back of his head. "God, the room is spinning."

"We've got him," I assure him, clutching his face.

Police sirens blare from outside. Cole runs the palm of his hand down the side of my face, pressing his forehead briefly to mine before looking to his brother. His eyes widen as much as they can under all that swelling.

"What on earth?"

Gabby pats Cyrus on the head. "It's okay. You should never send a man to do a woman's job. We've got this."

Cyrus struggles to get free, his growls loud through the ball gag.

Cole grabs the pan from the floor, staggering to his feet. He sways, and hisses when he pinches the bridge of his nose. "You took everything from me. *Everything.*"

Cyrus stops, a smug look crossing his features. And I know if the ball gag wasn't in place, he would be saying something cruel.

Glass crunches under Cole's shoes. "I hope you rot in prison for the rest of your life," he grits out, before swinging the pan up, aiming at Cyrus' head. The sound and the sight of blood turn my stomach, and I turn to the side, emptying the contents of my stomach all over the floor.

Cole drops down beside me, holding me close.

I fall into him as the police file into the home, yelling orders and demands.

It's over.

It is finally all over.

The adrenaline leaves my body at that notion and my eyes roll to the back of my head as I fall to the side, everything going black.

39

EMILY

The ambulance carrying Ben pulls out of the drive, lights flashing as they leave. I wrap the blanket the paramedics gave me tighter around my body.

"You're going to need stiches," the kind paramedic reveals, handing me a bottle of water.

"Thank you," I whisper, my focus on the puddle where the rain falls. "My friend—the man who left in the other ambulance; will he be okay?"

"I can't tell you. He was in stable condition when he left, but until the surgeons assess him at the hospital, it's too soon to know."

"Why are they keeping my friends and Cole inside the house? He needs medical attention too."

"I think the police just want to ask them a few more questions," she offers.

"But *he's* still in there with them. Why?" I plead.

She places her hand on my good leg. "You were unconscious when we arrived. Your injuries take precedence. Once my colleague has finished clearing the assailant for transport, we will take you to the hospital."

"Will he be coming to the same hospital?" I ask, placing the water down beside me.

"No. He's been diverted to St Andrews," she assures me. "He will be travelling with police escorts."

I nod, turning my attention to my surroundings. There are over two dozen police cars here, another two riot vans, and some unmarked cars, one of which I recognise as Inspector Douglas' vehicle.

Two policemen step outside the house, a handcuffed Cyrus in the middle of them. They hold his arm, leading him to one of the vans as he limps.

I stand up from the back of the ambulance, my breath leaving me in one whoosh. He meets my gaze, smirking. "I will come back for you," he roars. "I will be back."

Cole glares in his direction as he steps outside. It's brief because then he begins to scan the front garden, searching for me. I know it because the relief on his face at seeing me is palpable. He rushes towards me as I limp a few steps away from the ambulance.

A choked sob slips through my lips as he pulls me into his arms. The blanket falls to the ground at my feet, forgotten.

"Thank God you're okay," he breathes, his voice cracking. He pulls back, brushing my hair away from my face. "You scared me."

"I scared you? You scared me," I choke out, clutching him. "Are you okay?"

"Sir, we need you to ride to the hospital with us," Detective Douglas announces, interrupting us.

"Are you actually fucking with me right now?" he replies, his words sharp. "I'm not leaving Emily."

"It's vital that we speak to you both alone, and it will be best to do it whilst it's still fresh in your mind."

I place my hand on his chest. "Go. I'll meet you at the hospital."

"I'm not leaving you again," he retorts.

"Sir, it's either you or Emily, but going by the nasty gash on her eye, she needs to see the doctor."

"We both need to see a doctor," I snap, hating the way he used my injuries to manipulate Cole. I cup Cole's jaw. "I'll be at the hospital. Come see me when you're done."

Detective Douglas steps aside for his colleague. "PC Sweedy will be riding with you to the hospital."

"Why do I feel like more of a criminal than Cyrus right now?" I snap, wincing at the pain in my ribs.

"I just need to ask some routine questions. I'll take note of the injuries whilst I'm with you, so I won't take up too much of your time," PC Sweedy promises.

Cole bends down, kissing me on the lips. "I'll be with you once I'm done with them."

"I know you will," I assure him, kissing him once more. It feels like heaven to be able to kiss him again. To touch him. To hold him and be held by him.

I turn to PC Sweedy. "Will my friends be able to come with us?"

"They're sitting down right now talking to another officer."

I nod, and the paramedic takes my arm. "Come on. We need to take your vitals."

"I'll see you there," Cole promises.

I sit down on the gurney, shuddering from the cold. "I'll see you there," I whisper as the doors close.

And then the fun begins.

Questions after questions are asked—like I'm the criminal and they're trying to catch me out on a lie I've not even told.

———

THE DISTINCT SCENT of disinfectant fills the air. It clings to the robes the nurses fitted me with upon my arrival, and to everything I touch. It's making me nauseous, but then, that could be from the doctor, who has just finished stitching my leg up. He places the tape over the bandage before sitting back in his chair. "You can't get them wet for at least seventy-two hours."

"I want to see my friend," I hear Harriett demand, and I glance up to the curtain.

"We've answered all your questions," Gabby remarks. "A billion times to multiple people, if you need a refresher."

The curtain is pulled back, and I relax at the sight of my friends. "Have you seen Cole? Is he okay? Are you three okay?"

Gabby sighs heavily. "When I said getting kicked in the vagina doesn't hurt, I lied."

"You got kicked in the vagina?" I ask.

"Fucker woke up," Gabby replies.

Olivia rolls her eyes. "Gabby goaded him into it."

Harriett snorts. "She kept asking why she wasn't picked, but Trixie was."

"What?" I ask, shaking my head.

Gabby shrugs. "Look, my dad said I was a mistake. I have issues. I wanted to be special."

"She wanted to goad him into hitting her again," Olivia amends.

Gabby laughs. "Yeah, but in my defence, I was hoping I would get to hit him back again. I enjoyed it."

"Why were you all there?" I ask. "Not that I'm complaining."

"She had a feeling," Olivia replies, pointing to Gabby first. "And she had a gut feeling."

My eyes widen. "Woah, your feelings really haven't been wrong."

Gabby puffs out her chest. "I know."

"Are you okay?" Harriett asks, placing her hand on my shoulder.

"Getting stabbed really hurts," I admit.

"I need to stitch your eye, and you can't move. One wrong move and I could get your eyeball—which can cause blindness," the doctor warns.

"Okay," I shakily reply.

"I don't think I can watch this," Gabby admits.

"I'm just going to numb the area. It will sting a little bit."

"Okay," I whisper as a nurse passes him a needle. I whimper at the size, every muscle in my body tensing.

The girls murmur amongst themselves as the doctor preps my eye. The minute the first stitch is made, Cole walks into the room, and all hell breaks loose.

"What were you thinking?" Harriett snaps.

"What happened to being able to handle yourself?" Gabby demands.

"I get that you have questions," he explains.

"You bet your arse we do. You break her heart and then the plan fails," Olivia yells.

"Please, calm down," the doctor demands. "Or leave the room."

"You think I don't know that?" Cole bites out. "Believe me, I do."

"She shouldn't have been there."

"And what were you doing there?" he snaps. "You could have gotten yourselves killed."

"Bit of a good job we were there," Gabby argues.

"You were supposed to be watching my daughter," he barks at Harriett. "You could have led him right to her."

"Don't put this on me. River has her. She's safe. But our friend wasn't."

"They need to calm down," the doctor warns, adding another stitch.

"Pause," I order, before screeching. "Please, can we support the doctor stitching up my eye before I'm permanently blinded."

Cole places his hand on my leg. "Are you okay?"

"I will be a lot better if you could all stop whilst the doctor is doing this. No one but Cyrus is to blame for what happened tonight. None of us knew what we were walking into and none of us can truly say we would go back and change it. Everything that happened was bad, but look where we are. We're alive. We're safe. And Cyrus has been stopped from killing another person."

"Go ahead, we'll stop arguing," Harriett promises, taking my hand. "Have the police said what will happen next?"

Cole clears his throat. "With regards to Cyrus, no. He won't get out if that's what you're worried about. He's being transferred tomorrow morning. He needs an operation on his knee and hand."

"Good," Gabby mutters before clearing her throat. "Will we have to testify?"

"I don't know how it will be done. They have all the evidence they need. We added extra security the day we came back from the lodge so it's all on camera."

"It's really over," Gabby whispers.

"Hey, are you okay?" Olivia asks.

A sob echoes through the room. "I'm fine."

"You aren't fine," Olivia replies softly.

"My nightmares have been about him coming back for me or for one of you," she breaks. "I've been living in fear that he will finish what he started. I watched him torture Trixie and he found joy in it. Every time I saw him in my dreams, he would do it to me. Then even awake I couldn't hide from him. I saw him in every male, and it scared me. I didn't want to leave the house because I was so scared I wouldn't come back. And now I don't need to be scared anymore."

The nurse aiding the doctors loses her composure, and I notice tears slipping down her cheeks.

"Gabby," Olivia whispers.

"No other victim got away, but we did. We did, and I'm supposed to be happy about it. And I'm not. Because there are so many others who won't go back to their families, to their friends or life. It's over for us, but it will never be over for those who are still mourning the people they lost. I don't know if I can be happy about that."

The nurse clears her throat. "It's survivor's guilt you are feeling. I know because I felt the same thing. My parents were murdered in our home. I nearly died with them, but I didn't. And I spent years suffering with survivor's guilt."

"What did you do to make it stop?" Gabby whispers.

"I lived. We can't change the actions of those around us. We can only change what we do. And I believe that to make the world a better place, you have to start with yourself. Then the rest will fall into place. I got my nursing degree to help people. I volunteer at the Salvation Army and other charities."

I notice Gabby wipe tears away from her cheek. "That sounds like a lot of work."

"It is, but it's worth it," the nurse responds.

Olivia snorts, knowing Gabby's response is more of an 'I don't want to do all of that because I like my free time'. "Maybe we can help at one centre. Start there."

"Sounds good," Gabby breathes out, resting her head on Olivia's shoulder.

"All done," the doctor announces. "Keep it dry for seventy-two hours. You can dab some warm water over it after then but not too much. We'll take them out in a few weeks."

"Thank you."

Cole moves to replace where the doctor was, taking my hand. "I'm so sorry I brought you into all of this," he swears.

"It's not your fault," I assure him. "How are you doing?"

He brings my hand up to his lips, pressing them lightly against my skin. "He killed my biological parents and sister," he chokes out. "He admitted it."

Pain fills my chest as he closes his eyes in anguish. "Cole, I'm so, so sorry."

"He did all this out of miscommunications and fake notions he built up in his head."

"He's sick," I respond softly.

He meets my gaze, his eyes filled with unshed tears. "How did you know he wasn't me?"

"Because when I look at you, I see a future, and the world beyond today. When I looked into his eyes, all I saw was darkness. I know who you are, Cole Connor, and it is nothing like him."

He turns to my friends. "Thank you for saving her. Saving us."

"We didn't do it for you. We did it for her," Gabby announces.

"Gabby," I whisper. I know she means well, but he's been through enough.

"No, she's right," Cole replies. "I'm so sorry for how I did this. I put you in danger anyway."

"I would have always been in danger no matter what the plan was," I admit.

"But that's not what Gabby means," Harriett adds. "We're not just her friends. We're her family. When you hurt her, you hurt all of us. She has been bounced around from other people's emotions and needs all her life. She doesn't need that anymore. Not from you or anyone else."

"I know. Which is why I bought this ring a few weeks ago," he announces, pulling out a tiny, blue, square box. We all gasp at the sight, and if my eyes didn't already hurt enough, I would be crying right now. "When I met you, I knew you were different. You weren't someone I needed to conquer or have warm my bed. I didn't know what it was back then, but I do now. It was a bond that connected us in every way possible. I love you, Emily. I've made mistakes, but I'm prepared to fix them until my last dying breath. I wouldn't be the man I am today if it wasn't for you. You are the very best of me, so will you do me the greatest honour of becoming my wife?"

He pulls out a ring, and I fail to keep the tears at bay. Damn the stinging and pain. "Yes," I rasp as he slides the ring on my finger.

He kisses me, stealing my breath and my heart all over again. He has always had all of me, but now it's for keeps.

It's forever.

Because I never want to let go again.

EPILOGUE

EMILY

Today is the day of the town's Spring Festival, and it feels like our entire town is in attendance.

It's a beautiful day to be outside. The sun is warm but not too warm. People are laughing and having fun. And I'm going to be with everyone I love.

I gaze over to the swings, where Joe and Georgia push their granddaughter on the swing. Poppy throws her head back, screaming for them to push her higher. It brings joy to my heart knowing she has this. She gets to feel how I do every day knowing her grandparents love her. She gets it all, which is everything I ever wanted for her. My parents will never be in our life again. The courts granted our restraining order, and Ben made sure they knew if they went against my wishes again, he would tell the police it was them who broke into my home. They didn't know there wasn't any proof, and they didn't need to know. I'm just glad I don't have to deal with them ever again. The money I got from my grandma's estate got donated to an Alzheimer's charity. It's what she would have wanted if she knew I had Cole taking care of me.

I spot Harriett and River in the crowd. She waves, a big smile on her lips. "Have you seen them yet?" she calls, speaking about one of the reasons we are here. But that's for later, when everyone is here.

"Not yet," I reply as they reach me.

She glances around the park, her nose twitching. "Where are the others?"

"It's Gabby and Olivia. They'd be late to their own funeral," I answer, smiling. "Hey, River."

"Hey," he grumbles, and helps Harriett take a seat on the picnic bench.

Because my girl is five and a half months pregnant. We had the baby gender reveal last week, and she's carrying a boy. She's come a long way since she found out. Harriett has had her entire life mapped out, and a baby is something she was never prepared for at this time in her life. She has just finished her degree, and she was scared she would lose her status at work by taking time off so soon into her job, but they have been just as supportive as all of us.

The only one who still seems to be a nervous wreck is River. He's scared that our antics, and the trouble we can cause, will put them in danger. But if there's one thing he should learn about this, it's that Harriett is fiercely protective of the people she loves. She will never stir anything up that would cause harm to her or her baby boy.

"How are you feeling?" I ask.

"I feel like I could eat a burger and some cheesy fries," she replies happily, letting out a heavy breath. "My tits hurt like hell."

"Give it ten and she'll probably be vomiting behind a tree some-where," River adds.

"Where's your husband?" Harriett asks.

I smile at her calling him that. My husband. Our ceremony was beautiful. We had it outside his family home a few months ago, keeping everything simple and the theme neutral, from the flowers to the décor to the dresses. His mum and sister knew exactly what to do and had the wedding organised within months. The day I became his wife was also the day we signed the papers to officially change Poppy's last name too.

Then we spent two weeks up at the lodge because the place held a

346

sentimental meaning to us now. It's where we finally let go and shoved everything aside to just be with each other. Our time there the first time, and again when we were married, are times I'll never forget.

"He's just finishing up some bits at work," I explain, before turning to River. "Thank you for helping him and Ben with the charity."

"It's for a good cause. Too many children grow up to be the way they are because they're lacking the mental health help they need. The waiting lists are too long, or there are not enough resources. I got lucky. I used my fighting to get rid of my anger, and I dread to think what would have become of me if I didn't have that."

Harriett runs her hand up his chest. "Handsome, have I told you today that I love you?"

He grins, flashing his pearly whites. "Don't go crying on me again," he warns.

She rolls her eyes, pressing her lips to his cheek. "I'll pretend that didn't hurt."

She hates being emotional, and being heavily pregnant, she is feeling a lot of emotions.

I spot Gabby up ahead. "They're here," I state.

Harriett and River turn, and I grimace when Gabby nearly takes out a bunch of small children with the pushchair trying to get to us.

"Don't you dare," Olivia warns, racing further behind to catch up.

Gabby stops close to us and holds up her hand. A ring sparkles against the sun as she cries. "We're getting married."

I get up off the bench whilst River helps Harriett off hers. "Oh my god, congratulations," I cheer, hugging my best friend.

"I told you I wanted to tell them together," Olivia snaps.

Gabby, uncaring because she's so blissfully happy, shrugs. "I couldn't wait. Sorry. People need to shower me with love and gifts."

I laugh as I move over to Olivia, pulling her in for a hug. "Congratulations. I'm so happy for you."

"I'm beginning to rethink my decision to ask," she warns, narrowing her gaze on Gabby.

Gabby arches a brow. "There are no takebacks now. My mum knows."

"You told your mum before us?" Harriett cries.

"She came to the house to tell us we can move into the new one," Gabby responds. "She was practically foaming at the mouth when we told her."

"And, we're having papers drawn up so we can officially adopt the kids as our own," Olivia announces.

Gabby pouts at the announcement. "I wanted to tell them that."

"Aren't they already yours?" Harriett asks, her eyebrows pinching together.

"I'm their guardian," Olivia explains. "Now, I'm filing for adoption, and Gabby is going to be on the papers too."

"So, if she tries to leave me, I can take the kids," Gabby adds.

I laugh, hugging her once more. "I'm so happy for you both," I cheer.

"I'm not calling you Mum," Lee declares, lowering Ellie to the ground.

"Give it time," Gabby argues. "I'm like the mother of dragons now."

"Stop calling yourself that," Olivia snaps.

"Why? They practically breathe fire in the morning. Did you smell Lee's breath? It smelled of smoke," Gabby defends.

"I'm going," Lee announces loudly. "I'll be back later."

"I want to be excluded from this conversation," Kayden declares, parking his arse down on the bench.

"Are they okay with this?" Harriett asks.

"Yeah, they're okay with it. I mean, they aren't going to call me Mum or anything—although Ellie said she wants to, but with the engagement, and the fact Carter will see us differently than them, we wanted them to know they are still our main priority. It's unconventional, but we make it work."

"I'm so happy for you," Harriett tells her, her eyes brimming with tears.

"God, don't do that," Gabby warns. "I can't handle more crying."

"Who's crying?" Cole asks, and I melt at the sound of his voice.

I turn, taking in my gorgeous husband. We're at a park and he's still wearing his navy-blue suit. "Hey, husband. We were just congratulating Gabby and Olivia on their engagement and their plans to adopt the kids. Harriett is just emotional."

He pulls me into his arms, planting a kiss right on my lips. I melt into him, happy to kiss him back. "I've missed you," he informs me.

"I've missed you too."

"Urgh, pass me a bucket," Gabby cries.

"Can I go play with Poppy?" Ellie asks.

"She's right over there," I tell her.

"Stay where we can see you," Gabby and Olivia call out.

"Congratulations," Cole greets, placing his arm around my waist.

"Thank you," Olivia replies.

"Before I go over to see our daughter, I thought you might want to see this," Cole announces, pulling out a white envelope.

My breath hitches as I meet his gaze. "Is that what I think it is?"

"Baby, you got in. You start your course in September."

I squeal, jumping up in his arms and wrapping my legs around his waist. I kiss him, blissfully happy. "I got in?"

"Yeah, and I had no doubt you could do it," he reveals.

"I love you," I declare, kissing him once more.

He lowers me to my feet, his eyes twinkling with happiness. Which I'm thankful for. The weeks after the night his brother attacked were the worst. He got really depressed and it took a while for him to pull himself back out of it.

"I'll leave you to explain to your friends," he tells me, kissing me once more.

"Come on, little man, let's go play on the swing," River gently orders.

Kayden raises his brows. "It's dirty."

River pulls out a pack of disinfectant wipes. "I got you covered."

"Okay. But you should know statistics show more children get injured during outdoor play than they do indoors," Kayden responds.

"They also show seventy-eight percent of children are happier when they take part in outdoor play," River responds as they walk off with Cole. He's going to be a fantastic dad, and I'm so glad Harriett has him.

I turn to my friends. "I applied to start a hairdressing course in

September. With so many school leavers applying and needing spaces, I didn't think I'd get in. But I have."

"Congratulations," Harriett cheers, followed by Olivia and Gabby.

We all hug, standing in a huddled circle. My smile is wobbly, tears threatening to fall. "Who knew we would be here right now, having all that we do. I've always felt richer from knowing you. I'm so overwhelmed with love and joy and it's because of you three. I wouldn't have what I do if it wasn't for you guys. You made me stronger and wiser."

Gabby's eyes begin to water. "This feels like a goodbye, but it isn't."

"Winnie the Pooh once said: 'How lucky am I to have something that makes saying goodbye so hard'," Harriett reveals.

"Guys, this isn't goodbye," Olivia argues, wiping under her eye.

"No, but things will definitely change. Olivia and Emily are going back to school, Gabby will be running the new coyote bar for Cole, and I'm having a baby. It might not be goodbye, but it feels like we've closed a door on a chapter of our lives."

Tears slip down my cheeks. "But a new chapter always begins. Our lives may be changing, but we never will. We will always be together," I admit.

"And River and Cole have just gotten used to being in a four-way relationship. You get one of us, you get us all," Gabby declares. "Let's not screw up a good thing."

"I love you guys," Harriett chokes out. "Thank you for being my ride or dies."

We all turn to the commotion happening at the food trucks, standing side by side, our arms wrapped around the person's back next to us.

Sam—Gabby's homophobic next-door neighbour—is inside the food truck. Sweat beads his forehead, dripping through the white hat he is forced to wear around the fast food he is making.

"I'm not gay," he screams, as a friend of ours dressed in drag tries to hand him his number. "Why are you people doing this to me? Leave me alone."

"Sugar, you weren't saying that last night to me."

"Stop!" Sam roars. "I don't even know who you are, you faggot."

His boss walks up to the truck. "Sam, you were on your last warning. Leave. You're fired."

"But he's harassing me," Sam defends. "I need this job. I have bills to pay."

"Then go and see if Jimmy needs help cleaning the porta-loos."

"What?" Sam rears back, disgusted. "I'm not cleaning up shit."

"Leave before I call the police over to remove you," the man shouts.

Me and my girls huddle closer as another frenemy walks past with a litter picker. Colin stabs the rubbish into the bag, his expression thunderous. Once he disappears into the crowd, we all huddle back into the circle.

"That was so worth it," Gabby splutters, laughing her head off.

"They can't say they were never warned," Harriett adds, laughing too.

"No one messes with the girls from Tease," Olivia announces.

"Ride or dies, bitches," I holler.

We all make our way back to the table, discussing our plans for the future.

This is the life I always dreamed of having. And now that I do, it's everything and more.

Lives have been lost along the way, but they will never be forgotten.

Love has been formed that will never be broken.

And our friendship… it will never fade away.

Because our friendship is like a four-leaf clover. Hard to find but lucky to have.

Nothing will ever come between us.

ACKNOWLEDGMENTS

I am so very grateful to everyone who stuck by this series and supported me whilst I finished the trilogy.

It saddens me that the series has come to an end. Being a writer is not easy at times. There is a great pressure that comes with giving readers what they want and getting it out on time. I've always prided myself on not writing to a trend that is popular. And I've done it that way so my stories are not lost in a mass of other great reads.

I have read so many romance books that have impacted my life in some way. I've been inspired by them.

Then during Charlotte – A Next Generation Carter Brother Novel – I asked myself what made me love writing her story so much. And it was the friendships and what they would do for each other.

People tell you friendships are easily made but harder to keep. And in a way, those people are right. I've had great friendships in my life, ones I wish never faded away. It can be a great loss, one you will you always grieve in some way. But those friendships still impacted my life. They impacted my children's lives in a way that can never truly fade away. I miss them terribly, but without that loss, I wouldn't be where I am today.

Writing Tease was so meaningful to me because of them.

Friendship shouldn't be a tally chart of who did what.

It shouldn't be about who contacted who first.

It shouldn't be built with jealously in your mind.

It should be about what you can do for them and not what they can do for you.

It should be about being able to pick up the phone and talk like months haven't passed.

It should be about celebrating their wins and comforting their losses.

Friendships are about sticking together in times of need and celebration.

And I hope I portrayed this in my words.

Thank you to everyone who made this book possible. Without you, this wouldn't be happening. So please, share some love on their socials if you are reading this.

Harper at Dark City Designs gave these books life with her covers. Her talent speaks for itself and without her help, these would not have been possible.

Stephanie Farrant at Farrant Editing, you already know how much I love you.

You guys have been a huge support for this series, so thank you.

And to Michelle Carder and all my alpha and beta readers. Thank you for taking a chance on me.

And to my mum—Melanie—thank you for being my biggest supporter. I love you to the moon and back. I wouldn't be where I am if it wasn't for you.

Thank you to everyone who has supported this series and taken a chance on a trope you wouldn't normally read.

I hope you will take the time to leave a review on the appropriate platform—whether it be good or bad.

Please share with your book friends and on social media about this series. You might not think your words have reach, but they do. And I'm truly grateful to every single one of you who help spread the word.

You can now see other works and reading orders on my website.

WWW.Lisahelengray.co.uk

Until the next time…

Printed in Great Britain
by Amazon

40252360R00202